THE PORTAL

THE PORTAL

Keith White

LITTLE
MOOSE
PRESS

Beverly Hills, California

THE PORTAL
KEITH WHITE

This is a work of fiction. References to actual geographical terrain and
historical records are intended to give the fiction a setting in historical reality.
Names, characters, places and incidents are entirely the products of the
author's imagination. Any similarity to real persons, living or dead, is
coincidental and not intended by the author.

First Edition

Library of Congress Cataloging-in-Publication Data
White, Keith, 1959-
The portal/ Keith White.
p. cm.
ISBN 0-9720227-2-4
1. World War, 1939-1945—Fiction. 2. Time travel—Fiction. I. Title.
PS3623.H5785P67 2004
813'.6—dc22
2004048991

ISBN 0-9720227-2-4

Published by Little Moose Press
Beverly Hills, CA

www.littlemoosepress.com

PRINTED IN THE UNITED STATES OF AMERICA

Acknowledgements

To my reading committee: My good friends Paul Holling and Mary Ann Flannery, my mother, Margaret White, and my sister and unofficial editor, Lynne White, I cannot thank you enough.

And to Bill Bergeron who first triggered my enthusiasm to consider writing, and Horacio Marchand in Monterrey, Mexico, who added to it.

A special thanks goes to Ellen Reid at Ellen Reid's Book Shepherding who took on the flood of details that it takes to get a book from a final draft to a book store, a task as big as writing it itself.

Also I want to thank Roberta Tennant, Ken Debono, Michael Levin, Dottie Albertine, and Laren Bright who added to the effort.

Most of all, I thank my wife, Michelle, and my son, Kristopher, who put up with me sitting in front of the computer for uncounted hours.

CHAPTER ONE

End of September, 1943

UNDER HEAVY WIND SHEAR and driving rain, the small, single engine Ballanca floatplane appeared lost—dwarfed beneath the tempest mercilessly tossing from above and between the jagged cliffs threatening on both sides. The granite walls precariously funneled any advance toward the canyon's end, hidden in the mist ahead. Pushing eastward through the dark sky, the pilot struggled against the violent conditions in the gorge, the aircraft strained to the limit.

A bolt of lightning shot across the sky, the jagged shape striking a nearby cliff, then came the thunderous crack as the brilliant flash instantly changed the sky to blinding white. The Ballanca's cockpit and two faces inside the craft instantly lit up, their expressions frozen in time.

Ray Dobbs had flown this route many times in all kinds of weather and marshaled a cautious respect for the mountaintops imbedded in the clouds around him. He also knew his plane's limitations, limitations that had been exceeded long ago. At any moment he expected the storm to deliver a final blow, a pummeling strong enough to snap the plane's wings clean off. He squinted

7

forward unable to tell the fog on the windshield from the clouds outside.

His passenger was stoic, his expression cold, focused and determined. If he felt fear, not a trace showed in his face.

The plane thrashed sideways abruptly. Ray crabbed it back to stay in the center of the canyon, but knew they were ultimately at the mercy of the violent elements. A second gust followed, battering them hard and the airframe groaned with a sickening sound. Ray tightened his seatbelt strap once again to keep himself within reach of the controls. His fingers ran over the door latch to confirm it was fixed. It was a mechanical motion, an automatic habit that he nervously replayed every minute or two. He wished he could climb higher, but that was impossible. They were hemmed in by the ceiling, which was rushing past only a hundred feet above.

The pass for which he searched was approaching, but was still some minutes farther on. Ray knew the weather would be better on the other side, as the mountains nearly always blocked these storms, but he'd been in the grip of the winds for almost an hour and the few remaining minutes seemed like forever. He knew that between them and the pass the ceiling would sink lower even as the canyon tightened like a funnel, its cliffs closing in precariously, creating a crucible that would cause the winds to accelerate and the conditions to deteriorate even further.

Chaotic air currents suddenly jolted the plane upward and it disappeared into the soup overhead. Everything became a fuzzy gray void, and Ray's heart skipped a beat. He pushed the yoke in and fought the plane back down out of the obscurity. He did not have the instruments to fly in clouds. If he lost sight of the ground, he would become disoriented in seconds.

The sound of the wind increased as the plane plunged downward. Added to the engine's roar at full throttle, the cracking thunder and the raging gale, the mix became deafening. The ground reappeared suddenly, the jagged cliffs shrouded in clouds: a mixed blessing, giving Ray a bearing, yet awaiting his slightest mistake. He fought the plane to a semblance of level with no sense of relief.

It started to rain. An extreme blast of air hammered them unexpectedly from the right. Instantly the plane was at a standstill, turned on its side, and balanced on its left wingtip. Ray let out an uncontrolled shout. There was the twisting groan of metal as they hung in momentary limbo. The distortion popped Ray's door open and the cold wind and rain roared into the cockpit. Before Ray could react, the plane's forward motion stalled, and it tumbled downward into an uncontrollable spiral.

The jolt slammed his passenger's head against the panel beside the twin yoke. He clutched his seatbelt tightly but made not the slightest sound as he eyed Ray sternly. "Do you know what you're doing?" he shouted in nearly perfect English with just a trace of a Teutonic accent. Ray fought the controls, trying to regain authority of the spiraling plane. He had no time for answers. "What is the matter with this plane?" the man demanded.

"It's not the plane!" Ray shouted as he righted the craft momentarily. "It's all that, out there! Can't you see what we're in?"

"And your airplane—it cannot take it?"

"I don't know," Ray hollered. His voice was frantic. "I've never seen it this bad. There's only so much these wings can take before they break." He tried to slam his door shut but the twisted frame wouldn't allow it. He left it erratically slamming at his side, figuring it was only a question of time before it blew off into the storm.

The passenger's name was Heinz Bodecker. He claimed to be a German war dodger. Ray wasn't convinced. He had seen others, and knew not every German was a devoted Nazi eager to die for the Fatherland, but Bodecker did not fit the bill. Ray put it out of his mind. There were a growing number of German colonies throughout South America, so such men easily blended in.

Bodecker looked irritated. "Do you even know where we are?" he shouted over the wind.

Ray could feel Bodecker's piercing stare. He had enough to contend with already and didn't need to be badgered. He wished the kraut would just shut up. "We have to make that saddle," he answered, motioning with his head toward a distant notch in the mountain range now back in view. The deeply cut semicircle was sandwiched between the clouds and the canyon rim as if a giant had taken a bite out of the mountaintop. It was higher than they were, in these conditions, impossibly higher. The situation seemed obvious enough but apparently not for the German.

Ray didn't like Bodecker. He was arrogant and overbearing, but that's what Ray thought of all Germans. Well, he wasn't paid to like the passengers. Just to get them to their destination, and to get him and the plane back in one piece.

Ray Dobbs did not fit the image of a veteran pilot. A brown leather patch covered the socket, which his right eye once occupied. Beneath it a grotesque jagged scar extended to his right ear, a disfigurement that he hid underneath a baseball cap. The damaged tissue pulled taut the skin of his cheek and gave his mouth a habitual asymmetrical strained appearance. Despite his handicap he was still a good pilot. His depth perception had been affected, but his skill and years of experience more than compensated to keep him in the air.

He was normally a friendly and gregarious sort who loved to talk. His head was constantly cocked and turning with a quick twitch much like a caged bird's head. His movements were more exaggerated than those of others as he fit the same field of vision into his one good eye that most managed with two. This manic tendency kept him in perpetual motion and easily tired those around him.

Ray's reflection in the mirror was a constant reminder of his accident, a fluke incident caused by debris flying into the spinning prop of a nearby aircraft. Severed splinters rocketed into the side of his head fifty yards away. It was a chance occurrence with a most unlikely outcome. But being at the wrong place, at the wrong time, seemed to be the story of Ray's life. And it was looking increasingly to him as if another, and final, chapter was about to be added.

Storms here were temperamental, something Ray had hoped would work eventually to his advantage, but this tempest would not let up. Instead, it continued with incessant indifference and volatile fury. The little plane bobbed like a cork on an angry raging sea. Between them and the approaching saddle, the sky was black. The boiling ceiling billowed downward like inverted mushroom clouds, concealing the highest summits around them.

Suddenly, the sky opened with a renewed deluge. "Shit! What next?" Ray shouted. The huge drops quickly turned to hail, which pelted the windshield. The clatter overtook the roaring engine and banging door. The wind and water sprayed through the doorway and visibility was now all but gone. Without warning the plane plunged downward in a powerful current.

"More power!" Bodecker screamed. "We're still a thousand feet below the ridge!"

"There's nothing left!" Ray shouted over the racket. He shoved at the throttle with his hand to prove it would move no further. He was drawing all the power there was.

Bodecker rubbed his right temple. From the corner of his eye, Ray could see that the blow he had taken had caused him to bleed. "I didn't come here to die in the mountains of Colombia, with an incompetent idiot pilot like you!" The German looked as if he was about to strike him. Ray sensed the animosity and pulled away. He had enough trouble keeping them alive without having a fistfight on his hands as well.

Almost twice Ray's bulk, SS-Standartenfuhrer Heinz Bodecker's six feet two inch frame was tightly squeezed into the copilot seat. His loose fitting clothes did nothing to hide his muscular physique. His facial features were strong and angular, with ice-cold blue eyes that pierced through all they confronted. His blond hair was cropped short in quasi-military style, and on his left cheek was a vivid scar extending from his temple to his mandible.

But it wasn't Bodecker's size nor the deep scar gouged in his massive jaw that made Ray wary. Ray figured he had him beat in a disfigurement contest. It was the German's lack of fear in their predicament that concerned him. Conspicuous in his every motion was the man's fierce determination to get what he wanted, when he wanted it—or else.

The wings rocked ceaselessly and the nose pitched violently. More lightning struck, and the ensuing cracks of thunder delivered shockwaves that shook both men to their bones. As the canyon walls closed, the resonating shudders became even more brutal.

Finally Ray broke. "That's it! This is too rough!!"

"What do you mean?" Bodecker shouted to be heard.

In answer Ray banked the plane hard for the 180. "The plane won't stand much more of this! We're going back to Cali," Ray shouted with resignation. "We'll try again when the weather clears."

Bodecker flared instantly. "Keep going, you coward! We must not waste any more time."

"Coward!" Ray exclaimed, taking the storm in with a sweep of his head. "If that's what you want to call it, that's fine by me. But we're going back!"

Bodecker boiled in anger. "Turn this plane around at once!"

"You don't seem to know the difference between cowardice and stupidity, do you?" Ray said. Bodecker lurched for the yoke, but a hammering blast of turbulence slammed him back in his seat.

Shocked by his boldness Ray snapped, "The storm doesn't care who you are, or where you want to go!" He continued fighting the bucking plane as he made his turn. "This storm will swallow us up and spit us out if we don't get out of here!"

"*Nein!*" Bodecker's German slipped out angrily. "Go back now! Or I'll make you sorry you were born!" His words were laced with vengeance.

A flash of lightening illuminated the cockpit momentarily and for an instant Ray saw clearly the demon beside him. His once pale face was flushed red, his fist closed and ready to strike. Under the strain of a tightly clenched jaw his veins stood out on his neck like pulsating ropes. There was no fear in the man, only an imposing anger on the verge of exploding. It was but another reminder for Ray of why he disliked every German he'd ever known.

He waited for the blow that he expected to the side of his head at any second. *What kind of idiot would attack his pilot in mid air—in*

13

a storm? He thought. *A nut just like this guy,* he decided. And for a moment, Ray realized he would have cowed, if he'd had a choice, but he didn't. He had to return; the raging storm had made his decision for him.

"We'll die if we try to go on!" Ray said, trying to reason with the German. "There is no choice. Can't you see for yourself?"

"You'll die if you don't turn back," Bodecker threatened.

Ray licked his lips. "Then who will fly the plane?" Bodecker did not answer. Ray suddenly wondered if he could fly. He kept turning. "We'll never make the saddle in this storm!" He shouted, trying to get the guy to understand.

Bodecker shifted in his seat. Again, Ray thought the man was about to strike him and recoiled to absorb the blow, but instead he felt the German fumbling at his seat belt latch. Ray panicked. *He's gonna push me out!* He thought. The door was still battering back and forth, refusing to close, refusing to fly off. Without his seatbelt he'd fly through the opening any second. He grabbed the German's hand and pushed it away.

Bodecker eyed him. "Turn around, or get out! I don't need..." Bodecker did not have to finish. Ninety degrees into the turn Ray's heart sank. Going back was no longer an option. The mountains they had crossed over only ten minutes ago were even worse. The storm there was a solid wall of black. He had to press on to the east now, if they were to have any hope of surviving.

"There! You see!" Bodecker gloated, his face shiny from the rain, his eyes aglow at the sight of the storm in front of them. "The decision has been made for you. You have no other way out but over the pass." He was clearly pleased by Ray's quandary.

Reluctantly, but knowing he had no choice, Ray resumed his former heading, pressing on again toward the pass, worrying about the canyon walls towering on either side. Outside, he combated the relentless elements; inside he had to deal with a madman. The battering was taking its toll and his disfigured face showed it. A sudden current tossed the plane side to side. *This is it. I am going to die here with this maniac,* Ray thought. *No one will know. No one will care.* He allowed himself a moment of self-pity. His girl in Panama City would never know what had happened to him. Hell, they weren't that close anyway. She'd forget him soon enough. He just wished these last moments were with someone in whom he could find solace. He'd be better off alone.

Ray snapped himself out of it. If he was getting out of this he had to gain altitude. The canyon's dead-end was approaching rapidly. The pass was now closer and intermittently visible through the rushing clouds, but still much too high. He placed his hand on the throttle again. It was wide open. Fierce winds swirled the clouds around rocky spires on the rim, creating condensation trails like streamers twirling in the wind's wake. The canyon walls closed in even more. It was too tight now to turn back. They were committed. But even at full throttle the oxygen-starved engine did not put out enough power for them to climb. Their impending fate seemed inescapable, awaiting them on the sharply rising rock. Its barren surface was jagged and lethal. "Something good better happen soon or we're dead!" Ray cried out.

"Pull harder!" Bodecker ordered, as he yanked on the yoke himself. It slowed the plane even more. Ray knew that without sufficient wind under the wings the plane would stop flying and go into a stall, even with the engine racing.

"Stop it!" Ray fought him. "You'll stall us!"

Bodecker backhanded him. "Then you do it, fool, or nothing will matter!"

Ray grasped for options. There were none. Beside him Bodecker's piercing glare was agonizing. Ray was coming to fear him more than the weather. Under his breath he prayed, his eyes fixed on the looming cliffs. "Oh God, I need your help. I have been less than…"

Before he could finish there was a slamming jolt from below. Ray lost all control as his immobilized body sunk into the seat that was being shoved upward. Something was lifting them. The plane creaked dreadfully under the pressure, again on the verge of snapping. The cliffs ahead seemed to reel downward.

Bodecker glanced at the altimeter. Its arms were spinning wildly, indicating a climb of 4,000 feet per minute. They were caught in an updraft on the windward slope. Within seconds the invisible elevator of rising air rocketed them up, shooting them above the looming rim with explosive speed. The turbulence abruptly vanished, but the fast moving current continued, sweeping them quickly towards and over the saddle. Then it spit them out beyond, like a leaf tossed about and forward by the autumn wind.

Ray drew a deep breath. His aching muscles relaxed for the first time in an hour, and he gazed at the ground beneath them. The tranquility was short-lived as an equally violent downdraft awaited them on the leeward, where descending air turbulently sucked the plane down. The wings rocked sixty degrees in either direction; the door continued to batter back and forth. The cumbersome floats, hanging below the fuselage like pendulums, were all that stabilized the plane preventing it from flipping on its back and spiraling into the mountain.

Bodecker glared at Ray to take action, but he was just waffling indecisively, paralyzed with fatigue. With the engine still redlining, he grabbed the controls and pointed the nose to the sky. The altimeter now indicated a 3,000-foot per minute descent. He had to put distance between them and the mountain to escape the downdraft before it hammered the plane into the ground. The deafening wind rushed by the fuselage. The plane pitched back and forth, struggling to clear itself from the mass of rock. Finally, they broke from the grip of the churning gale, and as if a switch had been flipped, the rough air vanished.

Ray knew he had failed. Bodecker had saved them. He breathed a second sigh of relief as he took back the controls of the airplane. He felt Bodecker's unforgiving eyes bearing down on him. When would this nightmare end?

Beyond the influence of the storm the wind stabilized and the clouds thinned. Ray glanced at the fuel gauges. They were lower than expected, but the engine had been running at full power for almost an hour to fight the storm. He pulled the throttle back to cruise, trimmed the plane for a gradual efficient descent and turned south. The half tank remaining would have to get him back over the same mountains tomorrow. He grabbed the handle of the door and the third time it slammed shut and held.

Sunshine broke through the clouds, splattering spectacular patches of light on the receding mountains. Blue skies in the distance beckoned them out of their perilous crossing. Dropping slowly, Ray looked with relief at the ominous clouds behind, still pulsating with movement and flashes of lightning. He was exhausted and wondered how they ever survived the maelstrom.

CHAPTER TWO

Two hours had passed since leaving Cali, and now that they were clear of the storm the views had become spectacular. Mountain streams gushed through crags in the cliffs, and the rainforest to the east was an endless sea of green. Since their departure there had not been the slightest hint of civilization. This land was, for all practical purposes, as untouched and remote as when the Spanish conquerors had first passed this way.

In the storm's aftermath, Bodecker and his pilot pushed onward over rows of steeply rising ridges, which passed smoothly beneath them. Between the outcrops, lush tropical valleys, extensions of the rainforest, invaded the foothills like fingers, their advance stifled only by the rising rock. There was no repetition of the tension and threats during the storm, but Ray was taking no chances. He decided to hold his peace for the rest of the flight, though it did nothing to quell the fear he felt.

Finally, over a ridge much like the many others they had crossed, Ray pulled back on the throttle. The 120-horse power radial engine slowed to idle and the plane dropped quickly. Somewhere below, scattered into the rugged folds of these foothills, the seemingly ordinary settlement of the Picayulta Indian tribe lay waiting, their village only recently rediscovered just off the snaking bank of the Ortenguaza River.

"Is this it? The Ortenguaza?" Bodecker asked curtly, though he could not mask the excitement in his words. They were the first spoken by either of them since the storm.

"It is," Ray answered coldly. He watched Bodecker survey the valley with greedy eyes. In the seven years that Ray had been flying into the remote locations of Central and South America, he had never felt so uneasy about a passenger.

He had sensed trouble out of Bodecker from the start, and the recent confrontation had only confirmed his initial impression. Most of his fares were friendly and talkative. Few could keep from looking at and appreciating the splendor of the colossal mountains, the infinite coastline, or the vast rainforests. Many could talk of nothing else. Bodecker could not have cared less. He had neither interest in nor appreciation for the natural beauty of the land.

Ray had never liked Germans, and since the outbreak of war, he felt his prejudice had been justified. His boss, Hank McDermott, on the other hand, ferried any passenger with a dollar.

Most were hunters, searching for the ultimate challenge, the South American Jaguar. A few were biologists looking for new plants with medicinal potential. But there were also those who came to save the Indians as well as those who came to steal from them. From what Ray had seen they all ended up stealing, in one way or another.

To Hank, it did not matter. With a pocket full of unpaid bills, what he wanted was cash. And with the right amount, personal information became an unnecessary formality. Bodecker had gold. It had been good enough for Hank, even if he was a

German. There had been more of them recently he rationalized, as the German fortunes of war grew less propitious.

But neither Hank nor Ray had been able to fathom the true purpose of Bodecker's journey into the depths of the Amazonian basin. Even had they had a better idea of what the SS-Standartenfuhrer was up to, they would never have presumed to know who had personally dispatched him.

Having survived the worst storm of his flying career, Ray had only three goals: to make his destination, drop Bodecker off, and get out. True, he didn't know Bodecker's intentions, but at this point, he didn't care.

Dipping below the ridges, the plane gracefully descended into a valley indistinguishable from the others, though not to Ray's keen eye. He prepared for landing and as the plane dropped lower the temperature inside rose rapidly. The valley air was heavy, motionless and stagnant.

Ray leveled the plane just above the green canopy. The floats skimmed the treetops, which rose a hundred and fifty feet above the forest floor. The impenetrable foliage passed quickly below them. Startled birds frantically took flight from their perches.

Ray added flaps. The plane lifted, then slowed down even more as the engine dropped nearly to idle. Suddenly through a breach in the tightly woven fabric of trees and vines there was a momentary glimpse of water. Ray cut the power completely. The engine sputtered and the plane dropped hard toward the surface. Just above the chocolate colored water, he pulled the yoke back. The plane flared, steadily slowing until it settled smoothly on its pontoons, instantly transforming from airplane to boat.

The idling engine turned erratically as the water brought them to a standstill. Ray cocked his head and surveyed his surroundings. A dead tree jutting from the water gave him his bearings and he added power. He pushed the pedals with his feet, activating small rudders on the pontoon's aft undersurface to steer the plane.

The water's edge merged with the vegetation, concealing its true banks somewhere beyond. They taxied along the impenetrable border searching for an opening. Ray knew the place well. He turned the plane and sputtered up a cove no different in appearance from any other. Here the canopy completely engulfed the waterway. In a moment they had gone from the wide-open world to confines illuminated only by filtered light. They passed through the tunnel and rounded a bend to a break in the foliage and a small earthy beach beneath the trees.

The landing area was crude, a bank of mud where a pair of dugout canoes was beached, and another lay swamped, just breaking the surface. Ray cut the engine. The sudden silence was abrupt. The only sound was the water lapping gently against the floats as the plane's momentum carried them slowly toward the overhanging branches of the riverbank.

"End of the line. Picayulta International," Ray said with fatigue. It was the phrase he always used when delivering his passengers to their remote destinations. It normally lightened the mood of the long journey. Not this time.

Bodecker did not so much as acknowledge the pilot. Instead, as the plane slid gently onto the bank, he grabbed his bag, flung open the door and leapt to the muddy ground. "You will wait here until I return," he ordered.

"The deal was only to bring you. I leave tomorrow first thing in the morning if you're planning on going with me." Ray looked at the overheard canopy, wishing there had been enough daylight to leave at once.

Bodecker's scowl as he walked off left no need for words. He paused after a few steps and surveyed the vacant landing. Ray watched from his seat, waiting for the man to go off and find his Indians. Finally, he eased himself out of the plane, grabbed a rope and began testing overhanging limbs for strength to secure the plane for the night. He didn't look forward to a night aboard the plane but he'd done it before. And it was a lot safer than sleeping ashore—or near the crazy German, for that matter.

Bodecker crouched down, and for a moment studied the soil around a footprint at a trailhead. He stood up, and with a final scan of the landing site homed in on Ray and the plane.

Ray looked down at the painter he was fastening, not wanting to let on that he had been watching. He heard a branch snap, and when he looked up Bodecker had vanished.

CHAPTER THREE

Ray sat quietly in the same position for a long time, watching the trailhead, suspecting something unexpected might happen any moment. He didn't know what but Bodecker gave him the creeps and seemed capable of anything.

His muscles were weary as he finished fastening the tie ropes to a branch. He looked over his shoulder as he worked, certain Bodecker was lurking behind him someplace. Occasionally he held his breath, and listened closely, but the jungle was quiet; only the calls of a distant bird and the buzz of the nearby cicada were audible.

Ray sat back on the pontoon and drew a deep breath, finally allowing himself to relax now that he was rid of the German. It had been a long arduous day; he was too tired to think about it any longer. Bodecker was somewhere, hiking up the trail toward the Indian village—and that was okay with him.

The sun dropped quickly as it did in this part of the world, and the riverbank grew noticeably darker. Ray wondered idly just what the German was up to, if he was coming back to the plane for the night, or if he'd be here in the morning. *Well, he better be,* Ray thought, *because I'm off at first light.* He checked his tie downs then settled down on top of a float to eat. He unwrapped a sandwich and took a bite. The bread was stale and the chicken tasted like it had been sitting in Hank's icebox for too long. Ray spit it out into the river. Ripples sprang from the water's surface as fish scavenged the refuse. Ray took a swig from his canteen to get rid of the taste, then peered back into his lunch bag to see what else had been packed. All he saw inside were a few strips of dried fish in tissue and a banana. He shook his head with disappointment, then took a bite of fish. It had been that kind of day from the start. Why would it change now?

Every jungle howl or slight shift in the sounds brought Ray to full alert as he quietly finished his meal. When it was apparent that Bodecker was not going to return that night he climbed into the cockpit of the plane, secured the door and the windows, and shoved a blanket over a hole in the fabric skin behind the back seat. He made a mental note to check the entire plane for damage in the morning. Fully enclosed, he knew it was the best he could do against the tropical mosquitoes. At sunup he planned to be gone without notice. He leaned the seat back to full recline and in moments slipped off into a deep sleep.

•

Since leaving the plane Bodecker had forged his way up the trail toward the Indian settlement, and as he did, he scouted out the area. It was a quarter-mile before he came upon a couple of palapas, huts with thatched palm frond roofs. He could see that they were in disrepair from where he was. A crucifix leaned against the wall of one, and the place was unexpectedly quiet. Obviously abandoned. He scaled a tree to the first low-lying branch and patiently spied the place for movement. Beyond the huts a native walked unsuspectingly across the open space. His lower lip hung down unnaturally, distended by tribal self-mutilation.

Bodecker's attention was diverted from his vigilant perch to a nest of newly born Bushmaster serpents. This particular species of Bushmasters was one of the few snake species that bore living young instead of laying eggs. A dozen or so of the young reptiles were slithering over each other in a perpetually moving ball, each serpent plunging itself back into the center of the living sphere.

Bodecker watched them for awhile, his eyes fixed on their constant movement as if mesmerized by a dancing fire. He knew the species well. The young snakes' concentrated venom was even more deadly than that of their adult counterparts. He respected how they would grow to be patient stalkers, waiting for the perfect moment to strike at their unsuspecting victims, with fatal consequences, and without remorse. He felt a certain kinship with the deadly vipers and considered that they shared a common place in the hierarchy of the universe. Like him, they were more than just the survivors of their environment. They were the conquerors.

Preparation and patience were the rule in the killing game, and to Bodecker, that's what it was—a game. He prided himself on being innovative and yet unpredictable. Sometimes he used his ingenuity to overcome his opponents in ways they never would have suspected, other times he acted with pure and unadulterated brute force. It was this technique of preparation and study that he believed gave him his perfect record. First, he would manipulate his victims into vulnerability, then he ruthlessly crushed them.

Bodecker dropped to the ground for a closer look, and for another moment watched the snakes in fascination, then scooped the wiggling ball into his satchel and disappeared into the night.

•

The night belongs to the amphibians. Mournful baritones, mostly milk frogs, provided a deep doo-wop chorus to the tree frogs' hysterical cacophony. Add heat and humidity to this syrup of sound and the night was palpably thick, suppressing the movements of most of the larger jungle animals.

Ray was too deeply asleep to hear the night sounds. A single mosquito trapped inside the cockpit buzzed around his head, but even the high pitch of the little pest was not enough to wake him from his slumber. Soon, it too was motionless as it rested on the skin of his neck and sucked the blood from an exposed vein.

Ray did not hear the frogs stop croaking, or the airplane door as it opened briefly. The last thing he failed to hear was the ball of slithering vipers as it was rolled out of the sack onto the cockpit floor before the door was refastened shut.

The reptilian mass immediately fell apart and frantically began searching for a way out.

Bodecker sat patiently on the bank with a smug smile as he waited for his handiwork to take effect. The choir of frogs resumed its rhythmical chanting, and continued briefly until interrupted again, first by a loud slap, then by a shrill scream, which was followed by moments of slamming, thrashing, and yelling within the plane. But that commotion soon ended.

Bodecker closed his eyes to imagine what was transpiring, quietly savoring the moment. When it was over, he opened the airplane door. Several snakes wriggled out and fell into the river as he inspected his handiwork. He enjoyed new and original ways of carrying out his trade. After a brief moment of self-admiration he collected his pack, and headed back up the trail. There was one less American now with whom to deal.

CHAPTER FOUR

Professor Hubert Jenkins slouched idly in his comfortable stick built chair, keeping a distance sufficiently far from his thatched hut, a rough bungalow with a wide veranda, to properly oversee the mending of its roof.

The dark-skinned Indian he employed clung precariously to the thatching with one hand while making the repairs with the other. His pace was lethargic and sluggish, like that of a sloth, the professor thought. But the natives were unaccustomed to the concept of employment, and the professor, like it or not, had to content himself with whatever little he could squeeze from them. What authority he did have over the Indians meant the work would get done eventually. Progress would soon halt anyway, as the rising midmorning heat crept past tolerable, and sapped even the slightest hint of motivation.

Jenkins fussed monotonously with a bit of breakfast caught in his poorly groomed beard, then glanced down at his spindly white knees. His fair skin was barely exposed between his wrinkled khaki shorts and his tightly pulled knee-high white socks. He didn't like the sun. In his youth he had burned too many times and now his fair skin was paying for his indiscretion with sores and blemishes. His long sleeved shirt, with countless rings of perspiration staining the armpits, and his dirty safari hat constituted the rest of his ever-present protective sun barrier. They were pointless precautions against the dim filtered light penetrating to the floor of the rainforest.

A loud crack brought him out of his stupor. The native laborer had slipped from his place and was scrambling for safety, his ball of twine and materials falling to the ground. Jenkins lifted his eyes, but did not get up. Instead, he gave him a curt reprimand in his native language, shaking his head with disgust throughout the tongue-lashing. Indifferent to the scolding, the Indian resumed his slow work and Jenkins resumed doing nothing. A faint background of insect noises with an occasional distant call from a parrot or howl of a monkey were all that broke into the otherwise silent morning.

The professor pulled a gold watch from his pocket and turned it over repeatedly in his fingers; a chain attached it to his shirt. He inspected it carefully before opening its ornate cover. Inside where a picture could be placed, there was none. The second hand ticked slowly around the faded face. Jenkins let out a sigh. "Five o'clock," he said to himself, "somewhere." The piece had not kept time accurately in years. It didn't have to, as there was no time here. There were no Fridays, Saturdays or Sundays. And thank God, Jenkins thought from time to time, there were no Mondays. Amusement was now the watch's only value. Its loud ticking and rotating second hand were quite a novelty for the Indians.

An anthropologist by trade, Jenkins had spent the last thirty-nine years of his life traveling the world on assignment for the National Geographic Society. He was an academic sort, typifying his profession. At sixty-four years of age, and headed for retirement, he was disgruntled by this, his last assignment. There were more comfortable places he would have preferred. Hawaii had had an opening to study the disappearing natives, as had Tahiti. And someone of his tenure with the Society almost always got to choose his final assignment.

Jenkins had not been so fortunate. He was paying the price for a previous inaccurate account he had submitted, and the magazine had published, three years before. His editor had suffered the embarrassment of the blunder and exiled the scientist to what was considered a tropical jungle work camp, an assignment no one else within the Society had wanted.

Nearly three years ago now, Jenkins still felt betrayed. He shifted in his chair, passing this day like most, sulking bitterly. He'd always loathed the home office and had never trusted the management. On return home from each assignment there was always a new supervisor, with a new agenda, and with no regard for the men in the field—or so it was in Jenkins' paranoid mind.

Ever since learning of the assignment Jenkins had harbored his resentment, and the jungles of eastern Colombia had provided the ideal solitude to foster and perfect his consuming bitterness. He spent much of his time replaying the "what ifs" in his head, imagining the challenge to his editor that never materialized, the argument that he was too gutless to have, and the stand he was too spineless to take.

Though it never figured into his calculations, the only true constant in Jenkins' career was his cowardice. Dreading confrontation, and in the final days of his career, he had meekly accepted this last assignment and had become resigned to his role as a trampled company man.

His ultimate revenge had been that in his two and a half years here, he had accomplished virtually no research. Instead of studying his subjects, he used and manipulated them to promote his own comfort and convenience, for here he was the big fish. It didn't matter to Jenkins that the pond was insignificantly small. Over the years he had developed nothing but contempt for the primitive savages, as he now saw indigenous people. He expected them to serve him as slaves serve their masters. After the way he had been mistreated it was only his due.

Movement on the river trail interrupted his daily pout. Jenkins squinted and with no surprise watched a white man emerge from the jungle. He'd heard the floatplane land and wondered when his visitor or visitors would arrive. His one fear was that it would be someone from the Society wanting to review his work. Jenkins straightened in his chair for a better look. "Hello there," he called out.

Bodecker looked up and waved, as if the hike up the rise had been strenuous, and he was too tired to reply. Jenkins grabbed the walking stick leaning by his chair and pulled himself to his feet, then approached the stranger. "Professor Hubert Jenkins," he said pompously, extending his hand, although he was still too far away to shake. "Do you speak English?"

The German stopped, as if to catch his breath. From his shirt pocket he pulled a set of wire frame spectacles, and slipped the ear loops onto his ears, which were hidden by an out of style hat. It was like the one worn by Sherlock Holmes, made of plaid fabric with a small visor and a short tassel on top. The combination gave him a less aggressive, more academic demeanor, one of a man out of his element, exactly the image he sought to convey. He tipped his hat without removing it and studied the Professor. "Dr. Heinz Bodecker," he answered.

"I expected you last night shortly after I heard your plane land."

"Yes, well, it has been a difficult night." Bodecker paused. "Mr. Dobbs, the pilot, had an unfortunate accident as he disembarked from the plane."

Jenkins looked down the empty trail. "Oh?"

"I'm afraid he slipped on the bank and rolled into a nest of snakes."

"Snakes!" Jenkins looked concerned. "Do you know what kind?"

"Bushmasters. Newborn ones I believe," Bodecker said solemnly.

Jenkins was wide-eyed. "Was he bitten?"

Bodecker nodded. "Numerous times."

"My God! Then he must have…"

"Yes, I'm afraid so," the German said with a slight quiver in his voice. "There was really nothing I could do. Fortunately, he didn't last long. I tried to come up, but by then it was late and dark, and the trail was difficult to follow so I thought it best to stay with the plane and wait until morning."

"And Dobbs?" Jenkins inquired.

"I left him in the plane to protect him from the wild animals."

"Damn shame," Jenkins said, shaking his head at the somber news. "He was a good fellow, that Ray Dobbs, always friendly." His words were slow and thoughtful as he remembered the one-eyed pilot who had flown him in and out several times over the years, and delivered supplies and correspondence every few months. "Just another victim of this damn valley," he mumbled under his breath.

Bodecker strained to hear him. "Victim? Of the valley?"

Jenkins did not immediately answer. Finally, he nodded and replied, "Yes, sooner or later the valley…it gets us all."

"Us? All? Who is 'us'?" Bodecker asked.

Jenkins did not look directly at Bodecker as he answered. "Outsiders—non-natives. The Indians call us intruders. They claim spirits protect this valley. By coming here, they say, we are condemning ourselves to death." He stood quietly for another moment, leaning on his staff. "I would have never guessed Ray to be next." Abruptly Jenkins spun around and started up the trail. "Well, no use standing about in the heat," he said. "Come on up and rest. We'll send one of these savages to deal with Dobbs later."

His bungalow now stood alone and quiet. The Indian had used Jenkins' distraction as his chance to escape for the day. Jenkins was used to the shiftless ways of the locals and gave it no thought. There was always tomorrow. The first visitor, other than Dobbs, he'd had in a year now had his undivided attention—a civilized person at that, one with whom he could speak English. He motioned Bodecker to a veranda chair. "You must be exhausted. Please sit." He beamed with pride over his native-built dwelling but the place went unnoticed by Bodecker.

"There is so much I haven't heard—and want to know. It's been over a year since I last spoke to someone from outside, other than Dobbs and he had no interest in events outside his narrow realm. The occasional newspaper and magazine I get are always so out of date." He picked up a kettle. "Tea?"

Bodecker smiled. "How nice. Thank you." From his pocket he drew a packet of small cigars and lit one, the smoke acrid and sweet.

Jenkins curled his nose at the odor but said nothing. He fluttered about to find matches and lit a small stove. It had taken but a moment for him to forget his ill-fated pilot friend down by the river. He considered asking about the war but Bodecker was obviously German and he had no wish to alienate his visitor. "So, what brings you to this forgotten corner of the world, doctor?"

Bodecker leaned back in his chair. "I'm on assignment for the Archeological and Anthropological Department at the University of Berlin." He drew a lung full of smoke then exhaled through his nostrils.

"Berlin?" Jenkins hesitated. With the war raging in Europe the last option he'd considered was that a university in Berlin would still be conducting anthropological research.

"Yes. My director came across some long forgotten diaries."

"Diaries?" Jenkins perked up. "Whose?"

"A Spaniard. Don Diego de Vasquez." Bodecker noticed Jenkins was curiously puzzled. "He was a missionary."

"Weren't they all," Jenkins snickered.

Bodecker removed his hat and set it down, his forehead bright from the heat. "He came out here with twenty-two men to build a mission a hundred and eighty-three years ago. Two years later, he and one other younger man returned to Spain, as the party's only survivors. Upon arriving they reported directly to the Arch-bishop in Madrid. The younger man was never heard from again." Bodecker had Jenkins's full attention. "The church sent Don Diego into seclusion to a monastery in the Pyrenees, not far from the French border. They claimed he had contracted a disease in the Americas, some kind of jungle madness, and spoke only gib-berish. He was quarantined in a room for fear of contagion, or at least that was what the church maintained, and was allowed only pen and paper. Most of his days he spent writing to friends and high-ranking officials begging for his freedom. His letters never left the monastery." Bodecker paused. "Don Diego died in that same room eighteen years after his return."

"And his letters?"

Bodecker grinned. "Long gone, all of them. But the diaries he wrote, he had kept in secret, no doubt. They survived. They were discovered thirty years after his death in a vault, behind a stone block in the wall of his room. The old priest had carved out the hollow and stored his recollections and experience in a series of journals."

"A last act of defiance against overbearing superiors," Jenkins chimed in supportively, feeling a kinship to the oppressed Spaniard.

"Two years of memories recounted..." Bodecker paused. His tone was distant. "The journals described the fateful trip, and the experiences that he and those with him met with here on the banks of the Ortenguaza. They included precise accounts of a tribe of Indians living in the valley closest to the headwaters. The papers reported the tribe as having a supernatural power. A power so incredible that it could have only been given to them by God himself."

Jenkins shuffled a little, growing uneasy with Bodecker's words and tone.

"The priest believed the Indians to be a chosen race, like the Jews claimed to be, uniquely blessed, and virtually unchanged over the centuries by the outside world."

Jenkins chuckled sarcastically. "That had to please the Archbishop," he said. "Why did no one return to the Ortenguaza when the journals were discovered?"

"Those were dangerous times. As you know, the monarchy just to the north, in France, was literally losing its head, and the peasants were on a rampage against any form of wealth and power. No one was safe." Jenkins listened intently. "The church and clergy had been among the worst offenders in the corruption circles, taking and squandering money for missions that never happened."

"But they were not in France."

"The Archbishop in Spain was worried the unrest would spread south. The manuscripts were sealed and posted as sensitive material, and then moved to the restricted underground chamber of the National Archives in Madrid. They have gone unread for more than a century."

"Until now," Jenkins supposed, slowly digesting what he had heard.

There was hardly an anthropologist in the world unaware of the Nazi obsession with ancient works, especially of the supernatural. Reichsfuhrer Heinrich Himmler, head of the SS, was a nut on the subject. He was said to have regularly attended séances before the war.

The professor never would have guessed however, that less than two months prior, Bodecker had been standing before Himmler himself. There the former chicken farmer, now most powerful Nazi in the world after the Fuhrer, had given Bodecker his orders. The assignment seemed far-fetched, but Bodecker understood the chain of command, and he remembered the Reichsfuhrer's eyes still glowing from his meeting with Hitler who had personally sanctioned the mission. No matter how unbelievable, Bodecker was decided. He would carry out the mission with which he was now entrusted.

Jenkins was fascinated by the story as he had heard parts of it before. "I searched for those very journals," he mentioned with a hint of jealousy in his tone, "when I was first given this assignment."

Bodecker's eyes narrowed. "Did you now?" He'd heard nothing of it in his briefing. He lit another cigar.

Jenkins squared his shoulders. "Yes, I was chosen by the National Geographic Society to conduct research in the area." He made it sound as if he rigorously competed for and won the opportunity. "I knew there had been a Spanish expedition here and thought there might be some record." Bodecker nodded. "The Society has many of its own resources," Jenkins continued haughtily. "I traveled to Spain initially to search the archives for background on the Indians of this region, any facts or knowledge accumulated by the explorers and missionaries."

"But you found nothing?"

"No, not really."

"What do you mean, 'not really?'"

"Well, there was something, but I heard of it in New York, not Spain. And it seemed to refer to those Journals you mentioned in particular."

"Yes?" Bodecker asked with interest.

"A colleague of mine for the magazine, Larry Beakle, had done a piece on the eighteenth and nineteenth century Spanish church. In the process, he dug up bits and parts of a legend..." Jenkins stopped abruptly. His enthusiasm to tell his story had suddenly vanished, as if he had said something he would have rather not revealed.

"A legend?"

"Yes." Jenkins winced, realizing it was too late to take back his words. "Just stories passed down by monks over the years; incomplete tales, backed by these supposed but then elusive journals."

"What did your colleague say?"

"The details were vague at best, and unverifiable without the journals. He told me to go first to the town of Triste, in the Pyrenees, and find the order of the Brothers of San Gabriel. That's where I could get firsthand the rumors he had heard. Then he recommended I follow them up in Madrid with the journals that should be stored in the National Archives." Jenkins thought a moment and then added, "Larry was of the opinion that if there was anything to be found about the Indians of this area that's where it would be."

Bodecker cogitated thoughtfully. "He seems to have put it together."

"Larry was a smart guy. He did a lot of research. It was the only place he had ever seen the Picayulta tribe mentioned."

"Picayultas!" Bodecker reiterated enthusiastically. "This is the tribe I am searching for. Are they close by?"

"Yeah. They're my neighbors...just up the trail." Jenkins pointed to the continuing path.

The German looked at the path with longing for a moment, then asked, "Did you go to Triste?"

"I tried," Jenkins said disappointedly. "But when I arrived, there was a civil uprising, echoes of the civil war, and the military had blocked all passage into the foothills. The monks I ran into further south claimed to know nothing." Jenkins paused. "I didn't believe them, but figured I would question Larry more when I returned to New York."

"What did he tell you?"

"Nothing. Regrettably he was killed in a car accident while I was away."

"Most unfortunate," Bodecker mused.

The two men sat in silence for a moment, lost in their own thoughts until Bodecker broke it. "So what exactly are you studying here now, professor?"

Jenkins poured each of them a cup of tea. "Like you, I imagine, I am studying the locals, stuck still in the Stone Age. But how did you get hold of the journals? I'd thought it a dead end. The librarian at the Archives three years ago refuted their existence. I could tell he was lying, but it was like hitting a brick wall."

Bodecker sipped his tea. "Well, much as I disapprove of the German occupation of most of Europe, it has given us German scientists a rare opportunity to study *all* the archives of the mainland countries. No one, frankly, is in a position to deny archives to us. As a human being I abhor the tragedies of the war, but as a scientist it is hard to deny myself the chance of a lifetime to study many of the files which have never been made publicly available."

Jenkins pondered the thought of unobstructed access to all the archives of the continent. Far removed from the war and its horror, he focused more on his own little realm and personal wishes. It was obvious he envied Bodecker's position. "Why the Picayultas? There are many primitive tribes much easier to access," he finally asked.

"It is their supernatural beliefs, legends if you will, that intrigued us. The journals were specific and detailed. The Indian's unique beliefs fascinated the director at the university. My mission is to verify and document their validity, or at the least determine on what they are based, even if only on a concoction of Vasquez's fertile imagination."

"In the middle of a world war?"

Bodecker smiled arrogantly. "I'm sorry to inform you, as you are an American, that Germany has the war well in hand. It is not necessary for us to dedicate all our resources to that end." Jenkins said nothing but Bodecker could see the disappointment on his face. Cut off as he was, he had no choice but to accept his visitor's judgment.

"Well," Jenkins said, changing the subject, "'unique' certainly describes the little savages. Totally isolated by the mountains and the wilderness, they are virtually unchanged, and have managed to keep their independence from the outside world."

Bodecker leaned forward. "Tell me about them."

Jenkins drew himself up in importance. "As Don Diego had inferred, they believe themselves to be a chosen people, protected by a supernatural god." He paused. "And true to their legends, this valley has provided for them, and protected them from outsiders. They live a charmed existence, and possess an uncanny clairvoyance…it's downright eerie." His voice trailed off in reflection.

"Professor, your objectivity escapes you. They are surely just tales," Bodecker said, raising his eyebrows skeptically. "You sound as if you were starting to believe them." He then added in a disbelieving tone, "I see no dangers here."

"Tell that to Ray Dobbs," Jenkins said with a trace of sarcasm.

Bodecker bristled. "It was an unfortunate occurrence, but hardly supernatural."

The professor looked down, shaking his head. "Yes, just one more unfortunate occurrence. I've seen many in the last two and a half years."

"My point exactly," Bodecker pointed out. "You have been here two and one half years! You look just fine to me."

"Unlike the others, I keep my distance. I observe, but never interfere. If I am not wanted, I leave. And I've learned the language. It is this respect for their privacy that has made me tolerable to them. Others have not been so prudent."

"Others? What others?" Bodecker's tone perked up. "Were the Spanish not the last to visit here?"

Jenkins laughed. "Oh, there were others here—before me. The Wilson party. There were three of them. They arrived several years ago, led by a Reverend James Wilson. He was Pentecostal, I believe, one of the stranger branches of Protestant churches, if you ask me. Like his Spanish predecessors he was certain he had a direct connection to God. But it was through him that the Society discovered the existence of the Picayultas in the first place. Naturally, they wanted to study the Indians before the reverend and his band of do-gooders ruined them entirely."

"I see. That would tend to explain your presence here."

"My fear was the missionaries might have already force-fed the Indians new beliefs, altering them and their customs forever." Jenkins wore the smile of a passionate unbeliever. "And that is how you come to find me here. It is a strange world in which we live." Jenkins gazed pensively towards the landing area. "Even Ray considered the missionaries a half-cocked lot. He always tried to keep his distance from them during his supply runs here." Jenkins continued, "They were a strange bunch for missionaries. Two of them, Wilson's assistants, were supposed to be reformed alcoholics but it didn't take. Though most Pentecostals are teetotalers, they were known to partake of their home-grown moonshine, and when they did they could be downright mean. Even then, I don't think there would have been any trouble except one day Reverend Wilson became unhinged. I don't know how else to explain it."

"Just who was this Reverend Wilson?" Bodecker asked curiously, stabbing his cigar butt out in a coconut shell.

"Reverend James Wilson was an American. He and his two misguided backsliders set out to convert these savages into good God fearing Christians.

They'd been here a year already when I arrived and the damage to the Indians was already evident," Jenkins said with disgust. "Shortly after I settled in, his daughter Kelly joined them." Her name brought a smile to Jenkins' face. "She was a prize. Since the age of seven, she had traveled with her father on his missions in Africa, China, and South America. Uninterested in a career in religion, she was more focused on finishing her college degree in world culture and social development. Occasionally, she would skip a semester and tag along with her father," Jenkins reminisced contentedly. "She was bright and exciting, and the Indians loved her as much as she loved them. Things weren't so bad while she was here. But after just eight months she left. The U.S. government took an interest in her knowledge of certain tribes in North Africa. I suspect they were anticipating war there even then. The assignment sounded exciting; she would have been crazy to pass it up," he said, rationalizing her decision.

"What about the reverend?" Bodecker asked.

"He too was an interesting sort, in his own way. I believe he and his accomplices really did want to help these poor Indians, but they lacked the necessary diplomatic skills. And their fire and brimstone approach to religion was harsh. Something had destabilized the reverend. I don't know what, but I think that was why Kelly was trying to stay close to him. They pushed too hard, too fast, on these prehistoric jungle dwellers, ranting and raving around the village, throwing out accusations of sin on the elders and their families. Why, they even threatened their host, the chief," Jenkins said incredulously, "with doom and destruction if he did not change his sinful ways." Jenkins shook his head. "The year following Kelly's departure, I watched the village go from a peaceful if primitive commune to a nervous body of headhunting savages. Families feared leaving their huts as tribesmen wrestled with the tension. They looked to the elders for help, and the elders turned to the chief. Finally, the chief consulted his ancestors for the answer." Bodecker perked up but said nothing. "Wilson and his two helpers died thirteen months ago at the hands of a hostile mob of Picayultas," Jenkins testified somberly. "Although I did not like them very much, I was sorry to see them put to death. At the very least I enjoyed having someone with whom I could speak English."

With a look, Bodecker beckoned Jenkins to go on. The professor shook his head. "I don't know what triggered the final violent act, but having sat through a couple of Wilson's sermons towards the end, more than likely the zealots got what they deserved." He smiled dispassionately. "The story is that the chief pridefully keeps their shrunken heads impaled on sticks within his hut." Jenkins paused for effect, obviously enjoying an audience. His eyes were hollow; a callous smile was pasted on his face, as if the image of the missionaries he was visualizing excited him. "I think the reverend is happy there. I knew he would do whatever it took to get 'on staff' at the chief's meetings." He chuckled through his beard.

"Why didn't they kill you while they were murdering the white men?"

"I was never one of them and the Indians knew that. They are savages but they are not stupid or unreasonable."

"So you stayed on?"

"To finish my work, but with a new respect for the Indians, their customs and their privacy. And I was always mindful of their limits for tolerating outsiders."

"You do not feel vulnerable?"

"Vulnerable? Yes. Threatened? No. Not as long as I keep my distance."

Bodecker leaned back and pondered Jenkins's account.

•

An Indian servant appeared and served a supper as the afternoon turned into evening. She was a young woman, bare breasted and shy. Her lower lip was already extended with one of the wooden plates everyone in the tribe used. Bodecker looked at her with disdain, examining her perked breasts as he would the udders of an animal.

Dinner was spicy mint soup of cooked vegetables, followed by capybara and taro root stew. The meat was tough, tasteless and greasy. Jenkins noticed Bodecker pass on the stew. "Don't like river rat soup, eh?" Jenkins asked his guest.

"I don't know where the rat has been. I believe I'll just finish with the desert."

"Cinnamon bread sticks. Probably the only truly acceptable dish here. But here you eat what you have to, to survive." The steam from the stew clouded Jenkins' glasses as he spoke. He tore a piece of meat from a bone and chewed with relish. "Luckily there's the *chichi*." He poured a glass of a fermented root drink. "You might not like it at first, but it'll grow on you." He took a sip. "The women make it from crushed taro roots and spittle. It's aged for a few weeks, then sweetened with honey and spiced with bark. A lot like the *balche* that Mayans made, but with more kick."

Throughout the meal Jenkins asked about current events. Bodecker fed him bits of war news, hardly more than propaganda. Jenkins hung on the words though he was not without his suspicions. This was a German, after all. Bodecker avoided Jenkins' questions about the reason for his presence, asking instead for more about the obscure customs and rituals of the tribe, though he no longer had a real interest in them.

There was something more that he wanted something specific, and significant. He wondered if the professor was being sly in avoiding the subject, or was he so obtuse he had no knowledge of the legend that was his reason for traveling halfway around the world to come to this forsaken place. He dug deeper with his questions, and his words became more direct. "Your colleague in New York, the one who collected fragments of a legend..."

"Larry Beakle?"

Bodecker nodded. "Yes. What else did he learn about the journals?"

"Just those bits, I assume...nothing I could make sense of, but I'll never know, will I?"

"No names?"

Jenkins thought a moment. "No, none that I recall."

The intensity of Bodecker's interest increased. "What about objects or artifacts?"

Jenkins straightened in his chair and his answer was defensive: "No." Bodecker backed off. The professor knew. He was craftier than he looked. "What is it, exactly, that you're searching for?" Jenkins asked.

Bodecker leaned forward and looked the Professor directly in the eyes. It made Jenkins uncomfortable. He drew one of his sweet cigars from its pack and slowly lit it, then said forcefully, "Are you quite certain he said nothing about a small statue? A doll... about so big?" He held his hands out just over one-foot apart.

Jenkins fidgeted uncomfortably, but said nothing.

Bodecker pressed on. "Don Diego described it in his writings. It was simply carved, adorned with a gold headdress and imbedded with jewels. And," he held his breath, "the stone from which it was made was said to look like something from another world. The Spaniard thought it came from the Devil."

Jenkins nervously reached for the *chichi*. Beads of sweat formed under his nose, and his hand trembled as he lifted his glass. "Never heard of it," he said, flustered, his drink dribbling into his beard.

"What about 'El Chiflon?'"

Jenkins was taken aback, speechless. His face was white as chalk. A moment passed as he tried to regain his composure. He fiddled with his glasses. He checked around to see if any of the natives were within earshot.

Bodecker asked, "Are you alright? You look like you've seen a ghost."

"I'm fine," Jenkins answered.

"Professor? My question?"

"Yes. I've never heard of it," he said, dodging the real issue.

"Your expression betrays you. Certainly you have. You cannot have lived here nearly three years and not have learned of it. Don't treat me like a fool."

"Oh...ohhh, that! It's just an unimportant superstition these foolish Indians have," Jenkins stuttered unconvincingly.

Bodecker smiled. "Of course it is. They all are, but that is what I am here to study."

"Well, I really don't know much about that one. The natives never speak of it, and as I said, I don't press where I'm not welcome," Jenkins said, still shaking nervously.

"Professor, are you sure you are all right?"

"I'm fine," he answered, though he looked on the verge of a collapse.

"So then tell me," the German pressed. "I'm going to learn it one way or another. What do you know about this El Chiflon?"

The mention of the name again made Jenkins wince and seemed to push him over the edge. "Enough, Dr. Bodecker," the professor stated emphatically. "Simply uttering those words aloud could get us killed. You don't know what you are saying. It is late and I am exhausted. You are welcome to stay here on the veranda hammock if you wish. It is the most comfortable place to sleep I can offer."

Bodecker hesitated, then accepted the invitation with excessive grace. He would drop the subject for the time, but they both knew their conversation was not over.

CHAPTER FIVE

With the passing days Jenkins listened more and more closely to the afternoon sounds. That's when the planes usually arrived. And that's what Jenkins so eagerly wanted to hear, the sputtering of an engine throttled back for descent, followed by the louder revving as it maneuvered on the water toward the trailhead on the riverbank.

He paced the perimeter of his veranda like a caged ferret, and the knot in his stomach grew more and more burdensome by the day. Five long weeks had passed since Bodecker's arrival and each day had become more arduous. Jenkins forced himself into a chair to calm down, but his mind swirled on in agitation. The only thought to which he could cling was getting out. Before he realized it, he was back on his feet again, pacing.

How could things have changed so quickly? He thought. *Why is Bodecker making life so difficult? Even the Indians' mood has changed. What could be his true motive in coming?*

After that first night Bodecker had been cordial and unassuming. He had brought several bottles of good quality rum with him, which he generously shared with the professor. It was a treat Jenkins had grown accustomed to several times a week after supper. Smoother and sweeter than the local harsh *chichi*, it offered him an escape, if only in spirit. But accepting it had its price, requiring a compromise of his principles, and Jenkins's mounting dislike of Bodecker wrestled with his growing desire for the occasional nightly sousing. In the end, Jenkins would always appear on the veranda with empty glass in hand, prepared to sell out the instinct of his better judgment.

Bodecker rationed the supply diligently and served himself only modest amounts, thimblefuls at most. Jenkins' portions, however, he made stout. Jenkins consumed them eagerly. Each evening after supper, through the sweet, acrid cloud of smoke about the German, the men spent hours in discourse, covering everything from politics and the war in Europe, to astronomy and the rich botanical treasures of the rainforest. Jenkins's mind moved ineptly, more like that of a slug than a research scientist. He had been isolated for too many years in the rainforest. The copious helpings of rum did not make him any sharper. Bodecker often left the professor feeling inferior in their exchanges. Ineffective in his arguments, or maybe it was just laziness, Jenkins often swayed toward Bodecker's point of view.

Uncertain of what to make of the German, Jenkins was convinced there was more to him than he was letting on. Bodecker did not follow standard research protocol, that is, the universally accepted hands-off-observe-without-impact approach to his subjects. Often he had tried to communicate with them directly, but the Indians had flatly rejected him. It may have been his imposing size or the intensity of his scowl. Or, it could have been his indiscriminate spying and periodic invasions that spread the nervousness through the tribe. Now however, no Indian wanted to run into Bodecker, much less speak to him. All discussion passed through Jenkins. He was a known quantity; the person they did not consider to be a threat.

The village mood had changed dramatically going from uneasy to paranoid. It was unlike anything Jenkins had seen since the last days of the Wilson party. Worse yet for Jenkins, he was reluctantly compelled to be a part of it all, since Bodecker insisted he serve as interpreter.

Jenkins wondered if research techniques had changed so much in three years, or maybe it was just different in Europe, though he knew that wasn't the case. There was another reason altogether for Bodecker's visit to the valley. And whatever he was truly searching for was eluding him, causing him frustration. His demeanor reflected it, making him ruder, more demanding and more agitated by the day.

Jenkins now did everything he could to steer clear of Bodecker, that is until evening, when like clockwork, he would promptly appear for supper, mustering the needed courage to endure Bodecker, courage motivated by the rum which Bodecker always provided.

Around the veranda they sat with the lighted Cabashi: a ceramic firebox that resembled a lantern, an Indian device that burned dried root chips. With the top on, the chips smoldered for hours. From the Cabashi's side holes a trace of smoke oozed, rising slowly in the room before escaping through the thatches of the roof. Its pungent smell hung in the air, deterring the invasion of the marauding mosquitoes. Initially Jenkins had turned his nose to it, thinking it disgusting. But slowly he had grown accustomed to it, and after two and a half years he actually thought it pleasant. Bodecker's focus never wavered; he just tolerated the stench.

Night after night the ritual continued. Bodecker was patient and his questions were carefully planned. He knew that Jenkins was reluctant, but with the booze flowing he hoped to loosen the professor's tongue. He'd had no luck working directly with the Indians. Once Jenkins was primed, Bodecker inevitably manipulated the discussions to theology, then more specifically to the beliefs of the Picayultas. Ultimately, as the night wore thin and the professor was most susceptible, he more directly steered the conversation toward the legend of El Chiflon. It was the topic the professor feared most and Bodecker knew it, but one way or another he intended to extract everything he could from his colleague.

Jenkins felt the pressure and during his sober days he speculated as to the ulterior motives that Bodecker might be harboring. He noticed the pattern, always leading to the legend and the statue. Only the night previous, bombarded by the attempts and dulled by the alcohol, he had been on the brink of admitting to the depth of his knowledge, but in the last moments he found the will again, clammed up and claimed ignorance.

Bodecker knew he was lying and the supply of booze, usually an effective device, was dwindling. Down to his last bottle, he had decided the time had come to push the professor over the edge. He had hoped to secure his innocent cooperation but needed results. Tonight he would not ration the rum; Jenkins would be allowed his fill.

But tomorrow, it would be gone. If the night did not bear fruit, Bodecker would resort to other means, alternatives the professor would find much less pleasant. It wasn't that the idea of hurting Jenkins bothered Bodecker; he had tortured many people these last years—men, women, once even a classroom of Polish children. The kids had been between six and twelve years of age, and after witnessing the execution of their teacher, they were too scared to cooperate. He had ordered the schoolhouse burned to the ground and there were no survivors.

It would be no different for Jenkins, just inconvenient; Bodecker hated inconveniences.

•

Where the hell was Hank? Jenkins thought. *Surely a search plane would have been dispatched by now,* he mused resentfully. *It should be just a matter of time. What was he waiting for?*

Jenkins had made up his mind; when the next plane came, he was going to be on it. Feeling old and tired, and having long since given up on his research, he had decided the assignment was finished. For two and a half years he had paid the price for his editorial blunder. Enough was enough.

It was raining, the water running off his roof in small rivers. As he paced on his veranda, he spoke to himself loudly: "What more could they want from me?" He raised his hands as if conversing with someone. "And what could they do? Fire me?" He shook his head. "No way. They wouldn't do that," he assured himself with forced conviction. "Anyway, I'm just leaving a little early. And I'll be retired in only a few short months."

He reassured himself that he had compiled sufficient information early on in his assignment. With it he could provide the magazine with an acceptable report and be done. It would be his last, so why should he care if inaccuracies were later discovered in it? He'd be long gone by then. But his confidence was shallow, and he succumbed to nervous uncertainty. After his last debacle they'd double-check his work. There was no way they'd publish him without being certain of his findings.

Jenkins resumed his pacing. "Where is that search plane? It should have arrived by now." His voice was growing louder by the second.

"Perhaps Mr. McDermott has no other planes," a voice answered from the rain. It was Bodecker. His head poked from around the side of the hut. Jenkins spun around quickly. He'd thought he was alone.

"He has two," he said, trying not to look surprised. "A red one and a blue one. I saw them when I first came out."

Bodecker laughed, then stepped in from out of the downpour. "I hope the blue pile of canvas and wire I saw in the hangar two weeks ago was not the other one." His smirk irritated Jenkins. "If it was we may never leave this place."

Still, he seemed unconcerned. "Mr. McDermott did complain about being short of pilots. He said Ray was the only one he could keep on with the war and such. That leaves him with no one to investigate the disappearance of his one functioning plane and, of course, to determine our fate. The Colombian government has no resources to conduct a search and certainly no interest in doing so if it did."

Jenkins didn't want to hear that. He'd feared as much. And he was sick of Bodecker breathing down his neck, demanding he be available at his beck and call to interpret with the Indians. The natives refused to make any effort to communicate with the German directly. It may have been his imposing size or the intensity of his scowl, but all discussion had to pass through Jenkins. He was a known quantity whom they did not consider a threat.

For all this Jenkins resented most his loss of authority and was unaccustomed to actually working. But Bodecker's demeanor was now significantly more aggressive than it had been that first day, conveying an unspoken expectation of obedience. Jenkins, like the Indians, sensed he was someone to be feared. He had yet to threaten anyone outright. The impression came more from his manner and his overbearing tone, which inferred an unpredictable and dangerous reaction, if not obeyed.

•

Intermittently the October winds in Colombia blew from the west. Descending from the heights of the Andes, the cool air reached its dew point over the jungle, turning the humid low land soup into a dense fog, making the rainforest even darker, damper, and cooler than usual. It was at such a time that Bodecker broke out his last bottle of rum.

On the veranda that night, Bodecker repeatedly left the bottle unattended in front of the old man, pretending to go and relieve himself each time Jenkins' glass neared empty. From the thicket he watched the professor first eye the bottle, then look around to see if Bodecker was watching. Then he quickly splashed more rum into his glass.

The bottle of rum took hold, loosening the professor's tongue more than ever. And, on that particular evening, on Jenkins's veranda, the pearl for which Bodecker had patiently waited was yielded. It was late, and Jenkins was glassy eyed. His body had slid down, slouched in his chair. The Cabashi burned next to the almost empty bottle of rum, when under the German's relentless prodding he finally spoke the words the German had waited patiently to hear.

"There is a rock," Jenkins slurred, though with intoxication he was even more loquacious than usual, "a sacred rock, in the high country, to the west—beyond the headwaters of the Ortenguaza, where the rivers flow north instead of east. There, thirteen thousand feet above the steamy jungle, in a mountain basin, is a world of contrast, one that is rocky and lifeless. Bone chilling winds howl night and day unremittingly across its barren floor and snow capped peaks loom down upon it. To the Picayultas, it is known as the Valley of the Wind, accessed only by a steep, torturous trail, which even they seldom travel." He licked his lips, took a sip of rum, then resumed.

"Ominously mixed with the incessant winds are two distinct sounds. One, shrill and agonizing, cuts painfully across the valley. This agonizing scream is said to be the cries of the uninvited who have been captured and condemned to wander the mountaintops for an eternity of pain and suffering. The other is a deeper drone, permeating every corner of the valley like the Australian Aboriginal wind instrument, the didgeridoo. Mournfully resonating down upon the valley, it is said to be the great Picayulta chiefs of the past, on their ever-present vigil to guard the sacred rock and its secrets, which lie on its summit. Together they are so horrifying and lonely; they intimidate all but the foolish and the insane. No man, outside the Picayultas circle of elders, has ever ventured up into the valley and returned to tell the tale."

"The sacred rock." Bodecker pondered. "It is El Chiflon, just as the Spaniard wrote." He drew out his pack of cigars, saw the professor's disapproving stare, then slipped them away.

Jenkins raised his hand to not be interrupted. It had been some time since he'd last delivered a lecture. "From the valley entrance, below the constellation of Orion during the dry season, and among the surrounding towering gray and white summits is the rock formation—if that's what it is—called El Chiflon. The Indian name for it is so sacred, I've never heard them speak it. The fifteen hundred-foot single section of rock is embedded in the slope of an even higher peak. Its distinctive shape is like nothing around it: a half dome with a somewhat flattened crown, its side's sheer cliffs to the valley floor. Its color too is a unique deep charcoal-blue with a translucent quality that looks like black ice. The Indians claim it fell from the stars, placed there by the gods to protect them." Jenkins smiled and added, "That really pissed the Rev off."

Bodecker leaned back in satisfaction. "That correlates with Don Diego's account of the rock's composition. Where did you learn this?" Bodecker inquired, pouring more rum in the professor's glass. "From the Indians, yes?"

Jenkins lost his smirk. "Never in my years here did I hear the natives utter a word regarding their sacred rock." His voice lowered to a hush. "And personally, I wish I had never heard any of it at all. As will you." Bodecker's eyes sharpened. "In fact, the only time I ever heard the name…" Jenkins paused, looking for eavesdroppers, then continued almost inaudibly, "El Chiflon articulated at all was from those meddling missionaries. They were the ones who extracted the legend from the Indians. And they were responsible for their behavior to change."

"What are you talking about? What changed?"

Jenkins stretched his neck uncomfortably, his head extending forward to expel a muffled burp. "Everything!" Jenkins voice blurted edgily. "The demeanor of the natives. The way they spoke to us. Even the way they *looked* at us."

"So what did Reverend Wilson tell you?"

The lamplight flickered in the old man's glasses. "I remember the night they told me like it was yesterday." His mood turned solemn, apprehensive.

"Professor?"

Jenkins took another swig of rum. "It was late, a year and a half, maybe two years ago, around their campfire. The reverend, his boys, and I had killed off a couple of jugs of homegrown brew. Unlike this," he said holding up his nearly empty glass; "it was horrible stuff." He shook his head with a severe grimace. "Rough as it was, it was our only diversion, an escape from this forsaken hellhole." He stalled. "And the hangover that followed was certain to bring you to your knees the next morning."

Bodecker's face contorted impatiently.

"Anyway, in his compromised mental state, Wilson recounted having stumbled upon a peculiar pagan belief, one he had pried from the Indians during one of his interrogation sessions. Those bastards were no better than their Spanish predecessors."

"Yes professor, Yes. Go on." Bodecker demanded.

"I suppose Wilson was a good man at one time, but the claustrophobia of the jungle, his poor mental health, and his obsession with the legend turned him and his boys into fanatics of the worst sort. He was convinced that if he could gain control of the statue he could end the world's misery, and hated the fact that pagan Indians controlled such a source of power and used it only to see to their personal comfort and security."

"Yes, yes, but what about El Chiflon?"

Jenkins winced, again scanning his surroundings nervously. He leaned closer to the German and continued in a hushed voice. "Italcalpu, the medicine man, had reached his limit. Tired of my fanatical friends' pressure to make him commit to Christ, he climbed the village temple. It's a small pyramid of stone in the village center. The ruckus caused a scene, and a crowd gathered. There, before the tribe he denounced the missionaries, their intentions, and their God. He urged his fellow Picayultans to do the same, and to oust the trespassers. Wilson looked on, and as he did he worked himself up into one of his states.

"Italcalpu chanted a curse summoning the powers of the little statue that lived in El Chiflon. He begged the spirits to rid the tribe of the intruders, believing the idol to be their omnipresent protector. He hurled his threats directly at Wilson, assuring him that their opportunity to leave unharmed was quickly fading. His words promised a horrible death to all outsiders." Jenkins raised his eyebrows. "Being one of them myself, I was troubled by the news."

"Around the campfire, Wilson's idiot friends listened to him recount the story with drunken glee. They mocked the medicine man, dancing and hollering like madmen, shaking pretend rattles and pumping pretend spears. They dismissed Italcalpu's threats and the statue's powers as foolish native folklore. But Wilson was not so cavalier. The savage's threats and reliance on pagan gods were absolute insults to him, and undermined all that he was trying to accomplish. They precipitated a series of events from which there was no turning back."

Jenkins poked the embers inside the Cabashi to rekindle them, then continued. "Wilson lost patience with the Indians and their resistance to conversion. He believed destroying the idol in front of the tribe would be the ultimate confirmation that his God was the true God, and their gods were nothing more than impotent folklore."

"Although the missionaries were outnumbered, they somehow overpowered the tribe, much as the Spaniard, Hernando Cortes, and his little band overpowered the great Aztec nation. The Indians, intimidated into inaction, allowed Wilson to exercise his dominance. Feeling empowered Wilson began to harass Italcalpu and his family, trying to coerce him to repent and to reveal the location of El Chiflon. But the elder held fast, unwilling to bend." Jenkins paused to reflect. "Somewhere in the process, Wilson lost touch with reality. It became personal between him and the elder. He confined him and pressed even harder, furiously bent on breaking his resolve."

"In retrospect I realized I'd seen it coming for some time. Wilson had crossed a line, and the tormenting escalated to physical torture in the style of the old Inquisition. But I guess that sort of thing is justifiable if it's in the name of God." Jenkins digressed with a smirk, then continued. "The elders finally came to the medicine man's rescue, but by then it was too late. In agony Italcalpu had broken, repenting his obstinacy and spilling his guts as to the location of the spirit statue. In the wake of their impulsive actions the meddlesome persecutors realized they had gone too far, but they could not take back what was now done."

"Wilson regained some semblance of normalcy, and it was on the night after that he recounted the details of the incident. He described in detail what they had extracted from Italcalpu. His eyes blazed demonically, reflecting the firelight, as if the episode had possessed him. As he spoke, the empowering right that had gripped him again showed through."

"Tell me, professor," Bodecker asked in a hushed voice, "what did the reverend learn about the Valley of the Wind?"

Jenkins continued, "He said there was a trail that leads across the valley to its treacherous final leg, up the huge monolith of El Chiflon. This final path is a narrow switchback, cut into the rock, with some areas only able to accommodate one foot on its breadth at a time. A false step would send the unwary traveler hundreds of feet to his death. Those that successfully negotiate the perils of the footpath arrive at its zenith, a level platform of rock a courtyard in size. Beyond it, at its far end, the rock projects even higher, forming an apex. In the side of this projection stands a pyramidal temple built of stone, with an altar crowning its top; it has been carved from the stone itself by the long gone ancestors of the Picayultas.

"The natural projection of rock just beyond the temple is thin, a sliver only five or six feet in thickness, maybe ten feet in width, but it juts thirty feet into the sky. The erect slab is pierced in its center, the opening passing all the way through to its opposite side. The Indians call the hole 'El Ventorrio.' Through this aperture, on its other side, is a precipice, the bottom lying more than a thousand feet below. There, overlooking the Valley of the Wind and the heavens above, is the magical and mystical destination that has sparked the tribesmen's interest for centuries. And it is there that these savages are drawn twice each period of approximately sixty-one years for their ritualistic changing of the guard." Jenkins seemed suddenly sobered as he set down his empty glass. "El Ventorrio means window. To the Picayultas it is a window in time."

"A window to the future?" Bodecker interrupted with fascination.

"Exactly, but more than just a window."

"How do the Indians explain it? And if it's not just a window, then what is it?" Bodecker asked.

Jenkins again raised his hand. "The legend explicates that twice during each sixty-one year cycle, a fast moving star, referred to by the Picayultas as Huantanuco, or the prophet star, is summoned to this place on earth by the god of El Chiflon."

"The little statue?"

"Yes. The idol. And it is the same statuette that Italcalpu, the elder, had called on for protection from the missionaries. Supposedly, it resides behind the temple in the hole through the rock. Standing like a huge terrestrial antenna, El Chiflon attracts the star, drawing it closer and closer until it strikes the top, like lightning, I suppose."

Jenkins poured the last of the rum into his glass. He took a sip and savored it, enjoying the amber liquid as much as this transitory feeling of authority that he was experiencing. He felt confident that while he continued to reveal the coveted secrets, Bodecker would be as agreeable and tolerant as a child getting candy. Jenkins liked feeling important. He continued.

"On the prophet star's first visit, the chief and the elders make the journey up into the highlands to witness the event. A young warrior, a boy really, who was previously selected to succeed as chief, accompanies them. There, during this visit, at the temple atop the dome there is magic and sorcery. Then a visitor appears at the altar, a lad of the same age as the one with them. The entourage receives him expectantly. He comes from the past, sixty-one years prior, traveling across time for this rendezvous. In the world he left behind, time is at a standstill, but for him it moves forward. The elders give him an accounting of the hardships and decisions that he will endure during his reign. The wars. The famines. The diseases. The droughts. After two days of rigorous counseling and history, he vanishes back to his time, returning as the all-knowing and wise chief, prepared to lead the tribe through the challenges he has been privileged to foresee."

"A chief with hindsight. How intriguing," Bodecker said, gazing into the distance.

"It is just a legend, doctor," Jenkins replied, uneasy with his colleague's tone. Then he continued, "During this ceremony the old chief dies."

"He dies? How?" Bodecker inquired. "Is he sacrificed?"

"I don't know. But no chief, as long as their spoken word has lasted, has died by any other means." Jenkins paused. He was tired.

"You said the star visits twice." Bodecker verbally prodded the old man to get him going again.

"Yes, yes. Not long after this first visit from the past, the star returns."

"*How* long?"

"I'm not sure, two, perhaps three months. But the Picayultas have long studied astronomy and know precisely when to expect its return. The elders, and that same young warrior who originally accompanied them, make a second journey to the temple on the summit. There, through the same supernatural powers, the union again takes place, the past with the present, the present with the future.

"This time it is to take their chosen one, the young man that accompanied them, into the future. He waits by the altar as the star approaches. During its sweep past the Andean Mountain tops, time stands still. In an instant he is taken and returned. For those who are with him it seems like only seconds, but in the future world he has spent two days." Jenkins' words were calculated and his voice low. "From that moment on, he is the enlightened and unchallenged chief who has seen the future through the window, the time portal if you will, until the star's next return. The death of the old chief and the ordaining of the new one is a scheduled event that unfailingly occurs every sixty-one years." He paused pensively. "Foolish stuff, really. Its obvious intent is to give each new chief unquestioned obedience. As the reverend himself said, it's just a folk tale." Jenkins sat quietly now.

"As are virtually all legends, professor," Bodecker agreed sternly. "Please go on."

"The Picayultas have protected themselves from virtually all disasters and from the need to adapt, using this protective clairvoyance. But it also leaves them vulnerable. Accustomed to absolute faith in their chief, they are lost without him. And without him is what they are during the months between the celestial visits. The tribe has no chief, no leadership. And the future is unknown. This period lasts only a brief couple of months, but they are in an especially susceptible state. And they know it. During this time, Wilson speculated, the Indians would probably become anxious, highly unpredictable, and likely dangerous, a paranoid mob ruled by uncertainty. In a distant voice that made me uneasy he said: 'I'm afraid we have opened up a Pandora's box.' Wilson's last words on the subject were: 'There are some things best never discovered.' Even with all his Christian beliefs, it was as if, deep down, there was a part of him that believed the legend."

Jenkins peered into his empty glass. "I sensed the reverend and his two associates knew they were in danger, and had foreseen their coming fate. There was no way for them to leave. That is why he passed the story of the legend on to me." Jenkins stretched. "I'm tired. This rubbish has been going on for countless centuries, and the Picayultas have changed little since possessing this window into the future. If they really knew what was coming, do you honestly think they'd have stayed in this hellhole?" Jenkins' eyes drooped sleepily.

Bodecker considered that. No, the natives would stay put. They'd be too frightened to leave their magical window into the future, to abandon the certainty of prescient leadership, to risk another tribe gaining the wisdom that went with it. It made perfect sense that they would have remained here. And he suspected to a native born and raised beside the river, this land was not a "hellhole." "How do the Picayultas say they came to have this power, Professor?" Bodecker asked, trying to revive Jenkins from fading away.

Jenkins shook himself from nodding off and answered, "A hundred generations ago the Picayultas lived at the mouth of a great river far to the east."

"The Amazon River?" Bodecker offered.

"Maybe, but it could also have been the Orinoco," Jenkins suggested, then he continued, "Small in stature, they were at a disadvantage to fend off the other more aggressive tribes. Their strength was in their intellect, and they possessed the best land on the delta, a small patch that was higher than its surroundings so that during the rainy season it was the only land that stayed dry. But they were outnumbered, more than a hundred to one, by their marauding neighbors. For years they would raid and plunder the Picayultas, taking slaves, stealing their food and killing many.

"The exodus from that land was precipitated by a massive offensive launched by their rivals who banded together. The tribe was almost completely exterminated. Only a remnant escaped up the river. The attackers pursued them until finally in a storm on the great river most of the boats from both sides were lost. Their enemies gave them up for dead and retreated.

"The Picayultas say they had a seer, even then, who was given a vision. He led them here to this valley, where they first saw Huantanuco, the prophet star. They claimed the god of mercy had bestowed the statue as a gift to the survivors; its power was to be used to shelter the remnant from future hardship, persecution and bondage. The elders maintain that if the authority of the idol was ever used for greedy or self-serving reasons the idol would be lost and the tribe would plunge into an abyss of everlasting hardship."

Jenkins had mesmerized himself with his own narrative. He pulled himself out of his self-induced spell and smiled, insinuating the entire story was nothing more than a ghost story. "The reverend told me that the chief dies when the young Indian traveler looks into his eyes, for it is upon his own older body that the boy is looking. Although Wilson inferred that he did not believe these folk tales, his voice betrayed an insecurity that I still hear to this day." Jenkins appeared exhausted by the story and sat quietly for a while.

"Is that it, professor?" asked Bodecker.

"I don't know much more than that. Now you can see for yourself it is pure foolishness."

The German smiled. "But of course. Still, I can't help noticing it does make you nervous to discuss it. Have the Indians ever threatened you?"

"Heavens no!" replied Jenkins. "They have no clue to my being made privy to their secret. The legend is taboo. If they suspected me of knowing, I'm sure I would be with the reverend and his boys."

"What makes you think that?"

"Because the day after my campfire chat with Wilson was the day that he and his friends were included in the soup du jour," Jenkins said, trying to lighten the mood. "These savages believe the statue is their 'goose that lays the golden eggs.' They aren't going to allow what they have to be compromised by the likes of me." He said this while again checking around for eavesdroppers.

"You seem jumpy, professor."

"Now that you know the story, you should be as well. Haven't you noticed? The tribesmen have been acting strangely these last days."

"No, but I have only been here two weeks. I don't have any past references."

"My usual servant has inferred that the elders are preparing for a journey."

"A journey! Where?"

Jenkins hesitated, then said, "My suspicion is, it is their journey into the mountains to meet Huantanuco. This is one of those times where I believe staying clear of them is prudent."

Bodecker could scarcely conceal his excitement. "When?"

"I don't know, a few days, maybe weeks, I suppose."

"A few days!" Bodecker exclaimed as if hearing wonderful news. "Professor! This is fantastic! An exceptional stroke of luck for us both!"

Jenkins looked confused. "What do you mean? This is a very dangerous time. If I could, I would leave, and be as far away from here as possible."

"Leave? Impossible! It is an ideal opportunity to witness this indigenous tribe practicing its customs and exercising its primitive rituals. This is exactly what I have been sent to learn, but I never expected the good fortune of witnessing first hand such a ceremony. My superiors will be so proud of me." Bodecker's voice quivered with excitement. "You cannot tell me you are not excited as well?"

"Of course not. Only a fool would take such a risk. What you suggest is crazy," Jenkins stood up and interrupted firmly. "You don't understand, doctor, there are no outsiders allowed. Not even regular tribesmen may be present. Only the elders, the chief, and the chief-to-be may be present."

"But we *must* find a way to be included! This is a phenomenal opportunity. We shall shower the chief with gifts and promises."

"I'll have no part of it!" Jenkins exclaimed, now both sober and agitated. He turned to enter the bungalow. "I've had enough for tonight. I am tired and wish to sleep, so if you'll excuse me, doctor."

"I understand. It is late, professor. We can discuss it more tomorrow."

"Humph," Jenkins grunted and went inside, angry that he had divulged so much, and leaving Bodecker alone and content on the veranda.

Bodecker was pleased. It had been a good night. From here he would redirect his strategy. He stretched comfortably in his chair and idly wondered how Jenkins would eventually die. Then his mind returned to how all this had begun, for him.

His last meeting with Himmler came to mind, and how the Reichsfuhrer, in his high-pitched tone of voice, had gone on about a re-occurring cyclical event that was to take place high in the Andes Mountains. The event, supposedly catalyzed by a statuette, would give an Indian chief power—-power to see the future and predict the challenges that his tribe would face during his coming reign. If such power truly existed, Himmler and his Fuhrer wanted it for Germany. They wanted it for themselves. Bodecker knew that is why they had dispatched him.

That German command would grasp at such straws was no surprise, for it had been a year of disaster for the Nazis. The army in Stalingrad had surrendered in February and sensitive army documents projected that victory was no longer possible. The best Hitler could hope for was a temporary stalemate, a stalemate that would inevitably lead to Germany's defeat. That summer the German U-boats in the north Atlantic had been devastated, and in May they had been pulled from those waters, giving the Allies an unrestricted pipeline to Britain to prepare for invasion. Sicily had been taken, and during the time Bodecker had traveled to South America the enemy had landed in Italy.

Bodecker knew Himmler truly believed in the window to the future, and that fate had put it there to grant Germany the victory it deserved. The leader had called on him because he was the best. His record for success was perfect, and extraordinary missions did not daunt him. There was of course, always the unfortunate problem of the death and destruction that he left in his wake, but those messy consequences were overlooked as long as he got results.

He thought about the mission. It seemed far-fetched, but promotions came through performance. If he wanted to continue being the youngest aspiring power broker of the Third Reich he had get this job done. At least, he would follow up on the legend, at best he would steal the statue for his Fuhrer.

He looked into the darkness beyond Jenkins's hut, his mind considering the Reichsfuhrer's final words: "Your mission may be the pivot in determining Germany's destiny. Do not fail, Herr Standartenfuhrer." The words stuck in his head.

Intrigued by the close correlation between the Spanish journals and the professor's account, Bodecker couldn't help but wonder, maybe Himmler was right. If there was any truth to the drunken American's story the fate of the Third Reich might very well rest with him. His chest swelled in pride at the thought. What rewards might be his!

Then another idea came to him on the professor's veranda. It spread throughout him like a fierce glow. What life might a man enjoy who had seen the future? The very thought was overpowering.

CHAPTER SIX

The crisp morning air of an early Texas autumn filled Jack Sullivan's lungs as he ran off the exercise trail at the Army's Air Corps training facility. He cut across tall grass, and his high steps returned him to the elevated track where the course started. The field it encircled looked different now.

An hour earlier, when the squad of forty had set out, there were only a new moon and the stars to light the way. But the early morning darkness had given way and the predawn sky had changed first from black to purple, then gradually transformed itself to a fiery orange, as the beams of the still not visible sun struck the underside of the scattered high clouds.

Jack glanced back. Still no one was behind him. Four times a week the squad endured the exercise, and each time, from the start, Jack broke ahead steadily, distancing himself from the pack to the very end. His drive and stamina fueled him to excel.

His legs pumped hard as he climbed the graded slope before him. Bleachers came into view, then the field; finally at the far end he spotted the finish line. Alone he crossed the field. It was the homestretch of the ten-mile march. He quickened his pace in anticipation of breaking the camp record.

There was a barrage of enthusiastic clapping coming from a solitary man pacing at the finish. "Let's go! Let's go!" he shouted. His middle-aged face was rugged and he wore the neatly pressed uniform of a sergeant in the Army. He raised his stopwatch to motivate Jack to finish strongly. "It's gonna be close," he barked.

Jack felt re-energized. He culminated his hour-long effort in an all out sprint, heading directly for the sergeant. His heart pounded surges of air rapidly filled his lungs and then blasted from his mouth, condensing into jets of vapor in the cold air. His legs ached, but determinedly he maintained his final explosion of energy.

"Damn it, Sullivan, don't quit on me now! Finish hard!" the sergeant ordered.

Inspired by the sergeant's enthusiasm, he pushed himself, his arms pumping back and forth in rapid rhythmical succession. As he sailed past, the sergeant pressed his thumb on the button of his stopwatch. "Way to go, Sullivan!" he exclaimed approvingly. "Fifty-nine twenty-five. You just broke your own record—again." With a nod of his head he motioned toward the other end of the field where the trail lay vacant, and he added with a grin, "Looks like you'll be finished with breakfast before the sissies show up."

Sucking air, Jack just nodded in acknowledgment. He clasped his hands behind his head and walked around in circles. The steam rose off his wet T-shirt like smoke billowing from a locomotive. He felt good. He felt lean. He felt strong.

All 180 pounds that Jack carried on his six-foot athletic frame were solidly built. His sandy brown hair, which was normally longer, now was a standard U.S. Government Issue crew cut. He had a face that was young for twenty-five, though thinner and slightly older looking now than when he arrived at the Army Air Corps San Antonio base flight school ten weeks earlier.

Jack was a hard person not to like. His brown eyes were friendly and inviting, broadcasting a happy quality, which was reinforced by his ever-present smile that revealed straight white teeth. The small town atmosphere of New Braunfels, his hometown just north of San Antonio, had much to do with his friendly nature. Hard work on his family's farm made him instinctively self-reliant and yet always ready to help others. It was a quality that made people quickly befriend him.

Even Sergeant Ryerson liked Jack. In his fifteen years as a flight school drill sergeant, he could not remember a better pilot candidate. In fact, he could not recall any pilot candidate who had come to the boot camp already knowing how to fly. And normally the trainees who excelled quickly became cocky and arrogant. It was an attribute the Sarge usually overlooked, for it was one that would keep many of them alive in the dogfights they would soon face.

Jack was different. He was quiet and reserved. Never making waves, he performed with unnatural perseverance. What the sergeant didn't know was these qualities didn't come naturally; Jack had developed them out of necessity and hardship.

"Two weeks, Sullivan. Two weeks and you're out of here. Off to travel the world, visit exotic places, meet interesting people—and kill them." Ryerson smiled. He envied the recruits. They were all champing at the bit to get into the fight. He had been in the infantry in the Great War when the use of airplanes was just starting. Now that he was an experienced pilot, he was too old to fly for the Army. This was as close as he was going to get.

"Yes, sir!" Jack called out with a rookie's enthusiasm as he finally caught his breath. He moved away from Ryerson, making his way around the track to cool down. "Damn right," he said to himself. "Only two weeks left. Please God, just let me get through them."

The words brought him a sudden uneasiness. They had rekindled the ever-present insecurity, which had forged Jack into the reserved young man that he was. His real thought was two weeks of fear, fear that the Air Corps would rediscover his old medical records. Fear that for the third time, they would reject him, and dash his dreams to serve his country as a fighter pilot.

The thought made him shudder with anger. Who the hell do they think they are? he said to himself. He was tired of living with the burden of rejection always looming over him.

For ten weeks such thoughts had consumed him. Every day that passed was one less that they had to discover his secret. He relished the day when the paper-pushing bureaucrats would no longer wield their impersonal powers over him, unable to snuff out his hopes of flying for the Air Corps.

Yes, the end was close, virtually at hand, but Jack wasn't going to allow himself the luxury of believing he was safe from the impersonal reach of the bureaucrats. He had done that before, and been disappointed. His distorted sense of safety would come only when he had been assigned to active duty and sent overseas. Once there they would not bother to discharge an obviously qualified pilot, at least not during a war that had already lasted twenty-three months.

Jack kept walking. The sun felt good on his face.

He remembered back almost two years to the 7th of December. He was at Stinky's, the bar where he and his friends congregated in New Braunfels. The words of President Roosevelt resonated in deafening silence as they gathered around the radio. The Japanese had treacherously attacked Pearl Harbor. Attacked them!

The voice of their leader reminded the small Texas town, like so many other towns across America, that despite their isolation, they were still part of a great nation. And that nation now bore the heavy responsibility of defending itself in a dangerous world. Initially there was only astonishment, but that was quickly overtaken by irrepressible outrage. The violation by the reprehensible Japanese had hit home. In minutes cries of war rang through the streets. Like the rest of the country, the people of New Braunfels were blinded by a patriotic euphoria to defend the country's honor, not yet fully considering the price in blood and tears which they would be asked to pay. Overnight the American public was energized. There was both fear and excitement. Like every other young man, Jack wanted to be a part of it.

On the 8th of December 1941, and for many days after, men from eighteen to thirty-five came from the surrounding farms, ranches and settlements to enlist. The lines inundated the single room recruiting office at the post office in New Braunfels, and stretched around the block, crowding the streets of town. Sixteen year olds were turned away while older men and children shouted patriotic words of encouragement as the volunteers passed. Pride, fear and unity brought a lump of emotion to the throat of each recruit, reinforcing their sense of duty. Special buses had been sent to carry off this first wave of enlistments. Jack and his friends, all in their early twenties, were ripe for the service. All went to join, and all were taken as they stepped forward in the line—all but Jack.

He remembered that day as clearly as if it were yesterday. The new recruits, a rag tag group of central Texas farm boys who had never ventured more than two counties away, were lined up at the square by the bus stop, having passed their preliminary physical. Some shuffled nervously as they prepared to leave on a journey from which they realized they might never return. Others put on fronts of toughness, believing the Japanese would cower at the mere sight of them. A few quiet words were occasionally uttered, breaking the silence a sergeant was trying to impose as they awaited the arrival of the bus that would take them to San Antonio and boot camp.

Then it happened. From out of the blue and without regard for humiliation, the recruiting sergeant looked at his clipboard and paused. "Sullivan!" he bellowed, looking up and down the lines. "Step forward." Bewildered, Jack did so, standing at attention before the man. "Mr. Sullivan, *you* are an asthmatic," he announced loudly. "You have failed the United States Air Corps' physical." There were gasps up and down the line. Jack was shocked with disbelief. He felt fine and was in great shape.

"But sir…" Jack said, but was cut short by the sergeant.

"Silence, Mr. Sullivan. You will speak only when called on to do so," he shouted, using the opportunity to intimidate the entire rank. "The service has no place for men who are not in fit fighting condition." Jack stood quietly, not knowing what to do. "*You* may leave." It was an order, not an option. A few snide remarks could be heard down the line, but the sergeant lit into the group with fury, threatening them with a misery that he was looking forward to personally inflicting upon them. He scowled at Jack who stepped away, ashamed, and left. The others stayed in silence, fearing they might be next.

Those words cut through Jack like a knife. He had never imagined that such an obscure detail from his past would be the basis for his rejection. It was true he'd suffered a number of asthma attacks as a child, and a couple even required hospitalizations, but it had been more than a decade since his last bout. He hadn't thought twice when he checked "Yes" on the health question-naire. He never suspected it would be a problem.

The sound of reveille in the compound broke Jack's thoughts. He continued around the track. The sky was now light and Ser-geant Ryerson stood at the opposite end of the field. There was still no sight of the rest of the pack. Jack was back to breathing normally. It was obvious that his physical condition was su-perb, better than any of the others, and that thought momen-tarily reassured him. But his fears would not be put to rest that easily. It had been the asthma that had interfered with his desire to play sports in high school. He had been one of the best players on the football team, and his school was renowned around the state for their tough program. The trophy case in the school en-trance hall attested to their record.

But during Jack's sophomore year a freak incident with a high school athlete in Houston had resulted in a student's death from an asthma attack. Jack, then as now, had not considered his con-dition life threatening. In fact, it had never been a factor, and he had all but forgotten that he had once suffered from it.

But the mayor, whose son was a second-string linebacker vying for the same position as Jack, picked up the news of the Houston death. Jack's medical records mysteriously appeared at the right time before the school board, and pressure was placed on them to avoid a similar tragedy in their district's athletic pro-gram.

It wasn't long before Jack's asthma was a hot topic of discus-sion at the local coffee shop. Heated debates pitted the coach and involved boosters against the board, the administration and, oddly enough, the mayor's office. It was common knowledge Jack was the best linebacker on the team, but in the end, the coach did not have the clout to sway the spineless school board into voting against the administration and keeping Jack on the team. The word was the school would not risk the insurance costs or tarnish their prized sports program no matter how good the player.

And the word stood.

Learning the board's decision was another day Jack remembered only too clearly. He continued around the track. *No matter where I go, this stupid thing keeps haunting me and destroying my life,* he thought. His desire to wear the wings of a pilot and serve the country he loved clashed with his anger against the bureaucrats and the officials who administered and controlled the system. His frustration bordered on explosive.

He could not understand it. He was already a qualified pilot. *And a darn good one,* he thought. He had done half the work for the government on his own. When Jack was a teenager, his Uncle Sully had taught him how to fly crop dusters, a form of flying which made him highly proficient at maneuvering a plane in many conditions, especially at low altitudes. He wasn't a technical pilot, but more a "fly by the seat of your pants" type, relying on instinct and gut feel rather than book-learned skills. In any case it was certainly more than any of the other candidates could claim.

And Jack figured it was his ticket to fly fighter planes. He was willing to try anything to get another chance. His second attempt to slip by the system was in June 1942. This time he purposefully did not divulge his past medical history. And he buried the emotions of anger and humiliation endured on his previous attempt. But two weeks into this second try, his record resurfaced. And his plans again were dashed.

Now, after almost two years of stewing and ten weeks of training, Jack was so close to realizing his dream that it scared him. During those two years his goal had become an unhealthy obsession. Not a waking hour passed in which his thoughts did not turn back to his aspirations, but they inevitably turned to frustration, then anger and finally despair.

Jack approached Sergeant Ryerson. Eight and a half minutes had elapsed since he had finished and he was fully rested now. He looked down the trail, then back at the sergeant.

"Still no sign of the girls," Ryerson said with a wry smile.

It's crazy, Jack thought. *I'm in much better shape than any of these guys.* The best in his outfit and two weeks to go; maybe this third try would be the charm. *Just two more weeks,* he kept thinking. Jack stood before Ryerson and said, "Permission to return to barracks, Sergeant."

"Dismissed, Sullivan...and nice job."

As Jack turned toward the barracks, he spotted Lenny working his way up to the field. A hundred yards behind him the rest of the squadron ran as a pack, their movements awkward and sloppy with exhaustion. A straggler struggled despondently in the rear.

"One other thing, Sullivan," Ryerson called out with unknowing indifference. "The CO wants you to report to the infirmary at eleven hundred hours." Jack froze in his tracks. He did not turn around to acknowledge the sergeant's words. "Sullivan, did you copy?"

Jack had a knot in his stomach and his throat had suddenly turned dry. *It couldn't be. They would have known by now,* he thought.

"Sullivan!" Ryerson repeated sternly.

Jack turned around slowly. "Yes, Sergeant," he replied, the words caught in his mouth. He tried to convince himself it was nothing, but the fear that he had been discovered again was too

strong to dismiss. Suddenly, the satisfaction of setting his new record vanished as did the promise of a good day. He walked away
preoccupied, not hearing Ryerson ripping into the group. The
sergeant's voice bellowed out rapid-fire insults directed toward
the straggling squad and their immediate family.

CHAPTER SEVEN

The infirmary waiting room was large and sterile. Two ceiling mounted fixtures and the sunlight through dusty aluminum window blinds were all that lighted it. Besides three rows of wooden chairs and an empty magazine rack, there was just a plain-faced wall clock mounted close to the ceiling. Its monotonous ticking was the only diversion the place had to offer, and it was as annoying as a slow dripping faucet.

Jack sat alone and nervous for almost an hour, awaiting the reason he had been summoned. The place was dead. There had been no other patients since he'd arrived. He fidgeted in his seat; his eyes bouncing from the clock to the door, then back to the clock as he tried to displace his suspicions. Finally the door opened.

A short overfed nurse with heavy makeup stood in the doorway. Her nametag read Puget. Like a guard of a maximum-security prison she scanned the empty waiting room, as if searching for a single person in a crowd. "Sullivan!" she called in a tone usually reserved for delinquent children. Jack rose. "Come on. The doctor doesn't have all day."

At the door he turned sideways to squeeze past the heavy woman, who hadn't moved. Her eyes glowered upward, following his moves scornfully, as if he were an incompetent underling.

A short distance down the corridor was the doctor's office. The doctor didn't rise as Jack entered. His desk was a pigsty of books and papers and an ashtray filled with cigarette butts. "Cadet Sullivan, I presume?"

Jack glanced at the nameplate on the desk. It read Captain Ryan Devereux, MD.

"Yes, Sir," he answered nervously.

"Take a seat, cadet." Devereux studied Jack thoughtfully as he sat down. Then he leaned back in his chair and carefully fitted his fingertips together. He brought them to his chin, pensively gazing at an indefinite point in the corner of the room. The silence grew uncomfortably long. Finally he asked, "How do you feel, son?" The question came out of the blue. Jack looked perplexed. The doctor rephrased. "I mean, are you healthy?"

"Yes, Sir. I think I so. Just this morning I ran the pants off the entire squadron."

"Oh, you're fit enough. I won't argue that," Devereux said, thumbing through the papers of an open file. "But do you really believe you are *healthy* enough for active duty combat?"

"I haven't been sick in years, sir." Jack's voice quivered. "Why do you ask?"

"Why do I ask?" the doctor slowly repeated while pulling one of the papers from the file. "You must recognize this form?" he asked, handing over a sheet.

Jack's stomach turned as his eyes flashed across his medical history form. "No, sir," he lied.

"Well, what about this one?" The doctor passed him another. "They both have your name on them."

"Must be a mistake of some sort. Maybe another Jack Sullivan or something?" Jack stretched.

"Cadet, you've hardly had a moment to read them. Your signature is clearly written at the bottom of both forms," the doctor said indignantly, pointing with a pencil. "There's no doubt, these are your medicals." He let a moment of silence pass, then added, "I know what you're up to. But listen, you have been turned down, not once, but twice by the US Air Corps."

"But sir, I *am* in perfect health," Jack interrupted, panicked to see his dream again being ripped from his grasp. He felt helpless. The doctor shook his head slowly while looking into the folder. "What are you going to do, Sir?"

"You've given me no choice, son."

Jack started boiling inside. "Are you telling me you are going to deny me the opportunity to serve my country, even though I am better qualified than any of the others?"

"Me? I'm not denying you anything," the doctor said curtly. "The Air Corps, on the other hand, will do what it has decided is necessary. And as for your being more qualified…well, that may be from time to time under certain circumstances. But war is a harsh environment and you do fall short on one qualification. The regulations are clear: 'Asthmatics are disallowed from serving as pilots in the Army Air Corps.'"

Jack shifted helplessly in his chair. He looked around as if searching for something specific that would convince the doctor to change his mind.

Dr. Devereux closed the file. "There are reasons for this regulation. Sound ones, I'm certain. It is my unpleasant task to inform you that as of today you are no longer considered to be a candidate for flight school." His tone was that of a messenger, powerless to overrule.

"But…"

The doctor lifted his hand, indicating there was no room for discussion, then swept it toward the door dismissively. "Take the rest of the afternoon to get your things," he said as he followed Jack to the door. "But be off the camp by supper. I'm sorry, son, but that's how it is." Jack stepped into the corridor where nurse Puget pretended to be working, then started for the door. "And Jack," Devereux added, "Don't try this anymore. You're just wasting our time and yours."

CHAPTER EIGHT

In the distance, Gordon's Ford pickup hurried north on the otherwise empty highway leading from San Antonio. Its rumble was muted by a strong northerly wind, which carried the sound away from the New Braunfels intersection. The truck swerved unpredictably, making no attempt to slow down around the curves. And it wasn't until it was on the turn-off that its loud noise shattered the tranquility of the early Sunday morning.

It veered off the blacktop, the wheels locked up, grinding gravel under the tires as the truck slid sideways to a stop. For a moment it just lingered by the roadside without movement inside. Its engine idled erratically, on the brink of stalling. Then the passenger door opened, the old hinges letting out a shrill high-pitched screech.

Jack's feet missed the running board as he slid off the torn cloth seat. He attempted to center his weight over shaky legs, but his inebriated state and the loose roadside gravel were more than he could handle. Helplessly he tumbled to the ground and rolled down into a drainage ditch. He lay still, resting on his back. Clouds rushed above him across the sky and for a moment he thought he'd be sick.

Then he propped his head up and focused on the truck through the weeds. His cousin, Gordon, was peering out the open door, laughing uncontrollably. He was as intoxicated as Jack was, even though he wasn't the one in the ditch. As Jack laboriously pulled himself up, Gordon pitched his duffel bag out of the pickup. It struck him on the head. A pair of empty beer bottles followed close behind.

"Forgot your trash, Sullivan," Gordon slurred, slumped over the steering wheel. "Hope school goes better than your luck with the Air Corps, cuz," he added.

Jack gave him a halfhearted wave. "Go on and get out of here, you shit."

Gordon wore a foolish grin. He had three days' leave, two of which he'd already spent getting trashed with Jack to console him. He'd spend the rest with his mother in San Marcos before going back to camp. "Enjoy the hangover," he said, and then floored the old truck. Jack shielded his face from the gravel flying up from the tires. The sound of his cousin's truck slowly faded as it raced over the bridge to San Marcos.

Jack gazed down the single lane road leading into town. The grass undulated in gentle waves as wind moved across the face of the field. The patterns they made brought memories of his days crop dusting. *I guess I'll always be just the son of a farmer*, he thought with resignation. He had never traveled past Austin, and the one chance he had to see the world was now gone, this time for good. He wasn't going to try again. He was tired of trying to outsmart the Army Air Corps' watchdogs.

And as much as Jack wanted to leave, for the moment it felt good to be home. New Braunfels was all he really knew and so far he'd found the outside world to be full of roadblocks. For now, the world would continue to be a place that Jack knew only from his uncle's stories.

A line of doves sped south on the leading edge of a northern cold front. During the fall the weather fronts pushed the birds south in waves. There'd be more before winter and it looked as if he was going to be here to watch them all.

Having misplaced his shirt, Jack was suddenly chilled. He noticed blood on his forearm, an abrasion from his fall. Tomorrow it would hurt. He climbed back to the road. Where was his shirt? He rubbed the stubble on his face. Suddenly, he was anxious. He had not shaved or showered in two days, and had the breath of a dragon. His remaining clothes reeked of stale booze. What would his mother think? What would she say? He had never done anything like this before in his life. His mind raced. "Crap!" he said to himself. "If mom sees me like this, it'll be hell till Christmas."

He had to get out of here before anyone spotted him. He staggered to his feet, hefted his bag and started hobbling away. He couldn't show up at home like this. Analore Sullivan was a caring woman and had always been a good mother to Jack and his sisters, but she was also an uncompromisingly straight-laced German Lutheran with high morals and rigid expectations. To see Jack this way would shame her, or worse, it would break her heart. First, he had to clean up.

It was cold in the wind and he took refuge under a bridge while he thought. He laid down using the bag for a pillow and wrapped his arms across his bare chest. There was only one place he could go in this state and get any kind of understanding, that was to his Uncle Sully's place. Jack fought to keep his eyes open, then decided to let them close for just a moment. He fell into a deep sleep.

•

At sixty-nine Sully was an interesting sort. His true name was Jack Sullivan, but it was replaced in 1896, when he arrived at Ellis Island from Ireland. In his prime he'd been over six feet tall. His salt and pepper hair was in need of a trim; however, his beard of the same color was short and neat. Deep creases around his eyes and forehead suggested wisdom more than age, wisdom gained through the many and extraordinary experiences through which he had lived.

There was a comforting quality to his dark brown eyes from which warmth and understanding seemed to flow. Qualities learned from mistakes committed in a reckless youth. A time that seemed like it had been part of a previous and altogether different life. Yet now he carried himself with dignity, and from him emanated unmistakable discipline and self-control.

He was an Irishman through and through, and both a self taught, self-made man. There were 'movers and shakers', and there were 'farmers and workers'. Sully knew he had to make some big sacrifices to break the chains that had bound his family for generations. Born to a potato farmer in 1873, he never cared for farming. After losing both parents and two sisters to typhoid fever during an epidemic that ravaged Ireland in 1895, he and his eight-year-old brother, Patrick immigrated to America to seek their fortune. They heard rumors of opportunity in Texas, and followed them to the German settlement of New Braunfels where they found harsh work as farm laborers.

Sully felt responsible for getting his little brother Patrick into the mess. Smart and resourceful, he knew he had to take a risk and do something extraordinary to get them off the "slave camp" on which they'd landed. He had heard talk of war and the need for volunteers. He heard that Teddy Roosevelt and Colonel Leonard Wood were enlisting volunteers down in San Antonio at the Menger Hotel. They called themselves the Rough Riders, a rag-tag mix of wealthy northeastern socialites and tough western cowboys whose only common thread was the ability to ride horses and shoot guns.

Being an adventurous sort at heart, Sully didn't take long to decide to join the group. Patrick was now ten and able to take care of himself on the farm. Sully figured he would stash the money he made, then come back to find his brother. Then they could buy their own small farm.

On route to Cuba for the war, the Roughriders were stranded in Tampa. Teddy Roosevelt was desperate to find transport from Florida to Cuba, as it appeared they were going to miss the war. It was here that the future President recognized the young Irishman's resourcefulness. From out of nowhere Sully pulled up in a large old boat. He explained that the captain had offered, under slight duress, to ferry them to Cuba. It was enough to get a large number of these volunteers and their horses to the island. Having proven his worth, Sully was assigned and fought at Roosevelt's side in battle. With an innate sense of direction, Sully used his navigating skills to guide the outfit through the dense jungle and to the taking of San Juan Hill. He emerged a hero in the Spanish-American War.

After Roosevelt became President, he sent Sully to Panama, to map the terrain of what Roosevelt referred to as his "Pet Project," the development of the Panama Canal. Sully's mapping work continued after the project was complete. His reputation grew and he became the chief civilian mapmaker for the U.S. government. His talents were especially important to Roosevelt's fast growing military, and he was sent world wide to map territories that held the government's interest.

The brothers stayed close and all the time Sully kept sending money back to his younger brother, who saved it, until finally in 1910, at the age of twenty-three, Patrick was able to buy a farm that they could call their own. He married the daughter of German immigrants. Sully continued to work for the government, stationed at Fort Sam Army base in San Antonio. Occasionally he helped Patrick on the farm, but it was reluctantly, as he still detested farming.

Instead, in 1915 Sully took notice of the newest invention sweeping the country—airplanes. He saw great application for his mapmaking and learned to fly. Using his own airplane, he continued his work, and by 1918, at the age of forty-five, he became the government's leading authority in aerial mapping, working primarily in Central and South America.

With the Great War raging, Sully was rarely around; he spent most of his time doing secret government work. But the understanding and affection between the brothers was lasting, for they had endured so much together. And as different as they were, they knew that in times of need they would always be there supporting each other. So in 1918, on the family farm in New Braunfels, Texas, Patrick named his first son Jack after his own brother.

•

The sun was past its midday peak; the air under the bridge had warmed and was humid. Jack awoke to the pain of the hard ground beneath him. He had slept for hours.

To avoid the main road he used side trails and cut across the neighboring farms, until he reached the familiar backside of his uncle's cornfield. It had been harvested, and the stalks lay collapsed in disarray. Jack had worked this field for more seasons than he cared to remember. He saw the farmhouse on the far side, and skulked through the decaying stalks, hoping the farmer next door, who now leased the field from his uncle, would not see him. He threaded his way through a cluster of small storage sheds, then crossed over toward the barn. The farmhouse where his Irish uncle lived in modest solitude was quiet.

Maybe he's napping, Jack thought. He stepped between rows of vegetables growing by the house. The garden was the only farming his uncle could bring himself to do. Jack peered through a window. Inside was dark and after a moment he raised his hand to tap on the glass pane.

"You're going to mash me potatoes b'fore they're pulled from the ground, Jacky-boy," a voice said from behind. Jack spun around startled.

"Sully?" The voice had come from the barn. Jack moved toward the door, which was ajar. Inside it was dark and smelled of gasoline.

"You look like hell, boy!" For all his years in America and all his worldly travels, Sully had never lost his Irish accent.

Jack's eyes adjusted and he saw his uncle perched under the unmistakable outline of his biplane, a sixteen-year-old fabric covered Stearman C-3, with a black stripe cutting across its faded red paint. Sully had bought it directly from Lloyd Stearman who had broken away from Travel Air to start his own company. He appeared to be glued to the engine, holding a fitting in place until it was fastened. "Well, don't just stand there boy, pass me that wrench."

Jack picked the tool up. "What's wrong with Chessa?" he asked. It was the nickname affectionately given to the airplane, after Sully's youngest sister, Francesca. She had died at five in the famine.

"Just some water in the fuel intake."

"Water! How?"

"She's been sit'n for months. Condensation builds up, water's heavier than petrol so it separates and sinks into the carburetor intake."

"Don't you fly her?"

"Not anymore. She hasn't gone up since you left." Jack looked surprised; flying was Sully's love. "I'm gett'n more like Pixie here," Sully said, looking at his old dog curled up sleeping. "Blind as a bat." At fifteen, Pixie was both deaf and blind. Sully finished tightening the bolt and stepped away, wiping his hands off with a rag. "It's good t'see ya, Jacky."

The two embraced. Sully frowned and stepped backwards. "Bit early to be sip'n the grog," he said. "And look at yerself." Jack was still shirtless, bleeding and covered with mud on his pants and chest. "Did you lose the fight?"

"It feels like it."

"Yer mum's go'n to be surprised at what they're teach'n you boys in that Air Corps." The voice of disapproval was poorly masked by the smile on his face and the twinkle in his eyes. Jack shrugged, but said nothing. Sully saw disappointment on his face. "They found you out again, ehh?" Jack looked away, but didn't deny it. "Well then," Sully said looking Jack over from head to toe, "I suppose yer mum'll be expect'n you home today. So we best get you back into a presentable fashion, or you'll be stay'n with me 'n Pixie for good." He glanced at the still comatose dog. "Take off those rags and wash yerself down out back. I'll make some tea."

No one had done more for Jack than Sully, and Jack treasured the relationship. Eventually he knew Sully would expect an explanation, but he would let it come on Jack's time.

The shower was out back. It was a roofless barrel shaped shed with a pipe and showerhead sticking out above its walls. A chain hung from the nozzle. Jack stripped and pulled on the chain. Frigid water fell on his already cold body. He let out a cry and took fast deep breaths. His wound stung as he lathered with soap. "Damn, Sully, this is your version of a shower?" he groaned.

•

Without Sully, Jack would never have had the courage to excel.

He had been like a father ever since Jack's own had become ill. In 1928, Patrick, Jack's father, contracted polio. From there, everything deteriorated. Jack was only ten, and keeping the farm going was hard. His mother spent all her time tending Jack's two younger sisters and her sick husband. Then the depression hit and money was tight. They were forced to sell off most of the land just to make it.

Patrick's bedridden condition only worsened. He rarely spoke and eventually became despondent. Jack needed a father and Sully filled that gap. He spent much of his time teaching and guiding his nephew. His mother had expected Sully to help with more of the "real work" instead of just talking and guiding, but Sully could not bring himself to help with the farming. He hated it so much. He used to tell Jack, "Ye 'ave ta change yer stars, boy. Thar's no future in farm'n." Instead, Sully taught Jack to fly his Chessa. He had engineered on to her pipes, nozzles, and a tank, a design he copied from a Mississippi associate who had been the first to spray insecticides on farm crops from an airplane. Sully called his rig a duster and it was the first of its kind in Texas.

Jack was a natural and by age fifteen Sully was hiring out his services to the local farmers. His mother feared for his safety.

Stories of accidents in flying machines were common, the majority of them befalling daredevil barnstormers and wing walkers. But the family had no other income and they needed the money, so Analore allowed it.

After Jack's father died, Sully seemed to shrink within himself at the loss. Saddened, he retreated, and had lived as a near recluse for the last eleven years.

•

Jack returned to the house, his body shivering and blue. "Hell, Sully, you need to build yourself an indoor bathroom!" he jested. "It's the forties, you know. Modern times."

"Ahh, you kids are all spoiled now days," he replied. "This place is like a castle compared to where yer father and I grew up outside of Dublin." Sully poured tea into two cups. Jack cradled the cup with both hands to absorb the heat.

"Come with me to the house for dinner this evening. I'll show you what a real bathroom looks like," Jack offered.

"Sorry, lad, but this eve'n I'm meet'n with some government sorts in San Antone who need me in a hurry, or so they say."

"I didn't know you still worked for them."

Sully had maintained his ties to Panama and other remote areas of the continent where he used to survey, and for years after his retirement the government called on him for consulting. "Well, I doon't, but they sent me a telegram this morn'n. Said it was urgent."

"What do they want?"

"Doon't know, but it's got me curiosity tweaked."

"Maybe they need you in Europe," Jack kidded. "You know those damn Nazis aren't giving up easy."

"Panama is what I know best, and I'm an old man. If they need me in Europe we're in trouble."

"Wish they needed me," Jack said.

Sully had no response. He took a sip of tea to let the moment pass. Jack picked up a telegram from the kitchen table. "That's another telegram," Sully said. "From a friend of mine, Hank McDermott in Panama."

"Military?"

"No, but he does help them out down there at times. He lost one of his planes and a bush pilot not too long ago. He runs an air service into the jungle."

"Weather?"

"He didn't say. I doon't think he knows. He just wanted information on the passenger," Sully said. "He was a German man."

"Civilian?" Jack asked.

"I think so. Hank has agreed not to transport any German military—with the canal and everything being so close."

"Maybe he was a spy?"

"Yer jump'n to conclusions, boy." Sully smiled, then sipped his tea. "Hank wouldn't transport any spies. That's dangerous country. Anything could happen out there." He left it at that.

After tea Jack bandaged his torso and borrowed a shirt from Sully. Then suddenly Sully hopped up. "Holy Jesus, it's getting late. I've got to get go'n to San Antone. You too best be on yer way, lad, or soon yer mum's go'n to wonder where the beJesus ye're hiding. And ye know her, she'll be worr'n," he said, escorting Jack out the front door and down the walkway.

Jack went out the gate alone and started down the road. "And stay out of trouble," Sully shouted with a laugh. "Yer mom'll blame me, you know."

CHAPTER NINE

"*Atuyalp! Atuyalp!*" a young brown skinned native called out as he ran from the village. He stopped abruptly just before the steps to Jenkins' bungalow. "*Atuyalp!*" he called again.

The young man's eyes darted from the windows to the door then back to the window again. For a moment, he stood quietly listening for activity. There was none, except for a monotone muffled snore coming from Jenkins himself. The Indian came closer. "*Atuyalp. Syntato nael prenento!*" he continued in his native dialect, clearly anxious to deliver a message.

From inside the snoring stopped and Jenkins growled. The ruckus had pulled him out of his stupor. He looked around the room, rubbing his eyes. Everything was blurry without his glasses, but he could see Bodecker was gone. There was no other sound and in the quiet moment Jenkins drifted back to sleep.

The messenger paced, visibly agitated. Finally he stepped up to the door and banged on it loudly. "*Atuyalp al mentento!*"

Bodecker heard the ruckus a short distance behind the hut where he was breaking down and cleaning his pistol. It was one of two routines that he preformed every morning without fail. The other was going down to the river to hand turn the prop of the airplane, a procedure that would keep the engine pistons lubricated and the airplane ready to go when the time came to need it. He knew that anything made of metal was quick to freeze up with rust, especially in such a humid climate.

Hearing the commotion he quickly reassembled the Walther PPK and returned to the hut. He peered through the back window and saw Jenkins fast asleep.

At that moment a hand slammed on the front door, this time almost knocking it down. *"Atuyalp!"*

Bodecker ducked out of sight. Jenkins was startled awake. "Whaaa? Who's there?"

"Atuyalp. Syntato nael prenento! Atuyalp!" the boy repeated, stomping on the veranda, shaking the whole structure.

Finally, Jenkins responded to the Indian in the boy's dialect. He slipped on his trousers and opened the door. Squinting like a mole, he looked down, making eye contact with the young messenger. At just over five feet, he was considered tall for a Picayulta. His dark skin was fully exposed except for a loincloth. Three gold rings piercing his ear and two through his nose indicated he was from a prominent family. And like all the Picayultas, he had a wedge of wood impaled through his lower lip, which hung like a wooden beard below his chin. His hair was jet black and all the same length, as if a bowl had been used as a template to cut it. The crown of his head was shaved to the scalp, like a friar from the Middle Ages, exposing a bald spot six inches in diameter. It was the mark of a male who had entered manhood and was ceremoniously performed on all Picayulta boys at the age of eleven, and then maintained for life.

The two exchanged words. At first Jenkins' tone was offensive. He pointed to Bodecker's vacant bedding as he spoke. But the native responded curtly and spoke rapidly. He stomped his feet again, then resumed pacing. He took his job seriously. To be a messenger for the elders was a sort of apprenticeship to ultimately becoming one.

Bodecker chose that moment to make his appearance. "Professor, is there a problem?" he asked as he stepped onto the veranda from behind the hut. He was buckling his belt and tucking in his shirt as if he was returning from answering the call of nature.

"We'll know soon enough," Jenkins answered.

"What does the boy want?"

Jenkins did not answer immediately. Instead, he reached into his pocket for his spectacles, then turned to Bodecker. "Humph," he grunted gruffly. He fit the wire frames around his ears. "You'll be pleased to know that the chief has accepted your request to see us." The disappointment, as well as fear, was clear in his voice. Three weeks had passed since they had requested the privilege of attending the sacred Picayulta ceremony at El Chiflon and until now there had been no acknowledgment of the request.

Bodecker's eyes danced with excitement. "Wonderful, I look forward to the meeting. When will he have us?"

"They are waiting for us now."

"Now!"

"That's right. The chief may keep his subjects waiting for months, but once he decides to see you, you are expected immediately."

At that the native reacted with agitation as if they were taking too long to get going. He motioned them to follow, then started up the trail toward the village.

"We had better follow him, or you may not get a second chance," Jenkins said, grabbing his walking stick and starting after the native. Bodecker took out after Jenkins, holstering his pistol out of sight beneath his shirt.

There were no signs of civilization along the half-mile trail except for two structures, which looked abandoned. The roofs of both had collapsed, and a fallen crucifix leaned sideways at the entryway of one. Plants grew from every opening, as the jungle quickly reclaimed everything not maintained. The trail twisted around giant Tamarind, Brazil nut and Mahogany trees. Their enormous bases were buttresses, spreading out widely and interlocking, creating a labyrinth for the men to walk around.

The two men followed the boy silently along the foliage-lined corridor, dodging branches that swarmed with fire ants, and root projections that stood up to trip them, until they came upon a living wall. It was a row of close growing mature Mahogany trees. Layers of parasitic growth hung on them, virtually hiding their upper trunks and branches. The wall spread out impenetrably in both directions, fading into a jumble of green vines and bromeliads, which grew out of every possible nook and cranny. Some of the colossal trunks were thirty feet in diameter at their base, and grew so closely to one another that most of their sprawling bases and branches had fused with those of their neighbors beside. The result was a mass, which no longer resembled trees, but instead a solid wall of growth.

Bodecker considered the surroundings. Defense would be difficult against deft archers disposed to unleash their poison tipped projectiles at them. He knew they would be gone before he could react, melting away into the forest unnoticed. He was not used to being at a disadvantage. He glanced over at Jenkins who appeared oblivious to the possibilities.

As they approached, other paths converged with theirs, making it one well-traveled thoroughfare. Then together they burrowed into the foundation of the barricade.

Bodecker saw the native ahead vanish into the entrance, like a mouse scurrying into its hole. The professor followed without hesitation, but Bodecker had to crouch to avoid bumping his head through the tight squeeze. The passage spanned seventy feet. It was dark, and the moist wood and damp sides resembled a cave. On the other side the light of the open sky blinded the two white men as they emerged. They raised a hand to their brow to shield their eyes.

"Behold, the lost city of Atlantis," Jenkins said, waving his free arm before him like a magician presenting his apparition. He was enjoying the shock effect, which overcame everyone the first time they set eyes on the hidden city.

Bodecker squinted, then scanned the scene panoramically. What he saw came as a shock; it was a well-developed, thriving community, nothing like what he had expected. Compact and well planned the village had streets ornately lined with carvings, ceramic pots and statuettes, and everywhere were decorations of flowers. The wall behind them extended in an arc in both directions, continuing to curve inward until the two met in the distance a thousand yards away. The one hundred and sixty-foot high green border could be followed all the way around the city. But inside the settlement there was not a single tree; the city was an island of sunshine, the natural vegetation carefully cultivated to achieve the desired effect.

The men continued on the path, which had become much like a real road, lavishly lined with ornaments and stone carvings. It intersected several access streets, wide alleys that followed circumferentially around the wall's inside perimeter. Down these concentric circle easements were the living quarters of the populace. The buildings were made with a mix of mud brick, wood and rock with palm thatch roofs. The density was such, that the dwellings shared walls and roofs. Flowers and woodcarvings adorned them all.

The three men walked in single file, first the messenger, followed by Jenkins, then Bodecker. Natives paused to watch as the strangers made their way to the settlement center. Bodecker was of particular interest to them, with his blonde short hair, white skin and towering size, which made him seem like a giant from another world. The men and women looked down as he eyed them back, but the children ogled him with fascination.

They proceeded into the interior of the village toward a clearing beyond the living quarters. Three structures dominated the open area near a small bustling market. To one side was the largest structure in the city, a well-marked playing field rectangular in shape and sunk twenty feet in the ground, with a sophisticated drainage system to keep it dry. A smaller, more elaborately decorated wall with stone carvings rose above the pit on all sides. Bodecker leaned over to look inside.

"What are the stone rings for?" he inquired, referring to the hoops protruding from the walls about halfway up.

"It's a goal. The Picayultas play their games here," Jenkins said.

"Impressive. What kind of game?"

"*Hualta*. It's a ball game. Their only sport," Jenkins explained. "It requires a ball made of a leather covered core and tightly wrapped with strands of the milky sap called latex, a rubber like substances which the locals get from indigenous plants. The players try to bounce the ball through the rings to score, using only their feet, hips, shoulders and elbows."

Bodecker nodded in comprehension. "A derivative of a similar game I heard of, played by Central American and Caribbean Indians that have since vanished."

Jenkins nodded. "Stakes were similarly high," he added. He saw that caught Bodecker's interest and continued. "The captain of the losing team is beheaded. His head is then ceremonially prepared, shrunk if you will, then wrapped in leather. It serves as the core of the ball used in the next match."

Bodecker smirked. "That will certainly motivate you."

"Players consider it an honor to be a captain."

"Do they still play?"

"Twice a year, on the summer and winter solstice."

"*Atuyalp!*" the boy scolded to prod them on.

To one side of the field was a pyramid, a temple built of ornately carved stone blocks, with an altar at its apex.

"That is where Italcalpu made his stand," Jenkins said in a hushed tone. They crossed between the playing field and the temple and moved toward the third structure in the open space. Built on a platform of stone, it was the least impressive of the three, but from it you could see everything in the city. "This is where the chief lives," Jenkins said, "and where the elders meet to discuss issues concerning the tribe." They followed the boy up the stairs. "We will not be allowed to talk," Jenkins warned. "The elders do all the talking."

"What about the chief?" Bodecker asked.

"He rarely says anything," Jenkins answered, "but at a certain point in the deliberations he'll end the proceedings. Once he speaks all arguments cease. He'll declare his decision, which is final."

Bodecker nodded. He studied the details of the compound as they walked. There were two other roads similar to the one they had used entering the village. Easy to defend, hard to escape if it came to that.

The guards at the chief's residence were young and muscular, ceremonially dressed, and holding decorative spears. The messenger announced their arrival in a grave manner and the guards stepped aside. The boy gestured for the white men to hurry forward. The door was low and both Jenkins and Bodecker had to duck to enter.

Inside there were two rooms. The first was large and stately, in its own primitive way. It displaced most of the building's size, and Jenkins whispered it was used for tribal meetings. A door at the back led to the other room. It separated the quarters in which the chief lived. Several torches burned mutely, casting flickering light across the chamber. Their amber flames illuminated colorful battle shields, feathered spears, and handcrafted bows that decorated the walls. The ceiling was lined with chains of ornate objects linked together on a cord, like pearls on a necklace. As the men's eyes adjusted to the darkness, the ornate objects took the form of miniature human heads.

Bodecker instinctively moved his hand to his pistol. Jenkins saw him, and with widened eyes he shook his head to discourage anything rash. Bodecker backed his hand off, but still stayed vigilant, never trusting any of the little men around him.

Against the back wall, the chief sat holding a well-worn staff. It occurred to the German that the chief might very well be the oldest man alive in the tribe. If the story Jenkins had told was true, some sixty years before he had already been a teenager. That meant he was in his mid-seventies, an age unattainable to most in such a jungle environment. But if he was seventy-five years or so, he looked one hundred, withered, shrunken and bent. Only his steel black eyes showed life. They were unnaturally sharp, still disturbingly bright as if he were a youth.

His throne was primitive, with legs that raised the seat only inches off the floor. And there beside him, true to the stories, were the shrunken heads of three white men impaled on sticks. It was the first time Jenkins had seen the Reverend Wilson and his cronies since their disappearance. Bodecker took in the heads, then noticed a music box at the chief's side. He kept it close like a treasure. It was the gift he had given the chief to gain favor.

The ten elders who formed a sort of advisory council sat on jaguar skins, lining both sides of the wall, five on either side. One, Jenkins noted, was Taotoe, the chief's dour younger brother. Like older clones of the messenger, they had bowl shaped hairdos bald at the crown and a lower lip pierced with a wooden rod. Their skin, however, was darker and more leathery, cured by fifty years of equatorial sun. Simple pattern tattoos covered their arms, legs, chests, and backs.

Objects shone from their heavily pierced faces, reflecting in the faint torchlight. From one man's ear hung a ceramic teacup handle. Through another's nose, a boar's tooth uncomfortably perforated the septum, leaving little room for air to pass through his nostrils. Gold, worked into wires and rods, adorned cheeks, brows and chins of others.

Complete silence filled the room. The gathering looked exhausted, as if deliberations had gone on all night. Several of the elders clearly were unhappy. The others sat with expressionless faces. The chief raised his staff and Jenkins and Bodecker were told to sit by the messenger. They did so, cross-legged as were the elders, on the floor.

Bodecker wondered what was in store. He had been shunned by most of the elders from the start. It didn't bother him. They were just underlings. It was the chief's decision that was most important to him. That is where he had focused his energy, with gifts, mainly trinkets. And until just now, he had not even been sure that the gifts he had been sending were getting to the chief. But the music box clearly had made an impact.

He waited patiently.

Finally the chief spoke. His words were few. Jenkins was taken with disbelief, as he comprehended what he was hearing. When the chief was finished more than half the elders respectfully stood, including Taotoe, and left, showing disapproval.

"What did he say, Professor?" Bodecker whispered.

A moment passed without reply, then Jenkins answered, "You have succeeded in getting your wish, Dr. Bodecker." His words came slowly; his tone was distant. He was preoccupied by the falling out that would come from the rift dividing the elders, and by the price that someone would pay for the disharmony. Jenkins rose.

"That's it," Bodecker asked. "We came all that way here for a two minute meeting?"

Jenkins nodded. "We leave at dawn." There was a quiver in his voice.

Bodecker grunted in approval. He was one step closer to his goal, and congratulated himself for his uncanny skill in manipulation. He had never doubted himself. The Reichsfuhrer's faith had been well placed.

CHAPTER TEN

J enkins experienced a deep sense of foreboding the next morning as the party of fourteen started upriver in two long dugout canoes. Using poles and paddles, they moved up the slow moving brown waters of the Ortenguaza toward its origin, the old chief leading the way. When the boats bottomed out in the shallows they packed their gear and slogged through boot sucking mud until reaching a hidden trail. A trail that would lead them upward and eventually out of the blurred world of electric greens and rain-soaked browns that they lived in.

The single file of intruders advanced in the heavy morning air, spooking piha birds that screeched loudly and drawing angry chatter from Woolly monkeys that then stole away into the foliage. It didn't take long for Jenkins and Bodecker to be drenched in sweat. Jenkins had made many such journeys through the jungle without incident. He knew that on such hikes, all he had to do was stay behind the man in front of him to keep up.

The pace on the narrow trail was slow and steady, and the strung out column moved with virtually no conversation, each man fixing his eyes on the one before him. The others further ahead and beyond were swallowed up by a spray of overhanging vines and branches as thick as anacondas dangling from the treetops. The sky was rarely visible.

Jenkins's first few weeks in this verdant world had been difficult. Like most visitors he suffered anxiety attacks, craving the open sky. In serious cases the situation could exacerbate into delirium. But two and a half years in the jungle had cured Jenkins of his claustrophobia. There were few escapes from the creeping vegetation: the river, the village—and the mountains, which until now he had never ventured into.

Like the Indians, Bodecker said little. He found the pace slow and wished they would move faster, but did not make an issue of it. He assumed the disgruntled elders would use any opportunity to create a commotion, or even an unfortunate accident, to remove him and Jenkins from their pilgrimage. He was going to give them no reason to reconsider their invitation.

As they moved toward the mountains, the river was no longer brown and meandering as it had been on the valley floor, but instead, it was a clearer tea color, rich in tannins, and it moved briskly with occasional rapids. And as they climbed out of the valley, the topsoil all but disappeared, the vegetation came to an abrupt halt and to Jenkins' relief the sky suddenly opened above them. It was good to be out of the gloom and heat.

Bodecker looked back and scanned the verdant jungle canopy with interest. The sky was a startling blue, dotted with puffy white clouds. He tried to spot the vast clearing of the Picayulta's isolated city, but the sunshine in the open space was blinding. He looked at Jenkins. The professor was out of his league; his face flushed from the exertion. He had his weathered straw hat pulled down low over his squinted eyes. Bodecker marched on.

The trail grew increasingly steep as the day passed and by late afternoon the party had reached the canyon rim. At the last opportunity the Indians produced axes and systematically hoed down small trees, trimming branches away until they were left with thick poles.

As the Indians worked, Jenkins and Bodecker regarded the vast Amazonian expanse. The clouds they had looked up to were now just overhead like a thick fog. Far to the east a thunderstorm swept its way across the jungle. And ahead to the west was another valley, this one in the mountains that led both higher and deeper into the Andes. A different climate already prevailed, and a much colder wind blew from the eastern highlands. They had left the farthest reaches of the jungle, and beyond them rock became the dominating landscape, choking out all but the lowest lying shrubs, which fought to keep a hold on the ridge.

Once the Indian's task was complete the party resumed its march upward into the next valley. At the far end, high mountains towered, forming the true divide of the Cordillera Oriental range. Black clouds swirled around their snow capped summits, which reached nearly eighteen thousand feet.

An hour later the sun dropped out of sight without warning and the shadows were long and dark. In the few moments they had before darkness the group stopped to eat and set up camp. They took shelter in an ancient depression in the stone, one with steps leading both in and out. Bodecker and Jenkins surveyed the barren highland valley they were about to enter. "Somewhere in those mountains," Jenkins said, pointing, "lies the answer to your foolish quest, Doctor."

"Do you regret having come, Professor?"

"I can think of places I would rather be," he answered with a chattering shiver.

"Relax. You worry too much. You sound as though we will not make the return trip."

"I'd watch my back if I were you," Jenkins said, throwing a look of distrust in the direction of the elders.

The Indians had brought densely woven blankets, which they were donning. On top of that they placed jaguar pelts and boar skins, which they tied tightly around their bodies. It was a tailor's nightmare, but an effective weather barrier. And it was the first time Jenkins had seen the natives clothe their bodies. They gathered sticks of firewood and lit a small fire that burned brightly in the clear air, though the heat it gave was meager.

In his customary safari outfit, Jenkins realized he was ill prepared. He wrapped himself in the single blanket he'd thought to bring, doing his best to block out the cold wind. Deep inside he knew something wasn't right. Bodecker had with him just a single blanket though he seemed entirely satisfied with it. He made himself comfortable not far away, his back to stone his eyes towards the Indians. Then he lit one of his foul smelling cigars and prepared for a night at the edge of two alien worlds.

Jenkins had slept little and awoke at first light. His body ached. He didn't know if it had been the exertion of the hike, or the hard rock surface he had slept on.

The elders were milling around, preparing for their departure. All of them chewed wads of coca leaves. It seemed to give them an inexhaustible supply of energy.

The dawn air was cold, and a mist formed from each man's breath. After a sparse breakfast of dried fish the group set out again into the high mountain valley. No sooner had they started than the sun broke the mountainous horizon. Jenkins welcomed the warmth on his back.

The group plodded steadily, this time with their added supply of poles, which they divided evenly. Groups of two carried the wood except for the chief who walked unencumbered.

As they crossed the new valley Bodecker noted the water in the stream now flowed northwest. Jenkins noticed nothing, preoccupied as he was with the pain brought on by the previous day's arduous march. By afternoon they had cleared the second valley and were climbing steeply into the mountains. That night's camp was a welcome rest for the anthropologist. As he rubbed his sore muscles he feared the next morning his body might refuse to go any further. He cursed himself for bringing just the single blanket, but he had spent so many nights in the steaming jungle it had not occurred to him the mountains would be so bitterly cold. Bodecker, on the other hand, gave no hint of being affected by the march. From his place in the line he just eyed the Indians and smoked his cigars.

The Indians sensed his vigilance, which heightened the tension and polarized the hikers even more. Everyone seemed more distant.

On the third day the party awoke to make their final climb into the last and highest valley in the range. It was large with steadily climbing bowl shaped sides, and was the place that the Picayulta Indians called the Valley of the Wind. The valley floor was flat, and from the moment the trekkers entered it, a steady, cold wind beat harshly into their faces.

In the rising slope of the far side, there it was, true to legend, the enormous monolith, peculiarly out of place with its surroundings and dominating the valley.

The fifteen hundred-foot granite formation stood erect, partially embedded in the side of one of the higher peaks. Its strikingly different colors of glistening charcoal and silver had a hue of bluing like the barrel of a rifle, a stark contrast to the gray granite everywhere else. The monolith appeared to have come from a different place all together, maybe even a different planet, as it

resembled no other geology on the continents. At the first sight-
ing of the curious summit the elders drew to a halt, then bowed
in reverence.

"So this is it—El Chiflon," Bodecker said in a hushed voice.

"Precisely as Wilson described it," Jenkins said to himself,
more than a little in awe. Fear firmly gripped his emotions.

Bodecker overheard him. "Professor, the setting may be accurate, but I doubt we are going to be visited by any prophet star,"
he said in a mocking tone, then added reassuringly, "Tomorrow,
we'll be marching back down this path, twelve disappointed Indians and two scientists who witnessed the ceremonial display of
a lifetime. Nothing more."

Jenkins was not so sure anymore. He removed his single blanket and wrapped his shoulders. He could hear an ominous high
pitched shrill in the distance. Wilson's descriptions were only too
accurate. If so much had been true, then what about the rest?

It seemed the winds howled with increased intensity as the
group resumed its march closer. Led by the chief, who seemed
unaffected by the trek, the men began the final ascent up the
spire following the foretold narrow treacherous trail. The climbers had no protection; any ill-fated step would send them falling
hundreds of feet to a certain death. Jenkins hugged the rock face
and moved with timid uncertainty while Bodecker behind him
watched with amusement. Moving at a snail's pace, the climbers
took all afternoon to reach the summit. They arrived just as the
sun descended. The wind and whistling had grown deafening
throughout the climb. To speak it was necessary for the white
men to raise their voices. Relieved that the journey was over,
Jenkins dropped onto a rock. Every part of him ached. Out of
habit he pulled his pocket watch from his shirt.

"On time?" Bodecker asked, smiling sarcastically as he sat beside him, eyeing the huddled natives not far away.

"I'm afraid so," Jenkins replied reflectively. His hollow gaze was fixed on the time piece, but he did not see it. There was pain in his voice and he winced as he straightened his legs. He ran his trembling fingers over his swollen knees. He knew he should be alarmed by their size, but he was too tired. The creases carved into his aged face had grown deeper, and his gray eyes were void of expression. They just looked old.

"So this is it. The sight of our supernatural rendezvous," Bodecker said. Jenkins did not answer. "If the legend is correct, it is here, on this micro-plateau overlooking the God forsaken Valley of the Wind with the heavens looking down from above, that these foolish Indians are periodically drawn for their ritualistic changing of the guard," Bodecker said, standing up. He was unable to stay seated, and wanted to scrutinize every inch of the small summit.

The German seemed different to Jenkins since they'd left the river. He had grown louder and bolder, more like he had been the night he'd forced the professor to reveal his secrets. *It can't be hypoxia*, Jenkins thought. *He has too much energy.* The journey did not seem to have weakened him at all. Jenkins glanced at the Indians. Even they looked tired. But not the German.

"Just as the good reverend described," Bodecker continued almost gleefully, spinning around to take it all in. He pointed to a simple structure built on the ledge against the rock wall, which continued up another fifty feet to the summit of the giant monolith. "It's the temple!"

For that, it was small, only ten feet in height. Steps led from it to an altar. Just across was *El Ventorrio*, the window through the rock from which emanated the shrill howling. Its source, Bodecker could see, was the wind roaring through the tunnel. Roughly triangular in shape with five feet to each side, the opening appeared to be a naturally occurring phenomenon rightly named, for only ten feet beyond it opened to a vast drop off on the opposite side.

And in the passageway was the statuette, firmly fixed in place, standing simple and alone. Made from the same foreign stone as the giant monolith it rested on, it was exquisitely carved with a head bigger than its body. A row of variously colored, roughly hewed gemstones lined its base. Its eyes were deep red rubies, its nose grotesquely large with a polished miniature boar's tusk piercing the septum. Upon its head was a simple headdress, the band made of gold with emeralds symmetrically embedded along its length. Its short arms were raised before it, as if reaching out to grasp its observer.

Jenkins did not like the uncanny precision by which the entire legend was revealing itself: the Valley of Wind, the peculiar monolith, the mountain temple, the window in the rock, and of course, the stone idol adorned with gold and gems. He shuddered, just thinking of it, as he watched the elders unloading their poles. They had brought them to burn here on this rocky summit. They placed the wood at the base of the temple in a pit, which from its soot blackened walls looked as if it had seen countless fires before.

Bodecker walked about in the flat area in which they found themselves, which was about one hundred fifty by one hundred feet. As he did, he surveyed the details and observed the Indians. The elders too, watched him cautiously, as they prepared their sacrificial fire at the altar.

Fatigued and feeling ill, Jenkins sat by himself, close to the place where soon a fire would burn, as if expectation alone would warm him. He clutched his blanket tightly about his body. A terrible numbness gripped his debilitated body. His eyes grew heavy. Too tired to care about the pending ceremony any longer, he fell into a deep slumber.

CHAPTER ELEVEN

The sun was dropping toward the horizon as Jack arrived at the gate of the farmhouse where he was born. The rusty hinge announced his arrival. He expected his dog, Brix, to come barreling up the drive at the sound, hopping and jumping to welcome his master who had been gone almost ten weeks. But the place was quiet.

Still, it was good to be home. There were two jack-o-lanterns on the veranda. The girls must have made them with their mother, he thought. Jack went around to the back and peered through the diamond shaped pane of glass in the kitchen door. His mother was alone, bent over a pan pressing dough for a pie. Jack went in and put down his bag. "Hi mom," he said. "Sorry I'm late." He leaned over and kissed her on the cheek.

She turned with surprise. "Jacky. I was starting to worry if you were all right."

"I'm fine. I just got caught up visiting friends before I left," he replied while giving her a hug.

"Well, I'm happy to have you home safely." She looked up from her work and flicked a strand of hair out of her face. "Go put your things in your room and wash up, we'll be eating shortly."

Jack climbed the stairs and dropped his bag on the floor. His room was unchanged. Medals and ribbons decorated the walls, and trophies crowded the dresser top. His days at school seemed distant, as did the satisfaction of winning.

He thought of his asthma and the rejections, and a knot tightened in the pit of his stomach. The nostalgia turned to bitterness as he recalled his most recent disappointment. He tried to push the thoughts away, but this only angered him more as he recalled his father's fight with near complete incapacitation. Jack wondered how he could be so selfish and insensitive. Then he considered his mother downstairs. She had been so preoccupied by her husband's afflictions that she never noticed her own son's depression. It was understandable.

Thank God for Sully. He had been Jack's mentor in these difficult times, and had shared the fact that Teddy Roosevelt had also suffered from asthma. His own family had considered him frail, but still, he'd gone on to become a Rough Rider and President.

"It was his fight to overcome asthma and what people thought of him that forged him into the man that he eventually became," Sully said. "And it was by those very trials which tried to break him that he found his true inner strength." His pride in his friend was clear.

When the anger and frustration became too much, Jack remembered those words. They gave him strength to push his body to both its physical and mental limits. On the farm, he competed against himself. Every day he exercised. Every night he read insatiably. A bruised ego was not going to let him justify surrendering his future. "If Roosevelt could beat it, so could I," he rationalized.

His mother called from the stairway. "Jack! We're eating." It snapped him from his thoughts. He joined his mother and two sisters at the table, but he was still fuming with resentment. "I'm sorry things did not work out at camp," his mother said.

"I don't want to talk about it." Jack said.

"It's just as well, Jacky; now you can go back to college," she continued, "and get an important job." Clearly she was relieved at not having the only man left in her life placed in danger.

"I don't want to go back to college. If I can't fly for the Army I want to fly for an airline," he snapped.

"Jacky, soon the war will be over. There will be thousands of pilots out trying to get those same jobs. Experienced pilots, who fought in a war. What are your chances as a crop duster being chosen over the fighter pilots? Go back to school," she pleaded. "Besides, Jacky, with your problem, you are better off not flying."

"My problem?" He snapped. "What problem? The only problem I've ever had was trying to do something without everybody interfering," he all but shouted. "My *problem* is everyone around me. My *problem* is not getting a fair chance to prove I don't have a problem!"

Jack's sisters were staring at their plates. His mother looked at him with shock. Jack stood up, knocking his chair backward onto the floor. "My *problem* follows me everywhere I go!" He stormed out the door.

His mother rose but his sister Lisa stopped her with her hand. "Let him go, Mother. He'll blow off some steam and it will pass. It always does."

CHAPTER TWELVE

Stinky's was a barn styled Texas tavern and pool hall on the outskirts of New Braunfels. The converted Texas Growers' and Ranchers' Association exchange was complete with a grain silo on the side and a stockyard out back. But the growers had moved their business to a modern facility by the new railroad almost forty years before, and this place just sat vacant, decaying in the elements. Until Barney Johnson, a pig farmer everyone called Stinky inherited the wreck. He repaired the barn and built a stage, kitchen and bar. In the back were three billiard tables. A jukebox against the wall held mostly country tunes.

Prohibition had been scarcely a hiccup locally, and the newborn tavern was the only excitement the farm town had to offer. With a wink to the sheriff and an envelope of cash every week, Stinky's became the rural equivalent of a speakeasy. For the younger local crowd it was the only place to congregate.

When Jack arrived, there was a bigger crowd than usual. It was a combination of drunks in wild Halloween costumes, farmers marking the end of harvest, and a blissful remainder rejoicing at the fact that the British had just taken back a large part of Egypt. Any positive news in the war was in itself a reason to celebrate. The air was heavy with the smell of beer and cigarette smoke.

Jack felt none of the joy. In the back of the bar, he spilled the last of the beer from a pitcher into his glass, set it down by another he had emptied earlier, then made his way around the pool table where he played alone. The outburst at the dinner table weighed heavily on his mind. His rash behavior distressed him; his mother and sisters didn't deserve to be dumped on like that. They had a hard enough life without him adding to their troubles. He felt selfish. He wasn't feeling sociable and had no desire to make small talk, so he'd spurned every request for a challenge game. Consumed by emotion, he just wanted some space, space to fester in self-pity.

It was late. Someone was wailing on the jukebox, and a few patrons were stumbling around the joint in disheveled costumes, talking loudly, and not making any sense. The farmers, for the most part, had gone home. A few of the die-hard regulars were clinging to the bar. Oblivious to his surroundings, Jack chalked his cue stick, leaned his weight on the billiard table, and lined up a shot with impaired concentration. From across the table in the corner came a woman's voice: "Don't they teach you how to use your stick in the Air Corps, fly boy?"

Jack raised his eyes. She was blonde and petite; she ran her tongue slowly and provocatively across the red lipstick of her upper lip, then took a pull on a cigarette. "Lucy Cleave," he said. "Didn't think I'd see you again."

With pigtails in her hair and freckles painted prominently on her cheeks, she pointed at her shepherd's crook. "It's Little-Bo-Peep tonight." She stepped closer to the table, with an exaggerated sway of her hips.

Jack could not help noticing how tight her jeans fit. He felt his throat dry suddenly. His eyes wandered, but he knew she didn't mind. Her blouse was a short blue and white midriff, the top half conspicuously unbuttoned. The lower corners were tied high in the front to reveal a sliver of her flat mid-section. Only Lucy could take the innocence of a child's nursery rhyme character and transform her into a seductive temptress of the night, Jack thought. She raised the butt of her crook toward the cue ball, took quick aim and popped it. The ball darted across the felt into the corner pocket.

"Dangerous as ever, I see," Jack said. "How have you been?"

"Okay, I guess." She paused. "Missed you, though."

"Missed me," Jack cut in abruptly. "It wasn't me that just up and disappeared last July."

Lucy looked wide-eyed in innocence as she said, "I had to go to Louisiana, to visit my aunt."

"You could have said something. Or sent a postcard at least." Jack knew Lucy was impulsive. She was also aggressive and self-assured. Once her eyes were set on someone, she was unstoppable. Last spring they were on Jack. June and July had been incredible for Jack. Lucy overwhelmed him with her worldliness; he'd never known anyone like her. He knew there were those in the county that referred to her as a slut, but he didn't like to think of her like that.

The nights they'd had were hot and heavy, and though it was never love, he liked what they'd had. She had been the most exciting relationship he had ever had. In fact, she had been the *only* one he had ever had. It had stung like hell when she vanished, but he'd come to understand that was Lucy. She'd just been looking for a fling. And the real problem wasn't that she'd had flings with others, it was her attitude in her relationships. It was too cavalier, and basically opposed Jack's core of values.

"Anyway, you were gone when I got back," she argued.

"I was called up to camp. I just returned." They looked at each other across the table in silence for a moment, then smiled at the same time.

"It's been boring without you around," she said.

"You? Bored? I doubt that."

Lucy pouted. "It's true, you were the last of the real men around here. The good ones are all gone fighting that stupid war."

Yea, he thought, *that's where the real men are.* "What about you? What's new?" he said, changing the subject.

"Not a little ol' thing," she said like a frustrated child. "Nothing ever happens in this stupid town. I'm gonna run away, disappear to Austin, or Fort Worth someday. Wanna go with me?" Jack shrugged his shoulders. "Oh come on, Jacky, don't be such a stick in the mud. Let's go for a drive. We can go to the river, by the dam—you know—and watch the fire flies if you want." Her mischievous smile insinuated more. "I can cheer you up," she said assuredly. "Promise." She dropped her cigarette butt in a half full bottle of beer.

"I don't know, Lucy. I'm really not up to it tonight."

"Oh, come on, Jacky. I've got daddy's truck." She pushed her lower lip out and pouted. "I'll make all your problems go away," she said with a childlike voice.

"Right," Jack said. "Unless something has changed, it seems that any time I was with you, problems didn't seem to go away. Instead, things always seemed to ..."

"Get more exciting." Lucy offered.

Jack eyebrows rose. "An interesting description for uncontrolled mayhem." He conceded. He chalked his cue and readied for a shot.

Lucy leaned against the table, her sultry eyes connected with his as her loose blouse fell away from her chest. It was just enough to give Jack, and anyone behind him, a teasing glimpse of the swell of her breasts. "It wasn't all bad? Was it?"

Jack fought to keep his eyes off her. A couple of boys, too young to be in a bar in the first place, moved themselves in a position to get a better view. "No, I suppose it wasn't," he said, getting increasingly uncomfortable with the scene. He heard the boys snickering in the background and felt a wave of jealousy. Months had passed since they'd been together. It drove him crazy. How could she still have a hold on him? She'd just up and dumped him. There had been someone else. With Lucy there had to be. He knew what was in store for him if he went down that road again.

"I really want to go for a drive with you, Jacky," she said in a low voice. Jack cleared his throat. "You going to take me?"

It was close to midnight when Jack found himself in the gravel parking lot of Stinky's, opening the truck door for Lucy to get in.

CHAPTER THIRTEEN

The dirt road to the Guadalupe River was narrow and bumpy, and the truck's headlights bounced up and down and from side to side, as Jack struggled to keep the vehicle on course. He had convinced himself early on that he wouldn't let things with Lucy get out of control, and that this little drive down to the river would be harmless. He'd told himself that it was good to get out of the smoke filled bar.

Lucy clearly had other plans. Since leaving Stinky's she had been a persistent tease. Her fast hands had not taken long to unbutton his shirt. Almost immediately they were roaming freely over his exposed chest. Then her fingers wandered lower, across his abdomen where they happened upon the top button of his trousers. She fondled the button teasingly, and Jack's muscles twitched tensely. He felt his resolve collapsing. Lucy continued fiddling with the button until it finally popped loose.

"Whoa!" Jack veered to get back on the road. "Sorry," he said. He had almost hit a tree.

Lucy looked up with an unconcerned smile. "Trouble concentrating?" she teased. She had left no doubt what she wanted, and by the time he pulled the truck to the river's edge, he had already justified to himself that he had no reason to hold back. He turned off the ignition and the engine rumbled to a stop. The quiet of the river took over, interrupted only by the banter or a giggle between the two. The air was warmer than usual for an October night, and a partial moon glistened on the still waters.

Jack turned to Lucy, who leaned back against the door. Their eyes locked as she worked her toes up his leg, massaging his upper thigh. She never broke contact as she skillfully found and then slowly pulled down on one of the ties of her blouse. The fabric pulled tight, and the knot got smaller and smaller, until finally it disappeared into itself, and her top fell open, exposing her breasts to the moonlight. She lifted her fingers to her mouth as if taken aback by the outcome, all the while wearing the smile of a disobedient little girl. "See anything you like?" she asked invitingly, her voice a whisper. She fumbled a cigarette out of its package and lit it with a large wooden match that flared in the cab, illuminating them both momentarily. The smell of sulfur was strong.

Jack gazed at her bared breasts. In the soft light he could see goose bumps on the smooth fair skin, which culminated in erect, hard nipples. His heart skipped a beat. He reached over and pulled her closer, then fondled her firm breasts, caressing the nipples with his fingertips. Lucy giggled, then squashed the cigarette in the ashtray and took the lead. Her mouth was wet and warm, tasting of tobacco and lipstick. The temperature inside the truck climbed quickly and in a short time the windows were clouded over. Jack's troubles, as Lucy had promised, were forgotten. He was consumed with thoughts of having her as she took him to higher and higher levels of excitement. Then abruptly, she pushed him away.

"What's wrong?" Jack asked huskily.

With mischief in her eyes Lucy answered, "Let's go swimming!" She had a way of turning on a dime—changing whimsically. It drove Jack crazy, especially when he could hardly control himself another instant. He looked at her perplexed. "Swimming?" Perspiration dripped from his body down on to hers. Swimming was the farthest thing from his mind.

"In the river, silly. I'm hot, and I love it in the water." She moved closer to him and licked his lips then ran her tongue down his neck to his chest teasingly and added "Pleeease?" She was all but naked.

"Okay. Alright," he said, a little agitated, but driven by the knowledge he'd see her completely nude in just a moment. Before he could get out of the truck, she stripped off the last of her clothes and tossed her panties in the air. Then there she was, naked, running for the river, hollering out to him. Jack watched her all the way into the water. Her panties drifted in the heavy air, landed on the truck, and slid slowly down the windshield. Jack scrambled out of the truck.

A small concrete dam held the river back here, and the pooling water behind it was warm. The lake, actually a reservoir, was a widened portion of the river that had been built by the local power plant just up the river to cool its equipment. The byproduct was a stretch of river water eighty-three degrees year round. It was a favorite swimming hole for children in the day and lovers at night.

Jack waded into the water toward her. Lucy splashed at him and sheepishly tried to play keep away as he approached. He chased her halfhearted efforts to escape as she faked cries for help. Finally, he lunged forward and captured her, pulling her hips close, pressing her against him. She threw her arms up in surrender as he ran his hands freely over her smooth, wet skin, exploring the curves of her naked body. She brought her arms down around him as his hands continued purposefully down her body, under the water. She liked what he had found and what he did. Her body quivered and she turned submissive as he finally took the lead.

In the windless night under a spectacular array of stars, Jack and Lucy lost themselves as they made love in the warm waters of the river. Engrossed in their passion, neither noticed the peculiar flickering light rising in the distant western sky.

CHAPTER FOURTEEN

Beams of sunlight radiated from behind the jagged Andean horizon, striking clouds from beneath, and lighting them on fire. The spectacle grew brighter as the color of burnt orange spread and enveloped the white cloud tops above. But the sunset was very brief, conceding rapidly to the advancing night. Darkness engulfed the valley, and soon only a dim glow demarcated the outline of the surrounding purple peaks.

The ensuing night sky was dark, and the cosmos spread endlessly. Thousands of stars glittered and vividly blinked in the clear mountain air. Their iridescence illuminated the ghostly shapes that lurked in the Valley of the Wind. In the midst of this bleak desolation was El Chiflon, the barren promontory that stood out ruggedly like a sentinel, seemingly to guard the cold windswept vastness of the valley.

At this high altitude, nothing was found that would nurture life. No lasting water. No warmth. No trees. Precious little oxygen, and no shelter. Fourteen men sat motionless around a fire's dark perimeter. They were tightly bundled against the bitter winds. Twelve of the fourteen chanted nearly inaudibly, their mouths moving in rhythmic unison, their words visible on their lips, but the sound was swept away by the howling wind. They intoned the chant as if in a trance. Only the deafening whistle of El Chiflon could be heard above the gale roaring about the mountain crests. Its call resounded through the valley as if summoning a remote spirit.

Jenkins starred vacantly into the dim fire, its hypnotic spell holding him in its grip. Suddenly he lost his balance and snapped back from the flames. He was cold and his weary body shivered violently. He pulled the wool blanket about himself even tighter, leaving only his deep-set dark eyes and bearded face visible. The windswept fire reflected in his wire rim spectacles. His cheeks were a pasty white, his lips blue. He felt ill, dehydrated, deathly fatigued, and weary to his very being.

The biting wind sucked every bit of warmth from Jenkins' body, its cold snap robbing him of his vigor and allowing him only restless slumber. A slumber from which he thought he might never awaken. In his state, he didn't care. He eased towards the flames to capture as much heat as he could, but only his cheeks felt the radiance. The rest of his body suffered the bitter cold driving through the weave of the thick blanket. Occasionally his apprehension would return, and his eyes would dart from face to face nervously.

Bodecker sat next to him, like a statue challenging the elements. He understood they were on a watch. The unfolding accuracy of the legend had continued to erode his skepticism. Now, with the Indians he waited with anticipation for the arrival of the celestial occurrence, or whatever it was that they had traveled so far to see. He had pondered the idea of it being a comet. It made sense, reoccurring every sixty-one years with such precise accuracy. Comets were known to be unfailingly consistent in their reappearance. Whatever it was, there was more to it than just a typical cosmic appearance. The Picayultas knew it, and so did

Bodecker. He was as expectant as they were to greet a time traveler, a traveler from the past. He reconsidered the implications of such an event, absorbed and fascinated as he watched the others shiver. It gave him twisted pleasure to see them tormented by the frigid wind.

Jenkins glanced over at him. *This German is not human*, he thought, wanting to have nothing else to do with him. The old professor regretted being here. He had come against his better judgment, that truth he would not dispute. It was his drive to witness this, the most sacred of sacred Picayulta ceremonies, is what he kept telling himself, but in his gut he knew he had come out of fear—fear of Bodecker, who had needed him to translate. He banished the thought, not wanting to confront his weakness—not here—not now. He preferred thinking he was a logical man. A sensible man. A scientist. And after all, the Indians had no magical powers.

Jenkins surveyed the others huddled by the fire. Elaborately decorated, they chanted on tirelessly. The younger one sharply contrasted with the group. He wore no gold. He had no headgear. His fifteen-year-old skin had not yet turned to leather, weathered by the harsh environment. He was the next chosen one, handpicked by the chief to observe the end of this cycle of reign. He needed to understand it all, for he would succeed as the next chief. Through him the knowledge and tradition would be passed down to the next generation of the tribe. And it was here, in this magical, mystical setting that the process would soon begin.

Jenkins' heart pounded. Panic and fear raced through his body. He wished he were almost anywhere other than in this place. The Indians with whom he had lived for two and a half years no longer seemed like the same people he had known.

Their faces expressed apprehension, something he realized he had never seen among them before. In the light of the fire, Jenkins saw the Indians fidgeting and exchanging meaningful glances. He suspected a conspiracy and eyed the men warily. Or, were his nerves so frayed that he was just imagining it all? He knew the importance of the ceremony and reassured himself that the natives had never exhibited hostility toward him. There had always been trust between them. However, the heads adorning the chief's throne flashed into Jenkins' mind.

This might well be one of those times when trust should not be taken for granted, he thought wearily. *Less than three months from retirement—what the hell am I doing here?*

His mind fought to stay alert, but his fatigue and the fire's hypnotic forces beckoned him. Again he became too tired to care, too cold to care. A comforting feeling filled his body as he gazed aimlessly into the fire. His mind wandered to when he first arrived. The new assignment, the remote village Ray buzzed over so that Jenkins could see his new home. The way Ray set the airplane down on the still waters of the Ortenguaza River. *Poor Ray*, he thought as he dozed off.

•

Six hours had passed since the sun slipped behind the Tularosa Mountains in western New Mexico. The night was clear and the air cold and dry. Patches of sparkling stars littered the heavens, like an angry artist's canvas spattered with paint. It was an ideal night for stargazing. Conditions such as these were typical west of Socorro, and were the reason why the U.S. government had built its largest and most modern observatory here.

The giant dome, like a sentinel, stood watch over the desolate landscape. Protruding from its crown and pointed toward the heavens, the telescope probed the outer limits of the universe, collecting photons of light whose journey through the vastness of space had begun hundreds of millions of years earlier. After crossing the infinite emptiness of the cosmos, they herded down the tube. The images they carried bounced off the curved mirror, to a lens, which then bent them, packaged them, and neatly delivered them to meet their abrupt end in the back wall of astronomer John Grigsby's eye.

Though just out of school, Grigsby was a disciplined scientist, fastidious in every detail. He counted himself lucky not to have been drafted and justified his exempt status with special diligence to his work. He noted everything he observed, from the most insignificant anomalies and flickers to the slightest movements, recording the data meticulously. All the t's were crossed and the i's dotted; anything less, he detested. A serious scientist required such an approach to his work because most nights were boring, tedious and uneventful. This one had been no different—until now.

Grigsby was ready for a break. His watch over the skies of New Mexico had lasted five hours; hours cooped up in the cage that swung with the telescope, fifteen feet above the observatory floor. Five hours of intense concentration into the eyepiece. He was tired. He stepped back and rubbed his eyes with his handkerchief.

Then he took another look at what was keeping him from his break. What he saw was only a dot in space, but it held his undivided attention. It was a light, a moving object, and it intrigued him because it didn't belong. It was uninvited, invading his orderly world of distant specks and data. He recorded the dot's coordinates from the grid superimposed upon his field of vision.

He had done this for an hour now, and the object continued to baffle him.

It was growing larger. He calculated and recalculated its movements. Finally he allowed himself the excitement of believing he was following an unrecorded comet. This was the first interesting event that had occurred since he was assigned to the facility three months ago. He wanted to be certain that it was in fact a new discovery and not an error on his part. A false announcement would make him the laughing stock of the scientific community.

Many scientists went their entire careers without a major discovery. Here Grigsby was, fresh out of graduate school, enthusiastic about using his new found knowledge, and he could hardly believe that he was on the verge of discovering an uncharted comet. And this was not a typical comet. It should have been spotted weeks earlier, much further in space. Instead, here it was, on earth's doorstep as if by magic. It made no sense.

He calculated the position again. He had not yet shared the news with his colleague, Adam Radcliff, mainly because the man was pompous and carried a chip on his shoulder. Radcliff was a veteran stargazer, and in his own opinion felt he had been stationed at this remote post far too long. Although the equipment was state of the art and in many regards he was envied by his peers for the assignment, he was bored with his profession.

At one time everything had been new and exciting, but time passed and he'd lost his purpose. Now it seemed that the hours spent staring into space had been wasted. It had been thirty years of hoping to find that something special, anything that would make him famous, that he could call his own. He had passed up the wife, the family, and the house with a white picket fence. And yet the discovery never came. His diligence went unnoticed, and his demeanor had soured. At fifty-four years of age he felt entitled to a more desirable, more prestigious duty, such as the Tamalpais scope not far from San Francisco. Now that would be something.

To Radcliff seniority was a privilege to be abused and so he assigned his duties to his rookie colleague, Grigsby. Most nights he never got out of his chair, but just mindlessly entertained himself with solitaire, which he played as he sucked on his unlit pipe. Beside him was a bottle of cheap whiskey, and as he emptied the bottle he became increasingly belligerent.

Grigsby, on the other hand, was like a puppy looking out the window of the back seat of a car. He wanted to see everything; always worried he was missing something important. When he'd first spotted the approaching object, Grigsby had been elated, but it soon troubled him and not just because of its sudden appearance. He checked its trajectory, then again recalculated his numbers. Each time they verified his fears. The comet was headed for earth. Thoughts of praise and awards vanished, replaced by alarm and trepidation. "Adam," he called out, "you need to see this for yourself. Hurry!"

Radcliff, parked in his chair, had polished off his usual quota of Scotch, and was reluctant to listen to the young astronomer, but after much pleading Grigsby managed to persuade him to leave his card game for just a moment and look. Reluctantly he made his way up the spiral stairs into the cage. He knew the controls well and, with levers, motored the big scope to the place that had upset his partner. He peered into the eyepiece, then examined Grigsby's notes. Without speaking he grabbed a paper and scribbled out his own calculations. And for a brief moment, his interest in his field had been rekindled.

"Adam," Grigsby said, "that damn thing is coming directly toward us, I tell you! And from my calculations it will collide with us before dawn!" His voice broke nervously, while he hoped his senior partner would prove him wrong. Radcliff did not answer as he stared into the eyepiece. "Did you get a course reading?" Grigsby asked.

"Same as yours, I'm afraid," Radcliff replied dryly. "Headed directly into the earth's orbit."

Grigsby licked his lips. "What's our chance of collision?"

Radcliff belched. He smelled of whisky but that was no surprise to his young assistant. "Inevitable, it would seem." He sounded unconcerned, as if this was a harmless and unimportant event.

"Shouldn't we alert someone?"

Radcliff raised his head from the eyepiece. "Who? The President?" His tone was mean and sarcastic. "And what would we tell him to do? Mr. President, you know those fattening desserts you've been avoiding? Go ahead and have one."

Grigsby ignored the black humor. "How long before impact, would you say?"

"Thirty, maybe forty minutes," Radcliff said.

"But with its size and speed, it could kill us all! Wipe out the planet," Grigsby babbled.

Radcliff smirked. "Yes, it could be the end of the human race," he said as if he thought they deserved it. "Perhaps the next civilization will be more responsible," he added.

"What should we do?" cried Grigsby.

Radcliff spun off the chair and made his way back down to his desk. Grigsby followed. The senior astronomer opened the bottom drawer and extracted an eighteen-year-old bottle of Scotch. He blew the dust off it and held it to the light before setting it down next to his cards. As he packed his pipe with fresh tobacco he said, "I've been saving this for a special occasion."

He could see Grigsby looked scared. "It's always possible the comet will just miss us." He said dryly. "At least we can hope so. In the meantime, how about getting stinking drunk?"

CHAPTER FIFTEEN

I n the middle of the warmed waters of the Guadalupe River, Lucy and Jack rested in each other's arms. Jack was exhausted, sated for the moment, his energy sapped from an uninterrupted marathon of sex.

Reclining placidly in a nook of natural rock just below the water's surface, he gazed up into the sky. For a long time neither said a word. The water embraced them with its warmth; the night was quiet and windless. The moon had set and the stars were stark against the black backdrop. The universe above seemed to be at a standstill, especially the Milky Way. Only an occasional meteorite flashing its brilliance across the sky as it streaked to extinction interrupted the calm. It was spectacular, and yet so peaceful here in Texas, on the river. It was hard to believe that on another continent, and across the Pacific, a war was raging. Which one was the dream?

Jack felt Lucy's hands fondling him gently. It was relaxing on those rocks, in that water, on that night. "They're beautiful, aren't they?" he whispered, so as not to disturb the moment.

"What? The stars?"

"Yeah. At training camp we learned most of the bright ones and all the constellations."

"What for?"

"To navigate. Over the clouds sometimes, that and your compass are all you have for direction."

"Wow. That must be scary. Do pilots ever get lost?"

"All the time. It's one of the Allies' biggest problems." Jack gazed into the darkness. "That one over there is Orion, the Hunter," he said as he pointed off in the rising eastern sky. "Those three stars are his belt, and from it you can see that cloudy thing—that's his sword, and the bright one is his shoulder." He pointed at Polaris, dead center in the northern sky. "That one is the North Star. The bombers use it the most." The thought of the bombers changed Jack's mood.

Below the water Lucy's hands playfully tried to get his attention back. "Look at that bright little group," she said without interest.

"That's a star cluster, the Pleiades. It's part of the constellation Taurus, the bull."

She looked at him with a blank look on her face. "The bull?" Then she giggled. "That's a bunch of bull?"

"Well, it does takes a lot of imagination to see some of them."

"They all seem pretty dumb to me."

Jack ignored the comment. Lucy's inability to appreciate the simple things, the natural things, was something he'd become used to last summer. He'd come to suspect she really wasn't all that bright, and more than once his rational side had warned him that she was not a long-term prospect. He continued scanning the night sky. Lucy, feeling the neglect, lost her playfulness and gave a sigh of discontent. If it wasn't one thing with her, it was another, Jack thought.

His mind drifted back to the guys, right now, up over Germany risking their lives flying missions. He could feel his frustration edging back but was determined not to ruin the moment with more pitiful resentment. He was tired of that battle. He started naming stars, as many as he could, in order to block out his emotions. One star in particular caught his eye. It was brighter than the others were, yet he didn't remember it being there before, and did not know its name. "You see that one?" he said, pointing to the northwest. Lucy looked up into the sky, somewhat lost. "There, in that dark patch," he added. "It's brighter than the others."

"Yeah, I see it." They watched it in silence for a moment. "It seems like it's moving," she said after awhile. Again, they watched silently.

"That's weird," Jack said. "It *is* moving. Real stars don't normally move like that, not individually. They move across the sky in a group…"

"It looks like it's coming closer. Do you think it's heading this way?" she asked timidly. Jack didn't answer. "What do you think it is, Jacky?"

Jack continued to contemplate the light, searching his memory for some explanation.

"Is it an airplane?"

"I'm not sure. I hope it's not something coming from the Japanese or Germans," Jack wondered aloud. There had been rumors of the Japanese shelling Long Beach, California, from a submarine.

"Can they shoot stuff this far?" she asked. "Like bombs or something?"

"I don't think so." Jack said, but he wasn't certain. "It's probably just one of our planes."

The object kept growing brighter. He reconsidered. "No, it's not a plane. It's too high, and if you look closely you can see it's got something like a tail coming off of it."

"I see the tail!" Lucy said proudly.

"It looks like it's coming toward us—and it's getting faster…" The celestial object seemed to accelerate. "A lot faster."

It grew quickly. Jack stared upward in amazement. "Look at it go!"

"What should we do? It's getting so bright!" Lucy cried, raising her hand to shield herself from the light.

Jack didn't have an answer. The object lit up the river and the trees, and the rural Texas countryside as if it were daylight. Jack felt a prickling static sensation on his skin outside the water. Lucy squirmed. "Uuuwe, that feels weird." Sparks darted around the branches of the trees like fireflies. "What is that?" she asked frightfully.

"I've no idea."

The air started to stir, and building up in the distance Jack heard a deep rumbling drone coming toward them. It was a powerful sound, yet quiet. He'd never experienced anything like it. "Wow!" Jack exclaimed, light reflecting off his astonished face. With incredible speed the radiant object passed directly over them. His head pivoted one hundred-eighty degrees as he followed the object on its trajectory behind them. Lucy buried her head in her arms against his chest.

The object continued south in the sky and began to move downward toward the horizon. As it dropped, its brilliance dissipated, and soon it had disappeared altogether behind the thicket of trees on the riverbank. The night's serene darkness returned as if nothing had happened.

Lucy looked up from her arms. "That was really scary, Jacky. You think it had Mars men on it?"

Jack gave it some thought. "No, I bet it was a comet."

"A comet, what's that?"

"I've seen them in books. There's one called Halley's comet. It's rock or something, moving through space, like a small sta—" He looked down at Lucy. She wasn't listening. Her attention fluttered like a butterfly, and was now sidetracked by another sound coming from somewhere in the distance. "Never mind." What more did he expect from Lucy? At that moment on the river, surrounded by nature and the cosmos, he realized how vacuous she was, and how silly it was for him to have anything to do with her. He thought about the object again. It was long gone.

Then he too heard the other sound. It was a car engine accelerating on the dirt road. Gravel crunched and popped loudly under its tires as it moved quickly down the river road. Headlights flashed through the brush as the vehicle approached.

"Jacky!" Lucy said, sounding frightened. "Somebody's coming."

"Yeah, so?"

"So! So? Why we're butt naked in the river after doing the dirty deed. They'll see us!"

Jack snapped out of his daze. "Right. We better get out of here."

They slid off the rocks and quickly swam towards the bank. As they waded in the shallow water and towards their clothes scattered by the truck, the car turned abruptly from the river road into their parking area. Headlights flashed across the water, momentarily exposing the skinny-dippers. It was an old Plymouth and it drew to a stop directly between them and Lucy's truck. Its dust continued forward swirling into the light beams. The driver turned the lights off.

Jack and Lucy stopped in their tracks. "What's this guy doing?" Jack muttered.

The car sat motionless with its engine continuing to idle. A radio played loudly inside of the vehicle. It was a honky-tonk tune Jack had heard in the bar earlier. He assumed it was another couple out to park. After a moment he resumed walking out of the water, angling around the car and toward Lucy's truck. "You'd think they'd have the sense to find their own spot," he grumbled with annoyance.

Lucy placed a forearm across her breast, her other hand to cover her pubis and followed beside him. As they drew closer the headlights went back on, this time with high beams. The light flooded the little beach area and the river beyond. Jack and Lucy's naked bodies were brightly illuminated, causing them both to freeze in their tracks, while they were still ankle deep in water.

Still no one came out of the car.

"What the hell?" Jack felt incensed and vulnerable at the same time. His blood was starting to boil. "This isn't funny any more." Shielding his eyes, he attempted to see who was inside, then called out angrily, "Hey, what's your problem?"

Still no one came out, but the radio continued to blast from inside. Jack waded in front of Lucy, placing his arm around her protectively. "Let's just go around them and get out of here."

Lucy followed without saying a word.

They were just out of the water when the music stopped. The door swung open, blocking their path. They froze. The driver stepped out and was caught in the splash back of the headlights. He was a short, overweight man in his late forties with tobacco drool glistening down his chin. Handcuffs, keys and a baton dangled under the weight of his sagging belly, and he had a Sheriff's Department star pinned to his chest. He looked at Lucy first, and then his eyes locked onto Jack. "Well, well. What the hell have we got here?" the deputy said with an irritating country accent. He turned his head and spit a wad of chew onto the dirt.

Moonlight reflected off something in his hand. Jack glanced down and saw a gun—pointed at him. He stepped back startled. "Whoa, easy now."

"Shut up!" the deputy snarled.

Jack froze, never taking his eyes off the pistol, forgetting he was naked.

The man shifted, gripping the gun tightly in his hand. He looked unpredictable, as if even he didn't know what he was going to do next. Then a look of recognition crossed his face. "Why if it isn't Jack Sullivan," he spat, "the fly boy. Thought you'd come back to our small town for a little rest and relaxation, did you?" He looked at Lucy and shook his head. "You college boys think you can have anything you want, don't you?" His tone was spiteful and sarcastic. "Well, you're wrong," he growled, tapping his gun barrel on his star. "This is my town!"

"Excuse me?" Jack answered, bewildered, but cautious not to set him off. He searched his memory for the man's name. He'd seen him before but never up close that he could recall.

"Don't sass me, boy. You know what I'm talking about. Why look at you now, stark naked and no way out of this mess." The deputy shook his head. "Yeah, boy! You gone 'n done it good this time." He spat again, then wiped the drool off his chin with the back of his hand. "But when I'm done with you, you'll have nothing left to be proud of." He waved the pistol at Jack's groin.

"Mister, I think you have me confused with another," Jack said, trying to bring some reason into the situation. Dullum! He remembered. That was it. Willie Dullum. "We've never met, have we? Did I ever do you some wrong?"

"Do me some wrong!" Dullum spat back, mockingly. "Do me some wrong! Nothin' that you don't deserve dying for, you little son'bitch." Hate filled his voice, and his breathing was hard and fast. He raised his weapon and Jack took a step back. The man's eyes darted over to Lucy. "And you, you little whore. Why do you go looking for that shit everywhere, when you—you—can get it at home?"

"Huh?" Jack shot a bewildered look at Lucy. "You two *know* each other?"

"Know each other?" the man repeated mockingly. "Why you sorry son of a bitch, don't act like you don't know what's going on here! A woman ought to know her own husband even if she is full of another man's juices." He shook the pistol uncontrollably, getting Jack's immediate attention.

Jack glared at Lucy who looked sheepish, repentant. "Jack… Uhhh…sorry, this is…my…Uhhh…my…my husband… Willie. Willie, this is Jack." She said it all with an innocent twinkle as if an introduction could get her out of this fix.

"Husband! Why you shit! You're…married?" Jack asked incredulously.

Lucy nodded and shrugged her shoulders. "I guess I forgot to tell you," she said as if she had been caught with her hand in the cookie jar. Then she turned to the deputy. "Oh Willie, take a breath. It's not what it looks like."

Jack turned to her, astonished. She was a piece of work. How could she try a line like that with the two of them standing as they were, and still have the audacity to use that tone? It seemed as though she was enjoying the heightened excitement of being caught. She sure wasn't acting guilty.

Her comment seemed to fluster Willie. "Get out of the water, you bastard," he ordered, waving the gun. Jack guardedly made his way out of the water toward the truck. "So you had your fun, ehh? You liked mess'n with my wife? You little prick. I hope it was worth dying for."

Jack glanced back at Lucy. She had done it again. In disbelief he hoped she would say something to defuse her husband. But Lucy just darted in and out of people's lives to wreak havoc. When it came time for solutions she was nowhere to be found. Jack realized this time would be no different. She did nothing, but stood helpless in the water. "Sorry, Jacky," Lucy finally said in a hurt but insincere tone.

"How was I to know she was married? She's not wearing a ring, she never told me. Hell, you're married to her, you must know the kind of woman she is."

The deputy wasn't even listening to Jack. Lucy's words had infuriated him even more. "So you like him, huh?" He cocked his gun. "Let's just get this over with here and now, so you can see what your little escapade has done." He took aim.

Jack instinctively lurched at Willie, bracing himself for a bullet. But Willie was not as decisive as he talked, and they fell to the ground in a struggle. They rolled first away from, then toward the water, Willie grunting and groaning as they tumbled. Lucy watched the fight with rapt attention, licking her lips with excitement. Then the sound of a gunshot fractured the stillness of the night, the blast resonating up the river valley. No movement came from either of the men for an interminable moment. Finally Willie's lifeless body rolled off Jack.

Jack got up and checked himself for bullet holes. He'd heard you don't feel one going in. Barking dogs could be heard in the near distance. Lucy was silent, staring unemotionally at her dead husband, then abruptly she became horrified. She ran to Willie's body. "Is he dead?" Then she stepped back. "He is! He's dead!

You killed him! You son of a bitch! You killed my Willie!" Jack was momentarily confused. She was acting as if he were the perpetrator. "Can't you see he's with the sheriff's department?" she shouted. "He was just doing his duty and you killed him!"

"His duty? What duty? The guy was going to kill me!"

"Willie was harmless. He doesn't have what it takes to go through with his threats. You could tell that. You didn't have to attack him!"

"But you saw what happened. I didn't attack him. I was defending myself."

"You did too! He was just waving that pistol around, that's all." Jack was taken aback by her words. "You're in big trouble. They're going to hang you for this. And I'm not gonna help you. You killed my Willie," she said spitefully.

Jack stumbled back, away from her. She was delusional. He looked around nervously. Voices had now joined the commotion of barking dogs up the road, and it sounded as if they were approaching. Jack grabbed his trousers and slipped them on. The racket had stirred some farm workers sleeping in a nearby barn. "Lucy, you got it all backwards," he said in a panicky voice.

Unable to look at him directly, and without a word, she shook her head, staring down at the lifeless body of her worthless late husband. She had herself worked up now and tears streamed down her cheeks.

"Lucy, talk to me. Tell me you saw it—the way it really happened," Jack pleaded. She had turned the entire incident around. Her account made him out to be a murderer.

"You okay over there?" a voice called out from the dark.

"If you know what's good for you, Jack, you'll get out of here fast," Lucy said.

"I can't do that," he said. "It'll make me look guilty."

"You *are* guilty, Jack," she yelled. "You murdered him! I saw it with my own eyes."

"Murder?" Startled voices cried out in the dark. Jack could hear the group of men talking just beyond his perimeter of visibility.

"Ma'am, you okay?" a man called out.

"No, I need your help!" she shouted. "He's got me here!"

"I do not! I'm not touching her," Jack answered reflexively.

"Quick, Bart, go 'n get the sheriff," someone said. A mumbled discussion followed among the group, which sounded like three, maybe four men. Then it was quiet for a moment. Jack saw figures moving with stealth in the perimeter. "All right, fella, why don't you just lay down on the ground and leave the girl be till the sheriff gets here."

Willie twitched on the ground and Lucy lost it. She began screaming hysterically.

"Let her go, boy," a voice called out in the bushes to Jack's far right, while the metallic clicking of a cartridge being loaded into the chamber of a shotgun sounded in the brush to his left. They were trying to surround him. His eyes darted nervously back and forth. He saw nothing in the darkness. "Now, boy, I don't know what you done here, but there's no need to make it worse on yerself."

Without Lucy's support Jack's position was hopeless. He had to get out of there. He darted toward the truck, scooped the rest of his clothes off the hood, and fled into the darkness.

The men rushed in to find Lucy crying over the body of her husband, not a stitch of clothing on her. "Where is he, ma'am?" one man asked as he gave her his coat.

Jack stopped in the darkness to yank on his clothes and could hear them interrogate her. "He's gone," she said, sniffling and pointing into the darkness.

"Did he rape you?" another asked eagerly as if he wanted to hear her say it.

The last thing Jack heard before running like hell was her answer.

"He tried, but Willie got here just in time. God bless him. And look what Jack Sullivan did to him for protecting my honor."

With two miles behind him he heard the sirens. There were three cars in a line with their lights flashing, all headed for the river's edge. They wouldn't hear the truth, or even care what it was. And it wouldn't be long before they were knocking at the door of his mother's house.

Jack was a fugitive now; he couldn't go home. Instead, he headed for Sully's place. He would help and the police wouldn't think of it right away. There at least he could hide until they got the story straightened out, assuming they were interested.

CHAPTER SIXTEEN

Professor Jenkins's attention was divided between the slicing sting of the bitter wind and a twinkling glow in the northwestern sky. He was no astronomer, but the light looked to be moving erratically in the distance. As time passed he raised his eyes again and again towards the object and realized it was growing brighter. He'd never seen anything like it before. A luminescent tail trailed behind it, and it was more radiant than any star. Along the jagged horizon, its prominence grew steadily. Either it was getting bigger or drawing nearer.

Could it be a shooting star? Jenkins wondered. Its movement was too slow, and he knew that meteorites burned out. They didn't endure like this. *Maybe it's a comet, or just maybe Huantanuco...*

Abruptly the object changed course, moving decisively faster toward the men on the summit. In its center Jenkins could now see a small, defined core of brightness, which increased in intensity as it approached. Soon the object dominated the night sky pouring out a light that illuminated the valley below. Unable to take his eyes off the spectacle, Jenkins raised his hands to block the brightness. His body tingled all over. The hair on his arms and head rose on end. Even the whiskers on his face bent oddly, tugging gently toward the celestial body. Its blinding radiance, he saw, was focused on the apex of El Chiflon.

Jenkins glanced down. The hair on the Indians' heads was also standing on end. Beside him, however, Bodecker's hair appeared unchanged—already, as always, and stiffly upright. Shrinking into his blanket, his eyes fixed back on the radiant object in the sky above them, Jenkins yelled over the howling wind, "What is it?"

"There must be a strong polarization occurring between the mountaintop and that object!" Bodecker shouted.

"That's a hell of a static charge!" Jenkins' skin now itched uncontrollably. He scratched without relief as a painful prickling sensation surged within his body. Ignoring the cold, he pushed the blanket off, inspecting his hands and arms, rotating them, first one side, then the other. His eyes filled with horror as he saw lumpy waves move across the flesh of his arms and legs. They pulsed and quivered like worms burrowing below the skin's surface. He opened his mouth to cry out, but remained mute.

Now sparks formed at his fingertips and bounced erratically across the skin of his hands before leaping in the air. For an instant they swirled in suspension just inches from his hands, but then they bolted away, accelerating toward the object in the sky. Their numbers multiplied rapidly until a flood of energy flowed between him and the thing overhead. Jenkins' face contorted in pain. Paralyzed with fear and gripped by the force, he observed the others being affected similarly. The fluorescing photons that darted like fireflies created a glowing halo around the men. Eventually, each broke free, and like the others before it, streaked up to the object, leaving behind a slow fading luminescent trail.

The howling wind increased in volume and the attraction grew stronger as the object settled into a hover just above the highest spire of El Chiflon. Jenkins now felt the invisible force drawing him like a magnet, upward toward the entity. He felt light, almost weightless, no longer sensing the ground below him. *Is it the wind pulling me up? He* wondered. He realized the others too, were suspended inches above the ground.

"I'm floating!" he yelled with astonishment to no one in particular, but again, no words came out of his mouth.

Then it all stopped. The wind with its thunderous roar, the deafening shrillness through the portal in the rock, and the electrical display—in an instant—were all gone, replaced with a deathly calm.

Jenkins's pain had also vanished. He fell to the ground sobbing in terror.

The fire had been squelched to a smokeless flicker and yet around them it was no longer cold. A warm light bathed the summit ledge, and the still air lost its crisp clarity, replaced with a strange opaque mist that surrounded all that was real and tangible. There was a smell hanging in the motionless air, a peculiarly sweet aroma like burned sugar. Time itself had ground to a paralytic halt.

They waited. For what seemed a long minute, perhaps two or three, no one spoke, no one stirred. Nothing happened. Then, from within the portal, the eyes of the statue illuminated with life, glowing a fiery red. Thick smoke quite unlike the mist oozed slowly from the statue's gaping mouth, forming a cloud that began to turn and fluoresce with churning, glittering particles. It grew rapidly before the statue, the sparkling gases rotating horizontally, pin wheeling like a galaxy in space. At the same time a whirring harmonic rhythm emanated from the object in the sky, and as it grew louder the cloud surrounding the statue spun faster.

Jenkins had never been so terrified. He felt the ground tremble, and the waves resonated through his body. For an instant he thought it was an earthquake. Stones jumped and bounced randomly in place, until the emitted energy created a vibrating instability so intense that the foundation of the mountain itself was quaking. He feared the entire mountain was preparing to collapse away from under them. Adding to the growing chaos, a river of sparks gushed forth flowing between the cloud and the object suspended above. It was a spectacular exchange of energy bolting rapidly back and forth. The two white men could only watch with awe.

"Jesus, it's real!" Jenkins exclaimed. "This thing is really happening."

"*Ja!*" replied the German, wide eyed for once. Himmler had been right.

Then the heavy cloud stopped turning, obscuring everything in the passage, save for the red glow of the statue's eyes, which penetrated the thickness. The slowing soup fell, pouring away from the portal down onto the temple's flat altar top. The creeping mass spread evenly over the surface like spilt liquid on a table, then cascaded down the temple steps. At the base, the cloud continued its expansion, flowing ominously toward the dumbfounded onlookers. It hugged the ground below the still air, where its weight smothered out the last flickers of the fire.

At that instant the mist lost its brilliance. And the object, still hovering above them, started to lift away. Then without further display it turned and departed smoothly into the heavens, resuming its cosmic journey.

Whatever it was had come and gone.

On his knees Jenkins was unaware of the dispersing cloud that still enveloped his lower legs. He looked back at the passage that the heavy mist had once occluded. There, before the statue, stood a young man.

"The chosen one from the past!" Bodecker whispered in awe. "That must be him. He has arrived!"

The elders did not look astonished. They had fully expected this to transpire just as they expected the sun to rise in the morning. The chief stepped forward, his legs smoothly slicing through the low-lying mist. The gases formed swirling eddies in his wake and residual charged particles scurried around his feet. The odor of burned protein now replaced the earlier sweet aroma.

Stoically the chief greeted the arrival, the embodiment of their legendary god. With only a moment's hesitation he climbed the steps of the temple and moved across the altar toward the boy. A tear rolled down his aged cheek.

Of course, Jenkins thought. *Could that boy really be the chief, sixty-one years earlier?*

Although standing upright, the boy did not appear conscious, and as the chief approached, the boy fell forward into his arms. The old man carried him down the steps, growing weaker by the moment, and the idol's eyes, which had continued to burn brightly, now began to dim. As they faded so did the magical night of lights and smoke, its only legacy a boy helplessly delivered from another time.

Life left the idol and the chief simultaneously. The old chief slowed, then stumbled. The elders caught the boy as their chief fell to the ground and without ceremony expired before them. When his body was still, a gust blew across the high mountain ledge, scattering the blanketing smoke from the ground. The night turned cold at once and darkness returned. The wind cut through all that was exposed.

●

John Grigsby slipped deep into his chair, his shoes propped up on the desk next to the empty bottle of whiskey. Unaccustomed to the effects of alcohol he shoved away from the desk with his feet, attempting to turn toward Radcliff who was still peering into the telescope, his still unlit pipe in hand. The chair spun around swiftly on its swivel, sending the intoxicated scientist crashing to the floor. "Oh God, it's hit us! Help!" he yelled in a panicky voice. "I'm hit! I'm down!" he slurred.

The older scientist had been sobered by the events and paid him no attention.

Slowly regaining his senses, Grigsby realized he had fallen on the floor and was in no immediate danger yet. He laughed like a drunken fool. "What's happening, Adam?" he shouted. "Shall we start a countdown?" He looked up from the floor, feeling no pain at the moment.

"Odd little bastard," Radcliff muttered.

"No need to get personal," Grigsby shot back, realizing for the first time how drunk he was.

"No, not you. I mean the comet. It was coming right at us, even disappearing behind the earth's curvature. The numbers indicate its impact should have happened ten minutes ago somewhere along the equator. By now I expected us to have been swallowed up by the devastating shock wave circumnavigating the planet."

"So it has happened? We're dead? Or gonna be soon?"

Radcliff ignored him. "But instead, it has reappeared," he said in a puzzled tone. "And it seems to be moving *away* from us."

Grigsby straightened his tie. "Perhaps it came in at an angle, so shallow, as to cause it to bounce off the atmosphere and return in to space."

"Impossible. I calculated the course. It was too steep. I've never seen anything like it! It's as if it defied gravity."

"Should we report what we saw?" Grigsby asked.

The older scientist turned toward his inebriated colleague who was still sitting on the floor. He peered over his glasses at the rookie. "Sure, but who's going to believe you, boy? Are you gonna get up in front of the board and explain how the planet was almost destroyed by a comet, but it just decided to go away?" Radcliff said sarcastically.

"Thousands of people must have seen it. What do you think we should do?"

Radcliff thought momentarily, wondering if any other observatory could have seen the phenomenon the way they had. "I think we should have another drink?" he answered.

CHAPTER SEVENTEEN

It was three in the morning when Sully heard tapping. He looked towards the window and saw a silhouette, the fuzzy outline of a man, peering into the house. The man banged on the glass again, this time harder. Sully fumbled over the nightstand searching for his spectacles. He looked again. It was Jack. What was he doing here at this time of the night? "Okay, lad, okay." He waved him over. "Go to the door." Sully went to the back door which was closest and opened it. "Come in. Come in. What brings you around in the wee hours?" Jack tried to speak, but nothing came out. "You look as if you've seen a ghost."

"Sully! Deputy Dullum, he got shot," Jack finally blurted. "He died—and everyone thinks I did it, but—" Jack gasped for a breath and continued, "I didn't do it, or at least not the way she says I did." He drew a breath. "And then the police came; they were everywhere so I just ran. I didn't know where to go and I couldn't go home so..."

Sully raised his hands. "Slow down, Jacky-boy. What nonsense is this that you're going on about? What police?"

Jack took a deep breath and tried to regain his composure. Then he started again, this time slowly. He covered in detail everything that had happened to him that evening. Sully digested the story thoughtfully. "Well, it doesn't look good for you at the moment," he said. "If you have done all that you said you have with this girl—what was her name?"

"Lucy Cleave, I mean Dullum."

"Yeah, Lucy, I remember her. And I recall Willie too. He's a mean one. I think you best lay low a while, at least until this whole mess gets straightened out. Lucy's a known liar and, sorry to say, she's been pretty friendly with a lotta boys in the county. People are going to wonder what really happened once they cool down. They know you're a good lad."

"I can't stay here. They'll be by soon enough. Where will I go?" Jack said in a panicky tone. "Where will I hide?"

Sully stood pensively for a moment. "They'll go looking for you first at yer mum's place. Hmmm. And yer right, it won't take the sheriff long to think o' coming here. We'll need some time to convince that girl to speak the truth of it."

The word "we'll" reassured Jack more than Sully could have ever imagined. He was not alone. For an instant he saw a ray of hope. Thank God, he could always count on Sully.

Sully sat in thought for a long moment, and then he looked up. "I've got it, lad!" He paused. "Panama!"

"Panama?" Jack repeated with uncertainty.

"Yes. My friend, Hank McDermott. He has an air charter service down there. And he's in need of another pilot." Sully looked for a reaction from Jack. "Remember? I told you about him just yesterday afternoon." He reached for the telegram that still sat on the table. "You can hide out there and fly McDermott's deliveries, while I get to the bottom of things here. I know the Cleave family. Lucy's a wild one but they are fair-minded people. And her father will get the truth out of her once he knows there's more to it than she's sayin' now."

"But—I've never been to Panama!"

"It doesn't matter. You've never been to a lot of places."

"And—I don't know Spanish."

Sully looked him in the eye. "You want to stay here, boy?" Jack stared wide-eyed. "Don't start getting picky with me, lad. Your situation is serious."

"How will I get there?"

"No matter how it began, it turned out it's your lucky day indeed, lad!" Sully exclaimed. "That meeting I went to yesterday afternoon, in San Antone, was a briefing, by Military Intelligence. Protection of the Canal Zone and such." Jack listened intently. "They're sending new orders and a supply of maps down to command in Colon," Sully explained. "They go down tomorrow—or I guess it's today now," he corrected himself, looking out the window at the predawn light on the horizon. "On a transport plane out of San Antone."

Jack said nothing.

"I'll make sure you're on that flight." Sully's look and tone left no room for argument.

•

Before the sun broke the sky, Jack and his uncle were driving south in Sully's Buick, headed for Randolph, the airfield in San Antonio where Jack had been in training only days ago. He felt odd as the whitewashed tower that stood over the runway came into sight. It was a haunting reminder of his still stinging rejection. Jack had hated the place when he'd been forced to leave, but today it was his ticket to freedom.

Sully parked at the tower and went inside. Jack sat in the car, slouching down as much as he could without looking suspicious. A pair of uniforms walked by and glanced at the car. Jack thought they were looking directly at him and shrunk lower in his seat. Finally, Sully came out and waved for him to come over.

"We need to hurry," he said as they walked briskly onto a huge slab of concrete. It was the tarmac where the active airplanes parked in the daytime. A trainer taxied off the runway, crossing their path as it went to its parking spot. The smell of fuel spewed into the air from its powerful engine. Sully moved with purpose toward another plane, a D-3, parked three hundred yards beyond.

"Are you sure they know I'm coming?" Jack asked loudly over the noise.

"The CO just gave me his blessing," Sully yelled back.

The trainer cut its engine. It sputtered, choked, then its prop stopped abruptly. The area was quiet. Jack couldn't help himself from repeatedly looking over his shoulder to see if the police were coming up to suddenly rush in and arrest him.

"Don't worry, Jacky. They don't know you're here," Sully said with compassion.

Jack wasn't as confident. Things were happening too quickly. "What about the CO?"

"I told him you were a replacement pilot for Hank."

"He was okay with that?"

Sully winked. "We go way back. It was enough for him."

As they approached the silver DC-3, the left engine gave a loud bang. A cloud of white smoke blasted from its exhaust and the propeller raced into motion. Engulfed in the fumes, Sully stopped on the tarmac and cocked his head toward the plane. "Better get in!" he yelled over the racket. "They're ready to go. We caught 'em just in time." He handed Jack an envelope. "Give this to Hank. He's a good man, and he owes me more favors than he can ever hope to repay." Jack gave him a weak smile. "Just do as he says and keep yer ass out of trouble. I'll see to things here."

They gave each other a big hug.

"I don't think Roosevelt had to go through all this, Sully," Jack said, forcing a smile.

"Chin up, lad. You'll get your name back," Sully said with determination.

Jack climbed aboard as the second engine fired. The crewman, wearing his baseball cap with the bill sticking straight up and chewing a wad of gum, closed the door behind him, and immediately the engines revved. It was too loud to talk, so with a big grin he just pointed at a place for Jack to sit. The tail swung around roughly, and the plane lurched forward, sending Jack leaning into some cargo nets. The crewman took it in stride. Jack worked his way into his seat as the plane wobbled onto the runway. He looked out of his small window and saw Sully waving from the tarmac as the plane rushed down, then lifted off the runway. All that had happened had not yet sunk in. His mind was racing in disbelief at his predicament. Other than his nap at Sully's yesterday, he hadn't slept in three days. His eyes were heavy and his mind numb. He closed his eyes. Maybe it was all just a dream, a nightmare.

CHAPTER EIGHTEEN

The elders rushed the boy into a chamber within the temple. Only Bodecker, Jenkins and the lifeless body of the old chief remained outside.

Stunned, Jenkins said, "What should we do?" His teeth chattered from the renewed cold.

Bodecker pulled his coat tightly about him. "Let's see what they are doing inside," he said. He motioned to a light coming from a small round window in the temple. Together the men peered through the window, only to be met by an acrid cloud of gray powder blown into their faces by one of the elders inside. Jenkins inhaled the powder even as he tried to back away. He remembered staggering around the rocky ledge and seeing Bodecker fall to the ground unconscious, before everything went black for him.

•

Through cracks in the door the afternoon sun pierced the eyelids of the exhausted anthropologist. Jenkins did not know how many hours had passed since he had collapsed. Now he lay on the cold rock floor of a small dark chamber. His body ached everywhere and he shook violently with alternating fever and chills. He tried to shield his eyes from the light, but found his hands were firmly tied behind his back. He wiggled, noticing his feet too, were bound. It was then he realized the chamber stank of urine and excrement.

Bodecker also, was tightly tied. Conscious, he stared at the wall. Jenkins was drained. He lay silent and shut his eyes against the light. The stone blocking the doorway was rolled away and a cold wind swept in. Jenkins listened with his eyes closed as Bodecker threatened his captor, demanding to be set free. He jostled and thrashed about in anger, shoving Jenkins' pain ridden body into the wall. Then Jenkins heard blowing and smelled the acrid powder again. Bodecker went still.

Now the professor listened closely to voices somewhere else. He caught only bits and pieces, but clearly it was the elders instructing the new young chief. The sessions went on for hours as they prepared him for his future. In less than two days the boy would return to his own time, alone to be chief.

Jenkins was satisfied to be out of the wind; glad their attention was elsewhere. Any spark of interest that he once might have had in gathering intellectual information had long vanished. He was broken and feverish. Even his will to survive was evaporating.

Two days passed without food or water. Jenkins tried to follow Bodecker's lead of licking moisture from the rock walls, but his condition continued to deteriorate. He slept all but a few hours of the day, and doubted his ability to make the journey home.

During the few times Bodecker was lucid, he seemed to possess limitless energy and whispered intently about plans of escape, but the Indians apparently feared his size and continued to tranquilize him with their powder. By the end of the second day their senses were completely deadened to the vile smell and condition in which they were detained. Jenkins slowly became delirious.

It was that afternoon when a bright light suddenly filled the room as the Indians rolled the heavy stone door of the cell open. Jenkins raised his head to the blinding threshold. He struggled to focus on what seemed to be several figures. In his delirious state he thought he had died. The bright light appeared to have angels within who were calling for him.

The truth was quite different. The faces of the elders were contorted as they tried to escape the stench permeating the room. Finally one reached in and violently grabbed Jenkins. The delirious man screamed in horror, frightening the Indian as badly as he himself was frightened.

These are not angels, he thought. *They're demons. I've gone to hell!*

Then, with his eyes wide open from the rush of adrenaline in his body, he recognized them. They were neither angels, nor demons; they were his captors, the Picayultas. *Hell could not be much worse than what he had experienced the last few days*, he thought.

Still bound the two white men were dragged out. Their bindings were adjusted so they could stand. Jenkins scanned the area. There was no longer any sign of the ceremony. The idol sat quietly perched back in the passageway of El Ventorrio. And as for the time traveler, he too was gone. Jenkins had said nothing to Bodecker about what he had overheard. What would have been the point? Whatever business the Indians had come for in this desolate land was clearly accomplished.

•

The white men's hands were left tied and in loose rope leg shackles they were herded into the single column formed by the Indians. Without ceremony or explanation the group began down the narrow mountain trail. The descent was equally treacherous. The whistling of the great, perforated rock again echoed its melancholic call throughout the valley. The wind was strong and steady, but the morning sun took the chill off the air. Bodecker showed no sign of fatigue, and was full of questions. "Professor, what happened after that night?"

Jenkins didn't want to talk. "I don't know. I too, was overcome by that drug."

"You've heard nothing at all about the boy from the cloud, or their meeting after his arrival?"

"Nothing," Jenkins lied.

"Where is he now?"

"Gone, I suspect. Back where he came from." Jenkins was amazed that Bodecker was still focused, considering their current predicament. "Into that same cloud of whatever it was that spewed him from the statue, in the first place."

"So the boy was the old chief? In his youth?" Bodecker paused waiting for an answer. When it didn't come he continued, "Where is the chief now?"

"Now? Now he is dead. You saw it yourself the night of the arrival. The Indians no longer have a chief. And they won't for two more months." Jenkins stopped, short of breath. "When the comet, or whatever that thing is, returns and takes Nuepotal here..." Jenkins pointed to the young Indian leading the way down, "into the future, then, and only then upon his return will they have a chief."

Jenkins's illness and exhaustion left him weak. His mind was tired and his poor concentration caused him to stumble often on the narrow trail. But Bodecker continued with his questions, wanting to know exactly what had transpired on the mountaintop.

Jenkins foot slid on loose gravel causing the nervous professor to fall and halting the line's progress. Helplessly he lay tied on the ground unable to get back on his feet. An impatient Indian ordered him to get up, then pulled him to his feet and shoved him down the trail to move on. Bodecker moved toward him threateningly and the Indian backed away to a respectful distance. Even with his hands tied, they feared the German's imposing size.

"Who will lead the tribe during these months?" Bodecker asked.

"How should I know? I can barely walk this trail."

Once off of the huge monolith, the group continued, this time in a new direction that led them out of the high valley. The hike took them several hours into the mountains to the north where finally they came to a stop. One elder, the chief's brother Taotoe, pointed to a flat rock lying on the ground and spoke sharply. They listened intently.

"What are they saying, professor?" asked Bodecker.

"They appear to be debating what to do with us." The elder glared at the white men as he spoke. "Taotoe there, wants to lower us into a place called El Cuarto de el Diablo, the Devil's Room," Jenkins whispered.

"What the hell is that?" asked the German.

Jenkins looked ashen. "It is part of a huge maze of caverns—basically a bottomless pit, a cave where the Picayultas have taken invaders and raiders of the sacred mount to be banished forever," he added, recalling tales of the late Reverend Wilson. "The entrance is under that rock."

"What is the other option?"

"Shoving us over those cliffs."

"Neither choice seems desirable. So, it is safe to say that either way they aren't considering our best interests?" Bodecker said dryly, without the slightest trace of fear.

"I'd say that was an accurate assessment." Jenkins was beyond caring.

There was much discussion between the indecisive elders. But without a chief such a decision was not easy. Uncertainty prevailed, and Taotoe was quick to attempt filling in the void, even though he would never be chief. His overbearing manner did not go over well with the others.

"If Taotoe gets his way we'll be eliminated one way or another," Jenkins added. "You may recall he was against our presence here from the start." The elders continued to argue then seemed to arrive at a consensus. "It doesn't look good, doctor," he told Bodecker as the two men watched three of the Indians push the huge slate of rock from its resting place, exposing the opening to a dark cavern.

In a few practiced motions by the Indians, Jenkins found himself bound to a rope, then felt himself dangling, slowly spiraling as the Indians lowered him into the darkness. His body settled roughly on the sharp uneven rocks of the cavern floor one hundred feet below the aperture in the ceiling. He looked up at what would surely be his last view of the outside world. His lifeline to the surface dropped down like a lifeless snake on top of him. Silently he waited in the dark surroundings for the German who he expected would follow him soon after.

Bodecker had worked his ropes loose during the march down the mountain. Biding his time, he kept his hands behind his back, still appearing to be bound. He had no intention of allowing these little men to lower him into oblivion without a fight. He was actually rather happy that they had eliminated the old professor first. It had saved him the trouble of doing it when he got back.

When Taotoe released Jenkins' rope the elders turned to Bodecker cautiously, respecting his aggressive manner and physique. Then two of them approached to fasten a rope about him. As they came within range Bodecker reached up his left sleeve with his right hand and pulled out a long thin blade. Its six-inch razor edge was so sharp that it sliced through his first victim's carotid artery before the man realized he was being assaulted. The burst of warm blood brought the man down without so much as a whimper.

Bodecker's moves were smooth and fluid. He spun around gracefully to face the other Indian, sliding the blade across his abdomen. So clean was the cut, the man felt no pain as he stood shocked for a moment, then dropped to his knees trying futilely to catch his intestines. In moments the man keeled over lifelessly, leaning on his assailant.

Glancing at the others with contempt, Bodecker reached down and cut his hemp shackled feet free. He kicked the disemboweled native away, then crouched down, preparing to do battle with the others. Blood stained his arms up to his elbows, but his face was cold and expressionless. Another elder charged with a spear, only to have it impaled into his own rib cage. In unison the rest charged. With thoughtless speed Bodecker dashed to the edge and hurled himself down the mountainside, sliding on a steep slope of loose gravel. The elders attempted to stop him, but Bodecker's youth and agility left them far behind.

Below, Jenkins waited, lying on the wet stone. He heard a slight commotion above, but could only see a small window of blue sky through the hole. His fever raged worse than ever and he fought bouts of delirium. "Where's the German?" he wondered aloud.

As he waited he kept reminding himself that he shouldn't have gone on this journey. Only months from retirement. What was he thinking? But he was already resigned to his fate. He knew he wouldn't make it back even if the elders changed their minds and pulled him out. The journey was too long and arduous, and he was too ill.

"Why haven't they lowered the German?" he muttered again, looking up towards the opening. Then a loud rumble echoed off the walls, which were hidden in the darkness. It was the large rock being moved slowly back over the entrance, blocking out the few rays of light which were able to squeeze through the small aperture. Jenkins' heart raced. *This is it. I am to die here, alone,* he thought. The last point of light vanished and the rumbling stopped.

Now he was by himself, in total darkness, and total silence. He tried to prop himself up for comfort, but was too weak, so he lay there in his misery breathing the damp stagnant air. It was cold and he felt the warmth being sucked from his body. The hours passed slowly. It was quiet. Jenkins heard only the ticking of his pocket watch. In this world of silence its sound seemed inordinately loud. It went on and on until, finally, it stopped.

A drop of water fell from the ceiling, resonating in a small pool somewhere. Jenkins was thirsty but lacked the energy to search for the water. In the silence the professor was able to hear the sound of his heart beating. As he lay there helplessly, he had only it to listen to. It seemed to beat slower and slower. In his last conscious thought he heard it beat no more.

•

Bodecker made his way down the mountain late that same day. As he approached the edge of the rain forest he paused and

CHAPTER NINETEEN

The afternoon sky was clear except for a scattering of cotton ball cumulus clouds that dotted the ground below the descending DC-3. Jack stared vacantly out the window not noticing the vast jungle stretching across the Panamanian isthmus.

It was his third day with only a few stolen hours of sleep. The tangle of events that he'd collided with kept his mind racing. But the drinking, the sex, fleeing the police, together with the rare emotion he experienced at being summarily discharged from the service, were all catching up to him fast.

He was running on empty. On top of all of that, there were the long tedious hours in the plane, flying slowly over Mexico and Central America at one hundred-fifty miles an hour. He'd grabbed a box lunch of cold fried chicken, at their first stop in Mexico City, and was glad to have gotten it. Another meal was brought to him at the second refueling stop in Costa Rica. Afraid to leave the plane to forage for himself, the pilots had offered to bring him something from town. Otherwise the pilots and young crewman had kept to themselves. All through the flight Jack kept thinking and rethinking of ways to undo the damage. Nothing made sense any longer. Sleep wouldn't come, no matter how often he tried. He was a fugitive, running from murder charges. His future was shattered. His life was in shambles.

Jack closed his eyes to rest. The plane crossed a gash of water slicing through the jungle-covered hills. It banked southward and the doors to the wheel wells opened loudly. The vibration brought him back to reality. He saw an ocean liner under the tow of the mechanical mules paralleling the banks of the famous Panama Canal. It all disappeared behind them as the plane continued downward. Approaching the ground, they skimmed a swampy wetland. It was a marsh dotted with the hulks of dead and dying trees.

The nose pitched upward. Jack could feel the plane slow as it settled on the runway with an imperceptible tug, then the engines came to life, racing in reverse, and the cargo around Jack shifted forward in its bindings as the plane came to a halt. *This is the start of my new life*, Jack thought dejectedly.

The airstrip was just ten miles southeast of Colon and bordered the Canal Zone. It had originally been a labor compound housing the Antillean blacks who made up the bulk of the work force during the construction years of the Canal. But upon the Canal's completion, the facility was abandoned and fell into disrepair. The U.S. Army took it over during the Great War and bulldozed most of the barracks to make way for the runway. It became a base to protect the ships as they made their vulnerable transcontinental crossing. But the Panamanians didn't like having the Americans on their soil, so after a decade the Americans closed this airfield and removed their troops. There were other airfields now within the Zone, better ones, and there was no need to reopen this dinosaur.

Weeds sprouted through the joints in the concrete tarmac and potholes were scattered at random. The impoverished locals had scavenged the wood from the remaining bunkhouses. Rotting piers and a few collapsing walls were all that was left of the original place. In 1933 Hank McDermott leased the last remaining building to operate his shoestring air taxi service into the wilderness. It was a single hangar with the officers' barracks attached. With peeling paint and rot-hollowed walls, it was in need of repair, but got none.

The plane taxied to the hangar and stopped close to a derelict tanker truck. Its tires were flat and deformed, and looked like it hadn't been driven for a decade. The place looked deserted. The DC-3's engines coughed, and the props wound down to a stop.

"This is it," the copilot announced, stepping from the curtain dividing the cockpit. He walked past Jack to the rear of the plane and lowered the door. Jack stooped through the opening. The sun was hot and bright, and the air was thick, humid soup. Jack was already sweating. *This has to be the end of the earth*, he thought, stepping on the tarmac. No one would find him here. Who would even think to look? Only a few days ago Jack had expected to be preparing to go to Europe with winter coming on. It was already cold there. He never expected to be hiding in a hellhole like this.

The copilot pointed to the building attached to the dilapidated hangar. "That's the office over there," he said. "You'll find McDermott inside."

"Thanks," Jack said and headed for the door while the pilots and crewman unloaded their cases. He opened the screen door to the office. It almost fell off of its hinges.

"Careful with the door," grunted an elderly man reading at a desk. His hair was white and tired bags underscored his eyes. Stuck in the corner of his mouth was a foul, unlit cigar. The office was stark, with only a desk, chair and single file cabinet for furniture. A bare light bulb hung on a wire from the ceiling. Without looking up from his magazine, the man said, "What do you want?"

"I'm Jack. Uh, Jack Sullivan?"

The man looked up through his glasses with suspicion. "Yeah... So what?" Jack wasn't sure how to respond. The man put the magazine down and took a moment to assess Jack, then said, "Look, if you expect us to fly you somewhere, you're out of luck. I can't take nobody nowhere." He looked disgusted. "I've got a plane and pilot missing for weeks, and the only other plane I have is a piece of shit." He waited for a reaction, but Jack said nothing. "Until I find them, and get my one operating plane back, no one goes anywhere." His tone was curt. "If you were smart, you'd get your ass back on that plane, and get the hell outta here when it leaves."

"Actually, I was looking for Hank McDermott."

"Oh yeah? What do you want with Hank McDermott?"

"I was sent here to find him."

"By who? And where are your papers?"

That did it. "Papers? What kind of papers?" Jack asked as innocently as he could manage.

"You don't travel from country to country without a passport, boy!"

Jack didn't know what to say. Everything had happened so fast and Sully had said nothing about papers.

"Well?"

"I don't have any."

"You don't have any?"

"No."

"You can't just show up here without papers. You best get back on that plane and go home, if you know what's good for you."

"I came here on Sully's recommendation. Do you know where I can find Mr. McDermott? I need to talk to him."

"Sully? Sully Sullivan?" The man's tone changed at once.

"Yes, Sir," Jack said with the beginnings of relief. Jack handed the man the letter Sully had given him. He tore it open, then took what seemed an inordinately long period of time to read it, Jack thought.

"So you're Sully's nephew, huh? Well, you shoulda said so in the first place, boy!" The man smiled. "*I'm* Hank McDermott. How's the old bastard doing?"

"Fine."

"Sorry to give you the runaround. In these parts you can't be too sure why someone is looking for you." He read further. "Sully says you're a pilot, looking for work?"

"Yes, Sir," Jack answered.

"That's good. Sit. Sit," Hank said, pointing to the chair. "Got yourself in a scrape too, huh?"

Jack shrugged his shoulders. "It was a misunderstanding about a lady. Well, she wasn't really a..."

"A woman, huh? You've got more than a little of your uncle in you." Hank grinned. Jack was about to start at the beginning with an explanation, but Hank raised his hand. "Don't want to know. Less said the better. Just keep your nose clean down here. Any friend—er—nephew of Sully's can't be too bad. Besides, I could use the help. Ever land on the water?"

"Uh, no. Crop dusting mostly."

"Well, that's okay. I can teach you soon as we get my plane fixed. As I said, I lost my one pilot and my only working plane last month."

"Sorry. What happened?"

"Dunno. Ray just did not come back." Hank paused, then added, "He had more hours logged than any pilot I've ever had. He was good. He knew these jungles like the back of his hand. Poor guy," Hank reminisced. "Couldn't get a job anywhere after he lost his eye. I was the only outfit that would hire him—never told him it was because I couldn't get anyone to stay longer than three weeks." Jack could see why. "Hell, once this damn war broke out, I was glad he was missing the eye, otherwise he would have left like the others, to fly in the war."

Jack didn't want to be reminded. "Has anyone gone looking for him?"

"I'm it here! And I'm too damn old to fly. I can't even get that old bird in the hangar to turn over. All I could do is alert the Colombian authorities, for whatever that's worth."

Jack nodded. Sully had said Hank was a pilot and had spent half his life in Panama. He was a tough, self-reliant pioneer, one of the few original surveyors during the American effort to build the canal and an authority on the territories from Mexico to deep down into the Amazon basin. But Jack could also see he was feeling his years.

"You any good with a wrench?" Hank asked with a spark of excitement.

"I know a little," Jack said modestly. "I did all the maintenance on Sully's plane. But what about those papers you said I needed? Someone's bound to ask."

"Aw, hell, don't worry about it. We'll write up something official looking, and you can say it's a special permit. Most of these idiots can't even read. There's plenty of Americans running around out of the Zone and they don't carry their passports on 'em. Keep your cool and you'll be fine. If you have any bad luck just use my name. C'mon, I'll show you the plane." Hank walked Jack out to the hangar.

The pilots had just fired up the DC-3 for the return trip to Texas. They waved as they pulled away from the building. Hank waved back then turned to the hanger. Beneath a cover was the only plane remaining at the airport. The wings and tail stuck out of the sheets, and there were engine parts strewn all over the concrete floor.

"These all part of her?" Jack asked, pointing at the mess.

"Yeah, from the engine. She's easier to take apart than to put back together."

"Can she fly once she's all in one piece?" Jacked asked with concern.

Hank just smiled and pulled off the cover.

"A Stinson SM-1." Jack said.

Hank was impressed. "You know your airplanes." He shifted his unlit cigar to the other side of his mouth. "She's all I got left. A bit old and raggedy, but with a little tuning and some patching she'll roar like a lioness. And for just $350 she's yours out the door," he joked, using the pitch of a car salesman.

The plane was constructed of canvas and lacked support wires. Instead, it had struts sustaining the single high wing, and retrofitted floats replaced the wheels. Jack knew she was a good airplane. He'd read somewhere the SM-1 had set a lot of records, but that had been a long time ago. This wreck sat unnaturally lopsided on the concrete with its canvas torn, and mildew growing on its under surfaces. It was going to take a lot of work to make her airworthy.

"Ray jerry-rigged two extra tanks on the wing to increase the range," Hank explained. "That and the floats make it easier to get into the boonies. We use the water over there to take off. You know there are no airstrips out there. But water—you can find that almost anywhere. You just gotta watch the tree trunks." Hank smiled, but clearly wasn't kidding.

"What did all those add-ons do to the center of gravity?" Jack asked.

"Well, she's a little squirrely at slow speeds, but you get used to it."

"When was the last time you cranked her over?" Jack asked, pulling debris from an air vent.

Hank pondered. "Maybe six months?" he answered, uncertainly. "What month is this?"

"November."

"November! Jeeez, then it's been a good year at least."

Jack took a look inside. It was all but gutted. The sparse panel included a fuel gauge hanging out of place by the wires and a tachometer with a broken glass face. Behind the controls were three uncomfortable seats fastened to the rusty frame. There was room for luggage, but the large hole through the canvas in this compartment made its arrival with its owners questionable at best.

"Can you fix her?" Hank asked.

Jack was accustomed to old planes, and jerry rigging them was an art he had mastered. He nodded. "If everything's here, but it'll take a while."

Over a supper of chicken mixed with local spices Hank told Jack what he knew—or didn't know—of Ray Dobbs' last flight. While they ate, they poured over maps and speculated what might have happened and where Ray might be. Jack could tell

Hank liked Ray and was more concerned about him than the plane. "Tomorrow we'll start getting the old bird ready for action," Hank said, rejuvenated by Jack's arrival and the possible resumption of his operation. "Then we'll go find my pilot."

•

Late November, 1943

The last of two days of thunderstorms had just moved off of the eastern coast of Britain and with it had gone the lightning, which had interfered greatly with HYAC's ability to intercept enemy radio transmissions. HYAC was a special wireless unit that monitored the airwaves from the north side of Holland through Belgium and as far south as Brittany.

The station's twelve radio surveillance operators on duty were all women. They had grown bored with no one to listen in on, and some had wanted to go into the nearby village of Walmer on the coast, but the weather had been forbidding. So mostly, they just read and slept in their quarters, waiting for Colonel Meilandt, the station's commanding officer, to call them back once the atmospheric conditions had improved. At 10:00 p.m. Alice Quiney was two hours into her shift, part of a skeleton crew of two listening for the resumption of reception. It was tedious duty, waiting for voices to return to the airwaves. Like the day before, she had heard nothing more than the steady white noise of static, occasionally interrupted by the popping and crackling interference of the receding storm.

She thought longingly about her family in Suffolk. Tomorrow they would be celebrating the American holiday of Thanksgiving. They always did, ever since visiting their cousins in Virginia. Alice wished she could be there. With rationing as it was, it would not be the feast that they had enjoyed in the years before the war, but they would all be together, finding whatever good cheer they could, if only for the day.

She felt alone in the quiet room. She looked at her partner, Saundra, who had dozed off from the monotony. Alice couldn't blame her she was bored too.

Then a voice broke through the static, snapping Alice from her daydream. The transmission was garbled at first, and then, just when Alice could almost make out the words, a high-pitched chirp stepped on it. She had missed what was said, but it was definitely German.

She turned the dial to squelch the chirping squeal, and leaned forward to listen more closely. As the chirp receded the voice was still there to be heard. Alice made out the words: "Standartenfuhrer Heinz Bodecker…" and then the voice faded, sounding more and more distant until it too disappeared into the background of sounds.

She waited a moment for its return, but there was only static.

Another minute passed, and the static subsided. Again, it was there: "Have just returned from Colombia. Our discovery could definitely change the outcome of the war and history itself."

The statement sobered Alice completely. She wondered what she was on to. She picked up her pencil, preparing to scribble some more, but again the voice was gone. She was not sure if it was the storm blocking the reception, or the person at the other end had finished.

"Saundra, wake up." She nudged her dozing partner. "We're back on."

"Whaaaat?" Saundra returned.

Then once more, it was back. "We're picking up the Krauts. Listen."

"Am certain the Picayulta Indian legend is based on fact. The statue of 'El Chiflon' is unguarded in an Andean mountain temple. Suggest retrieving it for the Fatherland. Over." This time the voice was crisp and clear. Again there was silence. The response must have been coming from farther inland, in the direction of Germany, and its transmission did not have the power to get all the way to Britain.

"I'll get the Colonel," Saundra said, perking up instantly.

She got up and left just as it started again.

"Herr Himmler was right about the comet. Relay the message. I will stand by in France awaiting his orders. Over and Out." Then the signal went dead.

Alice grabbed a pencil and started scribbling quickly. She copied everything exactly as she had heard it. That was her job. It would be up to others to decide how important it would be.

In moments Colonel Meilandt barged in. "Things finally clearing up, ehh? What have you got, Quiney?"

She handed him her notes. The Colonel studied them a minute. "Is there more?"

"No, sir. Reception just came back on. I think it's only the tail end of the transmission, but it sounded important."

The Colonel ran his hand over his unshaved face. "Picayulta... El Chiflon...Andean mountain temple?" he mumbled slowly. "Certainly a strange communiqué."

"What do you think the man meant by 'Himmler being right about the comet,' sir?" Alice asked.

"Don't know. It is highly irregular; however, it might be a set of code names for something," he mused.

The Colonel put on a headset, and they both listened to see if any more was to follow, but after five minutes of silence it seemed to be over. "Hmmm...they seemed to be finished," Meilandt said.

He re-examined Alice's notes. "You haven't forgotten anything, have you?"

"No sir, this was everything I heard."

"Because this will go directly to MI 5. Any message with Himmler's name needs to be examined by the higher ups."

"Yes, sir."

Meilandt picked up Alice's notes and turned for his desk, then stopped. "Have we copied anything from this Bodecker fellow before?"

Alice shrugged her shoulders. "No, sir, not that I know of."

"Well then, good job." He continued, "Carry on. I'll get this off."

Alice saw that Saundra had returned with several other sur-veillance operators. Their spirits seem lifted as they donned their headsets. She too felt better. It was good to get back to work.

CHAPTER TWENTY

The elevator jolted to a noisy halt, announcing its arrival on the third floor of the Military Intelligence building's Office of Strategic Services wing. The accordion cage door rattled open noisily, followed by the main door.

It was 7:30 in the morning. Kelly Wilson stepped out into the long empty hallway carrying a box of personal belongings. MI's building had the sterile look common to all military structures. The Army had annexed the old complex to accommodate its quickly expanding war operations. Rampant inefficiencies and confusion had plagued the many departments scattered throughout Washington's Metropolitan area. The Pentagon had been completed just months earlier but many sections were not yet ready for occupation. It was the largest building in the world and the Joint Chiefs hoped consolidating military operations there would turn it into a finely tuned machine. Until MI's turn came, however, this place would have to do.

The doors closed loudly behind Kelly and the elevator's whirring motor faded downward. In the remaining silence, she heard the hushed mumbling of a conversation coming from an open door. It was the only sign of life on the Special Agent's floor, as it was called.

Dressed simply, but impeccably, she started down the empty corridor, searching for her new office. Her long legs moved her slender body smoothly down the hallway, and the echo of her high heels resonated ahead of her loudly. A door closed somewhere and the murmuring voices disappeared.

Kelly was a tall brunette in her early twenties with straight hair that bounced on her shoulders as she walked, and a face pretty enough to turn heads. Her high cheekbones and small nose were fine, and gave her an air of sophistication, but the faint dotting of freckles added a touch of warmth and friendliness.

She tended to be full of life, and it was contagious every place she went. She exuded a combination of innocence and happiness.

What her appearance and manner concealed was that she was a tomboy at heart. The high heels were new and killing her feet, and reporting daily to a boss in an office building was a confining exercise she had never before had to do. Her self-confidence shone brightest in the field where she worked for the government as a liaison, or interpreter, to tribes in North Africa, and in the jungles of South America where she had worked with her father. That is where she had spent most of her life as a young girl and that is where she was most comfortable.

At two, Kelly lost her mother, and her father, Reverend Wilson, devoted to his work, had them living the world over. Raised in remote areas, travel and change were Kelly's element, and any manners expected of a young urban woman she attained only with great difficulty. When faced with the subtle politics of a social event her self-assurance quickly disappeared. Not that she was awkward, but certainly she was more reserved.

Kelly had moved so often as a child that she had few long time friends, and the acquaintances she had accumulated as an adult tended to be superficial. With her pleasant looks, many men had been attracted to her, but she always left them at a distance, partly from the insecurity that lack of experience in such situations brings, and partly from disinterest. It was easier to focus on her work, and it was certainly more predictable. She did not mind. She liked her work.

Ahh, Room 312. My very own office, she thought.

The door to the windowless cubicle was open. She stepped in. The room was drab and musty with faded paint, and its splintered wooden floor was heavily scuffed. There was a standard Government Issue gray metal desk centered in the poorly illuminated room, and a bare wooden swivel chair on rusted casters to match.

Kelly didn't care. In fact she was elated. Only yesterday she had been given the unexpected news of her promotion from a civilian clerk to that of Special Agent. To become an agent had been her ultimate goal since she had been recruited eighteen months ago. This sudden leap up the ladder at the OSS had her puzzled, and she was preparing for a backlash of resentment from the other agents. It had taken most of them at least five years, but more commonly seven to eight years, to work their way up to agent status. But she couldn't be alone, she believed. The war had advanced many careers at a much faster pace.

On top of everything, she had been summoned to meet with the General in command, a man she knew better as Uncle Smitty throughout her childhood. The fact that the General was her uncle would make the fast move up the ladder even more suspicious to other agents. In truth the promotion had surprised her more than anyone. She had known nothing about it, and up to this point no one had told her anything, including how to get to

General Smitson's office, where she had been told to report first thing in the morning.

Kelly plopped her box on the desk, sat in the old chair and looked around at her modest surroundings. A grin spread across her pretty face and she spun around as hard as she could.

•

Like a statue, General Alex Smitson stood at the window of his office gazing out across the lawn. His eyes were fixed on a gardener meticulously tending roses. The rotund General possessed a stern, imposing personality. A man who saw action in the Great War during his youth, he was now content to do his part from behind a desk. He was well read and believed there were powers greater than men that actively molded and influenced the course of history. It was these beliefs that would not let him dismiss the latest and most bizarre intelligence report from Germany. In fact, contrary to most in his command, he was actually intrigued by the information, and the fact that it had been intercepted from within the highest circle in Nazi controlled Berlin made it even more alluring.

He stood pensively, disregarding the entourage of officers and agents to whom he had his back turned. He was waiting for the group to be complete. The large office was silent; the tension within was high. The General didn't mind, in fact he enjoyed it. The others sat silently, some waiting to discover the details of the unexpected mission, which had brought them together on this early December morning. Some already knew.

•

As Kelly finished arranging her drawers for the third time, she glanced at her watch and realized she was late. *The newest member to the department and already late to my first meeting,* she thought.

She grabbed her satchel and the map of the building and dashed out the door down the hall.

In his office the General slowly raised his arm to examine the watch on his wrist. The action was an expression of unspoken discontent. By unconscious habit he took a half step back and performed a relaxed about face. His eyes traveled silently across the group, heightening everyone's anxiety.

Anxiously Kelly hastened her pace down the hall. She caught disapproving glances as she hurried past staff members in the corridor. Finally, she saw the room numbers were favorably approaching the one she was searching for. The General's door at the end of the hall stood out, with flags on both side and a star on its face. In haste she shoved the door open. It swung wildly. The knob slipped out of her hand. She almost fell over trying to catch it before it slammed, but it was too late. The crash against the wall captured the immediate attention of all eyes in the room. Quickly up righting herself, she tried to gain her composure. She scanned the room full of solemn people in uniform. No one moved. *I'm two minutes late, yet they act as if I had stood them up for hours*, she thought. Chills ran down her spine as eyes followed her every movement. The door closed behind her.

The General, again gazing out the window, did not turn to greet her. But a colonel glanced at his watch, then looked at her to register his discontent.

"Sorry. I know I'm late," she said quietly. The apology was directed to the group.

The General turned, then extended his hand toward the only remaining chair in the room. It was beside another agent, a civilian named Donald Thornton. He was an eight-year veteran of the War Department whom Kelly had met at a department function. The only things she remembered about him were that he was the son of a senator, that he had made a crude pass at her, and that he was terminally arrogant. As an underling clerk she had just let the incident slide.

Thornton looked at Kelly as she sat next to him. He appeared particularly aggravated by the wait she had caused. Insecure and almost thirty, he came from an old money family, which partly explained his terminal hubris. His abilities as an agent were at best average, but he was predictably pompous and quick to demean his fellow agents. It was at his mother's request that his father had pulled strings to keep their little Thornton safely away from the dangers in Europe and the Pacific.

The General scanned the group thoughtfully, his eyes stopping last on Kelly and Thornton. "The two of you have been chosen for a low profile operation in South America," he said without preamble. "Sources have intercepted accounts of active German interest in a remote South American Indian tribe, specifically in a golden statue, an idol as it were, which they would like to possess. The Colombian government has German sympathies and is cooperating with them. We do not know very much about the tribe, but our source indicates that if these reports regarding this idol are true, Himmler's belief that it could vastly affect the outcome of the war may be true."

Thornton shifted in his chair and rolled his eyes, visibly annoyed. Kelly listened with keen interest.

The General continued, "Rumor is that this statue can provide a 'window' to the future." He waited for a reaction, but got none so he continued, focusing on Kelly and Thornton. "I want you two to go there and find these Indians. Validate if in fact this statue does exist, and explore any value it might have to our government. If, by chance, you find out someone else has been down there poking around, find out who and why. Last, get home safely." This last part he directed at Kelly.

Thornton fidgeted but refused to make eye contact with the General. Smitson knew he wouldn't like the assignment, but didn't care. "You each have been chosen because of your unique qualifications for the job," he added with a disrespectful look at Thornton whom he saw as a draft-dodging coward. In fact, in the General's mind, Thornton added little if any value to the mission, at best he would give the general's niece a cover. Beyond that, his only qualification was his father, the senator who was comfortable abusing his influence to pressure the General into sending his worthless son on worthless, and safe, missions.

Kelly, on the other hand, possessed real skills. She was not only the best qualified, but possibly the only person qualified for the mission. She had lived with these Indians for many months, while helping her father, Reverend Wilson, the missionary who rediscovered the tribe. She was the only living person known to speak the language and understand their culture.

The General opened a folder and continued, "We intercepted the report of an incident that occurred 31 October. A German officer claimed to have witnessed a supernatural occurrence in the Colombian Andes, an event of cosmic proportions of which we have no precedent, though the tribe claims it occurs every sixty-one years." The General's eyebrows rose, as he expected to see disbelieving faces. Thornton did not disappoint him.

With exasperation, he deflated his lungs loudly. "I suppose he saw Halloween ghosts and witches on broomsticks," Thornton snickered.

The General ignored the comment. "That officer was SS-Standartenfuhrer Heinz Bodecker, a notorious German operative. Bodecker is only assigned Himmler's highest priority missions. He claimed to have seen first hand a time traveler arrive from the past, a boy who for the last sixty-one years has reigned as the chief of the tribe."

Several listeners shifted uncomfortably in their chairs. "How did the Germans know about this—event?" one asked.

"We don't know. But they knew exactly where to go to anticipate it. And they knew the approximate day as well."

"How do we know that it actually took place?" Thornton snidely challenged.

"We don't. But on the night of the 31st our newest observatory in New Mexico did report an extraordinary occurrence, an astronomical phenomenon. A comet skimmed our atmosphere somewhere in the northeast of the South American continent. Thousands reported seeing it as well. It apparently deflected off the atmosphere and returned to space, continuing on its orbit around the sun." The group listened intently. "It is now racing around the sun and like a slingshot will be thrown back into deep space. Its elliptical orbit again has given it a path that will cause it to intercept the earth in exactly sixteen days. Our best scientists have concluded its trajectory could give it the same general coordinates of the first contact point in the Andes." The General paused. Thornton shifted. "In just over two weeks the second half of the sixty-one year event is to take place. During this period it is believed by the Indians that a person from our time will be permitted a glimpse of the future," he paused and then continued, "by traveling through time."

"Traveling through time!" Thornton burst out. "What the hell do you…?"

"Be quiet, Donald!" The General ordered. "I don't ask you to believe it, or like it. I'm just ordering you to investigate it." The room was silent. "If by chance such a phenomenon is possible, the time traveler could study the history of the war and return with vital information to change the outcome, and history itself. And that is exactly what the Nazis are hoping for. They know how the war has turned against them this year." The General paused, looking at the faces in the room. "I know what you people are thinking, but our source is extremely reliable. We do not know if there is any correlation between the comet and the incident which Standartenfuhrer Bodecker witnessed, but it's our best guess."

"General, are you really buying into this tale?" Thornton interrupted again. "It sounds like a hoax concocted by the Germans to mislead us, to get us to squander valuable resources."

"Perhaps, but we have reasons to think otherwise," the General answered. "First, our source is excellent, so we investigate. Second, Bodecker is a committed Nazi and one of their best operatives. Himmler would not waste him on a secondary mission. If Bodecker was sent, it's top priority and we can assume they believe there is something to be gained by it. Third, we have verified that the Germans have dispatched a unit of soldiers, right now as we speak, to the same village, presumably to coincide with the second coming of the comet. Their mission, we assume, is to steal the idol and return it to the 'Fatherland.'" Smitson spoke firmly with an attitude of "Don't question me again."

"They want to be the travelers to the future on the comet's return trip, to know the war's outcome and alter it in their favor. If there was any truth to it, no matter how unlikely, and we chose to ignore it, it would have devastating results for the allied forces. No matter how outlandish it sounds, if the Nazis think there is merit then we must, at the least, investigate what is taking place."

Thornton opened his mouth to speak, but the General raised his hand. "There are reports, many of you have seen them, that the Germans are developing rockets to drop explosives on targets thousands of miles away, that they have jet power fighters in the works, even a submarine that doesn't have to surface. We can't assume anything we hear coming from those people is impossible. So understand…We will investigate this; the decision is not open for discussion, no matter how farfetched it sounds. That's final."

"But…"

"No 'buts,' Donald. That's the way it's going to be." He addressed Kelly and Donald. "Now since this mission is on its face unlikely to be productive, it is low priority. We are going to have fewer resources than usual to work with. The military will only get you as far as our airfield in Panama. You'll stop first in San Antonio, Texas, to meet an old colleague, Jack Sullivan. He knows the area better than anyone does. He personally has made arrangements to get you transportation into the backcountry. It is the only outfit that can get you from Colon to the remote Picayulta village in Eastern Columbia." The General looked around. "Any questions?" No one asked anything. "That is all, then."

As the officers filed out, the General said to Kelly and Thornton, "You two stay." He closed the door behind the last officer leaving.

Thornton was fuming. "Why am I working with a woman?" he demanded.

"Because she has spent eight months in the area working with her late father. She has lived with these Indians; she knows the area." The General's tone was impatient. He found working with civilians always difficult. "Not to mention she understands and speaks the language. You don't."

Kelly said nothing. Instead she tried to hide her smile. General Smitson smiled at his niece to reassure her that she had his full support.

Thornton glared at her and said, "Well, I hope you can carry your own gear. I have no interest in dragging you all over the jungle on my back."

"Young man, try to make the best of this. You will get Kelly's full cooperation, I'm sure," the General said, trying to get the two started on a better foot. "And you'll need to get along. You'll be going down as a husband and wife botany team."

Thornton suddenly had a smug look come over his face. Kelly gasped. She did not like even the pretense of being married to such a moron. "But..."

"It is just to give you a non-military reason to be poking around down there. And the marriage is part of the cover. I expect nothing but good behavior out of you, Donald," the General threatened.

Thornton grinned at Kelly. "As a good wife, you better do as your husband says."

"Donald, sometimes I wish I didn't know your parents so well, so I could give you the ass kicking they never did," the General said as he handed them each a map. "You'll need this. As I said earlier, verify the statue's existence and the legend. If there's any truth at all to this, radio back so we can intercept the Germans and stop them from stealing it. I want no heroics out of you, and no confrontations between you and any soldiers. Of course, if possible, bring the little statue back to us." He looked at both Kelly and Thornton. "A complete description of the operation is waiting in your offices. Read, and know it, before leaving. Any questions?" They both shook their heads. "That's all, then."

As they were leaving the General added, "Oh, Donald, one other thing; take good care of my niece. Because if anything happens to her you'll answer to me, and I can absolutely assure you of transfer to a frontline combat unit." The smile on his face became a deadly serious look.

Thornton shook his head as he left the room like a spoiled child going to pout.

CHAPTER TWENTY-ONE

The mid-morning sun pushed the temperature to over ninety degrees. It was a suffocating heat, shiftless soup laden with vapor, which rose from the surrounding swamps and jungle foliage. In the shade of the hangar, removed from any breeze, Jack sweltered. His sweat tasted salty as it rolled off his nose. He looked around the place. Fernando, Hank's handy man, and his son had already disappeared for the next few hours.

"Lazy bums," he said to himself. "That's it." He was always the last to quit. Well, the plane was finally in good shape. He'd taken it up several times with Hank and was satisfied it would get him in and out of any place with enough water. He tossed his tools in the box, and grabbed his shirt, which hung on the wing. Crossing the cement floor, he called over to a mutt that had befriended him. "Come on, Stupid."

The dog lazed on the cement. Stupid got his name from being repeatedly bitten by the local vermin, never fatally to date; yet never seeming to learn to avoid them. He was lovable, but not all that smart. The dog didn't move, not even his head, but his eyes followed Jack's every move with a look that suggested that it was too hot for activity. Jack stopped short of the door and surveyed the lifeless airfield. The heat had sucked the energy out of the locals who had fallen into their daily siesta paralysis. *What a hellhole,* he thought.

He walked out over the threshold and into the sunlight, which glistened on his shirtless upper body. His lean frame had acquired a deep bronze tan during his six weeks as a refugee. His hair too was now longer than the military cut he'd had, wavy and bleached to a golden brown by the tropical sun. He walked to a group of palms by the runway where he usually slept the hot midday sun away. At least here there was a breeze. The dog plodded slowly behind him.

Jack stretched out on a blanket he kept in the shade and for the thousandth time considered his predicament. In the weeks that had passed he had received two updates from his uncle. The news had not been good. The warrants for his arrest were still out. The active manhunt had lasted two weeks. Now there was a $10,000 reward for his capture, the money put up by a police benevolent society. Lucy was sticking with her story and Sully had found out why. There was a pension she was guaranteed for the rest of her life—if her husband died in the line of duty.

Typical Lucy, Jack thought. She'd just dropped him onto her trail of wreckage. He wondered if she would ever come clean. He doubted it. It wasn't that she was malicious especially, but a life-long pension would be too alluring to let something like the truth get in the way.

But in his time here he'd come to blame himself more than Lucy. He'd had no business going off with her after the way she'd dumped him. Sure, he hadn't known she was married, but what of it? He'd known she was a lying little tramp who liked to play games and he should have known better.

Jack was homesick. It was the eighth of December, his twenty-fifth birthday, and he was all alone. He stared across the field where the airstrip lay smothered in the tall grass. Heat waves radiated over the concrete. It had a way of mesmerizing people. He daydreamed about being back home in New Braunfels, then fell fast asleep.

•

The engine drone of a landing airplane pulled Jack from his afternoon siesta. Its tires screeched as it touched the runway. The arrival was unexpected, but most of them were since there was no scheduled service to Colon.

The plane taxied loudly past Jack on its way to the fuel truck. He did not get up, but watched from the base of the palm tree he'd picked. He always waited in the background to see who disembarked and why. Would they be bringing the good news of his exoneration, or would they be the authorities coming to take him away in handcuffs? The tail of the DC-3 swung around, blocking Jack's view of the door. The engines slowed, then died. For a moment there was only silence. He heard the door creak open, but from his vantage point he could not make out who the newcomers were. Then Hank came out on to the sun-scorched tarmac to greet them.

That caught Jack's attention. Hank never got out of his chair to meet a plane. The highlight of his day was to watch passengers through his window, as they bumbled around trying to guess which of the doors in the old building they should try.

Jack propped himself up for a better look, not wanting to be conspicuous. Did they have uniforms? Police uniforms in particular were his fear. The thought made his heart beat faster. There was a man and a woman. He could see them talking to Hank as they shook hands, but Jack couldn't make out the words.

Immediately they headed for the shelter of his office where a fan and the shade gave only slight relief.

Jack's curiosity lured him over. He moved closer and closer in an effort to eavesdrop, until finally he found himself just outside the door. Beneath the door Hank saw the shadow of someone outside. "Come on in, Jack. There's some people here you should meet," Hank called through the closed door. Slightly embarrassed Jack entered. "Mr. and Mrs. Thornton, this is Jack," Hank said, removing his cigar and holding it between his fingers.

Jack wiped his hand on his pants and extended it to Thornton, who was the closest to him. Thornton, in his Ivy League blazer with pocket insignia, looked at Jack's hand, then continued his evaluation from head to toe. Jack was shirtless, dirty, and sweaty. Thornton's condescending glare stopped at Jack's eyes without acknowledging the hand Jack had extended for him to shake. "A pleasure, I'm sure," he said, with an imperceptible, but pretentious nod.

Jack lowered his hand, then looked over at Kelly. Staying at arm's length to retrieve some of his dignity, he just nodded. She looked tired. Even after the long journey, with crumpled clothes and disheveled hair, she had a natural grace and good looks that caught his eye. For a moment Jack couldn't look away. The moment became uncomfortably long before he realized it. Hank cleared his throat. It snapped Jack out of his daze and he gave Kelly an embarrassed smile. She returned the nod with cool reservation.

"Well," Hank said, in an effort to break a now awkward silence, "Jack will be the pilot for your trip."

"Hmmm," Thornton pondered, then evaluated him again as if judging a workhorse he was thinking about buying. "Has he ever flown an airplane?" his tone was sarcastic.

Jack returned Thornton's stare. "I have only crashed twice—this week."

"Ahhh, so he speaks English, and an American at that. What a relief. I thought we might have to communicate with primitive sign language," he said. Kelly rolled her eyes as the two men exchanged glares.

"Jack is a fine pilot, Mr. Thornton." Hank cut in defensively. "He's been flying for almost ten years back in Texas."

"He has, has he?" Thornton continued, "Then why is he here? Shouldn't he be fighting for his country like all the other healthy young men his age?"

"Excuse me," Jack said in a sharp voice. "I don't see you in uniform. I assume you've got a reason. So have I, and it's none of your business. Consider yourself lucky there's a qualified pilot here."

"Oh, I do my part, grease boy, just in a more civilized capacity, and at a more useful level, one which best employs the abilities that an educated man of my stature has to offer. Although it does have its downside," he paused, smiling pretentiously, "I am required to deal with every sort—even drudges. Most unpleasant at times. Hmmm. What do you think, Kelly? Is he scared to fight?" Thornton mused, his eyes glaring at Jack, "or is he some type of fugitive, running from the law?"

Jack glanced sharply at Hank, who indicated with his eyes that he had said nothing regarding Jack's predicament. But Jack clamed up hearing those words.

"It's none of our business. Like the man says, he has his reasons," Hank interjected.

"So, you mean to tell me that he…" Thornton said pompously, looking at Hank and pointing at Jack, "is *it*? Our only choice for a pilot." Thornton looked upset.

"He's your man."

"That's great! Just great!" Thornton said, raising his hands over his head. "I must risk my life in an airplane trusting the likes of a kid who probably struggled through the second grade."

Jack noticed Thornton didn't include his wife in his concern, then wondered why a girl as pretty as Kelly would marry a jerk like him.

"I said you'd be fine. You can take Jack, or try hiking your way into Colombia. There isn't any other choice," Hank said, tiring of Thornton's rude behavior. "Jack, the Thorntons want to be ferried south, across the Cordillera ranges in Colombia to a remote river valley up the Ortenguaza River." Then he turned back to his prospective clients, and said, "I'm sure you're tired. Jack will show you to your quarters. Tomorrow you'll want to leave bright and early to make the mountain crossing before the afternoon storms. It'll be more pleasant that way." He lifted his arm to the door and Jack grabbed their two bags. "And Jack, when you're done showing them their quarters, come on back. I'd like to go over some charts with you."

"Yes, Sir," Jack said dejectedly.

He led their guests around the hangar to a side building. The door swung open revealing sparsely furnished quarters. To the left was a table against the wall with a single straight back chair. To the right, a ragged partition separated two beds for privacy. And close to the ceiling a small window provided minimal ventilation. A ubiquitous mildew grew in patches on the ceiling and walls.

"The outhouse is around back and running water is under the holding tank," Jack told Thornton smugly.

As Thornton entered the room one of the enormous local cockroaches scurried across the floor. "Disgusting things," he said, stepping back. "God, what kind of shit hole is this?"

Well, Jack thought, *at least we agree on something.*

Kelly stepped forward and nonchalantly crushed the insect on the floor, then placed her handbag on a bunk and walked out. Jack set their other luggage on the floor, enjoying Thornton's reaction. "It's not much, but it's home. I think you'll like it here."

"Not for long," Thornton assured him.

"We leave at daybreak. I'll wake you a half hour before departure."

Thornton waved him off without turning around.

Jack stepped out and walked down the path back to the office. He saw Kelly alone admiring a flower. "So, you guys are going to Colombia?" he said, feeling stupid even talking to her.

"Yes. I think Mr. McDermott was pretty clear about that."

"What I mean to say is, what takes you down there? It's pretty remote country, from what I hear." He knew he was being a bore but couldn't help himself. She was the first American girl he had talked to since leaving the States.

"You, I hope, Mr. Sullivan. And as for my business down there, I don't think you would have the interest nor the need to know what it is that I am going for."

Her own abruptness took Kelly by surprise. It had been a long flight, and the more time she spent with Thornton, the more irritated she found herself becoming. She was coming to understand why unhappily married couples acted the way they did.

Jack raised both hands in surrender. "Just trying to be friendly, lady."

Kelly wondered why she was taking her frustration out on this hapless man instead of on the true object of her anger. She didn't like Thornton, and she liked pretending to be his wife even less. She was just tired. She decided to put it plainly. "Listen, I have camped in the jungles of Africa and South America for months at a time, Mr. Sullivan. I assure you there is little you can do for me that I cannot do for myself. So do whatever you want, but I'm tired, and I really would just like to be left alone."

She was a married woman and Jack had no expectations. He opened his mouth to correct any wrong impression he may have given, but paused. Each time he spoke he only made things worse.

"Good bye, Mr. Sullivan," she said.

Jack turned on his heel and headed back to the office, rolling his eyes. "Great. This should be fun," he mumbled. "Two abusive little rich brats."

●

Hank was waiting at his desk. Jack entered with a look of disgust. "Where do you get these people?"

Hank shook his head sadly. He'd just lit a fresh cigar and blew smoke at the ceiling. He insisted the disgusting habit kept mosquitoes away. "It comes with the territory. Besides, they're important. I don't know why, but I was told to give them priority."

"I thought you said they were botanists."

Hank shrugged his shoulders. "Important ones."

"Well, I think they're having marital problems. They don't say much to each other."

"You try spending a few days cooped up traveling with your wife, you'll see his point. And it doesn't matter one bit what she looks like." Hank changed the subject pointing to the map on his desk. "They want to be flown to the Ortenguaza."

"Isn't that where you said your pilot, Ray, was going when he disappeared?"

"It is. And this will be the first long trip for the plane since we finished her, so double check everything. I don't want to lose this one there too." Hank was kidding, as if the plane concerned him more than Jack. "But while you're going down, I want you to search the valleys…especially beyond Cali. We know they made it that far. My fuel boy's father, Domingo, reported they flew in around noon. Beyond that there was no word. He said the weather that day looked stormy over the eastern mountains, and said Ray looked tense, as if in a hurry to get over the summit." Hank leaned back in his chair. "Look for the plane in the water—or wreckage more likely," he added with hesitation. "After Cali it's mountains and jungle mainly, so it's not likely you'll see much, but check anyway. If you don't see anything, when you get to the village find a man named Hubert Jenkins. He's a scientist studying the Indians there. If Ray and his passenger made it that far, he'd know it. I'd sure like to know what happened to Ray. He was a good man," Hank said shaking his head thoughtfully. "Not to mention my airplane. It was the best one I had."

"Who was the passenger?" Jack inquired.

"A German fellow, mean as sin, said he was some kind of conscientious protester," Hank replied. "But he didn't look the type, big and brawny with a fierce scar down the side of his face. More like a soldier out of uniform. His papers were in order, though." Jack remembered what Hank had said about the value of papers down here. "Who's to say?" Hank continued. "Maybe he was a deserter; inquiring is just asking to be lied to. As for this Thornton guy," Hank said, changing the subject, "he's a real prick, that's obvious, but he doesn't know anything about you, or your business here. I'm not clear as to what he and his wife are up to, but they came with a clearance from the War Department, and a letter from your Uncle Sully saying we need to be as helpful as possible."

Jack raised his eyebrows at the mention of Sully's name. "Sully? Did he say anything else?"

"He didn't sound happy. Said your situation was gonna be harder than he first thought. Sorry, kid," he added, "I know you'd like to get back."

Dejected, Jack turned back to the flight plans. "So how much crap do I have to take from these two?"

"I know, I know. Its not gonna be easy, but they paid in U.S. cash. I don't get many like that. Odd…" he added with a puzzled tone, "the girl's been here before, several years back. Worked with her father. He was a missionary man. Stuck his nose where it didn't belong and got himself and his buddies killed, not long after she left." Hank paused. "Funny she didn't say anything about it, or act like she knew me."

"Maybe she's looking for answers to her father's death," Jack suggested.

"Right. With the blessing of the War Department," Hank said dryly. "I'm sure they've got nothing better to do right now than investigate a missionary dying in the jungle."

"Well, they're both brats."

"Regardless, stay out of their way. That Thornton guy is nothing but trouble and you've already got enough of that back home. You will probably need to stay down there for a few days so pack some gear, and keep your nose clean while they go about their business. When they're ready, bring them home. And be careful. That valley is bad news," Hank said with concern. "Stay with the airplane, clear of trouble, and you'll be fine."

•

It was a thud that woke Jack up that night. He lay in his cot; eyes open for a minute to see if he would hear it again. Then, another noise, this one different, but just the same Jack rolled out from under his mosquito net to investigate. "Darn rats," he mumbled, assuming the plague of rodents was raiding the food stores again.

Approaching the food locker, he heard it again, but it wasn't coming from the locker. Through the hangar window a flash of light outside caught his eye. He peered out and saw the door to the outhouse swinging shut. Inside it, the occupant's lantern light was still visible seeping through the cracks of the shrunken wood planks. *So, our wonderful Mr. Thornton is no better than the rest of us after all. Like us, he too has to lower himself to use the potty,* thought Jack.

With a gleam in his eye he sneaked over to an outdoor closet and gently opened its door. Inside, a nest of hundreds of huge jungle cockroaches lay dormant covering an old plank. Jack had been searching for something his first week here and Hank had told him to check in the closet. Everybody had quite a laugh at his reaction. He lifted the board gently so as not to disturb the sedentary giants, then walked softly toward the outhouse. In the darkness the insects lay motionless. The sound of the frogs chirping covered his footsteps as he came closer. Inside he heard Thornton humming nervously. With a mischievous smile Jack slid the plank under a gap at the base of the structure.

The lantern's light quickly energized the insects and they scrambled for safety. Some took flight; others just ran across every imaginable surface. In seconds, Thornton's panicky screams filled the compound, overpowering the now quiet frogs. The door burst open. Thornton came bolting out, waddling frantically and furiously brushing the monsters from his body. His pajama pants bound his ankles and he tripped on a root then careened face first into a puddle of water that remained after the daily rain.

Jack stole back to his bunk, with the commotion at his back. Lights went on in the office where Hank slept and in the passenger's quarters where he assumed Kelly was. The noise and outcome delighted him. He let a moment pass, then came out as if having just been awakened by the noise. Hank and Kelly were already trying to calm Thornton's hysteria. The American sat fuming with a mask of mud dripping from his face. Though he was hyperventilating, he attempted to explain what had happened. He saw Jack approaching and calmed himself enough to glare at him and say, "It was you out there, wasn't it? What do you have to say about it?"

"About what?" Jack asked innocently, wiping the sleep from his eyes.

"Don't play stupid with me! You know damn well," Thornton charged, pointing his finger. "I know you know." He wiped something from his face and flung it at Jack. Jack hoped it was only mud.

"I heard something outside that…that shit hole just before the swarm attacked me," he continued. "You were there, don't try to deny it."

Jack shrugged his shoulders and presented a bewildered expression to Hank and Kelly. "I don't know what you're talking about. You look fine to me, a little dirty maybe, but you'll live." He looked everyone over one more time and said, "You guys better quit playing around, though, and get back to bed." He yawned, then turned around and headed back for his own quarters. "We have a long day tomorrow." Walking away he could feel Thornton's anger on his back.

CHAPTER TWENTY-TWO

The Stinson lifted smoothly off the still water of the lake. It was a shallow swamp actually, an extension of the asphalt runway the D-3s used. Limited by the lack of wheels, the floatplane was confined strictly to landing in the water, but it was a minor limitation in reality, for south of Colon there were no runways. The old plane was showing her age and the engine was overdue for an overhaul, but with the recent care she had received, she was purring along smoothly. Handling sweetly at cruise, she was a pleasure to fly. Jack embraced the experience like a balm. While at the controls he was no longer a fugitive, just a pilot forming a synergy with his plane, and loving every second of it.

The flight south from Colon, Panama's primary Caribbean port, to Cali would take just over four hours. Kelly was dressed in twill pants with high boots to protect her from insects and snakes. Thornton had turned out on time dressed as Jack imagined he would on an African safari, pith helmet and all. He'd caught Hank grinning at the sight.

Thornton was tired. He hadn't slept much, having spent the late hours cleaning muck and bugs out of his hair and other places. When he finally managed to crawl back into his bunk, the thought of the roaches climbing all over his body left him bug eyed for the rest of the night. That morning he insisted on the back seat in the plane. It was a single seat, larger than the front ones, and more private. There he seethed in silence, but his fatigue soon caught up with him, and before long he had nodded off with his head flopping backwards, his mouth gaping widely.

That suited Jack who could see him in a mirror that mounted on the visor. He didn't want to deal with him anyway. Thornton was an insolent prick with a chip on his shoulder, the kind of man with unearned connections to power and influence. Jack had seen enough of his type in life to know that they could be dangerous, making rash decisions and stopping at nothing to protect the secret of their incompetence. He figured his run-ins with Thornton weren't over yet.

At nine thousand five hundred feet Jack leveled off. He looked to his side where Kelly sat quietly, looking clean and rested. He wondered again how she had ended up with a guy like Thornton. It must be the money, he figured. She had been rather snotty herself last night. They probably deserved each other.

Kelly had not been impressed with Jack at their first meeting. She judged him to be an unmotivated drifter, and after last night, a childish prankster as well. On her first assignment, in a new position, with an egotistical, haughty partner, to whom she had to pretend to be married, she didn't need some yahoo cowboy stirring up the pot.

Jack couldn't see any point in striking up a conversation again. Each time he opened his mouth things got worse. And to start a conversation would be inviting the subject of why he was out of the U.S. and not doing his part in the war effort.

So, for their own reasons, all three were content to keep to themselves. The trip was smooth, with only patches of clouds as they traversed the skies of the Gulf of Panama. In time, they skimmed the coastline of the Darien jungle, and the warmth of the rising sun was a welcome change. Further south, favorable winds pushed them gently above the coastal plains. Below was a lush green rainforest, hemmed in by Colombia's Pacific coastline to their right and the Cordillera Occidental, the country's westernmost mountain range, to their left.

Not until they turned east and crossed those mountains did they feel any bumps at all. And these were short lived, ending just beyond the ridge. Jack turned back and saw Thornton sleeping peacefully. He cut the engine and dropped the nose more suddenly than necessary. A squeal of panic and a lurching bang came from the back seat. The abrupt movement had torn Thornton out of his dreams. Jack smiled. Kelly grimaced.

Thornton looked out the window. "Where are we?" he asked groggily. The plane was dipping below the tops of some of the continent's highest mountains.

"That's Cali over there," Jack said, his head motioning to a valley beneath the right wing. In its center lay a patch of once colorfully painted buildings, old remnants of the colonial days that were now faded. The remaining sprawl was a monotonous maze of winding streets and earth colored ghettos, lining the banks of the Cauca River. From seven thousand feet it appeared lifeless. Within minutes they were just above the ground, clearing a stone dam, which held back a segment of the river. It was hot and windless, and the waters of the widened river were flat. The pontoons sliced two gashes on the undisturbed surface. The plane slowed quickly, its movements awkward as it settled in the water. Jack gunned the engine as he drove the lumbering plane toward the bank.

The commotion of their arrival stirred action on shore. Young boys and men came out, some running, to gawk at the only flying machine to visit their otherwise forgotten city in some time. The women looked from windows and doorways, preferring to distance themselves from the plane and the strangers. The engine died and the prop stopped; the late morning silence of the sleepy town returned.

Jack was hungry and ready to stretch his legs. From the pontoon he called to a boy who had stepped out of the crowd. "Simon?"

"Sí Señor," the boy answered eagerly.

"*Gasolina por favor.*" He threw a four gallon gas-can down on the bank.

The boy picked up the container expectantly. "*Sí Señor,*" he said. Then he hurried off with it.

Jack cut through the gathering crowd to a barren square that was sort of a park. The ground was dry and dusty, and the air quickly dried Jack's throat. Thornton and Kelly followed. "You can buy your lunch over there," Jack said, pointing to a vendor stand under the only shade in sight. "Hank recommended the beef or chicken tacos. The fish usually has worms and will make you sick unless it is overcooked," he added.

At the stand Thornton inspected the food. His face contorted. "It all looks utterly repulsive!"

Jack grabbed a warm soda and ordered the chicken. "It's not that bad." Thornton grimaced and followed his example reluctantly. Kelly being a veteran traveler ate some fruit that she had brought.

While Jack ate heartily, Thornton picked cautiously at his food, whining with each bite as he tried to identify each thing before he ate it. Finally in disgust he threw the taco down. "I'm taking a walk! See if I can find some real food."

"Don't go too far. We leave in half an hour," Jack warned. He wished he could leave him there, but Hank would blow his stack.

Jack and Kelly sat on a cement bench silently finishing their lunch. Out of the blue she said, "You know I saw you slipping back into the hangar last night. That trick you played on Donald wasn't very nice. It might have been someone else in there." Jack started to speak, but there was nothing he could think of saying, and he felt foolish enough. "I think I too, will go for a walk," she said, then breezed off coolly. Jack couldn't help noticing how pretty she was as she walked away, browsing the shops by the street.

It took Simon ten trips with the gas can and almost an hour to fully top the tanks. A half-hour later all three were back in the plane. "For your father," Jack said handing Simon an envelope.

"Gracias Señor."

Jack shot him a smile. "Now push us out, Simon," he said using body language and a Spanish accent as if it made him more understandable. Then he flipped him a coin.

Simon understood perfectly and with a grin he shoved the plane backward out into the river. Jack gave him thumbs up as the plane glided gently away from the edge. As they drifted out, he turned the plane one hundred eighty degrees, and the flock of onlookers moved closer to the bank. The kids, knowing what to expect, held their hands over their ears. Jack pressed the starter and the plane roared to life. Immediately they all cheered. He pushed in the throttle and a gale of wind and water blasted them. They laughed and played, jumping in and out of the spray, then watched as the plane receded swiftly down the river. Again there was cheering and clapping when finally it lifted off into the sky. Nobody left until it disappeared in the distance.

The second leg of the trip was as beautiful, windless and clear as the first. They flew east across the spectacular ridges of the Colombian Andes. Beyond those mountains they turned south. Green jungle blanketed the east, and rocky ridges jutted up on the west.

Jack explained to his passengers about the lost pilot and plane, and asked their help in looking for the wreckage. "Ray Dobbs, you say?" Kelly started. "He flew me…" then she clamed up, uncertain whether she should make known her past in the area. But Jack noticed her search efforts were diligent the entire trip down. From time to time he checked on Thornton. Back in a deep sleep, he was not going to let Ray Dobbs' misfortune bother him.

The floatplane skipped from ridge to ridge across the rising landscape. As it drew nearer to each crest, the jutting precipices mushroomed upward to meet the plane. The surroundings closed in, creating an illusion of acceleration. Each time the plane easily cleared its hurdle, leaving yet another valley behind. And with each passing ridge the earth again collapsed away, producing another gorge, with its own isolated valley and ecosystem.

It was Jack's first time this deep into Colombia and he hoped Hank's charts and directions to the valley were accurate. He had prepared Jack for the landing, describing it as a tricky act of faith, in which directions instead of instincts should be followed.

Find the ridge lined with six stone spires; there is a notch between the 2nd and 4th. Fly through the notch, and then immediately line up with a small cone hill on the valley floor while descending to a point between them. At minimum speed continue toward the hill, just above the treetops, until the river suddenly comes into view. At that moment cut the power completely and the plane will settle on the water.

When he reached the right location he set the instructions into motion. Thornton and Kelly watched wide-eyed as the small plane's floats skimmed the treetops. The landing place was no-where in sight. Jack wondered if he had the right valley. They had all looked quite similar. He hoped Hank's directions had been accurate. It didn't really matter now; there was only enough fuel to get back, but not enough to go searching for another valley.

"How many times have you landed here?" Thornton asked nervously.

"Including this time?" he paused, waiting for Thornton to nod. "One." Jack heard Thornton suck air, then moan as he moved back in his seat. Jack looked at Kelly. "Were in no danger," he said reassuringly, but she continued to look out the window without reaction. "Really," he insisted, but as earlier she seemed in no mood to talk.

Jack stayed focused on the hill ahead waiting for the expected break. Abruptly, a startled bird darted up from the foliage. The prop sucked it in and with a thud its broken body splattered onto the windshield. Kelly and Thornton both gave a yelp, and Jack recoiled instinctively as the bird's butchered remains dragged morbidly across the Plexiglas. The bloody stain diminished Jack's visibility drastically, but stooping low he continued his search for the break. Nobody spoke.

Then, exactly as Hank had described, the jungle opened sud-denly and the river materialized. Immediately Jack cut the en-gine, and the plane glided downward, then quietly settled on the water's surface. There was an unspoken relief inside.

The tricky part for Jack was finding his way through the maze of coves to where the Picayulta trailhead was hidden. *'Look for the huge tree trunk standing dead in the water. The inlet with the landing is just beyond it.'* Jack remembered Hank saying. Twice, Jack took the wrong path dead ending into the impenetrable foliage.

"Where are you going?" Thornton questioned impatiently.

Jack ignored him. He wondered if the dead tree may have been washed away. Or worse, maybe this was the wrong valley. His eyes darted nervously through the surroundings searching for the tree. His stomach started to churn. Suddenly, a wooden skeleton appeared.

Hopefully, Jack turned the plane toward it, then down a passage beyond it. The sight of several beached canoes lying by what looked like a trailhead filled him with relief. He cut the engine and coasted until the plane came to a complete stop. As he tied the back end of one of the pontoons to a nearby branch, he couldn't help notice the jungle was exceptionally quiet.

With their two bags of belongings, Thornton jumped to shore first. The mud was thick and slippery, and in seconds his boots were clogged with muck. "Gee—whiz look at this mess," he complained.

Kelly followed carefully side stepping onto weeds avoiding the mire all together. Then she scanned the jungle as if searching for someone. "Odd," she said, "someone usually comes down to greet us." After a few brief moments she added, "Maybe we should head up and meet them."

Jack reconsidered Hank's instructions to stay put. He didn't like the idea of Kelly off in the jungle, dependent on Thornton for her safety. Although he was her husband, he seemed terribly inept. Jack decided the plane would be all right alone, so when she and Thornton left for the village he tagged along. After sitting for so long, he told himself, the walk would do him good.

The trail to the village followed a small stream. Kelly remembered it well. It did not seem like two years had passed since she lived here with her father. In a few minutes they came to Jenkins's bungalow, which looked abandoned.

"Professor?" Kelly called from outside. A moment passed without response. "Professor Jenkins?" she repeated. She looked at Thornton and then at Jack. "This is where Professor Jenkins lives. He must be up at the village." Thornton stepped onto the veranda and pushed the door open. "Donald! It's his house. We shouldn't be barging in during his absence."

Thornton did not acknowledge her, but instead stepped into the hut. It was simple inside. There were the usual articles including clothing, a picture of the old man with a friend or family member and some books. "It's been a while since anyone has lived here!" Thornton exclaimed, examining the plants growing through the windows.

Kelly followed him in while Jack stood at the doorway. She picked up a notebook on a table by Jenkins's hammock. "It's his journal," she said, opening it to the beginning. She leafed through the pages, and then read for a few minutes. "Your pilot friend, Ray Dobbs—apparently he did make it here with his passenger." Kelly continued paging through the journal. Jack decided it wasn't worth the trouble to let her know he had never known Ray. "He wrote here that the man with him was a doctor from Berlin." She looked up. "I thought he was a deserter from the German army?"

"That's what Hank told me," Jack replied.

"Listen to this:

September 26th 1943.

The day before yesterday in the evening, Ray Dobbs flew in, with Dr. Heinz Bodecker, an Anthropologist sent by the University of Berlin. He's here to study the Picayultas. The Doctor reported that Ray's footing had slipped by the river, and he had fallen into a nest of Bushmasters.

"Lethal snakes," Kelly commented. "The area is infested with them." She continued:

This morning we buried Ray by the River. He had multiple bite marks on his arms and legs. He didn't stand a chance. I assume Mr. McDermott will eventually miss Ray and the plane, and will send a search and rescue plane out here. Until then, there is no way, nor urgency to report it.

Kelly paused for a moment. "That's too bad. Ray was a sweetheart of a guy."

"I saw no plane down there," Thornton interjected. "How did the plane leave without a pilot?"

"Well, I suppose we should find the professor, or this Bodecker guy. Maybe they can tell us. I know Hank would like to get it back," Jack said.

Kelly walked out the door. "The village is that way." She pointed and then started up the trail. There was nothing else to do but follow.

The three wound their way through the jungle maze, its thick walls enclosing them on all sides as they moved toward the walled village. There was no sign of human life anywhere along the trail. Kelly paused momentarily at the two dilapidated structures, which had been her father's residence and where she had lived, but she pressed on without comment. The path led to the wall of foliage and the tunnel entrance to the village beyond. Thornton balked and cleared his throat nervously to stop Kelly. "Where are you going?" he asked apprehensively.

"The village. It's on the other side." She smiled. "I've been through it a million times. It's no big deal."

"But…what about the bushwhackers?"

"It's Bushmasters, and I doubt there are any here." She went into the hole, her voice echoing out of the tunnel. "Though I could be wrong."

Thornton looked at Jack with hesitation. Jack didn't want to be stuck out here with him, so he disappeared into the hole and quickly caught up with Kelly. Thornton realized he was now alone in the jungle. His eyes shifted nervously from one jungle noise to the next, his cocky bravado vanishing rapidly in the wild. Anxiously, he scrambled through the passage, whimpering as he tripped and bumped down its dark course.

The entrance at the other end of the short tunnel was blocked with branches and debris. Jack pushed them aside to open the path. Then he poked his way through and helped Kelly out. "Where's your husband?" Jack asked.

"I thought he was right behind us," she said with no trace of concern.

There was a panicked cry coming from the tunnel. Suddenly, Thornton burst through the foliage, disheveled and irritated, carrying his pith helmet in his hands. "From now on let's stick together, okay?" he said, shaking his collar and wiping the dirt from his shoulder.

From the gateway they scanned the village. It was no longer the neat, orderly place she recalled and there were no Indians to be found. The streets were eerily deserted, the houses dark and still, and smoke drifted above them. Kelly felt as if she were walking into a place where something dreadful had happened.

"Somebody has certainly been here recently," Jack commented. He surveyed a group of nearby demolished houses and continued, "And they didn't come to make friends." They moved along the street to get a better view. A fire had destroyed more than half of the village, and some dwellings were still smoldering. On closer examination he spotted several Indian corpses, mixed in with the rubble.

"Oh my God! What has happened here?" cried Kelly.

"Looks like a war zone," Jack murmured.

"Perhaps a war with another tribe?" Thornton conjectured.

"I don't think this was another tribe," Jack said.

"What makes you so sure?" Thornton challenged.

Jack walked over to a corpse and crouched down. "These Indians were shot," he said, picking up a shell casing from the ground. "I doubt any natives, even their rivals, have guns in a place as remote as this."

"I know they didn't have guns," Kelly insisted. "Their only metal was the soft gold they used for their ornaments."

Jack pointed to the bullet-riddled body of a native just beyond. "Someone does." His eyes darted around. "And it wasn't that long ago. Those fires are still smoldering and these bodies are freshly dead."

Cautiously they moved forward, but for all the death and destruction there was still no sign of the living. It was a ghost town, without a single man, woman, or child, not even a dog. They paused at the edge of the destroyed buildings, which gave way to the large open plaza. The buildings across the way were also destroyed. And still, there was no one in sight. They moved across the opening toward what used to be the chief's court. No one said a word. There was nothing to say. Then they heard a shout. "Halt! Halt!" The command bellowed from across the compound. Before they could react, the powerful ricocheting of bullets tore the stone from the nearby walls.

"Shit! Let's get out of here!" Jack shouted, pulling Kelly into a nearby house. Thornton hurled himself in behind them. The popping bursts of bullets followed them. Across the way, there was yelling and commotion. Jack peered through a window. Men in the distinctive gray German uniforms and soft campaign hats were swarming like ants whose hill had just been disturbed.

He spotted the tail of an airplane over a high wall. "They've landed an airplane in here!"

"There are two more smaller ones over there," Kelly added.

"Looks like Main Street has been converted into a runway."

"What kind of airplanes are they?" Thornton asked incredulously. Jack looked at him, puzzled. "Military or civilian?" he clarified.

Bullets thudded into the walls around the window. "Military, from the sound of it." The high pitch revving of motorcycle engines distracted him. Jack spotted four of them tearing around a corner in the distance. "Looks like we're gonna have company, real soon!" More bullets struck around the window, breaking clay pots on a shelf behind them. Jack pulled back sharply. "What exactly are you guys here to do?"

Thornton's eyes darted toward Kelly, his mouth quivering. He was trying to say something, but was paralyzed with fear. Kelly interrupted, "It's a secret!"

"Well, it's no secret to them! We'd better get out of here quick, or we'll be surrounded."

The motorcycles, each with a sidecar carrying an armed soldier, were speeding towards them. Their drivers were making the chase while the soldiers in the sidecars unleashed their machine guns wildly toward the hideout. Jack, Kelly and Thornton bolted out the door, side stepping bodies to scramble through the rubble. Jack headed for the perimeter wall, darting one way then the other, but the exit to the river was nowhere to be found. Getting their bearings was hard with the village in total chaos.

The motorcycles bore down on them as they fled frantically, crashing into and out of destroyed structures. But each time they came out, they ended up exposed with yet another motorcycle in view, its driver fish tailing the vehicle, the rear wheel spinning, throwing dust in the air, to resume the chase. The riders were laughing and taunting them over the roaring engines. The sound was deafening. The pursuers tracked them on every street, closing the gap relentlessly. Confused and direction-less, the fugitives were herded like cattle. First circled, then trapped, and then allowed to escape and run free again.

Finally the three ducked into another bigger house. It was dark inside. The motorcycles zoomed past. "Germans!" Thornton whimpered.

"They beat us here," Kelly replied.

"What are you taking about?" Jack demanded.

Before she could answer, a mortar shell hit. The door they had just entered was gone, as was the entire wall around it. Sunlight streamed in, the churning dust lit in its rays. Thornton let out a hysterical scream and curled into a ball in the corner where he sobbed uncontrollably. Just then the motorcycle engines stopped. "Am I hurt?" Thornton sobbed. "I can't go on! I can't do this!" then added, "We should surrender."

Jack was incredulous. "Surrender! Did you see what they did to the Indians! Even the women and children! They aren't taking prisoners."

"Well...Well..." Thornton stuttered. "I'm staying here. I just can't run anymore."

Before Jack could say anything there were footsteps in the gravel outside. "Americans! Come out with your hands up!" a German sneered in broken English. "You have no escape." A moment passed. Then another said slowly, "We will make it painless." Several soldiers laughed. "You have one minute!"

Jack looked at Kelly. "Unless you want to turn yourself over to them we've got to get out of here." He motioned toward a small ventilation hole in the wall.

Thornton looked up at Kelly with pathetic eyes, tears streaming down his cheeks. "We'll be safe here. Stay with me, Kelly.
They are not allowed to hurt us; we are their prisoners."

Jack raised his hands in disbelief and said, "Talk to your husband."

"He's not..." Kelly paused, then snapped at Thornton, "Come
on, Donald. We have to go, or we'll die." Thornton couldn't even
talk. He shook his head with resignation and looked away.

"Thirty seconds," the German called out.

"We have to leave him," Jack said urgently.

"They'll kill him!"

"They'll kill us too, if we stay. There's really no choice."

Kelly looked at Thornton. It was no use. He was paralyzed
with fear.

Jack urged, "Come on. There's no time. Maybe from outside
we can come up with a plan."

With his eyes Thornton pleaded Kelly not to leave. "We'll be
outside, Donald," she said, "to rescue you when we can."

Focused on what they thought was the only exit to the building, the soldiers smugly waited for the seconds to tick away. The
outcome seemed certain.

Jack boosted Kelly up through the hole, then squeezed behind
her. Quickly they sprinted down a narrow side passage.

Then at a distance Kelly stopped and whispered, "Wait!" She
pointed to where they had just run from. Jack stopped too.
Perched in hiding, they could see the Germans closing in on
Thornton. They dragged him out into the open, and interrogated
him, yelling questions at him, then slapping him each time he answered. Kelly could see Thornton was sobbing. One soldier
pulled out his pistol and taunted him, prodding him to dance as
he shot bullets at his feet. Thornton jumped around to dodge

them, distancing himself from the shooter as he did. Then the motorcycles started up.

Trapping Thornton in the clearing, they circled around him over and over again, slapping and punching him as they passed. He continually scrambled to stay away, but they were just playing with him. Then a rider gunned his engine, and charged, kicking him hard to the ground as he passed. Kelly winced as she witnessed the brutality. From the ground, Thornton spotted Jack and Kelly in hiding. He looked tired and broken. He got to his feet and started toward them. His eyes locked on theirs pleading for help, but there was nothing they could do. He tried to run, but it was no use. Engulfed in the deafening roar, he was kicked down by another rider. This time his face was bleeding badly.

The barrage continued, each rider taking a brutal turn, and each time Thornton getting back up, his broken body pathetically moving toward Jack and Kelly. Finally, his legs broken, he could no longer stand. But on his knees, he begged, silently mouthing, "Don't leave me." He was looking right at Kelly.

There was nothing she could do. His lips continued to move slowly and awkwardly saying something unrecognizable. Then a soldier lifted his gun and sprayed him in the back. Thornton's body flinched repeatedly as the bullets ripped through him.

The German looked higher and made eye contact with Jack and Kelly. They snapped their heads back, both breathing hard, horrified by what they had seen. Before they could run, bullets were zinging through the air and thudding into the walls around them. They bolted through a doorway behind them. Its wood splintered as the bullets ripped it apart.

They rushed out into the street; suddenly there it was, directly in front of them, the path to the tunnel, and the exit out of the village. Kelly and Jack sprinted toward it. Behind, they could hear the screaming engines of the motorcycle catching up to them. The rider in the first sidecar had just run out of bullets, but the driver sped on aggressively trying to run them down. Just as he was about to hit them, they dove into the passage. There was a loud crash. The opening was too small for a motorcycle.

Jack and Kelly heard the Germans swearing at each other in disgust, but neither looked back. Popping out of the other end, they hustled down the trail for the plane, knowing it would be only moments before the Germans resumed the chase.

CHAPTER TWENTY-THREE

The path was very muddy. Kelly was out in front, moving with skill along the way. She had taken a shortcut from the village to the river, steeper than the way they had come. Jack's foot caught a root and his body twisted sideways. He crashed hard on his haunches and scooted downhill at her. "Woooee," he cried. His body accelerated as it slid. "Watch out!" he shouted then he clipped her from behind. She crashed down on top of him and let out a loud shriek. Together they hollered as they tumbled down the trail, where protruding roots and branches thrashed them as they passed. The wild ride ended abruptly as they careened into a rotting stump, stopping just short of plunging into the river.

Jack groaned. Dazed and discombobulated, Kelly rolled off of him. In moments, there were voices up the trail. Lots of them. "Hurry! They're already coming!" Jack said, pulling Kelly to her feet. Her eyes peered at him through a mask of mud. He too glistened with a coating of the dark brown slime. "Quick! The plane," he said, pointing. It was within sight, just down the river. Slipping on the unstable mud of the river's edge, they hurried toward it.

Jack didn't have to tell Kelly what to do. Simultaneously they lurched from the bank onto the closest pontoon. The Stinson jolted as they scrambled on to it and then into the cockpit. Kelly fumbled around looking for her harness. "Forget the seat belts!" Jack said, flipping several switches. "They'll probably shoot us before we can take off!"

He primed the engine. "What can I do?" she asked.

"Pray." Jack cranked the starter. The prop cycled once, then twice. Then died. He primed it again. And again, he tried to crank it. "Come on, girl. Come on," he begged.

Kelly stared at him expectantly. The engine turned, over and over with erratic whips, laboring to rotate the prop, but it would not fire. There was helpless panic on both their faces. Finally there was a click, and an explosive backfire, engulfing the cockpit in a white cloud. The engine roared to life. The gale from the prop blew the smoke backwards, vibrating every inch of the weathered fuselage. With relief, Jack pushed the throttle in. The engine raced and the front of the plane pitched up as they lurched forward. He whipped the nose around facing the open river. But in an instant it staggered, and nosed into the water.

"What happened?" Kelly gulped.

"I don't know." Jack opened his door and looked back. "Damn! We're still tied to that branch!" His mind raced. He pointed to the throttle. "See this?" Kelly nodded, "As soon as I say so, shove it in all the way forward and get us headed that way." He pointed to the open river.

"Where are you going?" she shouted.

"I'm going back to cut us free."

"But—I don't know how to steer!" she cried. But Jack was already gone without giving her the chance to refuse.

Outside, Jack found himself on the left pontoon; the plane was tied to the cleat on the right side. He had to jump across to get to the tie down. The plane kept violently lurching forward and jerking backwards, as the racing engine and well-rooted tree played tug of war. Jack fixed his sights on the moving pontoon. Then he jumped. He hit it at his waist, landing half in the water, then pulled himself out. With his pocketknife in hand, he crawled aft to where the painter rope was tied. The speeding propeller sprayed water everywhere, and as it tugged the plane continued oscillating, lurching forward, and then erratically recoiling backwards. Jack struggled to keep his balance. As he reached for the rope, shots rang out. It was the Germans. They hadn't reached the riverbank yet, but were firing from a clearing above. A bullet ripped through the float by Jack's hand and he dropped the knife. Without thought he thrust his arm into the murky water to retrieve it, but it vanished, just inches from his fingertips. More shots rang out.

His only option now was to untie the rope, but the knot was as hard as a rock, and the plane's forward motion only made it tighter. He tried anyway. The bullets continued to fly. It was futile. Then Jack heard a loud crack. The branch they were tied to had given way and the plane lurched forward violently. Jack lost his balance, and did a face plant into the pontoon, his legs landing in the river. Reflexively he yelled out, grabbing the handle on the pontoon's topside.

Kelly heard the yell and thought that was her signal. Biting her lip, she gunned the engine and powered forward. As they accelerated, Jack's lower body caught the water and spun backwards, dragging his dangling body from the waist down through the water. Bullets splashed around him, puncturing the aluminum float to which he was clinging. Fighting the drag, he held tight, then pulled up hard until finally he lugged himself out, back onto the pontoon. The water spray pelted him in the face as they sped faster. Bullets kept zinging into the water around him.

He locked his arm around the aft pontoon support as the plane kept accelerating, racing past the trail entrance to the river.

Struggling to his feet, Jack tried to inch forward, but couldn't keep his balance. He lunged for Kelly's door, grabbing it by the handle. It tore off its hinges, but not before he secured a hold on the doorframe. He pitched the door into the river, yelling, "Go!" Go! Go!" over the howling engine.

Germans were pouring onto the riverbank, all firing on them. The plane raced through a gauntlet of bullets. Some ripped through the windshield, others through the wings and dotted the fuselage. Jack looked ahead. He was still on the pontoon holding onto the doorframe, but he was on the wrong side. Kelly, in the copilot seat, was blocking him from getting in. There was no time anyway. The plane was moving too fast, and there was no time to switch. "Keep the throttle open! Steer with the pedals! Down the river," he ordered.

The plane's speed was enough to start skimming over the water's surface, taking short hops out of the water, but zigzagging so erratically down the river that each time it came down again, the pounding made it impossible for Jack to climb in. Water drenched his face as he crouched on the float, one hand holding the seat inside, the other holding the strut. Each time they came down he braced himself for another blow.

"I don't know how to fly!" Kelly screamed.

"That may not matter in a moment," Jack said, staring at the quickly approaching jungle wall. "Pull back the yoke!" he ordered. "Harder! Pull it!" A bullet ricocheted off the metal frame inside the cockpit and unconsciously she yanked it back hard. The plane leapt off the water toward the tops of the hundred forty-foot tree line ahead.

At that moment, free from the constant pounding, Jack thrust himself into the cockpit and onto her lap. It was tight, but he grabbed the controls just as they clipped the tops of the trees. Once they cleared the trees he slid over to his seat, looking back at the gunmen on the riverbank. "Nice job," he said. Kelly was staring ahead, bug-eyed and shaking with adrenaline. "You see," he said with a lopsided grin, "flying isn't so hard." Though he found it hard to believe they were still alive.

Jack kept the throttle wide open to climb as quickly as possible. They had to clear the valley walls. The windshield was cracked and riddled with bullet holes, and the door was gone. Maps, papers and debris swirled around in the cockpit thrashing him in the face. He squinted through the stinging dust to see his instruments.

Something didn't seem right, in the controls, and in the way the plane handled. It was bucking and struggling roughly. Kelly noticed it too. "Why is the plane doing that?" She asked, gripping the sides of her seat, her knuckles white.

"I don't know." He pointed at the tachometer. "The engine's running fine."

Kelly looked away. Fluid was running down the left wing and spewing off its back. "That doesn't look good," she said desperately. "What is it?"

Jack glanced out the missing door. "Crap! They hit our gas tank!"

"Is it bad?" Kelly asked.

"At that rate the left tank will be empty in no time."

"What about the right tank?"

He looked at the gage. "It's just half full. Not enough to get us anywhere important." Kelly looked at him for a better answer. "We'll never make Cali."

Kelly looked down. There was nothing but mountains and trees. "Where will we land?" she asked practically.

Again the plane pitched and rocked uncontrollably diverting Jack's attention. "I don't know," he answered, fighting the yoke, "but we've got other more immediate problems. Something's jamming the controls."

"That's not the sort of thing a passenger wants to hear from her pilot," Kelly said anxiously.

"I could lie." The yoke bucked forward, and the plane dropped a hundred feet. Jack fought the plane back to level. "But I don't think you'd believe it."

They came up on a scattered layer of puffy cumulus clouds and slowly climbed above them, the plane heaving and gyrating all the way. It took all Jack's strength to stay level. Then there was a loud bang in the tail section. The whole plane shuddered, and the yoke reacted. "We can't do this much longer." It did it again and then again. Each time, the plane shook and the nose swung wildly.

"Why is it doing that?" Kelly asked, never so frightened in her life.

"I don't know, but there is something wrong with the tail. Maybe they shot up the rudder." Jack tried to look out from his window, but the yoke bucked and the plane dropped suddenly again. "I can't let go of this yoke—not even for a moment. You're going to have to look for me."

Kelly turned around inside the plane. There was no back window. "I can't see anything."

"Not like that!" he yelled over the howling wind. "Stick your head out the side and look."

"Do what?" she asked incredulously. "There's no door!"

"Just your head. It won't hurt you."

Kelly looked terrified. "I...I can't do that."

The plane plummeted again. "You *have* to. I need to know what's wrong. If it's real bad we'll need to land..." He looked at her sternly and added, "Before something breaks off."

She wrestled with the thought, looking at him first, then out her open door, then back at him again. "All right, all right. I'll look." She turned toward the door, clutching the frame. The rushing wind was pulling her body outward.

Jack pulled her back in and yelled, "Seat belt!" Kelly's face turned pale with fright. She had forgotten it was not buckled. "Not too tight," he added.

The forced smile she returned was mostly to conceal her fear. She poked her head out, but still couldn't see the tail. She had to lean out farther. As she did, she caught a glimpse of something darting by below. It disappeared under the pontoon. To see it better, she would have to lean out even more. With a hand on the doorframe, and another clutching the seatbelt across her chest, she hung herself out as far as she could. The wind whipped her hair backwards, stinging her face.

Jack looked over; only her twisting waist and white knuckles clutching the seat belt were visible. Kelly spotted the problem. It was the rope, still attached to the cleat on the float. As they had bounced erratically on the water it must have flipped up over the tail and caught on the back wing. It thrashed wildly, putting pressure on the elevator and swinging into the rudder.

But then something larger came into view below the plane. At first it looked like a tree. It darted under the pontoon and then out again. Kelly couldn't believe her eyes. It *was* a tree, or at least a large part of the one that they had been tied to on the river.

"What do you see?" Jack hollered.

Kelly spun quickly back into her seat. "We've got a problem! It's the tie rope. It's still attached."

"I know that, but the rope alone couldn't affect us this much."

"No. I mean it's still attached to the *tree*! Or, at least a big part of it."

Jack opened his mouth. "That's impossible!" If they were dragging a branch, how could they have gotten airborne? He thought for a second. It really didn't matter. "Okay, okay. Whatever it is we've got to get free of it." A moment passed. The gears turned in his head. He fumbled around under his seat, then pulled out a coil of rope and handed it to Kelly. "Tie this around your waist—like a harness." She looked at him in wide-eyed astonishment.

Then again from under his seat he pulled out a small toolbox and sorted through it. He came up with a knife and handed it to her. "Here, this should cut us free." Kelly did not take it, but instead looked at him in absolute disbelief. He waved the knife handle closer to her hand. "Take it," he said.

Kelly pushed it away. "I'm sorry. For a second I thought you were suggesting I climb outside the airplane and crawl down the float to cut the rope." Jack did not answer. The plane lurched and he fought to keep it in the sky. "You weren't? Were you?"

He paused before answering. "It's our only chance."

She looked at him incredulously. "You might be crazy, but I'm not. I'm staying right here," she pointed at her seat, "in the plane." Jack kept looking at her. She turned away but could feel his eyes. Then in the next instant without warning she snapped, "Just get it out of your head! I am not going out there!" She was emphatic. She let a wordless moment pass. "And stop looking at me that way!"

A longer moment passed. Uncertain of what Jack was thinking Kelly finally broke. "What's plan B?"

"Plan B?" He thought for a second. "Plan B is I can't keep her under control and we crash and die. Or, I do keep her in the air until we run out of gas, but the drag from that branch slows us down enough that our shifted center of gravity makes us fall backwards, into a stall—from which there is no recovery—and we crash and die." Jack went on, "If you cut us free, we have a reasonable chance of controlling where we will land. If we're lucky we may walk away from it." There was another slam into the tail, and the plane lunged uncontrollably.

Kelly looked at him. "You're really serious, aren't you?"

He nodded. "I'm out of ideas, and sooner or later we're going to be out of gas." He looked at the gas still spewing off the wing. "My bet is it's going to be sooner."

Kelly sat frozen, looking straight forward, and contemplating. A minute passed, then another, the smashing got louder and the jarring even more violent. Jack gripped the control yoke tightly. "We're running out of time." It was a nervous plea. "I can't do it and fly the plane at the same time." He waited for a reaction. "Come on, Kelly." It was the first time he had called her by name. "You'll be tied to a safety rope. We have no choice if we want to live."

Her reaction came slowly, but finally, looking at the rope from the corner of her eye, then back up at him, she nodded in agreement. He reached over to her buckle and popped it open.

Contemplating what she was about to do, she tied the rope around herself, then braced herself, and snatched the knife out of his hand. "When we get back, I'm complaining to the management." Without a door to push open she rotated ninety degrees and stepped out in a huff. Her feet reached then planted firmly on the pontoon. At that moment, the full force of the wind pushed her backwards. In a flash of panic, she realized she had committed to something she shouldn't be doing. She looked back into the cockpit. The wind was deafening.

Jack made a cutting motion with his hand, mouthing the words, "Cut it!"

She turned her attention to the pontoon. The cleat seemed insurmountably far away. She inched back gingerly on the float's flat top. Her moves were shaky, but calculated. The wind was distracting, but she kept her eyes fixed on the knot, not wanting to see anything else. There was no going back, not until she reached it. Inadvertently her eyes glimpsed beyond the pontoon. Below, rocky cliffs sped past them. The motion made her instantly dizzy. She closed her eyes and pulled herself tightly against the strut, experiencing a swirl of fear and adrenaline. Another hard jolt forced her eyes open. It was the limb swinging wildly to one side. It dragged the rope across the elevator, and forced it down violently. The plane immediately plunged.

Kelly's stomach dropped with it and her feet flew up off the pontoon. She let out a terrified scream, locking her arms tightly to the strut with an unbreakable death grip, her body flailing weightlessly next to the plane.

Jack knew she was in trouble. He had the plane stable within moments, but he didn't know how Kelly had fared. He waited patiently to get a sign that she was still with him. A minute passed without a hint. It seemed like ten. He leaned over, but could see nothing. What had he done to her? How could he have asked her to go out there?

Outside, Kelly trembled uncontrollably. She knew she had to keep going. There was no choice. She tried to unlock her hands, but they didn't want to let go the safety of the strut. She took a deep breath, and forced herself to have courage. Releasing the strut, she grabbed for the pontoon support that was farthest back.

And with the knife in a free hand she reached for the knot. It was more than two feet away. She had to stretch farther, much farther, and she did so with all that she had, extending the knife toward the knot. But the blade was still inches away. To reach it, she had to let go of the support, just for a moment. If chance were not with her, the slightest bump would toss her off the pontoon. She pushed that thought from her mind.

Then she took a deep breath, wrapped her legs around the float, and in faith let go of the strut. Extending herself recklessly the blade landed on the knot. Frantically she started working it back and forth. The knot was as hard as a rock; only a few fibers springing apart at a time. The least he could have done was give me a sharp knife, she thought.

She pressed harder against the rope. Finally there was a pop, a large piece gave way, and it started fraying down its length. Kelly pushed harder and cut faster. There was a little bump. She couldn't quit now, she was almost there. The last fibers yielded with a snap and there was a jolting release of pressure. The branch plummeted with the severed rope trailing behind it. Immediately the plane stabilized and the violent shaking stopped.

Straddling the float and facing backwards, Kelly rested, her eyes fixed on the retreating branch as it tumbled. It disappeared into a cloud below.

At once Jack knew she had succeeded. Now all he could think of was getting Kelly back inside to safety.

Kelly continued to hold tightly, still facing backwards but inching her way forward to the cockpit. Suddenly there was motion behind her. She raised her eyes to look. Two fighter planes were barreling down on them, their machine guns blazing, the muzzle flashes sparking rapidly. Fear of heights suddenly became a secondary issue. Kelly sprang up on the pontoon and thrust herself into the cockpit.

Jack looked at her with relief. "That's better! We'll be all right now."

"No we won't!" Kelly hollered.

"What do you mean?"

"There are two planes behind—shooting at us." At that instant a barrage of bullets popped through the airplane. Jack could not restrain a yell of shock and fear. "Shit! Put on your seatbelt." Kelly strapped herself in and cut the rope from its attachment at the strut. Instinctively Jack put the plane into a dive. Kelly felt her stomach leave her. Their speed increased rapidly. Jack glanced at the airspeed indicator. They were diving at one hundred and fifty knots. But the fighters were much faster and closed on them within seconds. Jack pulled back hard on the yoke. The Stinson creaked as it leveled and then shot upward. In moments they were upside down in a tight loop and the faster planes flashed past.

Kelly was grasping the edge of her seat. "Is this safe?" she cried out.

"Safer than being shot at!" He looked into the short green-house-like canopy, as they came down behind the fighters. He could see a lone pilot in each. He recognized the aircraft from training camp. They were the G model of the Messerschmitt Bf109 series. The single engine fighters were the powerful main-stay of the German Luftwaffe.

Jack remembered his instructor talking about the Bf109G's armament with a mixture of fear and envy; it had two 20mm cannons mounted in pods on the wing, plus another 20mm cannon firing through the propeller hub, and two additional 13mm machine guns mounted on the cowling. These fighters, in their numbers, effectively dogged the allied bombers. And with their 1,475 horsepower Daimler-Benz DB605A engine, they reached speeds of 428 mph, fiercely challenging the Allied aircraft for superiority.

Jack watched the fighters break in opposite directions as they prepared for another attack. They were completely defenseless. "Now what?" Kelly cried.

Jack knew that it was quite difficult for a faster airplane to shoot at a much slower one. Their turns were much wider, and their targets moved up to quickly to get the tracers lined up in time. He had used it to save them this time, but knew their luck at that game wouldn't hold out. "We're safe for the moment."

"Not for long," Kelly cried watching the planes. They were sweeping around swiftly in wide-angle turns from both sides for the next assault. Jack had to think fast. Below, he spotted their only option. "We have to get into those clouds." He pointed the nose downward. The engine raced, and the airspeed indicator red lined. In seconds the Messerschmitts were behind them. The descent turned into a diving spin. Jack hoped to reach the clouds before the Germans. "God, what are you doing?" Kelly screamed.

"It's our only chance."

The barrage of bullets started again, singing past them under the wings. But in the same instant they plunged into the clouds, vanishing from the German's gun sights. The fighters broke off.

The cockpit inside the Stinson was suddenly transformed into a world of monochromatic brightness and disorientation. Kelly felt the plane oddly going into a roll to the right. It felt as if they would eventually be inverted. "We're turning over!" she said nervously unable to tell if they were right side up or upside down.

Jack's eyes were fixed on the panel. "No, it just feels that way. You have to trust your instruments," he said, pointing to the turn coordinator. It was the only instrument he had to keep them level. He took a deep breath and looked back over at Kelly. "You never did answer me," he said.

"Answer you?"

"Yeah, who are you guys? And why is everybody trying to kill us?"

Kelly was thinking of her answer, but her response was pre-empted as the cloud spit them back into the open. The Messerschmitts were out of position, but raced toward them at first sight. Jack saw another cloud and scurried toward it before they could reach them. It bought him some more time, but he knew he could not keep this up for long. He was low on fuel, and his plane was heavily damaged. Outrunning the German planes was impossible as they were grossly out-powered, and these rugged mountains offered no place to make a quick landing. Again they reappeared, exposed in the open. And again, they dashed for the cover of another cloud. Between them, they saw the fighters circling above.

"They're just waiting for us to come out long enough to make another run," Jack said.

Finally, the last of the string of clouds coughed them out. There were no others to run for. The Germans swooped down on their prey.

Jack looked to his left. Under the wing was a Messerschmitt barreling down and firing at will. He could see the flashes of its 13mm guns. He braced himself. Popping strikes pierced up the canvas fuselage. Two of the bullets ripped through the engine. The violent sound of metal tearing through metal was frightening. It deafened everything else. Horrified Jack saw a piece of his engine flying off past his windshield.

"We're hit!" Kelly yelled. "We're hit!"

Smoke immediately billowed out and swirled around in the cabin. The oil pressure dropped to zero. And in moments the engine temperature started to rise. Jack coughed and leaned forward to see through the smoke. "Hang on!" he shouted, expecting the wings to tear off from the damage.

The fighters backed off to watch as the crippled plane descend uncontrollably to its fate. The engine sputtered and backfired several times. Finally, it sputtered its last, and the propeller stopped. The smoke thinned, but continued to stream out from below. Only the sound of the wind remained.

The plane was sinking fast. Kelly looked at Jack. "My God! What are we going to *do!*" she shouted.

His answer came quick. "We can jump."

"Jump?"

"Jump," he repeated.

"I've never used a parachute before. I didn't even know you had any."

"I don't." There was a second of silence.

"You mean jump without parachutes?!"

Jack nodded. "I'll slow us to stalling speed."

"But the engines already stopped."

"No, stalling means to go so slow that the plane no longer flies. So basically we fall out of the sky." Jack paused, "The vegetation down there is thick. It'll make a good cushion. I think we can do it."

Kelly was speechless, responding only with wide eyes. Jack continued. "See that ridge ahead?" he pointed down to the flanking side of a higher mountain. She nodded. "The head wind we are flying into will increase just above the crest. On a normal afternoon the wind's speed could be thirty or forty miles per hour there." He looked at her to see if she was following him. "With flaps down and fully flared we'll be flying no more than forty miles per hour, maybe less. If I get close enough to the ridge and we time it perfectly, we can jump off at virtually running speed." Her wordless gape needed no explanation. It caused him to add, "Worse that can happen is we'll get killed, and if we stay here another minute we're dead anyway."

There was horror in her eyes, and her voice was frantic. "I don't know if I can do it."

"You have to. We won't survive a crash in these mountains. And even if we did they'll strafe us. We don't have a choice."

Kelly gulped and nodded in comprehension.

Just as promised, the wind increased as they closed on the crest, and the plane slowed dramatically. Jack added flaps, which increased the drag and slowed them even more. He cracked his door and looked at Kelly. He hoped she would find the courage to jump, because if she stayed behind she would die. Kelly understood there was no alternative. He was going to jump and if she wanted to live, she had to jump too. "Last chance," Jack said encouragingly.

Kelly resigned herself to getting the whole thing over with. She had no door to crack open, but unfastened her safety belt. Jack grinned. She looked at the ground. "We're still too high," Kelly cried.

"Trust me," he said.

The headwind increased even more just before the ridge and their ground speed dwindled to almost zero. Everything was in slow motion, and for a brief moment Jack thought, *This might actually work.* The plane dropped steeply advancing forward slowly.

Kelly focused on the approaching ridge and braced herself. Just before the crest Jack pulled the yoke full back. The plane slowed down then faltered as its wings started to stall. They were ten feet over the ridge and moving at a surreal crawl.

"Now!" Jack yelled as he pushed his door open and leaped. Kelly grabbed her satchel and followed screaming.

They sailed out of the lagging airplane, arms waving and feet gyrating, plummeting toward the ridge's short heavy foliage. The airplane continued westward, clearing the ridge and flying pilotless into the valley beyond. Both hit the brush hard. It provided a slight cushion. But still they tumbled and tossed over each other, through the bushes on the crest of the ridge, then down the other side, across more thick brush, and finally out on to a ledge.

In the turmoil Jack seized the short rope that was still attached to Kelly's waist. It snagged on a rock protruding from the ledge, stopping Jack abruptly on one side, but on the other side Kelly had more slack. She went sailing over the edge. Jack held on tight to the rope, which snapped taut. He took a breath and looked out over the valley beyond. His plane was silently receding in the distance. He felt the rope start slipping through his aching fingers, and tried wrapping it around his arm for security. Kelly's weight at the opposite end was pulling him into the rock.

Momentarily dazed, Kelly regained consciousness only to find herself dangling precariously over a precipice. Beneath her a cliff, three hundred feet straight down, dropped off before angling out into the canyon floor another thousand feet below. She tried to scream several times, but nothing came out. The rope pulled up tight around her chest making it hard to breathe. Finally the words came out. "Help! Help!"

"Hang on!" Jack cried. "I've got you."

Suspended and swaying, she cried again, "I'm stuck!" The cliff was out of reach. "There's nothing to grab." The rope was cutting into her sharply.

Jack's forearms were burning; his hands were bleeding. He shifted his weight and his grip slipped. Kelly let out a yelp of fright as her body jerked violently downward a foot. "What are you doing up there?" she cried, staring toward the cliff top; she was talking to a rope disappearing over the edge. Nothing else was visible. She searched the face of the cliff and spotted a crack. She extended her hand but couldn't quite touch it. "Hold me tight," she yelled. Then without waiting for an answer, and certain she was running out of time, she started to swing the rope back and forth.

The pain on Jack's hands was excruciating. She seemed bent on making things harder for him. "What are you doing?" he managed to holler.

"There's—a—crack," she said, one word at a time between swings. "Got it!" She locked her fingers into the crack, then jiggled her toes around, frantically searching for a second hold anywhere. She refused to give up and kept probing. Finally, she felt something, a groove in the rock face. She had found a ledge. It was small, but enough to support her weight.

The tension suddenly backed off the rope. Jack scrambled to anchor it better around the rock that had broken their fall. With the rope safely tied, he looked over the edge. Kelly saw him peering down. "Where have you been?"

Jack grinned, then braced himself and hoisted her up. Without a word, they rolled their battered bodies over to rest, leaning against the rock that had saved them. They gazed across the valley; their small plane was still gliding like a kite, way down and across the valley. It looked like a toy. Jack had heard what a remarkably stable craft the Stinson was and could only gaze in awe. But this last flight was over. They followed her until she smashed into a cliff. There was a fireball and a puff of smoke, followed by a distant muffled explosion. The burning wreckage rained down on to the rocky valley floor.

"The fighters are gone," Jack said, searching the sky. "I don't think they saw us jump." His voice was more hopeful than certain.

Kelly said nothing. She and Jack caught their wind and checked for serious injuries. Kelly was coming down from the exhilaration she had been experiencing since first climbing out of the airplane back at the river.

Jack was simply beat. It was all he could manage to look at her. "We'd better get moving," he said. "It'll be cold soon on this ridge." The sun was dropping behind the mountains.

"Solid ground. I never thought I'd be so happy to feel it under me," Kelly said. She was exhausted, too tired to move.

Jack lifted himself painfully to his feet and replied while turning, "Yeah, safe and sound..." but was silenced by the sight of eight German soldiers armed with machine guns only twenty feet away. He froze.

"Ohh...I could go for a nice hot bath," Kelly said, dreaming aloud. "That's what I want. And a bed. Yep, a hot bath and a big soft bed."

"I wouldn't start the water just yet," Jack answered, raising his hands over his head.

"What are you doing?" she questioned, puzzled, but then froze also at the sight of the gun barrels pointing in their direction.

A sergeant bellowed out in German and waved his gun wildly in the air.

"I don't think he likes your bath idea," Jack said.

CHAPTER TWENTY-FOUR

The march down from the ridge was brutal; made worse by the wind that turned cold as soon as the sun slipped behind the mountains. Jack stared across the barren slope. He saw Kelly on the trail ahead of him. Her hands, like his, were tied in front, restricted by another rope around the waistline.

Two German soldiers armed with rifles led the way. There were two more behind Jack. The path they were on was an imperceptible line of loose gravel traversing the slanted treeless landscape. It cut through patches of snow and clumps of a short hardy brush that was as stiff as wire. The bushes had a permanently swept-back shape, fixed that way by the unrelenting west wind. It was the only apparent life at this altitude.

Jack raised his eyes to the distance. The valley below was a purple monochrome of shadows. He spotted tents of an encampment and the flicker of several campfires. More Germans, he assumed. Distracted from the trail, Jack made a false step. With his hands bound he slid on the gravel, unable to regain his balance. To his right the down slope was an unobstructed fall for several hundred feet. Jack chose to fall to his left. He felt the rough jab of a rifle butt into his back.

"*Dummkopf!*" the sergeant behind him blurted. "Get up!"

As Jack tried, the sergeant shoved him again, smashing his bruised body back into the rocks. He crawled to his feet, then moved slowly the rest of the way toward the camp. A few soldiers glanced at the prisoners but no one paid them any special attention. It was cold and getting dark. Around the fires soldiers huddled, trying to stay warm, ready to settle in for the night. They approached the nearest fire where the soldiers with them moved quickly toward its warmth.

Jack was freezing cold despite the hard hike. He felt the fire's radiance and wanted to move closer, but paused when a large man emerged from a nearby tent. He was an officer with a pistol on his hip. From the badges on his field uniform he looked high ranking. He approached Jack and Kelly, examining them thoroughly, as he puffed on a sweet-smelling small cigar.

"Welcome," the German said with a mild accent. "I am SS-Standartenfuhrer Bodecker. I am in command. He paused. So...you are the acrobats my fighters chased earlier this afternoon...ehh?" He walked behind them, continuing his inspection. "The jump out of your airplane...I am impressed," he said with admiration. "My pilots radioed all the details. We listened with riveted attention." Bodecker continued his walk around them until he was back in front. Neither Jack nor Kelly spoke.

"It was your misfortune to leap from your plane straight into our arms, so to speak. I'm sure you didn't expect some of us to be up here on a little excursion." Bodecker smiled. "But in the morning we'll be returning to our base camp at the village... or, at least most of us will." He paused for a long moment, then continued, "I respect a man... and woman," he added looking at Kelly with piercing intensity, "of resource and courage. We Germans admire bravery." The firelight illuminated his face and reflected off the shiny scar that marred his cheek from the temple to the mandible. It gave Kelly the shivers; inside his eyes she saw evil defined.

"I'm very sorry about your friend, Mr. Thornton—that was his name, I believe, according to his identification. My men informed me of his fate…apparently he could not dance." Bodecker laughed, amused by the joke. Then his look turned deadly serious. "I am most curious however, to know what brings three Americans to this remote place on the planet, at this specific time?" He looked at Jack, who was wondering the same thing. Without warning, the back of the German's hand slammed Jack in the side of the face, sending him tumbling to the ground. Still tied, Jack was unable to soften the blow to his cheek from the rocky ground. "Who are you?"

Kelly looked at Jack, who was barely moving. She bit her lip.

"Could it be that you are here searching for the same thing that I am?" Bodecker speculated. He waited for a reaction. Kelly did not acknowledge him.

Then Bodecker extended his hand and an aide handed him a canvas pack. He flipped it open. "Maybe…something very old?" Kelly still said nothing but watched him closely. "Maybe, something…like this?" He continued slowly pulling a small stone statue from the pack. His eyes fixed on hers with anticipation.

The sparkling firelight reflecting from the embedded gems caught Kelly's attention. Her eyes grew wide at the sight of the little idol. Surprised of its existence, it had her spellbound in an instant. It was too late to disguise her interest.

Bodecker smiled. "I see you are familiar with this little artifact. But I'm afraid you are a somewhat late. It is now the property of the Third Reich." Kelly continued staring at the statue hypnotically. "It is beautiful—in its own way—isn't it?" he goaded her.

The simply carved stone figurine was exquisite, and the deep yellow gold adornments on its oversized head were intricately handcrafted. "Is it real?" she asked with covetous eyes.

The German laughed. "Very real, I assure you." Then without warning he slapped her.

Kelly felt the sting on her cheek and shot him an angry glare. "Who are you?" Bodecker demanded. "Or, I should rephrase: Who were you?" He looked at the statuette. "I'm sure you understand, now that you have seen this little jewel, I cannot just let you go free." He paused. "But still, I am interested to find out how you came across knowledge of it—and the legend that surrounds it."

Kelly could see he was studying her reaction. "Legend? What legend?" she asked with all the innocence she could muster.

Bodecker perked up. "Don't play me for a fool. You wouldn't be here if you had not heard of it."

Kelly considered her words, then asked, "So, is it true? The legend?"

Again, Bodecker laughed. "It doesn't really matter? You will not live to see it."

Jack groaned, lying at their feet. "Is *what* true? Does *what* matter?" he stammered, as a soldier pulled him roughly to his feet. "What the hell are you guys talking about?" He looked at Kelly staring at the statue in Bodecker's hands. "That's it! *That* is what this is all about?" Bodecker looked at him curiously.

Jack's astonishment broke Kelly's fascination with the statue. She could see he was struggling cluelessly. "He has nothing to do with this," she told Bodecker. "He is only a hired pilot."

"Most unfortunate for him."

A soldier interrupted, saying something in German, and Bodecker suddenly looked uninterested. He held the idol up to

Kelly's face. "Enjoy your look," he scoffed, then threw his cigar to the dirt and stepped on it, "since you'll never have the pleasure of possession." Replacing the statue in the pack he added casually, "I would kill you now, but I was in the middle of my supper when you arrived, and I do not wish it to get cold." He stepped forward, shoving Kelly aside as he passed. She fell into Jack, and like a domino he collapsed, his head striking hard against a rock. He was knocked out cold.

Bodecker paused to look down at him. He snapped his fingers at a soldier. "Keep them tied, and place them under guard until morning." He resumed his walk back to his supper, then turned around abruptly and looked at Kelly. "Tomorrow, I have a surprise for you."

•

The next morning came too soon for Jack. He awoke to the jostling of his bruised body on a gurney with two disgruntled German soldiers carrying him across the mountainside. Through the thin slits of his eyes everything was blurry, but he could make out the snow and rock they were traveling over. Ahead, Kelly was being prodded but still able to walk under her own power.

When the soldiers saw Jack was conscious they dropped him to the ground. His body screamed with pain; every inch was battered or bruised. A figure approached as he groaned, the sun shining directly behind the man. Jack raised his hand to block its brilliance, and then with an exaggerated squint he focused. It was Bodecker.

"Good morning. Nice to see you are awake," the German said. "I prefer not to tire my men. You can carry your own weight from here."

A soldier pulled Jack to his feet. He swayed for a moment before getting his balance. "Don't worry, we are almost there," Bodecker added callously. "Just a little farther up the mountain." He called out to his troops and they resumed the trek. Within fifteen minutes they had reached a level place with a slight depression on the mountainside. Several soldiers had forged ahead and were pulling back a heavy flat rock, exposing a cavern beneath it. The soldiers then took turns drawing close to the edge to glimpse down into the dark pit. The power of their curiosity was quickly replaced by dizziness as they approached the edge of the bottomless depths.

"I took the liberty to go through your things last night, Miss Wilson. I'm sure you don't mind." Bodecker looked smugly at Kelly. In his hand was her leather satchel. "Kelly Wilson, daughter of the infamous Reverend James Wilson, I presume. And now an agent for the American Military Intelligence. That career change was quite a shock for you, I would imagine." Kelly didn't respond. "I saw your father not that long ago, you know—with his pathetic cohorts—in the chief's chamber. He didn't look well at all."

"My father is dead," Kelly replied bitterly.

"I know. I know. From what I heard, it was his shortcomings in personality and communication skills that led to his demise," Bodecker chuckled callously, then looked away and mused further, "I think while your father was promising to bring God to these little savages, he was still searching for him himself. And, like most, his mind was closed to any variations from his already preconceived beliefs." Bodecker's prodding was relentless. "It's too bad, really. If he would have just considered the possibility of some truth in the legend, he might have come closer to God than he ever had imagined. But his mind was already set. He wasn't going to let anything like facts get in his way."

"At least what he did was with good intentions."

Bodecker laughed. "Good intentions." He smiled dismissively. "His intentions were no better than yours or mine." He paused. "Like us, he got greedy...too greedy for his own good. He wanted that statue just as we do; maybe not for the same purposes, but he wanted it just the same." Bodecker shook his head.

"When I want something I make a plan to get it. Lamentably, with your father's fumbling approach, he never even got to see it." Kelly was fuming.

"You are angry with me, yes?" Bodecker taunted. "Don't take it personally. You see, if you really want something in life, you must work people. Manipulate them. Make them believe they are going to get something they want—this way they will help you to achieve your goal." He lifted his hands as if he were preempting her certain interruption. "Yes, yes, I know what you're going to say. You don't like this sort of thing—it's lying, treachery and exploitation. Maybe so, but if those accusing you become a nuisance, you can always kill them." He chuckled cruelly and ran his hand through Kelly's hair, then caressed the back of her neck. "I hate to deny a pretty girl anything, but regrettably, like your father, you will never see the powers of the statue."

Kelly pulled away defiantly, but Bodecker closed his fist tightly on a handful of her hair, pulling her head tight against his hand. She could not move. He said nothing but gave her a piercing glare that left no doubt that he alone controlled her fate.

"You're lying," she managed to say. "The legend is nothing but a folktale."

"Believe what you will, Miss Wilson, but I assure you it is no folktale. I was there, and I saw it with my own eyes," he gloated, still holding her head in painful paralysis. "With your beloved friend Professor Jenkins." Bodecker released his grip, and Kelly stepped back.

"Professor Jenkins?" she said, "What did you do to him?"

"Oh, I lament admitting that I had nothing to do with the good Professor's demise; his fate was carried out by the savages... these so-called friends of his." He laughed.

Kelly wished she could burn a hole through him with the anger she was feeling.

Bodecker kept his evil smile. "Take heart! I personally punished them for their misbehavior. You saw the village when we were finished. As for you and your new friend, you will soon be visiting the Professor." He eyed the open cavern in the ground. "Lower them in," he ordered, tilting his head toward the pit. It was as if suddenly he had become bored with their bantering and was ready to move on with his day.

Bodecker opened the backpack and inspected the statue one more time as the soldiers pushed Kelly toward the pit. Jack stumbled behind her, barely conscious and being led by a soldier. With a rope attached to her waist, the soldiers lowered Kelly in, roughly at first as they allowed the rope to slide wildly.

"Gently, you fools!" Bodecker ranted. "I want her healthy down there, so that the fear of rotting to death in this anonymous hole can sink in."

The rope cut into Kelly, abrading her midsection. She hung helplessly, slowly spinning as she descended. The walls looked cold and wet, and the voices from above echoed against them distantly.

Bodecker stuffed the statue back into the pack and handed it to the largest of his men. "Guard this with your life." Then he looked at the soldiers. "Now her friend."

Jack's body came down in a series of jolting drops. His rope was not long enough to let him all the way down, and he hung suspended seven feet from the cavern floor as the soldiers above tried to decide what to do. It didn't take them long. They released their end of the rope and let him plummet to the ground. He let out a groan of pain as the rope tumbled down on him.

"Are you okay?" Kelly asked with concern.

Jack was groggy. "Yeah," he groaned sarcastically, "I'm just perfect. What the hell was he talking about? Statue, magic power?"

Before she could answer, Kelly's satchel slammed down against the rocks only a few feet from where they were. It was followed by Bodecker's voice from above. "There's no trace of you up here now!" His voice reverberated through the cavern. "I'm turning out the lights now. Good night," he said, laughing. A deep rumbling echo followed. The opening above shrank as the men pushed the big rock back over the entrance. The sliver of light above got smaller and smaller, and the chamber darkened quickly, until finally the last point of light disappeared into itself. Total silence and complete and utter blackness followed it.

A long noiseless moment passed. The darkness played tricks on Kelly's mind. It was so thick she could feel it like a musty blanket suffocatingly pressed over her face. She imagined the walls closing in around her, inside her panic and claustrophobia swelled. She heard nothing from Jack. Her voice quivered as she called, "Jack?" She heard him take a deep breath of the cave's cool air.

"I'm still here."

CHAPTER TWENTY-FIVE

The air was humid and stale, and cooler than on top. Kelly sat frozen in place, staring into the blackness, unwilling to venture into it. Jack too was afraid to move. He could see absolutely nothing. Even as the time passed, and his eyes tried to adapt, things did not improve. There was no light for them to gather. Time seemed to have stopped.

Finally, Kelly heard Jack fumbling around, and then he bumped into something. "Ouch! Shit!"

"What are you doing?" she quivered. Her heart was pounding so loud she thought she could hear it.

Jack's heart was racing too. "I don't know," he sounded exasperated, "but we've got to do something." He used his hands to touch his way from one rock to the next. "What was in the bag the kraut threw down here after they dropped me?"

Kelly thought for a moment. "Maps…Instructions…A compass." She listed the items off as if none of this had much importance to her now.

"Is that all?" Jack asked.

She paused to think what else might be in there. "An emergency kit, maybe. You know the kind the Army uses. First aid stuff, I think."

"You think! Don't you know what's in your own satchel?"

"It's my first assignment, okay?" she snapped. "And I was rushed. I've only been an agent for a couple of days." She paused. "And so far it hasn't been going too well."

"I hadn't noticed."

Again the two waited in silence.

Then Kelly blurted, "It has a portable light!"

"What?"

"My satchel! Donald told me there's a flashlight sewn into the side along with a few other emergency items!" She heard Jack trip in the darkness and tumble. Then there was a snapping crack of dried sticks followed by, "Ouch!"

"You okay?" she asked.

"I'd be better if you would help look for your bag."

Kelly joined him in the search. At first she moved slowly and cautiously, but the total darkness and the thought of the light soon had her scrambling frantically. "I found something!" Kelly exclaimed. She fumbled through the stuff with excitement. "I think its wood—sticks or something."

"Damn, I think I've been beaten stupid! I just remembered—I've got matches!" Jack said, feeling a box in his shirt pocket. "Gather the sticks in a pile. I'll work my way over, and we'll start a fire." He shook the box. The matches rattled inside. "I hope they're dry," he said, remembering the wet take off the day before. "There are only a few. We can't waste them."

Using the sound of Kelly's movements, Jack worked his way toward her, occasionally stopping and waving his hands blindly to feel through the darkness in front of him. He could tell he was getting close. Then his hand touched her arm.

Startled at first, Kelly jumped, but then she reached out and grabbed his hand back. It was rough and cold, but suddenly she didn't feel so alone. Jack held onto her hand the same way.

Neither willing to let go of the other, and neither was prepared for the surge of emotions that rushed through them at that moment. It was not an intimate exchange of passion or affection, but a feeling of companionship—another person, a comrade, in the midst of the darkness and despair, sharing the burden and thereby cutting it in half. They kept touching for a long moment.

"The matches," Kelly said finally.

"Oh, yeah," Jack replied. He released her hand. Instinctively she reached upward and held on to his bicep to keep the contact. She did not want to be alone again.

"Pass me one of those sticks." She heard his shirttail tearing, "This should make a fair torch." Then, slowly he opened the matchbox; he did not want to drop them. Carefully he felt for one of the little sticks inside. He took one out and closed the lid.

"What are you waiting for?" Kelly asked.

"Just trying to be careful." He pressed the match head against the roughened side of the box and snapped it across the surface. The phosphorous head ignited brilliantly for a second before Jack cupped it in his hands. Then he put the flame up to the fabric. The flame grew, and with it dim light spread through the obscurity, barely illuminating all but the farthest reaches of the cavern.

Kelly turned to the pile, planning to gather more sticks for the fire. As the glow from Jack's fire spread through the chamber, the sticks in her hands took a visible form. Her eyes focused on teeth, human teeth, firmly fixed to the kindling in her hand. She scanned the ground around her; to her horror she found herself standing in a crowded bone yard. Below her lay skull upon skull, with mouths gaping wide. She panicked as she felt their eyeless sockets glowering up at her. Her hand trembled and she dropped the jawbone in it, then stumbled backwards. It was as if she felt the presence of these long lost souls, victims of the pit, glaring at her accusingly of trespassing on their remains, invading their solitude and disturbing their peace.

Anxiously she looked upward and away, to avoid them; up into the huge dome ceiling. The mix of darkness, fear and fatigue gave her vertigo. In her mind everything started moving. The cavern walls rotated, first slowly, then faster and faster. Kelly lost her balance, tripping and stumbling backwards over the bones. Her foot kicked out wildly to regain control. It slammed into the satchel, sending it skidding across the dirt and rock floor. It stopped, teetering half way over the edge of an even deeper chasm.

"The bag!" Jack shouted as he watched it rocking precariously on the edge. They both held their breath as it wavered painfully beyond their reach. With their eyes fixed on it, neither wanted to move, afraid that the slightest vibration might send it over. A pebble beneath it fell away, and it teetered downward. Jack and Kelly both lunged, but as if in a slow motion dream, they helplessly watched as it tipped up and then dropped, falling away from their grasp and disappearing into the dark abyss below. With it sank their hopes.

A long moment passed before they heard the muffled sound of the leather bag splashing into water below. Jack picked up his improvised torch and revived it. It had almost gone out in the scramble. He held it out over the edge where the satchel had disappeared. It was a cliff straight down. The bottom was beyond the light.

"I guess we better not count on that flashlight," he said, then he turned to the pile of bones Kelly had gathered. There were ragged bits of clothes, rope, and hair as well as pieces of wood and broken clay vessels in the heap. He shoved his torch, a human femur with the burning rag wrapped around it, into the pile.

The mix quickly caught fire and lit the cavernous grotto in an eerie glow.

The chamber, Jack and Kelly could see, was enormous, its ceiling arching eighty feet above their heads. They were stranded at the center, prisoners on a huge rock, an island of limestone ninety feet across. It was a gigantic stalagmite, built up by minerals and debris that had dripped in with the water over eons. It jutted up like a pedestal surrounded by a bottomless pit and had tooth like projections on its perimeter. The cavern's walls were seventy-five feet beyond, out of their reach on all sides.

Judging from the number of skeletons littering the place, it had made an effective prison for some time. Jack and Kelly walked the perimeter of the rock inspecting the sides. All were sheer and smooth with no place to descend. Across the chasm it was no better, for even if they did get across there was nowhere to go. Returning to the center Jack looked at Kelly, "We're stuck."

Kelly's face turned pale. "Oh my God!" The firelight had illuminated the latest addition to the pit and its newest casualty. "It's Professor Jenkins." She squirmed at the sight of his decaying corpse slumped against a rock; his pocket watch still clutched in his hand. She had to turn away.

"We don't want to end up that way," Jack said matter-of-factly. "I'm gonna take another look." He walked the perimeter again, examining the gap that separated them from the cavern walls, hoping there was something he had missed the first time. He searched for ideas, but had none, then returned to the fire where Kelly had collected more bones. The flames of the fire danced erratically. They were creating a draft. "Do you feel that?" he said. "The air is moving."

Kelly took a breath. "It's not as musty in here," she agreed.

Jack looked up. "It's as if we were in a big chimney. The smoke keeps rising up and disappearing. It must be going out of the top."

"So?" Kelly questioned trying to see where he was going with this.

"So—the new air replacing it has to be coming from some-where—somewhere down here."

Kelly scanned across the rift at the cavern wall. "What's that over there?" She pointed to a dark hole on the other side of the moat. Jack raised his torch over the abyss to get a better look. He grabbed a burning bone from the fire and pitched it across the void into the hole. It landed inside, somewhere beyond the cave wall. Its flame flickered back and forth as the airflow caused it to burn faster. "That's it! That's our way out!" he exclaimed hope-fully.

"That? And what about this?" Kelly said, sweeping her hand before the expanse that spanned the distance between their dis-covery and the place where they stood trapped.

"That? That's just a detail." He looked down, then back over at Kelly. She was frowning. "Okay, it's a big detail. But that air has to be coming from somewhere, and if we find a way across, then there's also a chance we'll find our way out." Jack could see Kelly didn't share his optimism. "It's better than staying here," he added, looking at their dark surroundings. "Staying here didn't do much for these guys." He pointed at the bones.

Kelly could not argue that point. She scanned the litter of skel-etons, her eyes stopped on Jenkins. "Poor Professor. It must have been horrible for him." Then her tone became sincerely inter-ested. "So, how do we get there?"

Jack looked around thoughtfully. The ropes that the soldiers used to lower them into the grotto caught his attention. There were other ropes as well, in different stages of decay. They had been used for the countless other victims. He picked two up. "We'll start with these..." He tied them together. "And we'll make a bridge—of sorts." At its end he fastened a large femur and a rock for weight. "Pretty crude for a grappling hook, but I don't think we can be too choosy here," he said, testing the knots.

Climbing onto a rock by the edge, he looked across at his target. Between him and the passage was dark emptiness. He took a deep breath and began swinging the contraption like a cowboy preparing to lasso a bull. Then he released his hold on the rope and the heavy end sailed across the void, clunking loudly on the rock wall beyond and falling away.

"That wasn't even close," Kelly commented dryly. "I thought you were from Texas, where the men are all supposed to be cowboys."

"I'm a farmer, all right? Not a cowboy," he said testily. "Or, at least that's what everybody wanted me to be." His tone was short and there was a frustration that went beyond his missed throw. Kelly watched him for a moment while he prepared his next try. What did he mean by that? For the first time she wondered who he really was, and why he wasn't back in the States serving in the military? Well, now wasn't the time to ask. She refocused on the fire, keeping it burning while Jack kept trying his luck.

Jack's aim improved with each attempt. Several times the anchor actually disappeared into the passage beyond. On those tries their hearts jumped as they felt a glimmer of hope. Each time Jack gently dragged the contraption back out, hoping it would catch in a crack, or on a rock. Twice it actually did snag for an instant, but both times their hopes were dashed as the anchor broke free from its hold, reappearing at the entrance, then falling away into the chasm, where it swung back and crashed into the wall below them.

Finally, Jack threw a ringer. It went far deeper into the cave than any of his previous attempts, and this time it locked firmly onto something. Jack tugged at the rope. It seemed lodged. They looked at each other hopefully. He pulled harder. It still would not budge. Without a word they both pulled, knowing their lives depended on whatever it was that the rope had locked onto. It still held.

"Now what?" Kelly asked.

"We'll tie a second rope here," he said, pointing to the protruding rock he was standing on. He climbed off it. "Then I'll tie both ropes to my waist and climb down our side on this one." Kelly listened intently. "When I've gone down about forty feet on our side, about half the distance across, and the other rope has pulled tight, I'll start pulling myself to the other side. You'll need to start feeding out some slack on this rope so I can pull myself freely. In theory, I should move across the pit—like a spider in a web—until I'm against the wall over there." Jack pointed to the other side.

Kelly looked skeptical and visibly upset. "Like a spider! I think you've spent too much time in that barn of yours with nothing better to do." Jack had not expected such a reaction. He had had a hard enough time convincing himself it was possible. "I don't want to be stuck here by myself!" she admitted.

Jack could hear the fear in her voice. She did not have a better plan, so he continued, "Once I'm there, I'll pull myself up to the entrance."

"That won't be easy. Not in your condition."

"This sling will help," he said. He held up a loop of rope he had tied, and then threaded it through his belt. "I'll fasten it on over there. It's a step that I can slide up the rope, allowing me to shift my weight from my hands to my feet over and over. I'll work my way up slowly until I reach the top."

"What if the anchor gives way?"

"The other rope will catch me, swinging me back over to this side."

"You'll crash into the wall!"

"It beats falling." He looked into the abyss and added, "Into that."

"Use this one." Kelly said, untying the rope around her waist that was in better condition. In the firelight, he watched her dirt-smudged face as she worked to connect it to his waist. Absorbed in her knot, she didn't notice him gazing. How could she go through all this and still look so good? He thought. She was beautiful. "There," she announced, tugging on the rope and looking up. Her eyes caught his for a look that lasted an instant longer than necessary. Jack suddenly became uncomfortable, mindful of his staring.

Just then the fire collapsed and most of the light vanished within the chamber, rescuing Jack from the moment. He took two steps over to it and threw in the last of the bones and debris Kelly had gathered.

"Not much left to burn," she said.

"Yeah, it's now or never."

He stepped over to Jenkins body and tore away his shirt, then proceeded to shred it. Kelly looked on aghast. "We need these... to feed our torches," he explained, noticing her expression. He added the rags to a stash he had collected from other victims, then stuffed them along with another torch into his shirt.

With the two ropes hanging from his waist, one attached to the rock beside him, the other tied to an unknown anchor on the far side, he stepped up to the edge, turned around and lowered himself into position. At a loss for better words he looked up at Kelly and said, "Hope this works."

"Me too," she replied, holding a torch out so that he could see.

Then he descended into the darkness.

Kelly cautiously peered over the edge. Jack was gone. Only the tension stretched rope was visible. It moved erratically sideways, its end disappearing into oblivion. Suddenly she was afraid. Afraid of being left alone in this pit if something happened to him, but also afraid for him.

Jack reported his progress inch by inch as he descended. His voice was all she had left for reassurance. She kept her eyes pointed downward, hoping to get a glimpse of him to know he was all right, but it was too dark for her to see anything.

After a short time Jack looked up. He could see the dim flicker of her torch forty feet above. "I'm at the end!" he called out.

She could hear him breathing hard. "What do you want me to do?"

"I don't know yet." He grabbed his other rope, the one leading to the cave opening across the way, and he pulled out the slack. Then he tried to pull himself across the gap. It was impossible. He was too tired, too beaten and too bruised. "Untie the rope."

"Untie it!"

"Yeah, but don't let go, just feed out some slack." He paused. "So I can pull myself sideways across."

"Okay," she said uncertainly. The rope was already wrapped around the rock for leverage. Kelly grabbed the loose end and pulled on the slipknot. The knot popped undone with a jolt, and the rope jerked tight. Below Jack shut his eyes tightly, preparing for the worst—crashing back into the wall or even worse, down into the pit. "Hey!" he hollered as his body dropped a few inches.

Kelly gripped the rope tight so it would slide no farther. "Sorry." Then she noticed that his full weight was no longer on that rope alone. "Is that better?"

"That's good."

She felt jolting movements on the rope as it angled further and further out across the chasm toward the other side.

"I'm almost to the wall," He said.

The light of Kelly's torch dimly lit the opposite side. It was a sheer cliff. "I can see you!" Kelly yelled out enthusiastically. Jack was suspended like a spider between the two ropes. He continued moving at a painstakingly slow pace. When he reached the other side he attached his sling. Then carefully he worked his way up it, inches at a time, until finally his head broke over the edge of the passage. A gentle breeze flowing from the opening cooled his perspiring face. "I'm here!" he shouted, pulling himself over the edge.

On the other side, Kelly breathed a sigh of relief. Jack lit a new torch and untied his safety line. He inspected his anchor bone wedged in the rock and was unable to figure out what had held it in place. But he was relieved that he did not know it while his life hung in the balance over the chasm. He attached the rope to a better anchor, then looked into the passage.

"What are you doing?" Kelly asked.

"I'll be back in a moment."

"Jack, wait! Don't leave me here!" she called, but he was gone in a flash.

For a moment she could see the flicker of his torch, but that too disappeared. She felt alone, alone in the room full of corpses. She fed the fire to keep her mind off her fear.

•

A few minutes passed and the fire burned lower. When this fuel was gone there'd be nothing left to burn. Finally, Kelly heard a voice coming back from the passage. "You still here?"

"What do you think?" she said, relieved to have him back. "That wasn't very funny leaving me like that."

"I wanted to explore this thing, make sure it wasn't a dead end before you crossed."

"What did you see?"

"The cave seems to go on forever," he said. "And with this breeze coming through, there's got to be a way out. I'm sure of it. Measure out sixty feet of rope and tie it to yourself well. Go around your thigh and shoulder to make a harness."

"Okay," she answered getting right to work.

"Now tie the other side to the anchor rock."

"Okay," she replied, still trusting his judgment. She had placed her life in his hands more times than she liked to think about in the last twenty-four hours, and he had pulled them through the scrapes each time. Was it just luck she wondered.

"Now tie the rope from this side into the harness around you and pull out all the slack."

"Check." She looked across the void, and could see him in the torchlight. "Now what?" she asked, standing harnessed to the two ropes.

"Jump," he said.

"JUMP?" she shouted back, horrified.

"Yeah, jump. It's the easiest way."

"I'm *not* jumping. Don't you have any better ideas?" she exclaimed.

"The ropes are strong. And they'll work against each other. You'll slow down in an arc, over on my side. Then together we'll pull you up."

"But I'll be stuck, dangling in the middle!"

"Beats hitting the wall."

Grudgingly she looked back across at him. "Jump, huh?" she said, wanting further reassurance. "Didn't we just do something like this yesterday?"

"Yeah, and look, it turned out fine."

"You call this fine?"

"Just close your eyes and step off."

Kelly moved her toes to the edge. It was total blackness below. Her heart was pounding. "Just step off?" she asked, stalling.

"Yeah, step off!"

Psyched up to do it, she closed her eyes. She swayed forward, then held herself back. She tried again, drawing a deep breath. This time she leapt off. Her screams followed her loudly as she plunged into the darkness. The rope at Jack's feet snapped tight and jerked her into suspension. He looked down at her gyrating body. She was recoiling in the blackness. The echoes of her screams continued below, then they dwindled as she realized she was no longer falling. For a moment she just hung there swinging back and forth. She took a huge breath. "Get me out of here!"

Working together, she climbed while he pulled. Finally, she reached the top, emotionally drained.

"That wasn't so bad, was it?" Jack said with a smile. Kelly shot him a "How dare you" glare, and then without a word she stormed past him into the passage.

CHAPTER TWENTY-SIX

They wandered through a labyrinth of passages and cavernous chambers, occasionally climbing or descending, but always moving toward the source of the flowing air. As they entered yet another chamber, Jack's torch was petering out. He pointed to some rocks high enough to sit on. "Let's take a rest." As they sat, the torch expired, leaving them only a red glowing ember that quickly shrank away. A moment passed in darkness.

"Are you going to light another torch?" Kelly asked.

"In a few minutes. Let's just rest in the dark for now and conserve our last few rags," Jack said, feeling the dwindling stash in his shirt.

In the darkness everything seemed louder. Jack's breath was deep and heavy. So was Kelly's. As they rested, their breathing became shallower and quiet until eventually the two were sitting in complete silence. The rest felt good. Jack could sense the closeness of Kelly's body. There was comfort in not being alone.

Kelly perked up suddenly. "What's that?"

"What's what?"

"That noise." She paused, and they both listened.

Jack shifted. In the silence even the movement of his clothes seemed loud.

"There it is again, you hear it?" she said. "It sounds like dripping water, a stream, or something like that."

Jack listened harder. This time he did hear a noise. "It sounds like a squeaky wheel turning to me."

"No. That wasn't it," she said, having heard the same new noise. "That's something different. I heard water dripping before. I'm sure of it. Listen."

Both of them were tired and hungry, but dehydration was their worst problem. The thought of a drink of cool water was almost overpowering. They listened closely again. "I hear it!" he whispered, "I do hear it! I can barely talk. The inside of my mouth is parched!" he exclaimed, raising his voice with anticipation.

"So is mine," she concurred.

Jack fastened another rag to his torch and took out a match to light it. Kelly wondered aloud, "What do you think the other noise was?"

"I don't know." The flare of his igniting match burned brightly for an instant.

In the flash Kelly got a glimpse of something so odd she thought she had imagined it. It was a wave of motion traveling across the ceiling and down onto the walls. "What was that?" she asked anxiously.

"What?" Jack said, focused on getting the torch lit.

"The walls, they moved. I swear I saw them moving like Jell-O."

Jack looked around as his eyes adjusted. The flash was gone and only the small flame of the matchstick against the rag was giving light. He saw nothing. "You're tired." He paused. "We both are. Let's find that water."

The fresh rag burned bright, lighting the chamber much more than the previous dwindling rag had. The illuminated cavern took on three dimensions. And Kelly was right. The walls were moving. Patches of the ceiling vibrated with increasing intensity, and the squeaking wheel sound returned, but this time much louder. The whole cave became more and more agitated until parts began breaking away; the falling pieces hurling themselves erratically at the firelight of the torch, then the room came to life.

"Bats!" Jack shouted in the same instant that the entire ceiling collapsed. His voice disappeared, drowning in a sea of deafening squeaks and fluttering wings.

Thousands of the little mammals took flight, and by the hundreds bounced into each other and into Jack and Kelly. Jack waved his torch to fend them off, but that only increased the frenzy. It was pandemonium. Fluttering wings hit them in the face and hairy bodies bounced into them from all sides. Both Jack and Kelly screamed, wiggled and jumped hysterically as the flying creatures attached themselves to their clothes. Several bats caught in Kelly's hair; others used their sharp claws to cling to their skin.

The ground around them was littered with injured bodies, and Jack and Kelly felt them under their feet as they fled for safety. It was hard to figure out who was more scared, the bats or Jack and Kelly. The chaos lasted several minutes, but seemed much longer. Finally, the bulk of the creatures made their way out through a passage at the other end of the chamber.

The two stood shell-shocked. It took Jack another minute to regain his composure. "Let's follow them. They must have an exit they use when they go out to feed at night."

To her own amazement Kelly agreed, wondering what would happen next. They followed a few of the stragglers making their escape, and as they did they came across the stream they had heard earlier. It was every bit as good as Jack had imagined, quenching his thirst and rejuvenating his spirit. He had to force himself to come up for air. Kelly was enjoying the moment too, dipping her hair after she had drunk her fill. "It feels so good," she said with more satisfaction than yesterday's wish of a hot bath would have brought. The long day had lowered her expectations.

After they'd had their fill they followed the flowing water down the passage. Some stretches were so constricted they had to crawl on hands and knees to get through. Others were giant cavernous rooms with columns of stalagmites and stalactites they had to climb around. But there always were at least a few of the fluttering bats moving with purpose toward what Jack and Kelly hoped would be their exit.

Finally, the flowing water led them into the biggest chamber either had seen yet. In its high ceiling there was a confluence of holes. They were small and barely visible in the torchlight, but the obvious target of the fleeing mammals. One by one, the last of the stragglers disappeared through the openings and beyond, leaving Jack and Kelly stranded out of reach on the cave floor.

"How are we going to get up there?" Kelly asked disheartened. "And even if we do, those holes are tiny."

Jack too, was at a loss. It seemed an impossible feat. "Doesn't look good," he replied surveying the chamber's near vertical walls and high ceiling. He could tell that the draft inside was flowing from there as well, coming from the free and open world.

"We're so close," Kelly said quietly. Dejected, she sat on a rock and watched Jack contemplate their predicament. For a while she stared along the continuing passage and then an object caught her eye. She did a double take. There was something there, on the ground, at the edge of the darkness. "Look! Over there!" she exclaimed, "It looks manmade. It's metal, like a rail or something."

Jack moved forward with the torch in his hand. They studied the object for a second. It was rusted and incomplete, but there was no doubt—it was manmade. "It's a rail!" Jack said with renewed excitement. "We must be in a mine!"

It was their first sign of real hope. Kelly's attitude quickly transformed. She was suddenly filled with energy and allowed herself to believe that they truly might get out alive. They both started down the tunnel; their eyes fixed on the track that led into the darkness. The stream of water flowed between the rails.

"I bet this stream flows right out of the mine's entrance," Jack said optimistically. Their pace increased as their minds considered the possibility.

In some places the rusty remnants of the track disappeared, but the tunneled shape of the passage was now unmistakably a mine. Its walls were squarely carved and bore the telltale signs of drilling holes and pick-axes. They passed beneath a number of wooden support beams bowed down with rot. Around each bend they anticipated the glimmer of daylight, and the sweet smell of fresh air. Every step raised their spirits higher and higher, so much so that they hardly noticed they were sloshing through water which was halfway to their knees. Finally, Kelly said, "It's getting deeper."

The water continued to increase in depth and the ceiling came down lower. At last, the water was chest deep and Jack had to bend his neck to avoid bumping his head into the ceiling. Ahead they both stared at the occluded passage. "No," Jack agonized with distress.

For a moment neither spoke. Then finally Kelly said it. "It's a dead-end, isn't it?"

Another moment passed before Jack answered. "Looks like it." With despair he raised his hand, then slapped the water. Backhanding the ceiling and cutting himself as he did so. "Damn! Ouch!" he said as if one word. "It must have flooded." His voice was pure anguish.

With their hopes crushed, the cold water they were standing in became a stark reality. Kelly's teeth chattered uncontrollably. "Maybe we should go back and get out of this water." She said despondently. "We can't stay here."

She was right but Jack couldn't bring himself to accept that resignation yet. He searched for ideas. He noticed there was a current pulling him farther in. The water had to be making its way out somewhere. But how far was it to the exit? "Just a second." He tied the rope he had been carrying around his waist. "Hold this tight," he said, handing her the end. "And this," he added, giving her the torch.

"What are you doing? Where are you going?"

"I'm not sure," he answered as he waded further into the water. "Out, I hope."

Kelly watched as he surveyed the water below his chin. It was crystal clear. The mine seemed to continue beyond under the water. "Hold the light higher." He took another step, having to cock his head sideways between the water and the ceiling. "I'll be right back. Don't let go of the rope."

"Hey! You're not going anywhere without…" But before she could finish he had taken a big breath and disappeared, leaving her alone with the torch and the rope in her hand. She followed his submerged body as it moved off in the direction of the current. Quickly his form faded in the underwater darkness. The rope followed him dangling and pulling; it was his tether back if necessary.

For a minute it continued to feed out, occasionally stopping. Then it stayed still for a while. Kelly looked at the remaining rope. It was almost at its end. Jack had been gone for much longer than a person could hold his breath, Kelly thought. Something was wrong. She started to worry. Then there was more tugging on the rope, this time harder. She held it tight as Jack used it to pull himself back along its length. He shot out of the watery mine entrance, bubbles streaming from his mouth. His head burst through the surface and immediately he inhaled a much-needed breath of air.

"There is light! At the other end!" he exclaimed jubilantly, taking another breath big enough to get the words out. "I didn't get all the way to it, but I could see it through the water. I think it's the way out. We're gonna make it!"

"But I can't hold my breath that long!"

Jack rested a moment, still breathing heavily and then continued in a lower tone. "Don't worry. There are a couple of air pockets where you can catch a breath." He handed her the end of the rope. "The worst part is the darkness. You have to use your hands to feel the way." Kelly looked frightened. "You can do it," he told her reassuringly. "I'll go first, and when I get to the other end, if everything is okay, I'll tug the rope hard three times." He mimicked the tugging motion as he spoke. "Then all you have to do is take a big breath and pull yourself hand over hand along the rope until you reach me."

Kelly didn't look convinced, but before she could think of a way to stall him, Jack had moved back, close to the flooded tunnel opening. "I'll see you on the other side."

"No, wait!" Kelly said, but Jack had already disappeared below the surface. Her eyes stayed fixed on the passage and the rope wiggling in the water below. She held her end so tight in the one hand that she forgot about the other. The torch she held in it bumped into the ceiling, and the burning rag fell off into the water, extinguishing the flame. Kelly let out a gasping cry of panic. Her heart raced, and her breathing became fast and shallow. She could hear each breath echo down the mine tunnel, bouncing off the walls as it disappeared into the darkness. Around her everything was black.

Then the panic got worse. She realized the rope was no longer in her hand. She had let it go. Spontaneously she dove into the water and waved her hands frantically to find it. She could not let it get away. She fought to keep her wits; she couldn't allow panic to take over. The moment seemed to last forever. Finally she felt something hovering in the water beside her. She snapped at it quickly. It was the rope. Her fingers locked around it with a death grip that jarred Jack to a halt.

On the other end Jack was pulling toward an air pocket. The jolting stop caused him to fall just inches short of his breathing place. He was shocked when water instead of air rushed into his lungs. He coughed it out violently, and then lunged a second time for the air. This time he reached it, and coughed out the rest of the water before he could take a breath. What was that about? he wondered. Was Kelly in some kind of trouble? He waited a few more seconds, catching his breath. There were no more tugs. He decided to continue farther.

Kelly felt the rope start moving again, and allowed it to feed through her trembling hands. She kept a cautious grip as it moved, but was shaken by her carelessness. Her only connection to the outside world was by Braille. She had no other sensory perception. "That was close," she said, trying to talk herself into settling down. "But how much rope could be left?" She moved herself closer to the entrance. "Stay ready for the end, girl," she said to herself. "It's gotta be coming soon."

Her head was bumping the ceiling; her chin was touching the water. Was the cave longer than the rope? she wondered. At the very moment of that thought, the end slipped suddenly again through her fingers. Her heart sank as she felt her connection severed. Without a thought she took a huge breath and dove toward the entrance. Her hands frantically waved through the black water, again hoping to feel the end dangling before her. First once, then twice, but this time there was no rope. She tried again down lower, and then swam further into the flooded tunnel; still there was no rope. She was getting panicky when the rope finally brushed her hand. She grabbed it hard with both hands, and then started pulling hand over hand with all her might.

Thirty seconds of pulling passed, as she bumped and scraped into the rock walls. She detected the faint shine of silvery air pockets trapped on the ceiling above. But she was too frightened to stop. The fact that she could see anything at all meant there had to be some light. And with that was the promise there would be even more up ahead. She just kept pulling. Her air supply was running short, but the light at the other end was getting brighter. She couldn't stop now, and there was no way back. She just kept pulling, swimming as fast as she could to reach the light, and the air that she hoped would be there.

Finally her head broke the surface. She gasped a huge breath of air into her oxygen-starved lungs and saw Jack's silhouette in the light. But she could not get enough air to speak. She heaved a second big breath. Her lungs expanded the wet clothes that stuck tightly to her torso.

"Good girl! I knew you could do it. What was that pulling all about? You were supposed to wait for my signal."

"You were supposed to give me a longer rope," she scolded in a raised voice, her tone mixed with anger and fear.

"Are you okay?" he asked.

Kelly took another breath and looked at him with narrow eyes. "Part of me wants to kill you." Jack was taken aback by her reaction. Then she looked toward the entrance, overwhelmed by a sense of freedom. "But another part of me wants to hug you."

Jack grinned. "That part sounds better." He let her draw a few more breaths. "Not bad for a farmer, huh?"

Kelly moved closer to the mine entrance to look out over the sunlit mountains. She took another big breath. The sky was the most beautiful color of blue that she could imagine. She moved into the sunlight. It was streaming through the opening, pouring its warmth directly upon her skin. "That feels so good," she said with deep satisfaction.

The rays shone through the transparency of her wet blouse, revealing almost every detail of her firm shape. Jack could not take his eyes off her, and he could not help but think how good she looked.

CHAPTER TWENTY-SEVEN

The abandoned mine was nothing more than a perforation high on a massive and steeply descending rock slope. To the dismay of the miners who dug it, it had only served as a short cut for trapped underground water, and had converted their hard work into just another mountain spring.

The cramped entrance was knee-deep in water, which flowed into a deeper though small pool just outside. The standing water sat on the discarded tailings that had been pushed over the edge just beyond the opening. Its piled debris hung precariously, suspended above the steep slope like a balcony looking down on the valley.

Kelly waded out into the warmth of the sun's rays. She raised her arms over her head as she took in the majestic view. "You've got to see this, Jack!" she exclaimed, relishing her freedom. "It's beautiful."

Jack was behind her, his eyes still fixed on her wet revealing blouse. He was in agreement with the description of beautiful. He shielded his eyes from the brightness and pushed his way across to the outer edge of the pool; it was only eight feet across. He was exhausted. The mound holding the water back was just loosely piled gravel. It was thin and small, but it looked strong enough, so Jack pulled himself out of the water and plopped on his back to rest. He let out a sigh, and then lay still, basking in the sun. His eyes were open just enough to gaze up at the wide-open blue sky. It was good to be out. He did not notice the wall beneath him bow under his weight or the downward shift of the mound itself. Kelly moved next to him and straddled the mound. "Happy now?"

Jack turned onto his side, his head lying close to the water. "I am, but I'm too beat to show it." He looked at the water passing over the top of the gravel dam at his eye level and followed it past the edge. The drop off on the other side was steep, and the cascading stream quickly picked up speed as it careened down the mountainside. The water had created a slick trough cutting smoothly through the rock, first going one way, then turning abruptly another. It followed the descending contour of the slope perfectly. Lined with algae, which thrived in the sunlight, its surface was slick and frictionless, making a natural shoot for the falling water to blast down at high speed.

The dam shifted down a few more inches. Neither Jack nor Kelly noticed. Kelly leaned back on the crest of the mound and closed her eyes. A long while passed before either spoke. Finally Jack broke the silence. "What a day!" he sighed.

Kelly's eyes wandered and her gaze took her down the treeless slope, following the jet of water shooting through the low-lying bushes. Then something caught her attention. Her eyes grew wide. Jack was pulling himself up, but Kelly grabbed him by the shirt and yanked down hard. His tired body was unexpectedly pulled off balance and slammed down on the earthy dam. The thud jarred the mound, and a crack formed at the base where it rested on the rocky slope. Jack rolled into the water. "Hey! What's that about?" he said with astonishment.

Kelly recoiled into the water beside him and put her finger to her lips. "Shhh." She pointed over the tailings, indicating there was someone beyond. "Did you see them?" Water started to seep from the fault in the gravel below them, but neither was focused on the dam.

"See who?" he said.

"Quietly!" she scolded.

Crouched in the water, they edged back onto the gravel rim, Kelly insisting on caution. They peered over the edge, and she pointed down to where the shoot cascaded into a river a quarter mile away. "Them!" Suddenly the water felt colder.

It was the Germans. They were stopped by the stream, some eating, others cooling off and filling their canteens in the fast moving shoot. "Do you think it's Bodecker?" Kelly asked.

"Who else? There can't be that many of us out here," Jack replied. "I guess we didn't come so far after all."

"Look! That big guy," she said, pointing to a soldier heading for the stream with his canteen in hand. "He's got the pack. The one with the statue!"

"So?"

"So... What do you think we should do?" she said.

"Wait for them to go away."

"But what about the statue?"

Jack looked at her with disbelief. "The hell with the statue!" he said curtly. "That damn thing has almost got us killed twice already."

"But we need it. That's why we are here."

"We?" he snapped, "We? I'm only your pilot, remember? Nothing more." He paused a half second. "In fact, I'm not even that, because thanks to you I don't have a plane anymore." She looked at him with frustration. "Besides, do you see how many of them there are?" She kept on looking. "You don't get it, do you?" he continued, "They have guns, we don't. There must be twenty-five of them. There are only two of us. They are soldiers; they kill people for a living." Kelly didn't answer. "And what's with that damn statue anyway? Why are you and everybody else so interested in it when there is a war on?"

"Because..." She paused, then continued, "Because the legend says the possessor of the statue will know the future." She knew that sounded stupid.

"The legend!" He raised his voice.

"Shhh... Yes... It's a window...into the future."

Jack was incredulous. "What...like a time machine?"

"Yes."

"You expect me to believe...to risk my life for a legend!"

"Never mind," she said with disgust. "I shouldn't have expected more from a farm boy."

"I may be just a farm boy, but I'm not a fool."

Kelly knew Jack was right. He owed her nothing. If anything, she owed him. After all she had put him through; he had every reason to turn her down. "You're right," she said pensively, "I shouldn't be asking such things from you. This is my fight. I'll do it myself."

"Do what? How?"

"I don't know yet...but I can't just sit here."

"Look at the odds..." he said, but Kelly held up her hand.

"I don't want to hear it. It's my job. My country is depending on me." She said nothing for a while, turning her focus to other options, considering how she could go it alone.

Jack's emotions churned. Was it all that they had gone through in the last forty-eight hours, he wondered? Had they shared a closeness, or was he fooling himself? He shook himself suddenly. What was he thinking? Kelly had just lost her husband, witnessing him violently gunned down. The last thing she would be thinking about was the fleeting second of closeness that they had shared in that moment of fear. Still, he could not get her off his mind, and he didn't want to alienate her. But he didn't want to die for that stupid statue either. He hated the silence. Brushes with the opposite sex never went well for him. "So you and your husband—boyfriend—whatever he was, came all the way here for that st..."

"He wasn't my husband, and he wasn't my boyfriend!" Kelly snapped. "In fact, I couldn't stand the pompous..." She stopped, remembering his fate. "Look, just forget I asked you for any help at all. Okay?"

"He wasn't your husband?"

"No!"

Jack looked dumbfounded. "Let me get this straight. We risked our lives, and Thornton died—because of a legend! Don't you see a problem here?" he whispered loudly.

"If the legend is true, it could change the war. The Germans think enough of it to send soldiers and airplanes to destroy a people just to lay their hands on it. We can't afford to laugh it off." Kelly paused and looked at Jack. "Don't you think I know how silly it sounds?"

"That's what this is all about? Everybody wants to see the outcome of the war?"

"Exactly," she said as if it should have been obvious from the beginning. "If the war went against you, and you could learn how to change history and win, wouldn't you want to do it?"

Jack didn't answer.

"So it's become a race between us and the Germans to get possession."

"Well, that's great, and I'm a patriot and everything," he said, "but..."

"Are you?" she interrupted. "If you are, what the hell are you doing hiding in the jungle when your country is at war?" She turned to glare at him.

Her words cut deep. "If you only knew," he said, shaking his head.

Kelly could tell she had struck a chord that hurt. She sensed she had been unfair in her questioning. He had put his life on the line more than once to save her. He was correct, she did not truly know him, and she owed him only gratitude, not callous comments. But there was no time for this! She reconsidered the reality of the situation and concluded Jack's assessment was accurate. They were heavily outnumbered and outgunned. They didn't stand a chance of getting the statue. "Okay, you're right. When they're gone we'll go for help," she conceded.

"Good, now you're thinking," Jack said, shifting his weight one more time on the dam. The leaking water had significantly destabilized its support, and finally the loose dirt collapsed. Jack and Kelly suddenly dropped along with several tons of dirt and water into the narrow shoot. Instantly they accelerated in the rushing water, pushed faster and faster by the water-gravel mix which was barreling down behind them at full speed. Jack tried to grab an overhanging bush, but they were moving too fast. He tried to dig his heels in to slow down, but the surface was too slippery. The edges were just as bad, with no place to grab hold.

Another branch came up. This time he grabbed it. It slowed him down quickly as he stretched it to its limit. Just as he had stopped, Kelly crashed into him from behind. Together they continued their uncontrolled descent like riders on a luge in an Olympic bobsled competition. The watercourse rocketed them through tight-banked turns, and their speed threw them high against the smooth walls. Then they plunged down again in a different direction. Back and forth they went down the natural slide. With each twist and turn their bodies slammed jarringly against the sides, and the jolts impeded their ability to get another hold. A small drop off sent them flying in the air, first Jack, then Kelly, only to come crashing back down into the slot of speeding water.

They were approaching the end. Ahead Jack could see the soldiers, unaware of their uncontrolled descent. Within seconds they were upon them. Jack flew by the big soldier as he was filling his canteen. Instinctively, he reached out wanting to slow himself down, but all he did was hook the soldier's pack. The big man never saw him coming. Dumbfounded, on his haunches, he looked downstream at Jack and the pack speeding away and tried to understand what had just transpired.

Seconds behind came Kelly, screaming as she went. The big man turned toward the oncoming commotion upstream just in time to get clobbered by her foot that she had managed to extend at the level of his jaw. He fell backward, but her momentum continued unimpeded.

The jet of water ended its run in a single forty-foot cascade that plummeted into the white water of a large river below, a headwater of the larger Rio Magdalena. Jack looked ahead but saw only open oblivion. In an instant the world dropped out from below him. He sailed off the edge beyond the falling water. His arms and legs flailing as he fell, he plunged and disappeared into the swirling torrent below. Kelly came along immediately after, her long unbroken screams following her all the way down into the boiling water.

It had all happened so fast. Bodecker saw it unfolding and drew his pistol, but the two had disappeared over the edge before he could get off a shot. He rushed to the edge, barking orders. The men followed him frantically, then spread out along the cliff, scanning the white water.

The big man arrived last, rubbing his sore jaw. His lip was bleeding. He stood near Bodecker who was examining the bubbling water. The rapids moved swiftly and unabated, guided through the unforgiving terrain by sheer walls that bordered both sides of the river canyon. There was no sign of Jack or Kelly. They'd appeared like phantoms and disappeared just as completely.

The soldiers kept searching as the minutes passed. With no visible place for the fugitives to get out, Bodecker called them off. The speeding current had, by now, swept their bodies far beyond where they had fallen, and well out of sight. He glared at the big man next to him. There was rage in his eyes. "You are an idiot!" he hollered, "You let them escape with the statue. Follow them and get the statue back!"

The man looked puzzled, uncertain of what he meant. But before he could react, Bodecker grabbed him by the collar and flung him over the edge. The man tumbled like a rag doll through the air and was instantly enveloped by the boiling rapids. He never came up.

Knowing the man would be lost, Bodecker turned to the others, flushed with anger. "We must find them," he spat. The veins in his neck protruded like ropes under his skin. "I don't care how long it takes, or how many must die, we will find them and get the statue back."

"They could not have survived the fall, Sir," a sergeant speculated nervously, attempting to speak for his men.

Bodecker turned and approached within six inches of the sergeant's face. "Then we will search the banks below for their bodies. All day and night if we have to, and I will hold YOU personally responsible if we do not find them! Do I make myself clear?"

"Yes, Standartenfuhrer!" the intimidated sergeant said.

•

The water raged wildly for miles down the canyon. Trapped in currents of different speeds, Jack and Kelly were separated. A mile down the canyon several large branches were stuck in the middle of the river, wedged against a submerged rock. Jack, far ahead of Kelly, reached out and snagged one of the limbs. He held it tight, then pulled himself up out of the current. Coughing out a mouthful of water, he gasped and struggled until finally he was able to heave in a lungful of air. For the first time since the perch had collapsed at the mine's entrance, he had a chance to catch his breath.

Still far from safe and trapped inside the canyon in the middle of the raging river, he checked his surroundings. The cliff rose on both sides directly from the river. There was no place to climb out. He fixed his eyes on the current above, scouting the rapids for any sign of Kelly. He saw nothing but green and white water pouring over giant boulders. He prayed helplessly, hoping she had survived.

Then a cork-like object caught his attention, tumbling and bobbing on the water. It was Kelly. Her arms waved wildly as she headed for Jack's safe haven. Jack tied the backpack onto the largest of the trunks to free himself to help her. The swift water drove her directly into one of the limbs, jarring the amalgamated island of branches. Kelly clung to one branch while reaching for Jack's extended arm. Her added weight destabilized the complex, and the current slowly started rotating the matrix of branches around the rock, back into the faster moving water.

"Ohhh shit! Here we go again," Jack cried.

"What do you mean? I never stopped," she answered, coughing up water.

"Hang on," he yelled as they smashed into a boulder. The whole complex started to break up.

"Get onto this big trunk!" Jack shouted. Kelly quickly jumped from her branch over to his, and they continued the wild ride down through the rest of the canyon, clinging for their lives on the floating log.

An hour later, and miles down river, the Rio Magdalena spit them out of the canyon's mouth into what seemed to be a flat mountain valley. The current continued at a steady, but statelier pace. Fatigued by the trip, but wanting to put distance between them and the Germans, they decided to stay on the drifting log and sleep in the afternoon sun.

Kelly was exhausted from the ordeal and had nothing to say. She thought she had lost the statue. Jack had been too tired to remember the bag tied to the log.

•

As the afternoon grew late their log approached a village. It was a remote place; its outskirts inhabited strictly by Indians who lived on the water in floating huts and connected dugout canoes. Beyond them on the bank were more dwellings, these made of weathered scrap boards with thatched roofs, the paint faded and chipped.

One building had a sign painted on it in Spanish. "*Mercado,*" Kelly read. "That means store in Spanish."

"If they speak Spanish, they must be connected somehow with the outside world," Jack said.

They spotted a clearing on the riverbank between some houseboats and kicked their log toward it. When the water was shallow enough Kelly let go and waded toward the shore. Jack grabbed the backpack and followed. "Maybe it would be better if we stay out of sight," he whispered. But at that very moment a young woman washing clothes spotted them. Her gaze followed them inquisitively as they waded from the river.

"Too late," Kelly said. She turned to the woman, *"Buenas tardes,"* trying to make their sudden appearance look normal and benign. The woman only smiled shyly, never taking her eyes off them. "Try to act normal." Kelly said.

"Normal? That should be easy. This Indian girl probably sees two soaking wet Americans appear out of her river every day." Jack said sarcastically.

"Stop it, okay?" Kelly returned. "We need to just need to stay out of sight. There may be Germans here."

Dripping with water and shivering with cold, they slipped from one dirt street to the next looking for signs of Germans. All they found were speechless stares from the natives. Kelly approached an old woman whose face was deeply wrinkled by a lifetime in the harsh equatorial sun. She was squatting on the sidewalk weaving a basket. Around her were a number of others she had already finished.

"Look at these beautiful baskets," Kelley said suddenly shifting from fugitive to shopper. She smiled at the woman, who was chewing a wad of coca leaves in a toothless mouth. *"Buenas tardes,"* Kelly said. The woman gave her the same blank stare as the young girl, but without the smile.

"Does she understand you?" Jack asked.

"I don't know."

"*Soldados Alemanes—Aquí?*" Kelly said, pointing to the ground. "*En el pueblo?*" she added.

"What'd you say?"

"I asked her if there were any German soldiers in town… I think."

After a pause the old woman perched on the sidewalk shook her head. "*Aqui no hay soldados,*" she said and then went back to her weaving.

"She said, 'no,' " Kelly translated with relief. "*El centro? Donde esta?*"

The woman lifted an arm and pointed down the street, never looking up, eyes fixed on her basket. They followed her direction to the center of town.

CHAPTER TWENTY-EIGHT

Jack and Kelly moved down deeply rutted red clay streets toward the middle of town. There were no sidewalks and the alleyways smelled of raw sewage.

"Not the best of neighborhoods," Kelly said with her hand to her nose.

Suddenly there were two pops, like small caliber gunfire several blocks away. Jack jumped into one of the alleys and tried to pull Kelly in as well. "I'm not going in there!" she said. "It stinks."

"That sounds like gun fire. It could be the Germans."

Kelly pulled him back out in the street. "Do these people look worried?" She motioned to an old couple that saw him duck for cover. They were chuckling at his paranoia. "And those boys there." She pointed at two little boys walking toward them, one with a large lizard on his shoulder. He was chattering to his friend about his pet. "They don't seem very concerned either."

Then there was another string of pops just around the corner. Jack winced. The noise was followed by a group of wild children tearing around the corner laughing, one of them still tossing firecrackers. Kelly smiled. "Don't be such a worry wart!"

"Well, better safe than sorry," Jack said, feeling a little silly. Still he peered around the walls of each corner before proceeding to confirm it was safe. Kelly followed, less concerned. The number of townspeople increased as they got closer to the center of town, and as they rounded another corner they almost ran into five men carrying a live and not too pleased boa constrictor. The preoccupied men didn't notice them, but Jack and Kelly both reeled backwards.

"That's not something you see every day," Kelly said.

Rounding the corner, there was an old Spanish mission, and in front of it, a plaza. It was more a crude open space than a square really, but it was filled with a jostling, noisy crowd. They were actively making preparations of sorts.

"San Ignacio, I assume," Jack said, reading the bold letters on a banner that stretched across the street.

Men were stringing more banners and colorful flags from the roofs of the mission and several other buildings, stretching them into the trees and poles of the square. Women had booths set up to sell wares. And small children chased each other among the adults, playing cheerfully with carefree spirits.

"Not as sleepy looking as it first appeared by the river," Kelly said, noting the decorations and festive mood. "Looks like they're planning quite a party."

"I'll say," Jack agreed. Kelly started out into the crowd. Jack raised his hand to stop her. "Hold on. We better be careful. We don't exactly look like the cousins from out of town."

"Quit being so worried, Jack," Kelly said as she pushed past him. "Haven't you noticed? They've already seen us. They just don't care that much."

"I still don't think it's a good idea," he fretted.

She turned back at him, wearing a frown. "I know these people."

"You know them?" he said with disbelief.

"Well, not these personally, but I know the mountain Indians. By and large they are friendly. So relax."

"Okay, okay, but it doesn't hurt to be safe. Let's just stay on the sidelines."

Dusk was setting into the mountain village, adding a dark backdrop to the festive atmosphere. Kelly moved along with the crowd in the street, while Jack hovered on the fringes watching the townspeople with suspicion. A building opposite the church caught his eye. Suddenly he had a change of heart. He whisked over to her and grabbed her by the arm. "This way," he said, cutting through the crowd.

"Hey, what happened to 'low profile and stay on the sidelines?'" Kelly complained as she followed him.

"Like you said. I need to relax. Besides I have new priorities." He pointed at the building. The word "HOTEL" was written in faded letters over the threshold. It was the only two-story structure in the town. It bordered the square. Out front were two restaurant tables and chairs. "There could be food and a bed in there."

"So, what you're trying to say, but are having difficulty admitting, is that you were wrong?"

"No," he said with a smile, "but you were right."

"Alright, I'll settle for that," Kelly said with a smile. "It's a bit of a cop-out, but you're coming around." Inside, the place was charming and remarkably clean with polished tile floors and fresh paint on the walls.

"We'll stay the night here, and get an early start tomorrow," Jack said.

"What about Bodecker and his men?" Kelly asked.

Jack approached the door. "The only way they could catch up is if they hiked all night over the mountains, and then they'd still have the valley to cross." He pointed toward the distant mountains the two had left behind in their journey. Then he added, "I'd say that's a two day hike at least."

At the counter was a mustached man with features more Spanish than Indian. He was a good six inches taller than the locals, and thirty pounds heavier as well. He studied Jack and Kelly for a moment and then said in broken English, "Welcome to the Altamira. Would you like to stay here for the night?"

"Yes, please," Jack answered.

"You like one room, or two?"

Jack and Kelly looked at each other. "How much money do you have?" Jack asked.

"Money?"

"Everything I had was on the plane, and you know what happened to that," he said.

"Well, everything I had was in my satchel, in the cave." She looked at the backpack slung on his shoulder. "Where did you get the pack?" she asked. She hadn't noticed it until now.

"I took it from one of the soldiers by the river as we slid past."

"Which soldier?"

"I don't know. Everything was happening very fast. I just reacted out of instinct."

"What's in it?"

"Nothing but wadded paper, I think," Jack said coyly. "I figured we can use it to carry food tomorrow."

"Maybe there's some money," Kelly speculated.

"I don't think so, but I'll check again."

The expectant clerk cleared his throat then raised his hands waiting for their answer. "Un momento por favor," Kelly told him.

The two backed away from the counter to look at the contents inside. Jack unbuttoned the flap and pulled a wad of soggy wrapping paper from within. "Is that it?" Kelly asked with disappointment.

"Well, there's this little thing also," he said, pulling the paper back just enough to give Kelly a glimpse of the face of the golden statue. The clerk leaned over the counter with curiosity trying to see what the two Americans were looking at.

When Kelly saw what he had hidden she let out a yelp of excitement. "JACK! You got it!" She hugged him and impulsively gave him a kiss, catching them both off guard. She backed off quickly, but was still elated. "How did you do it?"

"It just happened. One moment I saw it on the riverside, the next moment it was in my hand."

Again the clerk fidgeted, this time with exasperation. "Excuse me Señor; do you want a room—yes or no?"

They reached in their pockets and pulled out change, a handful of small bills and coins, counting it on the counter. "Either one room and dinner, or two separate rooms," Jack whispered quietly to her.

"One room," they said in unison.

"Husband, wife? Yes?" the clerk asked, pointing at one and then the other.

Kelly shook her head. "No, we…" Jack stepped on her foot. "Ouch! What was that for?" she said, glaring at him.

"No married?" the clerk repeated. "No married… no same room. You must be married."

"Yes, married," Jack answered. "Just married, this week."

The clerk looked at Kelly. "Married? Uhh… Yes? Just…this week?"

Kelly got the picture. "Oh, yes. I did not understand." She took Jack's arm.

On hearing this, the clerk perked up, shaking their hands with a congratulatory look. "This week! Rosa!" he called. A woman came to the back door and peered through the bead strings. "They just married! They newlyweds!" he said with excitement.

Rosa was a short heavyset woman with a broad warm smile. But her smile quickly vanished when she saw them standing in wet clothes. "Your clothes, they are wet!" Her voice was both concerned and sympathetic. "What has happened?"

"Our boat turned over in the river; we lost everything," Kelly explained, tears forming in her eyes as if the honeymoon had gone sour. Jack was taken aback by how quickly Kelly had settled into the act. Rosa looked visibly upset. "It was terrible," Kelly continued.

"Oh, Palo, look at these poor kids." She raised her hands over her head. "You no worry about a thing," Rosa said with a maternal smile. "Mama Rosa, she take care of everything. You go upstairs and get dry. I bring you dry clothes, and take these to wash." She pointed at their soaked rags. "They ready in morning, okay?" she offered graciously.

Then Jack started, "Oh thank you, but you don't really..." This time it was Kelly that stomped on Jack's foot. "Ouch!" he cried.

Kelly smiled, wiping the tears from her cheeks. "That would be so very nice. Thank you so much," she said, accepting her hospitality.

"Palo, get them their room now," Mama Rosa ordered. "Can you not see they are cold and wet?"

Palo smiled warmly, grabbed the key for a room, and headed for the stairs to the second floor. The room was clean and simple with a window that looked out on the bustling square. Kelly looked for the bathroom. "Is there a shower?" she inquired of Mama Rosa's husband.

Palo looked briefly confused then got a spark in his eye. "Toilet, down the corridor, yes. With shower, yes, hot and cold, this very nice hotel."

"Down the hall?" she said with a worried tone.

He smiled a mischievous smile. His front tooth was gold and shone in the light. "Do not worry, Mrs. Sullivan. You the only guests this week. No else come upstairs." He paused, then turned to Jack. "This is the honeymoon suite. It is very nice, yes?" He patted the bed, looking at Jack to make sure he knew what he was supposed to do.

"Yes, very nice, thank you, sir," Jack answered, walking him out. The door closed.

"Well, he did say there was hot water," Kelly said, grabbing a towel and heading for the door. "I'll be a sport and make sure it's safe."

When Jack returned from his shower he found Kelly gazing out the window. There was music and commotion coming from the celebration that was in full swing in the square below. The lights from the fiesta came through the window and reflected off her face. Her neatly brushed hair fell softly on her shoulders, and she wore the dress that Mama Rosa had provided. It was a simple, but beautifully flowered outfit that fit Kelly's body snugly, hugging close to her curved figure. It was hard for Jack not to take notice.

"That obviously isn't one of Mama Rosa's dresses."

"Look, it's a gorgeous night," she said, ignoring his compliment.

Jack held out his arms, modeling the clothes that Mama Rosa had laid out for him. The jacket sleeves were too short, while the pants were bunched up and baggy. She had even provided him with a typical Inca derby hat that was too small and sat only on the crown of his head. "You got the tailor; I got the apprentice," he joked.

Kelly looked at his silly outfit and laughed. "You look like a hobo. I can live with the jacket and pants, but the hat has to go."

"Gone." He flung it onto the bedpost.

"I'm hungry. Let's walk through the fiesta, and find something to eat." Kelly suggested, looking out the window at the lights in the square. "It looks like fun."

•

The town was energized, and the square was the nucleus of activity. Families mingled with each other, the children running wild while the mothers and older girls laid blankets and picnic baskets on the sparse grass. The men stood in groups around the hotel and another restaurant that offered the same alcoholic brew *chichi*, which prevailed in the Andes. On stringers around the perimeter, an assortment of colored lights flickered in the dark sky. Banners were pasted on every wall with the image of the Catholic saint they were honoring. Dogs and cats moved freely through the crowd looking for scraps of fallen food.

Jack and Kelly walked out of the hotel where Palo and two other men stood smoking. Kelly looked stunning, and the men's eyes were fixed on her alone. As she walked forward they parted, tipping their hats to her as she passed. "You have a very pretty lady, Mr. Jack," Palo said admiringly.

"Thank you," Jack replied. "I think so too."

Kelly liked his answer, but she was out in front, so Jack never saw the smile that it brought to her face. Then the men wished them fun at the fiesta and went back to their conversation. Their remarks left both Jack and Kelly feeling welcome and invited.

Kelly stepped off the curb into the bustling street. "Isn't this exciting?" she exclaimed with a giddy schoolgirl's tone. She was feeling clean and refreshed, and her spirits were renewed. Women everywhere smiled at the couple as they passed. Mama Rosa had got the word out about the newlyweds.

At the corner by the square, a shriveled hag attended a rickety pushcart. Palo saw Jack and Kelly eyeing the crowd gathered around the old woman's stand. In her hands she was shaking a container vigorously, its contents rattling loudly. "She is a seller of potions," Palo said walking up behind them.

"Potions?" Kelly asked. "Like a witch?"

"Yes, yes, she is a *bruja*," Palo answered.

"And that thing she is shaking, is that one of her potions?" Kelly asked.

"Oh yes, of course," Palo answered. The woman stopped and poured the contents into a wooden cup. It was an especially distasteful looking concoction made of blended fruit, raw fish, whole quail eggs, and a fluid she squeezed from the ruptured globe of a bull's eye. "She makes many strange things." Palo screwed his face in disgust.

The old woman handed the concoction to a man standing before her. He took it, raised his glass to his friend, and downed the contents completely.

"What does it do?" Kelly asked.

Palo looked embarrassed, then said to Jack, "We call it the Levantador Andeano. It is very good for making…" He pulled his fists toward his hips, and glanced at Kelly. "Maybe you should have one for your honeymoon tonight…ehh?"

Kelly raised her hands pretending surprise. "Palo, I think I've heard enough, thank you." She looked at Jack. "Com'on let's go."

Palo laughed loudly, then walked back to help Rosa. Jack spotted the table by the hotel. "I'm starved," he said. "Let's eat."

"After seeing that," Kelly grimaced, "how can you be hungry?" But the smells from Rosa's kitchen caught her attention, and it reminded her just how hungry she really was. "How much money do we have left?"

He reached into his pocket. "Six pesos and twenty-five centavos."

"How far will that get us?"

"I don't know." Jack pulled Kelly's chair out for her. He could hear the women taunting their husbands in Spanish and could only guess that they were chiding them for no longer showing them such courtesies. Kelly enjoyed Jack's little show of manners. She felt pretty and special, and the festive nighttime atmosphere only made it better.

Mama Rosa was quick to arrive with a menu and a smile. "You look so beautiful, Miss Kelly." She beamed at the couple. "I will bring you a special bottle of wine that I wish you to have for your honeymoon night."

Jack looked worried. "But we don't have much money."

"I tell you, Mr. Jack. You worry about nothing. I take care of everything." She left with a broad smile on her face and blasted through the loitering men like a bowling ball through pins. She scolded one about something before she went inside.

"Doesn't this feel good?" Jack remarked, leaning back in his chair. He gazed at Kelly with pleasure.

"Yeah, no guns firing at us, no planes crashing, no caves, or raging rivers," she joked. "I could get used to this."

"You did great through it all," Jack said with admiration. He could not take his eyes off her, or her beautiful smile. It made her a little self-conscious, but at the same time she liked it.

"You weren't so bad yourself." She was quiet for a moment, then added, "I'm sorry for what I said earlier today."

"When?"

"Back at the mine entrance. About you and why you were down here." She paused. "I have no right..."

"It's okay," he interrupted, "really." He could tell she still wondered about him and his reasons for being here. "I've just had some bad breaks, and I'm trying to get them worked out. What about you?" he said, changing the subject. "Who sent you here? You don't look military."

"Well, I'm not really, but I do work for them as a civilian. I'm an agent for Military Intelligence." Jack recoiled a bit, and Kelly noticed his apprehension. "A brand new one," she added. "I just got the promotion five days ago, I think. I can't even remember what day it is." She chuckled. "This is all very new to me."

Just then Rosa barged in, a glass of a cloudy amber brew in each hand, both topped with a head of foam. "*Chichi*," she said proudly, presenting the glasses on the table. "It is our national drink." She took a step backward and waited. They inspected the beverage cautiously. It looked questionable at best. Then they looked back at her. She continued standing patiently, waiting for the couple to taste it. Her body language told them she would not leave until they had tried it.

Jack hesitated at first, but then he picked up his glass and toasted, "To my beautiful wife." Kelly blushed at his words, but the toast made Rosa beam.

"Not bad," Jack said, holding his glass to the light.

"To Rosa," Kelly added. Her eyes connected with Jack's and it was obvious there was something special about him that she liked.

Rosa could see it was time for her to go. And she did so, this time quietly and contentedly.

"So," Jack said, "If you're a rookie, why did they send you down here on such a dangerous mission?"

"No one guessed it'd be so dangerous," she replied. "In fact, Washington expected the opposite: the legend to be a farce, and nothing and no one to really be here or even care." She paused. "It was the lowest priority of missions, the kind you're supposed to get for your first assignment. As for me, they picked me because I was the only person known to speak the Picayulta Indian's language." Jack's eyebrows rose. His face displayed a mixture of awe and bewilderment. "I lived and worked with them a couple years ago," she said. "With my father. He was a missionary. God rest his soul."

"I'm sorry."

"He had been struggling with personal and mental problems these last years. When he learned of the statue and the legend that surrounded it, he became even more distressed. The distress turned to rage as he and his two like-minded associates egged each other on. They became fanatics on the subject. I thought I could do something about it but it was hopeless. When I left he promised he'd let it be, but…"

"This window thing with the statue, do you believe it?"

"I don't know. The logical side of me says 'No,' but then I wonder why have so many people, high up in the government, have invested so much time and energy on its retrieval? On both sides."

Jack pondered her question. "You have a point. The Germans sure went to a lot of trouble. Bringing those soldiers along with a transport, two fighter planes and a ground crew is quite a commitment."

Kelly smiled, "Well, for a simple Texas farmer, you sure were clever to get it away from them," she said, patting the pack slung on the back of his chair.

"It was luck."

"I'd say you have a lot of it going for you these last couple of days."

"I could have used it a couple months ago," Jack said.

His look suddenly seemed more distant to Kelly. She knew it had something to do with why he was out of the country. "What part of Texas are you from?" she asked. Jack looked uncertain. She could tell he didn't want to answer. "Well, it's not fair for you to get to ask all the questions," she pouted. "For Pete's sake, we almost died together several times! I owe you my life. I don't care what you're escaping from; I'm not going to turn you in. I mean, it's not like you're a murderer or something." She waited for his answer. "Is it?" Jack did not say anything. "Well, is it?" she repeated.

"No, it's nothing like that," he lied, but then wondered what she would think if she knew. "For the last two years I have been trying to get into the Army Air Corps as a fighter pilot. I've been turned down three times." His voice grew bitter.

"But why? You obviously know how to fly."

"It wasn't because of flying. It was for two asthma attacks I had as a child. They said I was unfit for the service, and claimed I would be a danger to others. The last attack was when I was twelve."

"That makes no sense."

"They think I'd be susceptible to attacks at high altitude. It's a regulation they have, and they don't bend it for anyone."

"But why are you here?" she pressed on.

"Back home, when I arrived from training this last time, I got into a situation which developed into an altercation. It was all a misunderstanding, but this guy, a deputy, went a little crazy. His pride was injured and there was no doubt he had it in for me. We got into a fight and he got hurt." Jack didn't feel like going into the part about Lucy. There was something he was starting to feel for Kelly and he didn't want to spoil it by bringing up old girl-friends.

"So?" she pushed.

"So... I got out for a while, and I'm hoping it'll blow over."

"No, I mean what happened to the deputy?"

"I don't know for sure. I took off running." He knew that was stretching the truth, but he really didn't feel like rehashing that part of the story either.

"Well, when we get back to the States, I think there will be a general or two that could pull some strings after all you have done here."

"I can't go back..." He stopped. "I mean, what kind of pull would you—no offense, but this *is* your first assignment—could you have with a general?" He waited. "And as for me, the Air Corps has already had enough."

"I have ways to get what I want," Kelly said smugly. Her girl-ish smile hinted mischief. Jack wasn't sure he liked the way she put that. She didn't seem like that kind of girl. A hint of jealousy stirred inside him. "And I don't give up easily," she continued.

Jack imagined a girl with her looks and personality could get just about anything she wanted if she was willing to compromise herself. Again the thought disturbed him. "No, really. You don't need to do anything like that for me," he stammered. "I need to get back to Panama anyway, and tell Hank what has happened to his pilot, Ray. Not to mention telling him that both airplanes are gone and he's out of business." He sat quietly for a moment. "Maybe I *should* go to Washington with you after all. Hank's not going to be too pleased."

Rosa returned with two steaming meals of pork, corn and a salsa that smelled perfectly spiced. The aroma of the fresh cooked food was almost too much for the famished couple. "Rosa, Rosa, Rosa, it looks and smells so good," Jack said.

"And the tortillas, Mr. Jack, they are fresh made of maize," she boasted proudly. Then she pulled a bottle of wine from her apron pocket and said, "This bottle is a wedding present to you from me and Palo." She popped the cork and provided two clean glasses from another pocket.

"Oh Rosa, you shouldn't have," Kelly said.

Jack turned to the doorway where Palo was perched, lighting a cigarette. He raised his glass to him, and Palo nodded back. Rosa again left them to enjoy their meal in peace.

"I feel a little guilty now with our charade," Jack said, looking at the bottle of wine.

"But look at her." Kelly motioned to the hotel patio where Rosa was enthusiastically talking with her friends. "She's having so much fun doing it up for us. We can't let her down now."

A band of Andean musicians played flutes, and the lights flickered as the two enjoyed the copious meal Mama Rosa had provided, and although it was a bit rough, the two managed to empty the bottle of wine. Its relaxing effects melded the sounds and the lights and the tastes of the night into a magical experience. Kelly and Jack had long forgotten their troubles and flight from the Germans earlier that day. As they finished their dinner, a procession of ghostly images and skeletons paraded through the crowd. It was a display of the mixed beliefs from both the Catholic missionaries and the old Inca religion that the Indians had blended into a surreal display of fear and gratitude. They chanted and mourned and played instruments to pay homage to San Ignacio, the saint they were celebrating. The square was small and to make the procession last longer than two minutes they marched back through two more times.

Then a space cleared in the street and two flute players broke away from the band. A guitar and accordion were added to the ensemble. The musicians picked up the tempo and the younger locals who had all had their fill of *chichi* began to dance uninhibited in the street.

"Take your lady out to dance," Rosa said with a smile.

"I don't know how," Jack said.

"Come on, Jack, let's do it," Kelly said, dragging him from his seat. "It'll be fun." Before he knew it he was doing his best to survive in the gyrating crowd of dancers. He watched Kelly move with fluidity and realized his attraction for her was growing stronger. After a few numbers of fast paced music the band slowed it down and the older folks joined in. Jack unconsciously took Kelly into his arms. He was shy, holding her loosely at first, not wanting to seem presumptuous. But Kelly shifted her arms further up and around his shoulders in what felt to Jack like a genuine embrace. Her weight hung comfortably on him.

Their cheeks touched. Her skin was soft and smooth. Jack slid his hands down her back; they settled just below her waist. Then he pulled her gently in toward him and felt her hips and breasts press against him. Her firm figure felt good to hold. He had wondered earlier what she would feel like. The time passed and the crowd dwindled. The musicians finally quit and all that was left were a few straggling lovers and a couple of drunks. Neither Jack nor Kelly wanted the night to end. It had all been so perfect.

Kelly watched the musicians depart. "Even Rosa has gone to bed. Let's go for a walk. Want to?"

"Sure," Jack answered. They walked a few short blocks to the river where the stars spread like an enormous canopy above them. Kelly commented on their beauty. She was the antithesis of Lucy, Jack thought as he recalled that fateful night in Texas on the Guadalupe River. Lucy was a bumbling featherbrain; Kelly was as smart as she was pretty.

When Kelly stopped talking, the silence grew until at last they turned to each other. She looked up at Jack. There was only dim light, but he could see into her dark eyes. He wanted to kiss her badly, but was nervous. Kelly could sense it as he leaned toward her then swayed away slightly, afraid to make the final move. She moved purposefully closer so he couldn't change his mind, and their lips met.

The kiss was soft and tender. Jack hands moved above her waist and held her gently. She kissed him back, her arms hanging invitingly on his shoulders. The kiss led to another, and Jack embraced her more tightly. His hands wandered cautiously over her figure. Kelly liked his touch. She felt a surge of desire. Their kisses became more passionate, and their hands traveled even more fervently as they explored each other's bodies both fearing that something would cause this magical night to end.

"Let's go to the hotel," Kelly whispered huskily. They walked briskly back, for the first time realizing the mountain air had cooled the night. The streets were empty; even sleeping dogs did not move to look at them.

At the room Jack hung the backpack on the bedpost. Immediately they fell back into each other's arms. They pulled their clothes off with anticipation, their hands moving over every inch of the other's body. Their heads were spinning with emotion, neither aware of anything else as their half naked bodies fell to the bed. Without thought or words they made passionate love.

CHAPTER TWENTY-NINE

The rising sun shone brightly through the window, and Jack could see it through his closed eyes. He could hear quiet voices in the street outside as villagers cleaned up after the festival. Their voices pulled him slowly back to consciousness. He turned to Kelly lying next to him in the bed, and it dawned on him, *it wasn't a dream.*

She was beautiful. Her hands lay upon the pillow cradling her face. A wisp of hair fell across her face, gently resting on her cheek. The corners of her mouth twitched upward slightly, hinting the innocent dreams of an angel.

The rays shining through the thin curtains warmed Jack. High on life and love, he had all but forgotten his problems back home. He had even managed to put the dangers of the last two days into the back of his mind. But the peace was suddenly shattered by loud forceful voices. They were Spanish words spoken with an unmistakable German accent. And they were directly outside his window. Reality came crashing back.

Jack sprang out of bed and peered from the corner of the window. It was Bodecker, a pistol in hand, intimidating the villagers below. His men were scattering down the streets and throughout the village with lightning speed. They pushed people aside and turned over stands. No one dared confront them.

"How could they have gotten here already?" Jack said to himself. He scooted back to the bed and whispered, "Kelly! Kelly! Wake up." He nudged her gently and quietly. She moved slightly, but only to adjust herself to continue sleeping. "Kelly!" he said, shoving her more forcefully.

"Uhhhh." Her eyes blinked open and a big smile spread across her face. "Mmmmmm…" she said, stretching first, then rubbing the sleep from her eyes. "Good morning."

"Kelly, we've got to get out of here. The place is crawling with Germans."

"What?" Her voice faltered groggily.

"The Germans. They're here." At that instant she heard Bodecker shouting below their window at the front of the hotel. It sounded as if he was insinuating something, and Palo was denying it. Kelly's eyes opened widely. "Quick, get dressed," Jack said.

There was more arguing in the street. Kelly listened. "He says he's going to search the hotel," She translated while fumbling into her clothes.

Downstairs Bodecker shot his pistol once in the air. "Get out of my way, you imbecile, or I'll kill you," he bellowed, in broken Spanish.

Jack hurried to the door and looked down the hallway. "We'll go out the back," he said, then pulled the back pack from the bedpost. "Can't forget this." They heard the door below being kicked in, and as they crossed the hall to an empty room on the backside of the building, boots stomped up the stairs. "Quick, out the window."

Without hesitation Kelly slipped through the opening and jumped to the ground. Jack followed. "Let's head for the river," he suggested. Darting across streets and hiding behind walls, they eluded the searching soldiers who were spreading intimidation with shouts and violence, so much so that it instilled fear in the townspeople to stay inside or flee for cover.

Several blocks from the hotel, and feeling temporarily safer, they stopped to make a plan. Jack looked up and down the street. There were no Germans in sight.

"Look, Jack, a bus stop. There by the river." They hurried across the street to the stop where a man stood nearby. "Is there a bus today?" Kelly asked in Spanish. The man nodded slowly. "When does it arrive?"

"Not long." He smiled.

"When?"

"Next week," he said.

"Next week!" Kelly exclaimed.

The man nodded. "Yes, but one just leave," he said pointing down the dirt road. He was proud that his town had a regular connection to the outside world. Jack and Kelly looked down the road. The dust was still settling from the departed bus. Then they looked back at each other with exasperation.

"Where does that bus stop next?" Jack asked the man. Kelly translated.

"Campo Alegre."

"How far?"

"Fifty kilometers," he said waving his arm down the river.

"Is there any other way to get there?"

The man smiled a toothless smile and pointed to a group of wooden boats pulled up on the bank of the river several blocks away. A boy sat atop one of the dinghies, which was flipped over beside a few others. Jack and Kelly shot a glance at each other, but were interrupted by a shout followed by gunfire. A German had spotted them. Still far up the street, and close to the square, the soldier started after them, quickly joined by others pouring in behind.

Jack and Kelly sprinted toward the boats. "How much for a boat ride down the river?" Jack asked the boy. Kelly translated.

"I no go. You ask father," the boy said.

"Where's your father?" Kelly continued.

"At the festival cleaning up," the boy responded.

"No time, I'll buy the boat. How much?" The boy shrugged. Jack looked around and spotted Kelly's gold watch. He reached for her arm, stripping it from her without asking.

"Hey! That was given to me by my father!" she said, protesting.

"He'll understand. Trust me." Jack shoved the watch into the boy's hand, not waiting to see if the terms of sale were agreeable. There was yelling down the street. "Get in!" Jack ordered as he pushed the bow off the muddy bank. More shots rang out and he leaped in behind Kelly. The boat drifted backward while he scrambled for the paddles. He tossed one to Kelly. "Paddle!" he ordered, with an eye on the soldiers tearing around the corner at the bus stop. The Indian boy looked panicked, and was urgently yelling something to Jack in Spanish. "What's he saying?" Jack yelled.

"I don't know. I can't hear anything," Kelly cried out over the sound of the gunfire. "Something about the second bridge—get out of boat—then—I—I don't know. I couldn't hear him."

Just then bullets zinged by, some shattering the top board of the wooden hull. They ducked down low in the boat, low as they could go. The boat floated aimlessly in the water, bobbing back and forth as the current sucked them into swifter water. Still more shots rang out, but they grew fainter as the current carried them away, quickly separating them once more from Bodecker and his men. Jack carefully peered over the splintered gunwale. "We're clear, for now," he said as the boat rounded a bend in the river.

They moved quickly down the river, which wound back and forth at first in small rapids. But soon the terrain dropped steeply and the river with it. The fast moving water had cut a canyon in the mountain with high banks to hem it in. Bend after bend, new tributaries poured in, and the river continued to pick up speed. The rapids were no longer gentle, but the little wooden boat held up well.

Jack took the oars and Kelly worked a paddle to help steer. A road followed closely along the bank and Jack assumed it was the one to Campo Alegre. As the rapids intensified, Jack spotted the bus up ahead. Its progress was torturously slow as it made its way across a bridge spanning the river. "Look! The bus!" he yelled. "We're catching up to it. In fact, we're going to pass it," he added as they approached the bridge.

"Maybe we can flag them down further down stream," Kelly added enthusiastically.

The boat bolted under the bridge and made a sudden violent drop. A hammering crash jarred the hull. It took all Kelly had just to stay in. The river began an even more rapid and turbulent descent. They shot past the dilapidated bus in a flash, smoke spewing from its tailpipe as it struggled its way down the steep canyon road. The passengers were peering out, their faces pressed against the dirty windows, awed at the sight of the two strangers being helplessly tossed by the swift river. The driver too stared at the boat through the space where once there was a door, his eyes were wide with disbelief. He took his foot off the gas pedal, causing the old engine to backfire violently. Waving a sign of disapproval, he honked his horn, then gestured to warn of approaching danger.

Unable to slow down or reach the riverside, Jack and Kelly quickly left the bus behind, plunging forward in increasingly violent surges. The river had become a giant washboard. The ripples became huge waves forming massive walls as the river rushed over giant underwater boulders. The tiny boat was thrashed about like a piece of cork as it was sucked down the slope of one mountain of water, then thrown up the next. Petrified by the river's force, the two boaters tried to keep the bow pointing down river so they wouldn't be swamped. Their drenched bodies trembled with cold and terror. Kelly's knuckles were white as her aching hands gripped the side of the boat. She was using all of her strength to keep from being thrown out. Jack fared no better. He worked the oars relentlessly, but the force of the water was so great that it made little difference what he did.

"I can't imagine it could get much worse," Kelly yelled over the thundering rapids. Then around her she heard random high pitched zings, directionless sounds emerging in an instant and being lost as quickly in the turbulence about her. The zings grew louder as the river mellowed into a fast moving flat stretch. Suddenly, they were surrounded by more of the plopping little splashes. In the background they could hear the muffled popping of gunfire.

"Damn! You spoke too soon. They're back," Jack swore, looking back at three boats of German soldiers in pursuit. With one man at the oars and two more with paddles, it still left two as snipers in each boat. They were busy peppering the water around them with rifle fire. Given enough time one of them was bound to make a hit.

At the head of another set of rapids a protruding boulder caught Jack's oar. There was a loud crack and the boat jerked around sideways, throwing the pair out of their seats. The right oar was gone, snapped cleanly from its mounting. They floated uncontrollably at the mercy of the river's current. The rapids intensified again and the German's crowded launches floundered as helplessly as Jack and Kelly's crippled boat. Ahead of them all, an immense wave loomed.

Kelly was facing downstream and felt a sinking feeling in the pit of her stomach as she eyed the giant wall of moving water. She tried to speak, but could not get the words out. Preoccupied with trying to replace the broken oar with a paddle, Jack was unaware of the trouble until his eyes caught her frightened face, and her lips trying to gasp the words. He turned slowly to follow her line of sight then looked upward to face what he sensed would be a disaster. He saw the giant wave just as they started up it, but a side current miraculously pulled their uncontrolled launch from its full force. They skirted the towering wave, spinning wildly like a pinwheel.

The first boat of pursuing Germans was less fortunate. The wave tossed their craft in mid-air as they crested the twenty-foot wave, flipping it over and sprinkling its human cargo out over the boiling water. Like miniature toy soldiers scattered by a child, they vanished into the raging swirl below.

The second boat, also propelled up the devastating wave, followed the first to a similar fate. But the third shared the same random mercy as Jack and Kelly. It skirted the danger and then continued the pursuit. Again the rapids abated and the paddling Germans slowly gained on them, shooting their weapons until they had exhausted all their ammunition.

In the calmer water, now absent of gunfire, Kelly heard a rumble. It grew louder and louder as they approached a bend in the river. The river had flattened, but the water was swifter than ever. As they rounded the bend she spotted a bridge. "Look, Jack! A bridge!" Kelly yelled over the amplifying roar. The bridge was no more than a set of ropes with slats of wood spanning the hundred foot wide river. It sagged in the middle to within six feet from the river's surface. Fifty yards beyond it everything disappeared.

"Waterfall!" Kelly shouted. Jack turned down river and looked past the bow of the boat. His eyes grew big at the sight of the water disappearing. "Quick, the bridge!" He grabbed the backpack and slipped the straps over his shoulders. "We'll have to jump for it!" he exclaimed.

The Germans, now just ten feet behind, were paddling frantically, their eyes fixed on Jack and Kelly. The gunless snipers, brandishing their bayonets, crouched on the bow ready to pounce for the kill. For a fleeting second Jack wondered if they were unaware of the looming waterfall. Surely they could hear the roar below.

As their boat passed beneath the bridge, Kelly and Jack leapt with all their might for the ropes, sending their boat skidding sideways. At that moment the Germans suddenly realized the impending danger of the waterfall. Their disposition changed from attackers to victims in a single second. The men dropped their weapons and began paddling furiously with their bare hands.

Kelly had a solid hold on the rope bridge, but Jack had only been able to grab an insecure wood slat that moaned with his weight. He shifted to secure the rope just as the board gave way. The pieces fell away into the rushing water below. Jack lifted his upper body onto the bridge, but his legs still hung exposed to the oncoming Germans.

The soldiers had now abandoned their positions as their boat slipped under Jack's hanging body. Several of the unnerved men scrambled to reach for his dangling legs. They needed to grab him, this time not to pull him down, or to kill him, but to escape from their doomed boat on its path toward the fall. He was their lifeline.

Two were successful, and Jack felt the hard tug of their weight on his legs. The rope burned him under his armpits from where he was supporting himself. He thrashed and kicked to get free, but the parasites held tight as their boat drifted out from under them. The rope bridge bounced wildly as the Germans fought to hang on and Jack thrashed to get free. Their bodies dragged in the current as they clung for their lives. The strain on Jack was all but unbearable.

A third soldier jumped for the human chain, hoping to save himself, but fell short, and the water dragged him away behind the doomed boat. Its two remaining occupants wailed and cried as they fatefully drifted swiftly toward the fall.

"Hang on!" Kelly cried.

"I'm trying," he said, as if it wasn't obvious. She reached for him and pulled, but it did nothing. "Knock those guys off!" he pleaded.

Kelly looked around for something to throw at the Germans. She pulled on a board, but it was too well fastened. She found another and this one broke away. She used the piece to pummel one of the men, but it did little as he held fast.

"Hurry," Jack pleaded, grunting under the strain.

Kelly slipped off her belt and began thrashing the German soldiers. They screamed as she belted them, but they would not let go, realizing what awaited them if they did. She grabbed another piece of wood and jabbed at one of the men's hands. "Ouch!" Jack hollered. "That was me." Kelly pulled the wooden plank back and stared. "Well, don't stop!" he groaned. "Beat the crap out of them."

With a combination of fear, anger and confidence, Kelly raised the board high and hammered it down on one of the soldier's forehead. "Take that!" she hollered. "And that, and that, and that." She continued relentlessly.

Jack could not see what she was doing, but it sure sounded good. Suddenly, the soldier's grip was broken, and he screamed as he plunged into the river below. Kelly grinned, then turned to the other soldier. There was fire burning in her eyes now as she raised the board to strike him. The man looked up at her with fear in his eyes. Exhausted by the fight, he resigned himself to his watery fate. He let go. His eyes never left hers as he vanished into the rushing water.

Jack pulled himself up. His muscles screaming with pain, coughing and heaving, he rolled on to his side, and watched the last soldier as he went over the huge fall. "Hurry!" Kelly called. "The bus is coming."

Jack didn't care. He just wanted a minute to lie still and catch his breath. "You go and stop it. I can't move another inch."

•

The bus trip was slow and torturous. It was the upper river valley's only link with the capital, providing a rare opportunity for the locals to trade for currency instead of bartering as usual. The driver, having seen their pitiful condition and having witnessed at least part of their boat ordeal, gave Jack and Kelly free passage aboard. Kelly's good looks didn't hurt in winning him over.

Space on the bus was precious, and Kelly had diplomatically negotiated two seats from the owner of four caged chickens and a pig. The man put one of the cages with two chickens in his lap; the other traveled on Jack's, while Kelly held the backpack, gripping it tightly against herself. The pig rode comfortably on the seat between Jack and Kelly, his head resting comfortably on her knee.

"He's kind of cute." She said patting the little pig. "Feel like you're back home now?"

"What's that suppose to mean?"

"Home? On the farm—Texas?"

Jack scratched the piglet's head, and it let out a grunt of satisfaction.

"I think he likes you." She added.

He smiled. "It wasn't that kind of farm."

She kissed his cheek. "I'd like to see it sometime."

Several times there was a high pitch squeal. It was the radiator of the bus boiling over, and each time the driver stopped, nonchalantly popped open the hood, and added water. His movements were mechanical as if it happened all the time, and the passengers all took it in stride.

The bus made several stops; some were villages others were no more than country ranch huts. The man with his chickens and pig got off at the first stop. It gave Jack and Kelly some breathing room, but the heat and smell, along with the constant vibration made them drowsy. Kelly laid her head on Jack's shoulder and soon drifted off. The bus continued its torturous stopping and starting all through the day and into the night. It wasn't until late that they at last pulled into Bogotá, the capital and final destination of the bus. With no money for a hotel, and too tired to care, they spent the night on the benches of the bus station with a score of fellow indigents. The benches were hard and uncomfortable, and at daybreak they were awake, still tired and very sore.

"Jack? You awake?" Kelly said.

"Yeah. I don't think I ever really fell asleep."

Kelly sat up and looked around. There were bodies strewn everywhere. Some snored. All slept. The air in the terminal was stale and smelly. "Let's get out of here," she said.

Jack stirred. "And go where?"

"First...to find a phone."

"You won't find a telephone in Bogotá. The best you'll do is a telegram."

"Where?"

Jack thought a moment. "I'm not sure. I never needed one. Hank just told me if I ever needed to contact him from here that was the only way." He paused. "I guess I should give him the bad news. Let's try the train station."

It was still early and the city appeared closed. As in all Latin cultures, the people of Bogotá stay out late, but come morning they are slow to start. They wandered the empty streets looking for the station. After forty-five minutes of aimless walking they came upon some tracks. "Well, we know the station is either this way, or that way," Jack said, pointing down the tracks.

"Town is back that way," Kelly said.

They walked on the tracks, ending up almost where they started. On the building in large letters was written, "*SANTA FE DE BOGOTA*," and to the side there was a door on which was written "*Correo y Telégrafo.*"

"There," Kelly said, pointing at the sign, "that's it." She scanned the hours of business. "What time is it?" she asked, looking at her bare wrist.

Jack peered at the wall clock inside the window. "Seven-thirty."

"They open in an hour."

"There are some benches in that little plaza. We can wait there."

Eight-thirty passed and so did nine-thirty. It was quarter to ten before they heard the clerk's jingling keys as he opened the door. Jack and Kelly were there waiting by his side.

"*Ocho y media?*" Kelly said, pointing at her wrist with exasperation. The clerk looked at her with bloodshot eyes and shrugged his shoulders. It took him several minutes to get organized, hampered by what appeared to be a crippling hangover. "*Quiero mandar un telegrama a USA,*" Kelly said. He did not respond. "*Y quiero recibir dinero también.*"

The man finally nodded. "*Sí, Señora, Sí. Un minuto,*" he said apathetically, handing her the form to fill out. Kelly scribbled the words: "General Smitson. Golden Idol successful. Have statue. Thornton dead. Need money and passage home from Bogotá for two." The clerk took the paper and after a few moments started tapping away at his key with agility. Jack and Kelly waited for an hour in the plaza. Still hungry, they smelled the aroma of food being cooked nearby. "I would give anything to have just a taste of whatever that is," Jack said.

Kelly took a whiff of the air. "It does smell good."

Then the telegraph clerk from across the street came over and interrupted. He handed Kelly a paper. She took it and glanced at the message. "It's our answer. Someone's on the ball in Washington." Jack moved behind her to look over her shoulder. She read:

"Good job. Glad you're safe. Money voucher enclosed. Get to Cartagena. Tickets for two await. Pan Am Clipper to Miami. Call from Miami. Want to know who's with you. Love, U S."

"Love, U S?" Jack said jealously. "Who's U S?"

"The General, silly." She smiled and said, "Uncle Smitty."

"General Smitson is your uncle?"

"Yep, that's why I suggested the night before last that you return to Washington with me. He's very good at fixing things, like whatever trouble or mess it is that you got yourself into back in Texas." Her tone was half cocky, half proud, but it left Jack knowing she rarely abused the privilege. Then she bounced up off the bench and started across the street toward a bank that the clerk had said would deliver the transferred funds. Jack was dumbfounded. In mid-street Kelly stopped and spun around. "You were right." She took a deep breath. "That does smell good." She waved the papers in her hand. "Want some lunch?"

Jack perked up at the invitation and realized just how hungry he was.

CHAPTER THIRTY

The train left at six o'clock that evening. It was an all night trip to the lowlands, and it stopped frequently at the numerous towns that lay between. By morning they were pulling into a station by the waterfront in the center of Cartagena. The harbor airport was but a short distance from the train platform. From there they could see the three hundred year old walls of the fort that guarded the entrance.

After a quick inquiry the two made straight for the ticketing booth where they found a ruckus at the counter. Some waiting passengers had gathered to listen. Kelly cut through the group. Behind the counter was a petite woman agent defending her position in denying two passengers their seats. She waved away the man and his wife with whom she was arguing and motioned Kelly forward. They backed off, complaining and fuming bitterly with anger. "Two tickets to Miami, please," Kelly asked at the counter.

"For today, Miss? The plane is full. We have no more seats," the agent said, brushing Kelly off with a "tough luck" attitude. There was still muffled grumbling in the crowd. "My name is Wilson, Kelly Wilson. Are you sure there are no reservations for me?"

"Ah, Miss Wilson," the agent's tone changed quickly to charming. "Of course, your tickets, I have here."

At hearing this, the disgruntled man bolted back from the crowd and resumed his heated argument with the agent, but to no avail. When she was finished and the man had left she said to Kelly, "I am sorry, Miss Wilson. The man would not listen. I was instructed to give his seats to you yesterday," she said, as if inconveniencing the man was no big deal. "They tell me it is important. I just do my job. He not like that."

"Well, I understand. I wouldn't like it either," Kelly said, a bit embarrassed that the General had pushed the man and his wife off the plane so Jack and Kelly could go. The agent just shrugged. Jack and Kelly felt the glare of the small crowd as they walked away with their tickets. They decided to wait for their flight at a nearby and nearly empty café. Almost immediately a waiter arrived to take their order. "Coca Cola, *por favor*," Kelly said.

"Make it *dos*," Jack said, holding up two fingers.

The waiter turned and bumped into a well-dressed European man who had just stepped behind him. "*Pardon*. Excuse me, *Señor*," the waiter said, while catching a glass that tipped on his tray. The man waved him away politely, sat down with his back to Jack and Kelly, and started to read his newspaper.

Kelly sipped her soda and watched the bustling dock. It was busy with a gang of laborers forming a human chain. They were slowly passing sacks of grain down the line, the sacks ultimately disappearing into the hold of a small freighter. Jack was fidgeting with the statue in the pack. Some of the gems at the base had come loose, so he decided to remove them all and put them in a small pouch for safekeeping.

Just beyond, but within sight, a large plane floated at a nearby dock. It was a flying boat, a Pan American Martin 130 known commonly as the China Clipper. Its massive size caught almost everyone's eye the first time they saw it, and it had become of special interest to a group of local boys that had gathered at the dockside pretending to be pilots.

"That's our plane?" Jack asked, looking at it with a pilot's interest.

"It better be," Kelly said. "The agent said there are only two flights out of here a week and they're both to Miami."

"When do we leave?" Jack asked.

"In about an hour or so," she answered. "But the agent reminded me nothing here is ever on time. She said it would likely be closer to two. Let's go for a walk. We're going to be cooped up for a while." As they passed the man at the adjacent table, he folded his paper as if finished with his reading. He waited a moment before he stood and followed them. Before he left he nodded to another man, a native in greasy overalls, down on the dock. The native acknowledged his signal and with his toolbox headed for the airplane.

•

Trash and oil covered the water's surface in the harbor, and neither pilot noticed the fuel spill mixed in with the mess, nor the fact that their fuel gauge needles had been jammed. Both gauges read full.

As they taxied into the harbor, the last remaining gallons of fuel sloshed around inside the otherwise empty tanks. The pilots throttled forward and the heavy plane skimmed over the calm waters of the bay, lifting off with Jack and Kelly into a beautiful Caribbean afternoon. She reached over and took his hand. For the first time since he'd fled Texas, Jack felt as if he was going to be all right.

The clipper climbed steadily to five thousand feet and South America was falling out of sight when the right engine choked and sputtered. There was an immediate loss of power and a sinking sensation. Nervous yelps echoed in the cabin and many passengers made the sign of the cross. "Is that normal?" Kelly asked nervously.

"A little rough maybe, but he's probably just leveling off," Jack said, trying to be reassuring.

Kelly looked out the window. "The propeller isn't turning!" she said, startled.

"That is definitely not normal," Jack said stating the obvious.

Other passengers noticed as well, and in seconds there were screams in the cabin over which no one could hear. The frightened co-pilot appeared from the cabin and said something about crash landing. He tried to go over the life vest procedures but there was so much pandemonium few understood. Jack donned the backpack and then put his life vest on over it as he supervised Kelly getting into hers. They tightened each other's straps, then turned to help those around them.

"Are we crashing?" Kelly asked Jack fearfully.

"We shouldn't have to. This is a boat plane. If the other engine holds we can land on the water and stay afloat until help arrives."

"But out here?"

"We should be okay. The weather is good," Jack said, looking out at the waves below.

The clipper glided steeply toward the water. "I would like to land where I'm supposed to just once when I fly with you!" Kelly said over the screams, shouts and prayers around them.

"I guess I should be thankful I wasn't let into the Air Corps after all," Jack joked.

The plane leveled, hung as if suspended for several long seconds, then hit the water hard, parallel between swells, its hull banging loudly on the surface. The panic culminated in loud screams. The plane bounced into the air and hung for an instant before its outboard pontoon buried itself in the next wave. Baggage flew like projectiles throughout the cabin. The second jolt spun them ninety degrees, before slamming them to an abrupt stop.

Then it was quiet. No one said anything that first moment, unsure of their status. But the next wave was soon passing under them, rolling them back to reality. The big plane creaked, leaning first to the left, then to the right. The seas were relatively calm, though the rolling was uncomfortable. Jack looked out the window and decided they were in no imminent danger.

There was more panic, though not as loud as before. Passengers scrambled to gather their luggage, constantly returning to a window to reassure themselves that they weren't sinking and to look for help. The co-pilot came out and told everyone to calm down. He said there was no reason for panic, and help was on the way. After that everyone waited. Kelly gripped Jack's hand like a vice, even though he told her several times they would be all right. It was a well built ship and given the light seas they could stay afloat almost indefinitely.

In less than an hour someone shouted they could see a ship heading directly toward them. Jack looked out his window and to his shock spotted a submarine moving toward the marooned airplane. A man appeared on its mid-ship superstructure and waved as the sub advanced toward them slowly. Impatiently, some of the passengers opened the door. When they saw how slowly the sub was approaching some dove from the floating airplane to swim the fifty-foot distance. But most waited until the submarine's bow was within jumping distance to board. Two sailors assisted the passengers as they jumped across. Kelly, like the others, boarded the sub's forward deck. Jack followed, thinking it odd but fortunate that a submarine was in the immediate area. The deck was small and quickly filling with the refugees.

Immediately after Jack stepped across, one of the sailors raised his hand to the next passenger to hold off for a moment. He signaled the man on the tower and the submarine's engines vibrated to life. The boat pulled back from the plane.

The remaining passengers were puzzled at first, thinking a wave had separated them; they waited patiently at first for its return, but the boat kept its distance. As time passed the stranded passengers grew impatient. They waved and pleaded for the submarine to return, but it became clear it wasn't going to. Their pleas turned to hostile yells.

"What are they doing?" Kelly asked, bewildered, "Why aren't we going back to get the others?"

Jack tapped her on the shoulder. "That's why."

She turned to see three German soldiers climbing out from the submarine's tower. It was Bodecker followed by two gunmen. "Miss Wilson. Mr. Sullivan. Welcome aboard," he said politely. "We have all had quite an adventure." He paused and smiled. "However, enough is enough. And it is time to end it." The soldiers stepped behind them and separated them from the others. "I believe you have something that belongs to me," Bodecker continued, snapping his fingers. Like guard dogs, the soldiers were all over Jack, one holding him tight while the other tore the pack from his shoulder.

"How did you find us?" Kelly asked in disbelief.

"It was not difficult. Our man in Bogotá followed you to the telegraph office. The clerk there was reluctant to help at first, but was persuaded to be cooperative. Why, he was answering questions that weren't even asked of him." Bodecker smiled. "You two should be a little more discreet. You left a trail any idiot could follow."

"That certainly explains how you managed to find us," Kelly snipped.

Bodecker slapped her across the face. It caused Jack to boil over with rage. He tried to retaliate, but the soldiers held him firm. "You have been quite lucky, I must say....but your luck has just ended. I'm afraid this has become personal for me. I am not in the habit of losing half my men to amateurs, and I will not be outsmarted by you again." Bodecker waited a moment waiting to see what they might say. Neither spoke, so he continued. "Oh, I must remember to thank 'U S,' whoever he is, for being so clear about your flight plans."

The soldier with the pack handed it to Bodecker. He unbuttoned it and poked through the papers inside. A smile grew across his face. "Good. You have done well to protect the statue."

Kelly interrupted his moment. "You must help the others. They are still stranded on the plane." She pointed to the wallowing airplane. A few of the remaining passengers were still frantically waving for help. Others had resorted to diving into the water and were swimming after the submarine.

Bodecker turned to the tower where a sailor stood beside a mounted cannon and nodded. It fired once, hitting the plane directly. From the passengers on the submarine deck came startled screams of horror. The explosion split the aircraft in half and within seconds the two halves had sunk below the surface. The remaining passengers now huddled in fear, crying and whimpering.

"You ruthless bastard," Kelly said, glaring at the cold-blooded Nazi. One of the passengers disengaged himself from the rest and stepped forward, interrupting her. He begged Bodecker for mercy, pointing out they were civilians and non-combatants. Bodecker had no interest in his or any other person's plight. He pulled his sidearm from its holster and fired a single round into the man's chest. There was a look of shock and disbelief in the man's eyes as he clutched his chest. He stumbled backwards and fell from the deck into the water. The rest of the group was now silent.

"Miss Wilson," Bodecker said, "you are in no position to argue. I have what I came for, and you have now outgrown your usefulness to me." Bodecker looked to the water where a shark had begun feeding on the man he had just shot. An inky cloud of blood stained the water. "It is important to be useful." He paused. "Even in death a use has been found for that man....probably a higher calling than anything he ever did in life." Then he turned to Kelly and raised his gun. "You should be so fortunate."

"It won't work!" Jack interrupted, speaking for the first time. Two soldiers held him fast. Bodecker looked at him, puzzled. "The statue, it won't work anymore," Jack repeated. Bodecker smiled disbelievingly.

Jack continued, "Really, it won't. The stones lining the crown were in a specific order. Like the crystals of a radio, they create the statue's ability to receive and transmit on certain frequencies."

Bodecker's smile vanished. He pulled the statue from the backpack and inspected it. The stones were gone. "Where are they?" he growled.

"They are in my pocket."

"Search him," Bodecker ordered.

The soldiers slammed Jack to the deck where he landed hard with a painful groan. With his face pressed into the deck, he felt them tearing his pockets open. A small felt bag fell from one onto the deck. It opened as it hit, and some stones spilled out toward the deck's edge.

"Carefully, you fools!" Bodecker scolded while catching one of the gems that almost fell into the water. "We need those stones." Bodecker looked at the little rock. It was a deep red ruby.

"You must replace them all, in the proper order," Jack groaned. "Only then will the statue tune in to the right frequency."

Bodecker grabbed the other stones on the deck, then picked up the open bag. He emptied the rest into his hand, counting nine different gems in all.

"Go ahead," Jack said, still pinned to the deck. "Put them back in yourself. There are eighty-one different combinations. So you have a slim chance of getting them right. And if you're wrong, you'll get another chance," Jack paused, "in about sixty-one years."

"Let him up," Bodecker ordered. Jack got to his feet, rubbing the parts of his body that hurt. He knew he would feel that in the morning. But that was a good thing, for moments earlier he doubted he would live that long. Bodecker looked Jack up and down. "You are resourceful, Mr. Sullivan," he said with a bit of admiration. "And this order of the stones, you wrote it down, of course?"

Jack shook his head and pointed to his temple. "It's up here."

Bodecker gazed out at the water. More sharks had joined the first in the feeding frenzy. "So, I was a little too fast to say you are no longer of value to me. I have gone to a great deal of trouble to track you down, and now this." Bodecker shook his head. "This misbehavior cannot go unpunished. Like a parent, I must show you, and my men, who is in command. Your mischief will be paid for by…" He paused, scanning to see who would pay for his inconvenience. His scarred face showed no emotion. "By them." He motioned to the huddle of humanity on the forward deck. "They will pay for the consequences of your actions."

"But they are innocent!" Kelly cried. "What will you do to them?"

"Nobody is innocent in life, Miss Wilson," he said, and then to one of the soldiers he added, "Take these two below."

The last thing Kelly saw before the soldier pushed her head down through the hatch was the passengers huddled on the deck crying and sobbing after witnessing the brutal murder of the others.

Jack and Kelly waited below, under guard, in the main operations room of the submarine. The air inside smelled of diesel and the quarters were dingy and tight. At first, Kelly could barely see the other submariners moving in the dark interior. But as her eyes adjusted to the dim light, she could see they were pale and gaunt. They looked as if they had not seen the sun in months. Several approached the open hatch in the ceiling just to steal a breath of the fresh sea air. A slightly older man, no more than thirty, wearing a scruffy sweater and hat, stood to the side. Kelly assumed he was the captain.

Finally the two soldiers came below, followed by Bodecker. "Close the hatch," he ordered.

"What happened? What did you do to the rest of those people?" Kelly asked.

Bodecker looked at her directly and said matter-of-factly, "You would be proud of me, Miss Wilson, I did not hurt a single one of them." His tone implied there was more to come.

Kelly did not believe him. "Where are they?" she continued.

"On deck. And when I left them, they were in perfect health," he answered, then turned to the captain and ordered, "Take us down to thirty meters." The command was repeated, then followed by an alarm, which rang through the submarine to alert the crew of the ensuing dive.

"Engines one half," the captain added.

"Engines one half," the first mate repeated.

In seconds Kelly felt the bow dropping as the submarine pushed forward. "But the people! They'll drown," Kelly cried.

"Perhaps," Bodecker answered. "Miss Wilson, as you can see, ours is but a small submarine." He paused and then added mockingly as if it would be of consolation to her, "The strong ones will swim…for a while. The weaker ones…will quickly take their place in the food chain."

"Ten meters," the wheel man interrupted.

"I am busy now, but we will find time to discuss our matter of the statue…very soon." He looked at Jack threateningly. "I assure you. Take them away."

As they were escorted to a room converted to a brig, Kelly could not help but imagine the panic unfolding outside for the innocent people above her. She wondered how long any of them would last.

CHAPTER THIRTY-ONE

Nothing made sense. At first Jack was riding in a truck through downtown New Braunfels. It was Lucy's truck, and she was at the wheel. She turned to him, smiling. It was a false smile, the type that conveyed cruelty more than warmth. With her eyes fixed on Jack she spoke. Jack could see her lips moving, but her words were drowned out by the sound of howling wind. Jack was confused. He couldn't feel any wind.

The car was suddenly and forcefully banged and jostled. Jack looked forward beyond the windshield. There was a track in front of them, rising into the sky. It had a firm hold on the truck as it pulled them powerfully upward, like the beginning ascent to a roller coaster ride. At a dizzying height they reached the summit. From it Jack could see most of Texas. He tried to snap out of it, but felt powerless and vulnerable.

Lucy laughed at his helplessness, as if she was in on the madness. He questioned his sanity, but before he could answer, the truck plunged chaotically. Jack felt dizzy and sick. They hit bottom and Jack tossed about, struggling to get a grip on his senses. *It's a nightmare. This can't be real,* part of him thought.

As his senses gathered, Jack realized he was lying with his face buried in a pile of something coarse and fibrous, encrusted with salt which stung as it cut into his cheekbone with each movement of his body. Each breath he took carried a damp, stale stench into his lungs. Then from below, a force pushed up hard. His body pressed deep into the coarse bedding. He felt himself being thrust back into the darkness above. Everything hurt. He struggled to open his eyes to see where he was being flung, but he could not. His eyelids were heavy, as if glued shut.

"Wake up!" words from the darkness ordered. There was a sharp blow to his ribs. It was no dream; it was painfully real. "You heard me, you lazy *dumbkoff*. Wake up!" The accent was unmistakably German.

Jack forced his eyes open, then squinted groggily toward a light outside. His accoster stood in the doorway. Jack sat up slowly. It wasn't in Jack's mind. They were still at sea. It all came back to him: the airplane, the submarine, and the killing. "Where's Kelly?" Jack demanded.

"Shut up," the soldier returned. "Put this life vest on. The Standartenfuhrer wants you with him in case we sink."

Jack sobered quickly. "I thought we were on a submarine."

"We moved to this fishing boat two days ago."

"Where's Kelly? Is she all right?"

"The girl's still alive, next door," the soldier said, hanging onto the doorframe as another large wave rolled under them. "Put it on." He shoved the vest against Jack's chest, and then stepped out and locked the door.

In moments the hull of the hundred-foot trawler vibrated as the anchor chain was fed out. Jack dragged himself up to peer out the window. There was land in the distance. He wiped the fog from his breath off the windowpane and looked onto the deck. A crew of North African fishermen was frantically scrambling about. Two men on the bow were trying to secure the forward hatch, sealing it from the onslaught of waves crashing across the deck.

Threatening clouds blanketed the black sky. Beyond them there was still some daylight. Lightning struck, illuminating the next giant roller moving in on its prey. The vessel tossed in the angry black ocean as a wave crashed over the bow. The deck disappeared under the foaming water. When the sweeping waters receded, the two men who had been there an instant before had vanished.

The door opened, letting in the wind, water, and the cries of a panicked crew trying to regain control of their vessel. It was the soldier returning with Kelly. Their clothes were soaked, and they wore life vests. "Wait here," the soldier commanded, pushing her onto the piled nets next to Jack.

"Kelly, are you okay?" Jack asked. She did not answer, still too drugged to talk.

Neither Jack nor Kelly remembered much of the last twelve days. They had been sedated for the journey, and until now had been unaware of their transfer to this old fishing vessel sailing under the protection of a Moroccan flag. It was a perfect ploy to get Bodecker and his prisoners through the Allied surveillance and into occupied Europe. The Allies never showed aggression toward commercial fisherman, and certainly not toward those of an African nation.

The vessel did not have a true brig, so the watchman's quarters behind the wheelhouse had been commandeered for the job. The room was tight and uncomfortable, nothing more than a windowed closet containing a steel framed bunk, a table and a chair. It was also a storage hold for everything from engine parts to fishing nets.

Jack made Kelly as comfortable as he could, then shifted his attention to the room. He reached over and pried caulking from the window joints. His first thought was to escape, but he knew in the middle of the ocean there was no place to go. So he pocketed the putty, then searched the chamber for other items that might be useful later. He found a piece of wire, a broken sliver of glass with a sharp edge and some rusty fishing hooks. He stashed them in the cuff of his pants. Then, using a fishhook and thread from a net, he sewed his stash closed. Still blurry-eyed and nauseated, he needed all his concentration to sew on the tossing boat. He never noticed the engines slowing or the boat turning into the wind.

Suddenly, the door burst open. It was Bodecker. "Out! Both of you!" he barked. Jack looked up startled, wondering if he had been discovered sewing his cuff closed. "Move!" Bodecker shouted. He noticed Kelly was unable to move on her own. "You two carry the girl." Two African fishermen reached for her. "Hurry! We have to be there by midnight!" She moaned as they lifted her.

Sheets of rain drenched them on the deck as they moved aft. It sobered Jack quickly. Off the starboard side he could scarcely make out the hills through the rain, but there were lights. *Thank God there's land close by*, he thought.

Behind the stern was a small vessel frantically trying to stay close to the larger fishing boat. An enormous wave passed under the boats, slamming them together. The other boat was so close Jack could see the concentrating eyes of the pilot. He was also African, older and looked like a veteran of the sea. The dangers all about did not seem to rattle him. "You want us to get into that!" Jack said, looking first at Bodecker and then the soldiers in disbelief. The soldiers looked equally apprehensive.

"Shut up. I have no time to waste with you. Prepare yourself to jump aboard, or I'll kill you now and get it over with." He shoved Jack toward the rail. "Throw her across," Bodecker ordered the fishermen carrying Kelly. The Africans stumbled to the rail cautiously and swung her limp body back and forth, attempting to synchronize their throw as the two boats moved with the motion of waves, first close, then apart, then close again. One man slipped just as they released her. At that moment the boats pulled apart. Kelly flew out over the open water, barely landing on the deck of the other boat.

The man who lost his balance was not so lucky. He hit the rail and cart wheeled over the side, screaming hysterically as he splashed briefly between the boats in the frigid water. But the next wave came quickly and it slammed the boats back together like two massive hands. They collided violently, crushing him between their hulls. When they fell away the man was gone. The two soldiers looked at one another with apprehension.

"You next," Bodecker said, directing his order to both Jack and his men. When the soldiers hesitated Bodecker waved his pistol toward the boat, indicating he would tolerate no insubordination.

Jack had no intention of letting them take Kelly alone. He braced himself, judged the waves then jumped, as did the two soldiers, the next time the boats came together. Bodecker followed with seeming ease, carrying the well-worn backpack. With all on board the small craft broke away from the larger vessel and made for the distant land. The wind whipped hard as they crested each wave, blowing the tops into the air, adding saltwater to the falling rain. From each crest Jack could see the approaching land. Jack was soaked and cold to the bone. Kelly remained unconscious on a pile of burlap and he wondered if she was dead.

After what seemed an interminable time, the captain turned the small craft parallel to the steep shoreline, precariously close to the breakers. The huge waves lifted the launch as they rose to break. Jack could feel them pulling the boat as they toppled just beyond their course. He could hear their power pummeling the cliffs.

The captain made for a point jutting from the land, and fighting the uncertain waves, rounded it into a bay. The huge rolling swells of the Atlantic were replaced with smaller choppy waves in the agitated waters of the inland bay. Jack saw the soldiers looking at one another in relief.

In the calmer water Kelly slowly regained consciousness. The rain subsided as they drove deeper into the inlet. Kelly propped herself up and drew a breath of the cold Atlantic air. It was night by now. Along the shore the overcast sky permitted just enough moonlight to illuminate an island coming into view over the bow. It was rocky, but shrouded by mist and engulfed by the sea, it soared high above the mainland behind it. A layered marine fog cut the island in half, revealing only the rocky base below and the steeple of its huge abbey above.

Kelly glanced at Jack, who was elated to see she was alive. "I know this place," she whispered. "It's Mont-Saint-Michel, on the west coast of France. My father brought me here as a child, on our way to Africa."

"What is it?" he asked.

"A town with an abbey—heavily fortified to guard the entrance to the river behind it."

"This seems an odd place to bring us," he said.

The boat circled the medieval island. Jack surveyed its fortified walls and imposing towers. It was still another mile to the mainland, and the connecting causeway was covered by the storm tide.

The captain sped toward a small dock built into the face of the stone fortification. Bodecker glanced at his captives. "You are conscious," he said to Kelly. "Good. My men were getting tired of dragging you around." The captain cut the engine and the boat slowed as it settled in the water, then drifted to a stop at the landing. "Get off. We are moving on."

The guards pulled Jack and Kelly roughly to their feet and they stumbled clumsily on the bobbing boat. From the landing they were herded into the confines of a narrow passage that burrowed through the fifteen-foot thick wall. On the other side was a twisting cobblestone street packed tightly with centuries old buildings. The storefront windows were broken and boarded, and trash lined the otherwise vacant street. The place looked deserted, but when Jack looked closer a cracked shutter revealed someone spying on the strangers.

One window stood out from the others. In it burned a candle, and around the frame was a simple Christmas decoration. It was the first sign of Christmas Jack had seen. From the window's bottom corner a very young girl peered down. Her eyes connected with Jack's, and she smiled at him. He could not help but return it. A soldier pushed him forward.

The air was wet and the street stones were slippery. Kelly was still unsteady and had difficulty staying balanced. Occasional moonlight helped illuminate the winding path that rose above the ghost town. Jack glanced up the vertical hillside. Giant buttresses and Gothic arches of the abbey's imposing cathedral loomed over them. The church was the town's crowning structure. Constructed on three levels, it had been a flamboyant medieval learning center with finely decorated rib vaults and or-nate Gothic windows.

They came to the gate that once insulated the monks in their secluded realm from the town below. Outside it a helmeted Ger-man soldier, smoking a cigarette, stood guard over a gang of la-borers. And beyond them, just inside the gate, was a guardroom. It was built into the wall with a window to the en-trance passage. In it, a solitary guard was fast asleep in a chair tipped back against the wall. Bodecker knocked hard on the glass, waking the guard from his stupor. Upon seeing the Standartenfuhrer's uniform he tried to kick the chair upright, but the back legs slipped out from under instead and the man crashed to the floor. He jumped to his feet and stood nervously at attention.

"Germany's finest," Jack said.

"Worthless idiots!" Bodecker replied.

"Your fort here is not exactly well guarded; in fact, it's almost vacant," Jack continued, prodding his captor. "Things must not be going so well for the Fatherland."

Bodecker bristled. "It is inconspicuous, and that is precisely why we chose it for this particular operation. Nobody knows about it, and nobody knows about you...not even on our side. And when you are gone, nobody will miss you."

His words silenced Jack. They moved up the continuing street, which was now inside the walled abbey, and was more like a spectacular stone stairway. At the top the stairs opened onto a terrace high upon the hill's west side. From there the view was spectacular, overlooking the ocean and the mainland. The retreating storm was still visible, lightning illuminating the dis-tant sky. The terrace and the massive church were lit in the flashes.

A uniformed man hurried out of one of the church's huge wooden doors. Bodecker stopped as he approached. He wore a General's uniform, distinct with the red stripe down the trousers. "I was becoming concerned," the General said hastily. He was perhaps sixty years old, fit, and wore wire-rimmed glasses.

"Have I failed yet?" Bodecker asked curtly.

General Joachim Schwartz disregarded the Standartenfuhrer's comment, turning instead to the prisoners while still addressing him. "There is little time to waste. Do you have it?" Bodecker pulled the statue from his pack. The General's eyes lit up like those of a madman. "Let me see it," he ordered. Bodecker handed it to him, and the General ran his trembling hands over the little statue, lovingly caressing the object. "It's beautiful. Just like the drawings in the library." He paused at the pits where the stones were missing. "And the stones? You have them as well?"

Bodecker held up the leather pouch. "They're all here." He then explained how Jack had removed them from their sequence in the statue and refused to place them back in proper order.

Schwartz looked at Bodecker with something close to contempt, then turned his attention to Jack and Kelly. "It was a very stupid thing you did," he said, eyeing them both from top to bottom. "Don't you realize the significance of this statue and the moment in history that is going to take place tonight—on this very terrace?" Then he walked a wide circle around them, one soldier each holding them from behind as he did. He looked Jack in the eye. "Unlike the Standartenfuhrer, I am a compassionate man. And I am willing to give you one last chance to avoid a very long and painful death....but don't test my kindheartedness, because it has its limits."

Jack said nothing as the General studied him. "Our time is growing short," the General snapped. "Bring them downstairs," he added, pushing Jack back in the direction from which they had just come.

The General led the way back down. Upon arriving at the gate where they had entered the abbey, he stopped, then continued several steps beyond it. To the left and down was a garden outside the walled complex. It was about forty feet below. Jack could see two guards below smoking cigarettes.

The General called out to one of them. "Corporal Günter, get inside and open the dungeon." The Corporal snapped to attention, then hurried over toward a door in the wall.

The General spun around and said, "This way, please," his hand directing Jack and Kelly and his men back into the guardroom. The same lazy guard that had fallen was still there, anxious at the presence of his superiors.

"Come on, come on. In you go," the General continued in a pleasant, almost friendly tone. "We must hurry. A busy night awaits us."

The soldiers shoved Jack and Kelly through the room. Bodecker and the General followed. They filed past the guard, who stood fearfully at attention, and moved toward a small door at the opposite end of the guardroom. It opened into a dark stairway that led downward. A lantern burned on the wall just inside. The General grabbed it and entered. Bodecker prodded Jack and Kelly to follow using his flashlight. Between them, they illuminated the cut stone stairs of the steep narrow passageway that descended, spiral after spiral, inside the fortified wall. The only other light was the setting moon, occasionally visible through thin gaps cut lengthwise in the wall, sporadically shining through the clouds onto the ocean.

"These slots were many an invader's downfall," the General said, pausing to look out over the water. "From them archers rained arrows down on their assailants." At the bottom of the stairs was the same guard from the garden, seated at a desk. He was Nordic in appearance with blond hair and blue eyes. He snapped to attention beside the open comic book he had been reading by the lantern light.

"Is everything in order, Günter?"

"Yes, Sir. Cell eight, down to the left, is open and ready Sir."

"Good." The General held up his lantern and shined it down the passage that turned perpendicular to the wall and bored into the bowels of the rocky island. It was no more than a damp, musty cave carved from the underlying rock. "This way," he said, sidestepping a rat that scurried from the light. "And watch your step."

From the sides of the tunnel, a number of cells had also been burrowed out, each enclosed by iron bars that were imbedded into the surrounding rock. "Do you like my dungeon?" the General asked proudly. "During the French Revolution it was a prison for the more notorious political prisoners, few of whom ever saw the sun rise again." He stopped in front of an open cell with two wooden chairs inside it. Wordlessly he stared into the cell; the others waited.

General Schwartz lowered his lantern, flipped open the backpack, and admired the statuette once again. He extended his hand toward Bodecker. "Herr Standartenfuhrer, the stones." Bodecker tossed him a leather pouch. Then the General glared at Jack and Kelly. "Lock them in and tie them up."

Bodecker motioned them into the cell with a nod. The General started back toward the guard's desk then stopped and turned back. "After I inspect the stones, I will give you one last chance to reveal the order of their placement," he said this threateningly. "You would be foolish not to cooperate." Then he continued to the desk, where under the light of lanterns he carefully studied the gems and the statue, comparing them to papers he had brought.

Bodecker looked at Jack and Kelly. "From this pit, you shall never leave, I assure you."

Recalling the cavern in the Andes, Jack smiled mockingly. "You have said something like that to us once before."

Bodecker's face turned red. "Tie them up!" Immediately the two soldiers moved forward. Bodecker went to where the General was examining his artifacts.

"In the chair," a soldier ordered roughly.

Jack eyed Kelly. "Ladies first," he said, stepping out of the way.

"Thanks a lot!" she grumbled.

As Jack backed up, he caught his foot and stumbled, tripping on to the floor. He moved awkwardly to get up, tearing his cuff open as he did, removing the wad of putty he had hidden there on the fishing boat.

"Get up!" the soldier ordered, kicking Jack in the ribs.

"Okay, okay. Just give me a chance. After being on that ship so long, I still don't have my balance." He moved shakily, using the threshold of the cell door to pull himself up, and as he grabbed it, he shoved the putty into the space where the bolt of the lock would normally close. Then he fumbled over to his chair.

As the soldiers finished securing them to the chairs, Bodecker and the General returned. Nobody said a word. In the corner of the cell, while looking away from Jack and Kelly, the General took out a cigarette.

"You feel pretty smart, Mr. Sullivan, ehhh?" He waited a moment, then turned ninety degrees and struck a match against the rusted iron bars of the chamber. The pitted surface lit the phosphate head with a bright flash, and a plume of odiferous smoke rose to the ceiling. "We'll see just how smart you really are." His unlit cigarette dangled from his mouth. "Yes?"

He lit the cigarette, and inhaled deeply, holding his smoke while inspecting the lit end of the cigarette. He did this silently for an extended moment, then exhaled a thin jet of smoke up toward the stone ceiling. He leaned purposefully closer, squatting so as to be at eye level with Jack. "I think you are a fool!" he said forcefully.

Jack stared defiantly back at him. Again, the General let time pass. From a leather sheath he pulled a knife and brandished it before Jack's eyes. "But, we will see." He took another drag, deep and slow, and moved closer, just inches from Jack's face. Their eyes stayed locked on one another, this time the General exhaled his smoke into Jack's face. He didn't like Jack's attitude, Jack could tell by the blade pressing on his throat.

"You're a tough guy, are you?" The general prodded on, then he laughed sinisterly. "We will see….just how tough you are when your friend here is screaming in pain." Jack's eyes darted nervously over to Kelly. He could feel the General's breath on his face. Its smoky stench filled his nostrils. "I'll ask this question only once. If you answer promptly and truthfully, I'll make things fast and painless for you both. Right here and now. If, however, you choose to be stubborn, I shall give Standartenfuhrer Bodecker a week of leave from his duties, so that he may dedicate all of his time to your miserable demise."

The General's eyes burned sadistically. Bodecker, in the background, looked on with pleasure. "The Standartenfuhrer is a truly cruel man. I do not wish to imagine what humiliating violations you and…" He paused and turned to Kelly, extending the knife and popping the top two buttons from her blouse. "Miss

Wilson especially, will suffer before reaching your inevitable fate."

Jack again glared at the General.

"Now, for the last time. In what order were the stones placed on the statue?" Jack said nothing. The General allowed a very brief moment to pass. "Time is up." Jack was puzzled. He expected more strong-arming, but instead the General lost interest almost before he started. "Regrettably, for you, it turns out you really were not needed." The General smiled callously pulling out some weathered sheets of paper. They were detailed drawings. "These renditions made by the Spaniards were quite accurate, down to the position, and placement of each and every one of the statue's jewels. They have answered my questions sufficiently." He seemed pleased with himself. "Every game has a winner and a loser Mr. Sullivan. Unfortunately the two of you have gone far out of your way to make this more difficult, costing me much time and effort. Therefore your price for losing must be higher. I wish I had the time to deal with you now, but I am a very busy man, with a statue to repair and a star to catch." He took a step back toward the cell door. "But do not worry, this matter we will be taken up tomorrow, right where we left off…and it will be most unpleasant." He turned to Bodecker. "Herr Standartenfuhrer, time is growing short. Check that they are secure. We'll deal with them in the morning."

Bodecker stepped up to relish his turn at taunting Jack and Kelly. As he double-checked their ropes, he said, "Tonight, on the terrace of this rocky point in France, history will be written—possibly even rewritten." He paused. "Last night from the boat, I could see the Indians' comet returning, speeding back from its catapulting trip around the sun." He let the information sink in. "You know what I'm talking about, don't you, Miss Wilson? It all fits, just as it did two months ago, and as it has for centuries before. The comet will return seeking the statue. And together they will reunite as they always have to open the time portal."

"And who will be the lucky traveler? The person to travel forward sixty-one years into the future?" Bodecker's eyes blazed like those of a madman. He slammed his fist into his hand victoriously. "That person will be me!" he exclaimed with clenched teeth. Then he turned toward the light down the corridor where the General was reconstructing the statue. "In what will seem like no more than an instant here, I will vanish—into the future—to see everything that is in store for us. And yet only seconds later, before the comet speeds off back into space and the depths of the solar system, I will have returned....with knowledge. Knowledge to win. Knowledge to dominate." He paused and gazed over their heads, inspired by his own words. "It will give me alone, more power than any human has ever had—more power than any human could imagine. I will be unstoppable."

"You are insane!" Kelly blurted. "Your lust for knowledge is your weakness, and like the original sin, it will lead you to your own destruction."

"Quiet!" he returned angrily.

"You are naive to believe—"

"It is not a mere belief, Miss Wilson. It is real! I was there. I saw it with my own eyes!" Bodecker's voice rose sharply like that of a lunatic.

"You're mad."

"Mad! Hardly. But since you choose to refer to the Bible, I must agree, our God does work mysteriously. Does He not? Picking me, a simple soldier of the Third Reich. Me, of all people, a warrior." He laughed loudly. "Maybe I will be like Joshua, chosen by God to slay all who occupy the land destined to be part of the

Fatherland." Bodecker paused, thinking of his words. "But I will not fail as Joshua did, in removing the filth from the earth. With the knowledge I bring back, the Führer will fulfill his destiny and rid us of the weakness which has infiltrated the human race."

"You are a presumptuous fool!" Kelly exclaimed with angry frustration. "You, your so-called Führer and every last Nazi are scum, despised by God."

Bodecker slapped her hard. "Silence, you fool! What can you, a woman, possibly know?" He stood back trembling with anger. He turned and exited the cell, then looked back. "I see your jealousy," he said laughingly through the bars. "And I cannot blame you. My time, and that of the Aryan race, is approaching, as is yours. And while I will have brought victory and success to Germany, you will have failed your country. I shall leave you to ponder your failure in the good hands of Corporal Günter." He smiled and swung the metal door closed. The sound of metal crashing into metal echoed down the cave walls.

Bodecker barked orders to the guard in German, then spun on his heel and joined the General, who was working carefully to restore the gems in the statue. After a few minutes they were gone. Only Jack, Kelly and Günter remained in the dungeon. The guard looked blankly into the cell where they sat bound. "I have to go to the bathroom," Kelly said.

Günter smiled, but said nothing; he just wandered slowly back to his desk, and planted himself in his chair. There he re-opened his comic book, leaving them in the darkness of their cell.

CHAPTER THIRTY-TWO

"**I** wonder what he said to the guard?" Kelly asked Jack, not expecting an answer.

"He said he wanted us safe and alive until morning. Once certain that the window to the future has been opened, and that we have done nothing to damage the statue's powers, they can do whatever they want with us, as long as they don't kill us," Jack told her.

"Well, that's kind of good… I mean the part about not killing us."

"He told our friend, Günter, that he alone wanted the joy of killing us, then said something about making it slow and painful."

"Now that part is bad." Kelly thought a moment, then said, "Hey! I didn't know you spoke German."

"I'm not just another pretty face from Texas," he said, then added, "I'm only Irish on my father's side. My mother is German and spoke it to us as kids. My grandparents could barely speak English. I had no choice, I had to learn."

"There's more. General Schwartz told Bodecker while they were at the guard station that he would hide a box under the stone that supports the altar in the crypt of Jean-Claude."

"What's in the box?"

"It sounded like information of some sort, but I'm not completely certain. That was all I could hear." Jack rocked his chair back and forth, walking it closer to Kelly.

"What are you doing?"

Jack lifted a leg onto her lap. "There's a shard of glass in the cuff. Use it to cut your ropes."

Kelly looked at him wide-eyed, then maneuvered her bound hands to the leg on her lap. She could barely reach it, but finally caught the already torn cuff and pulled it open. The shard fell into her hand. In minutes she had cut through the ropes that tied her feet. She could not reach the rope that bound her at the wrists. But still holding the glass, she moved to Jack and cut the rope binding him to the chair.

"Hurry. Günter may come checking." Just then the ropes broke free. Quickly he untied his feet and moved toward the bars. Wedging his head between them, he hoped to catch a glimpse down the passage to see what Günter was up to.

"Hey! What about my hands?" Kelly whispered.

"Just checking on our friend," Jack said, returning to free her. They both returned to the bars, rubbing their wrists. Günter had settled in, prepared for a long and boring evening. His eyes were closed and his head wobbled as he fought to stay awake.

Jack moved to the gate and pushed. It didn't budge. Had the bolt engaged into the jam, he worried? If it had they were doomed. He pushed again, this time outward and against the hinges at the same time. Still nothing happened. He tried once more, harder and jiggling it as he pushed. Suddenly there was a click and the door flew wide open with him riding on it as it swung. Jack cringed as the hinges squeaked loudly. He saw Günter stir at the end of the passage.

"Shhh!" Kelly said with big eyes and a finger to her lips.

Quickly Jack jumped back pulling the gate as he returned. He was certain the noise had alerted Günter.

"I didn't expect it to go so far," he whispered.

"How'd you do that?" Kelly asked.

Before he could answer, Günter called out into the darkness of the passageway. "I'll tell you later," Jack said. "Get back in your chair with your ropes," he added, wrapping a piece of wire around the bars of the door and its door jam. He heard the guard getting up from his chair. By the time Günter arrived at the cell, Jack was back in his chair with his ropes haphazardly thrown over his body. Günter held up the lantern inquisitively. Its dim light barely illuminated the passage, much less the inside of the cell. He spoke German to them. Jack looked at him and wiggled, acting as if he did not understand. The guard grabbed the door by its bars and shook it hard, checking its integrity. The wires Jack had fixed held and the door did not move. Shaking his head and mumbling, he wandered back to his bench.

Thirty minutes of silence passed before Jack or Kelly moved or spoke. Finally, Jack pushed the pile of ropes off himself, and Kelly followed suit. The light in the dungeon was all but gone. The guard's lantern provided a mere flicker, but his snoring attested to the fact that it was not keeping him awake. Jack untied the wires on the door and this time gently eased it open. The two slipped out of the cell and down the passage toward the sleeping guard.

Günter never knew what hit him.

Armed with Günter's rifle and a pistol they found in his desk drawer, Jack and Kelly made their way up the stairs to the guard-house above. They found the small door leading into it from the stairs ajar. Over the last stair, at floor level, Jack peered into the room. It was heavily clouded with cigarette smoke. He backed away. "Looks like five of them. Four are playing cards, the fifth I can barely see by the door across the room. I think he's just watching."

"Any ideas?" Kelly asked.

"No. But if we're going to stop Bodecker and the General, we're going to have to get through that door." He looked at the pistol in her hand. "You know how to use that?"

"I've shot cans on my Uncle's farm in Virginia."

"That's going to have to do." He paused. "We'll storm in, and catch them off guard."

"Just like that?" she gasped.

"We should look desperate," he added, trying to bolster Kelly's confidence.

"That'll be easy," she said without hesitation.

With weapons drawn the two stormed the room. Jack bolted for the soldier by the door. He reached for his holster, but Jack slammed the butt of his rifle against the man's head. He went down like a sack of rocks. "Hands up!" Jack ordered in German.

Kelly stormed the table, holding her pistol with both hands. She waved it from one soldier's face to the next. For a moment it was a stalemate as the men considered their options. The lack of response made Kelly more anxious. She yelled at them in English, her voice high pitched, her eyes crazed, her motions jittery. Even Jack could not understand her. She looked dangerously out of control. The men's eyes were fixed on the barrel of her gun and her finger trembling on the trigger. It looked like it was going to go off any second. The men raised their hands very slowly above their heads. Kelly kept moving maniacally about them.

"I'll keep my gun on them. You strip them of their weapons, belts and shoes," Jack said to Kelly. Once they were stripped, Jack ordered them down the stairs. He used his rifle to point them in the direction of the door. They marched them down to the dungeon, the able ones dragging the unconscious one and picking up the still limp Günter on the way.

Jack removed the putty from the door jam as the last of them entered the cell, then swung the door closed. This time it locked tight. When they started back up the stairs, he asked Kelly jokingly, "Are you sure you haven't done this sort of thing before?"

"What do you mean?"

"I mean, I'm glad you're on my side. I thought you were going to kill them back there."

"It looked a lot different from where I was. I thought I was going to wet my pants."

Jack and Kelly cut through a maze of rooms and passages below the superstructure of the old abbey, hoping to gain more discreet access to the terrace above. They came on a room largely taken up by a wooden wheel fifteen feet in diameter. Rolling off its axis was a rope leading out a gaping hole in the wall. Beyond it was a pulley. Kelly stuck her head out and looked down the two hundred-fifty foot steep drop, which was composed of wall then hillside to the ground below.

"What's that?" Jack asked, joining her in looking over the precipice. There was a cart secured to the rope and resting on rails against the lip of the opening. The rails went vertically all the way down the wall to the ground below.

"This is how the monks once got their provisions. They had vowed total seclusion from the outside world. By using the cart they could keep their silence—sending notes and pulling up supplies.

"We could use it to go down," Jack joked.

"I think we'll find another route, thanks anyway."

Continuing up through the interior, the two crossed a kitchen and then entered a long narrow room lined with tall windows. "This is the dining hall where the monks, prohibited from speaking, silently had their meals while listening to the reading of scripture," Kelly told him.

"You know everything about this place?"

"I told you, I came here with my father on our way to Africa."

The huge tables of the empty hall were covered with maps and charts. "Looks like the General's been using this place as an office," Jack said." They passed through open doors, then into a beautifully manicured garden, surrounded by elegant marble columns supporting miniature Gothic arches and stone carvings. It was empty.

"Where do you suppose they are?" Kelly wondered.

"I don't know, but we're at the top," he said, pointing at the huge buttressed walls of the Cathedral beside them.

"There's a light over there. Just past the garden," Kelly whispered.

They moved across the garden toward the light. A strong North Atlantic wind had blown the storm south, and the moon had set, leaving the night sky dark, clear, and gleaming with stars. There was an opening in the wall through which they peered diagonally onto a flat terrace under the stars. A fire burned brightly on its cobblestone surface.

Five men were gathered around the blaze. Two of them were in German uniforms and had guns. They stood back and to one side, their faces impassive. One of the other three wore a robe resembling a religious garment of some sort, while the other two were in civilian business suits.

"Look. They have the statue! On the pedestal by the fire," Kelly exclaimed. "And isn't that man beside it, in the suit there, Bodecker?"

"Yeah. And those are the steps in front of the Cathedral where Bodecker met up with the General when we first arrived. You remember? Where the General said history was going to be made," Jack added. "Who's the guy by the stairs, in the fancy robe?"

"It looks like the General," Kelly said.

Jack scrutinized the gathering more closely. "So it is! They've got themselves a regular costume party."

The wind blew coldly over the terrace, whipping the flames into a frenzy. The firelight reflected off the statue's polished gold adornments, its red ruby eyes occasionally flashing brilliantly as the light caught them just right.

"Looks like they figured out how to put the gems back in place," Kelly observed.

"The order of the stones was just a bluff," Jack said. "I have no idea whether it would have any effect on the little statue's ability to do whatever it is that it supposedly does, or not."

"So, now what?" Kelly asked.

"I'm not sure. Let's just see what happens," Jack said.

The wind grew stronger and stronger, whistling through the stone buttresses and steeple. Its howl became so loud that Jack and Kelly could barely hear each other. Finally, a light in the sky caught Kelly's attention.

"Look at that! Over there!" She pointed to the light shining more prominently than the stars.

Jack looked up, immediately remembering that fateful night on the river with Lucy. "I've got a bad feeling about this."

Kelly didn't hear him. "It's moving!" she said. "I wonder what it is. Do you think it's a plane?"

"No." Jack paused. "I've seen this star...thing... before..."

"When?" Kelly asked.

"Let's just say, it didn't turn out to be my lucky star."

"What is it?"

"I don't know, but this star, comet, or whatever, must be what Bodecker and the General are here waiting to receive."

"It's the thing the legend of the statue is based on," Kelly said.

They watched together as it grew brighter. The wind howled relentlessly and seemed to grow in intensity. The robed General raised his hands, chanting inaudible words towards the sky as Bodecker looked on with a stone face, unaffected by the harsh elements.

The tail of the comet became more clearly defined as it accelerated toward the little island. "Maybe we should take cover," Jack suggested.

"Are you kidding? We need to stay here and see what happens."

"Then what?" Jack inquired.

"I don't know. Stop them, I suppose."

"You have a plan?" Jack asked.

"No," she said. "That's what I have you here for."

Jack looked at her with bewilderment.

"Well, we can't just let them go waltzing into the future and find an advantage over us, can we?" she added. "Besides, look at it, it's beautiful," Kelly said, gazing up at the comet's brilliance. The light poured over her like a spotlight, drawing her from concealment into full view of the terrace.

"Careful, Kelly, they'll see you."

The entire island was now lit by the object's radiance, which also reflected brightly on the ocean around it. Like the five men on the terrace, Kelly was unable to look at anything other than the source of the light. Bathed within the light, she felt no fear. Jack felt a strange itching and pulling. He looked at Kelly. Her long hair was on end, spread out like the spines on a sea urchin. Amazed by the phenomenon, he stepped from behind shelter to touch Kelly's extended hair. Sparks flew from his fingers toward her, then up into the sky above. "What's going on?" he muttered, watching the light flow from his fingers. Now that he was in the light, he too felt the pull exerted by the object.

"I feel as if I'm floating," Kelly said, almost in a trance.

"You are," Jack answered, watching Kelly's body weightlessly lifting above the ground.

"It's real. It's not a legend," she said, mesmerized. Her face was relaxed and bore a contented smile.

Abruptly Jack tore himself from the light. He reached out and pulled Kelly's floating body to him. Her feet dropped to the ground as they huddled in the shadows. "Stay out of the light!" Jack warned.

"But it was so beautiful," Kelly said, still in a daze of contentment.

"Snap out of it!" Jack said, slapping her cheek. "We won't be any good if we aren't in control."

Kelly sobered quickly, though they could still feel the force of the light on their skin, as it bent around the wall. "If it gets stronger it could get to us even behind this wall!" Jack said. "Quick! Take cover in there!" He pushed her to scurry for the church. They entered a side door, the howling wind slamming it closed behind them.

"Hurry! The front door!" Kelly exclaimed. "From there we can see what they're doing, up close!"

Stained glass lined the massive wooden church doors and the brilliant light shone beautiful colors through its colored mosaic on to the stone walls of the narthex. Kelly peered through a clear piece of the glass while Jack looked through a peek window built into the door.

On the other side the wind whipped and swirled the fire. In a surreal scene the five men hung suspended just above the ground, sparkling lights dancing around them. The soldiers and the smaller man in civilian clothes who accompanied Bodecker appeared alarmed by the comet's brilliant core. It began hovering above them. Its blinding radiance illuminated everything.

Bodecker was anxious, anticipating the next stage—the opening of the portal into the future. General Schwartz was equally enthusiastic, having no reason to doubt what the Standartenfuhrer had told him. Then it all stopped—the wind with its deafening whistle, the thunderous roar, the electrical display. All that remained was the mesmerizing light. What followed was neither a cold nor dark—only deathly quiet as if time itself was slowing down.

Frozen behind their perch in amazement, Jack and Kelly waited. A swirling cloud took shape around the statue, its gases rotating horizontally like the rings of a planet. Its energy caused the stones of the huge Romanesque pillars beside Jack and Kelly to vibrate. Increasing in intensity, the tremors spread to the ground and nearby cliffs. The soldiers backed away from the cathedral, fearing its collapse. Then the core descended into the cyclone around the statue, its light now within the swirling cloud. A hole appeared in the cloud.

Jack and Kelly saw Bodecker motion to the other civilian in the group. "Now! Follow me," he ordered. The civilian, of slight frame and much smaller than Bodecker, hesitated only a second, then the two stepped through the edge of the rotating transparent cloud into the hole. Inside, only the statue was visible, illuminated by the light of the core within. Sparks danced at the border where their bodies made contact. As the pair moved forward into the cloud they abruptly vanished.

"Hurry! We've got to follow them," Kelly yelled. She bolted through the huge doors, down the steps, and onto the brilliantly lit terrace, catching Jack off guard. Her hasty reaction left Jack without options. He had to follow her.

The two charging figures broke the mesmerizing spell that held General Schwartz and his two remaining soldiers captive. "*Halt!*" he shouted, his hand instinctively reaching for his sidearm. But there was only his robe. He turned to his men and ordered, "Shoot them! Quickly! They will ruin everything."

Gathering their wits, still shaking off the effects of the light, the soldiers reached clumsily for their weapons. As they did Kelly bolted past them, then hesitated at the changing cloud surrounding the statue. The soldiers now had drawn their weapons. "Kill them!" the General ranted. They opened fire, but in the confusion missed. "You idiots! Give me that gun!" he yelled, snatching the weapon from one of the men.

Jack saw the General's intentions, and leapt toward Kelly who didn't see him coming. As he flew through the air he scooped Kelly in his arms, and his momentum carried them into the cloud. Engulfed in a flash of a thousand lights, they disappeared into the swirl. Jack braced himself to hit the stone terrace hard.

The last thing he heard was the General's gun firing loudly next to his ear.

•

The hard landing never came. Instead, light surrounded Jack as he spun in total silence. He could see Kelly in his arms. The church, the statue, and the General were all gone, vanished.

"Where did they go?" he asked, but he could not hear his voice. Inside the cloud the lights were of all colors. Jack could sense motion about them, but could perceive no borders, no horizon. He was filled with a warm sensation of bliss.

Together they moved in slow motion down a passage that had yet to show its end. Jack could see Kelly's lips moving. She was trying to say something, but he couldn't hear her words. She looked at peace. Her expression was that of warmth and contentment. He too, felt that same sense of peace and tranquility. He wondered *did the General shoot us? Are we both dead and going to the afterlife?*

It did not matter; he had the woman he loved in his arms. If this was death, he welcomed it.

CHAPTER THIRTY-THREE

Maximilian Kudrnac had chosen the graveyard shift for the holiday season right from the start. At seventy-two he was the most senior watchman at the Metropolitan Museum in New York City, and always had first pick of shift on each new schedule. The junior watchmen thought him a fool to take the night shift on the holidays, but he had his reasons, reasons he did not wish to dwell on or share—the loss of his wife of fifty-three years.

Ever since her death he dreaded going home to his empty apartment, lying in bed alone while hearing life go on out in the street. It was particularly difficult during the holiday season. Besides, over the years he'd come to like the night shift. It was quiet, and he could read.

The museum had been closed for a full thirty minutes, but it had taken that long to shepherd the last of the straggling visitors out the door. The holiday crowd had been large and the weather outside was cold and windy. Peculiarly it was even threatening with lightning. Max finally started his first round through the southeast wing, turning out lights, securing exit doors, and checking to be certain that all the visitors had found their way out. This was the section of the museum used to display special touring exhibits on loan from other museums.

With that done and the place empty, Max decided he could settle in for another quiet night of reading. As he closed the door to the special exhibits hall, he backed into its sign which someone had moved. It clanged loudly on the marble floor, echoing throughout the empty building. Max grunted as he squatted, then lifted it up and moved it into place.

It read, "*South American Archeological and Anthropological Exhibit,*" and in small print below, "*presented with special effects talents of Josh Goodman.*"

"You okay, Max?" a voice asked from the other side of the hall room.

"Oh, Mr. Goodman, you're still here." Max paused. "Yeah," he said and brushed himself off as if he had been the one to fall. "Yeah, I'm fine. It's the base on this sign, it's all cockeyed."

Josh Goodman looked around, then up at the ceiling of the museum's second floor hall room one last time. He was a well-dressed, distinguished looking man of sixty with reassuring, fatherly looks. "Well, it's a wrap here," he said to the watchman as they walked down a hallway to the main entrance.

"All finished here in New York, Sir?"

"Yeah," Josh answered with a touch of satisfaction. "We're all done here."

They reached a balcony overlooking the museum's expansive entryway. Josh stared blankly down into the Great Hall, pensively recalling the tour he had been in charge of. "I think it went well."

"Went well? I should say so," Max said. "I heard Mr. Gaston saying your exhibit drew record numbers for the museum."

Josh Goodman enjoyed another moment and then humbly said, "Life is good, Max. I have no complaints."

"Where to next, Mr. Goodman?" Max asked, shaking his keys to free the one he needed to lock another door.

"This is the end of the tour. The exhibits will be returned to their respective museums from which they are on loan. And I will go back to L.A."

"What about your feature exhibit?" the guard asked.

"The Picayulta statue?"

"Yeah, where is it housed?"

"It goes back to Paris, to their museum of archeology in the Louvre."

"Paris? What's a South American relic doing in a French museum?" Max inquired.

"That's very perceptive of you," Josh said with surprise. Max straightened a bit and threw his shoulders back. It felt good to impress a man of Josh Goodman's caliber. "It is a mystery. No one is sure just how it got there, but an elderly French woman discovered it buried in her potted plant back in the fifties."

"In a potted plant!" Max exclaimed with disbelief.

"Yep. Her cat knocked it off the balcony and in the broken mess was the statue."

"Boy, wouldn't you love to find a prize like that in your yard?" Max dreamed momentarily. "You'd be rich and famous." He paused then looked at Goodman and concluded, "I guess you already are rich and famous."

The two men walked toward a window that looked out over Fifth Avenue and the park. A blanket of snow covered the ground and bundled pedestrians moved briskly in the cold wind. "Well, it didn't do her much good, Max," Josh said. "She died the following week, before anyone could ask how she came to own the potted plant."

"Wow! That's rotten luck."

"So, I guess we'll never really know how it came to be in France." Josh wore a mysterious smile, highlighted by a flash of lightning that came through the wall-sized window of the museum's second floor. "But it is mysteries such as these that keep us movie making archeologists employed."

"So that's it," Max concluded.

"I'm afraid so. I guess I'll head home." More lightning flashed through the glass. "That's quite a show of lights," Josh commented.

Max moved closer to the window. The flashes followed each other so closely that the park seemed to be in daylight. The spectacle lit up silhouettes of leafless trees in a backdrop of skyscrapers. "I hope you brought your umbrella. That's a real storm brewing out there," Max said, then added, "Don't remember anything quite like this in December." He paused. "Not in my seventy years here."

Josh joined the watchman at the huge window on the mezzanine level and looked out over the park. "That's odd. I don't recall any mention of rain or snow in the morning forecast, let alone lightning." He shrugged. "The shippers will arrive at five thirty in the morning to dismantle the exhibits, Max," he said, turning to leave. "Have a good night."

"Good night, Sir," Max answered, turning the main lights of the Great Hall off. The watchman started down another hallway to resume his duties, leaving Josh alone to watch the lightning. With only the diminished night lighting system operating, Josh made his way carefully around the balcony toward the stairs, the incessant flashes of lightning continually illuminating the Great Hall and the marble statues that loomed lifelessly within it. As he descended the stairs a hissing sound caught his attention. It grew louder, but its origin was unclear. It seemed to permeate from every direction, and then abruptly it culminated in a loud crash, which came unmistakably from the southeast wing.

"I thought everyone was out, Max," Josh called as he set out toward the disturbance.

A commotion was coming from within the doors of the special exhibit room. Max hurried back. "I just made my rounds in there, Mr. Goodman. There was no one."

They heard the door's locks being rattled and turned. "What the…" Max moved with purpose for the doors, rattling his keys loudly as he went. But before he could get there the doors of the special exhibit hall burst open, and two men in suits ran out, one enormous and obviously fit, the other much smaller with a pencil mustache. Confused and disoriented, they looked one way and then the other.

"Hey!" Max shouted. "We're closed. You clowns need to get out of here, or we'll call the police." For an instant, the men looked puzzled, then spotted the exit. Max was between it and them. "Out! Now!" Max ordered forcefully. He moved briskly toward them.

The men rushed toward him. "Get out of my way!" the bigger man said threateningly with a German accent. He straight-armed Max, sending him careening to the floor. The other man said something to his companion in guttural German. Josh stepped aside and let them past.

"Stop! Stop!" Max yelled from the floor.

Josh watched as they hurried down the stairs and made for the front door. In seconds the men were outside on the street. A taxi had stopped and a man was opening its door for his companion. The Germans pushed them aside and entered the cab. Josh could see the couple's muted swearing through the glass as their hijacked cab sped off. He wrote the number on the cab down on his hand. Then he turned to Max, who was just getting back on his feet.

"I'll chase them down, Sir," Max said with embarrassment. "I don't know how they got in there. The place was empty."

"It's okay, Max. They're long gone. They were empty handed; probably just a couple of drunken tourists who lost track of time."

"Shall I call the police?" Max asked, rubbing the shoulder he had fallen on.

"Don't bother, but I'm going to have a look around just the same to be sure. Why don't you finish locking up?"

As Max left to complete his chores Josh returned to the special exhibit hall. He first checked on his prized piece, "*The Picayulta statuette from South America*." It was resting safely on its display pedestal. After assuring himself that the statue was unharmed, he continued through the hall with relief. He made a mental checklist of the other valuables belonging to the collection. Everything was there. The men had taken nothing.

As he turned for the door he sniffed the air, detecting a peculiar odor. It was very faint, as if something sweet had been burnt. He discounted it as the lingering aroma of some cheap perfume. "Odd," he muttered.

•

Having come to grips with the realization that his life had ended abruptly, that the General's bullet must have struck him, and that he was now dead, Jack was trying to figure out where this surreal dream was taking him.

He and Kelly were moving down a dimensionless tunnel of pulsating blurred lights and vague motion. The walls that guided them were fluid and translucent, and each time they swayed close to one, the side would bow away as if avoiding the contact.

Were they in limbo, or were they actually in motion....going some-where specific, Jack wondered? It felt like movement, but he could not see ahead. At what speed they were moving, he could not tell. Time was distorted. And as he plunged forward into the un-certainty of his existence, he felt no apprehension. Instead, he was filled with a sense of harmony and well-being.

The peripheral motion was hypnotic, and for how long the journey continued, neither knew. Then something changed. The trajectory of their path began to oscillate erratically and the gen-tleness disappeared. They deviated roughly to one side. This time the surrounding walls did not yield. Jack felt a few bumps as they skimmed it. Abruptly they made a sharp turn for the oppo-site wall. There was a sudden sense of speed, and Jack braced himself as they powered into the side.

The nebulous border absorbed them into its mass. Plunging through turbulence they pushed forward. Then they hit some-thing hard, and were violently thrust through a barrier, the boundary of whatever it was that they were in. Jack felt pain again. His senses returned as he tumbled across the ground.

•

Resuming his way to the exit, Josh heard the return of the hiss-ing sound, accompanied by a deep drone. It was eerie. He spun around and scanned the room for the source, but again it seemed to be everywhere. It grew louder. Josh focused on the statue. It no longer rested quietly. Its ruby red eyes burned brightly and sparks spewed from its mouth. The air surrounding it took on a fluorescent glow.

"What the hell..."

Then there was a burst of thick billowing smoke which poured out of the statue's open mouth, flowing onto the floor before it.

Josh could not take his eyes off the spectacle. The dense cloud piled on itself, growing higher and higher, until it reached the level of the statue itself. It hovered in a mass, not spreading. Sparks darted from the statue into the cloud. The deep drone increased in volume, agitating the other exhibits to a frenzied vibration. One crashed to the floor. Josh could not take his eyes off the statue. The droning culminated in a loud crash and a bright flash that came unmistakably from within the cloud.

The sparks, the hissing and the deep drone stopped as if someone had flipped a switch. The suspended cloud continued to hover briefly before collapsing under its weight, dropping to the ground and spreading thinly across the floor. Josh looked down. The amorphous gas flowed around his ankles, and swirling eddies formed in its currents. Again there was that sweet smell, this time stronger. Motion drew his attention back to the statue, and there he saw two human figures, motionlessly enveloped in each other's arms, lying on the floor. Cautiously he approached, uncertain if they were dead. One moved slowly, groaning with pain. They were alive!

"What are you doing here? The museum is closed," Josh said nervously, and then quickly realized the stupidity of his statement. Whatever he had just witnessed was much more than late leaving visitors. He collected himself. Before him were a man and a woman, strangely dressed and looking completely bewildered. Both were now moving, dizzily attempting to get on their feet. Josh stepped backwards. "Who are you?" His tone was much more inquisitive this time. "Where did you come from?"

The disoriented travelers lifted themselves to their feet.

•

Jack ignored the man talking to him. He was unarmed and did not appear to pose a threat. He was more concerned with the General, who was firing the gun behind him. Jack spun three hundred sixty degrees searching for the General.

"What happened?" Kelly groaned from the floor.

Jack helped her up, still turning his head in all directions. "The General... He's gone!" he told her.

Josh stepped closer. "General? What are you talking about? And who are you?"

"Where are we?" Kelly asked Jack groggily.

Realizing there was no General, no Mont-Saint-Michel, and that they weren't even outside anymore, Jack and Kelly turned to the man standing before them demanding explanations. In unison they asked, "Who are you?"

"Excuse me, but this is my exhibit. I'll ask the questions here," he snapped. "A minute ago I was in here, searching the place. It was empty. Then wham! There was a big crash, and suddenly the two of you appear. Now if you don't start answering my questions, I'm going to call the authorities."

"Where are we?" Kelly asked.

"This is the second floor of the museum hall," Josh replied.

"Is this still the abbey in France?"

"The abbey! In France?" Josh exclaimed. "Have you been drinking?" But inside he was starting to understand that he had just witnessed something extraordinary. What it was he did not know.

Kelly looked at the statue. "Wow! It actually worked!"

"I guess it did," Jack answered. "The General's gone, and so has the fire on the terrace."

"There you go about a General again," Josh said irritably. "What General?"

"It's not a legend!" Kelly exclaimed. "We're really here!"

"But where is here?" Jack returned.

"Damn it! You're in New York City," Josh interrupted, not really sure why people wouldn't know the city they were in. But he wanted answers.

"New York!" Jack looked back at Josh, who was staring at the two intruders curiously. He could see that they too were in some sort of shocked and confused state of mind.

"Bodecker!" Kelly suddenly exclaimed.

"Did you see two men come through here?" Jack asked Josh.

"Two men? Why yes, there were a couple of German tourists who left hurriedly a few moments ago."

"German tourists?"

"Yes. They sounded German to me. My guard scared them off. They pushed him over as they fled, catching a cab out front."

"How could a German be a tourist in New York? We're at war with them!" Jack said.

"At war! What are you talking about?"

"Pearl Harbor?" Jack said. "Remember?"

"Pearl Harbor? Why, that was more than sixty years ago," Josh said, confused by Jack's statement.

"What year is this?" Kelly asked.

"What do you mean, what year is this?" Josh answered with exasperation. "It's 2003, of course. Who are you two? What year do you think this should be?"

Just then Max rushed in. "Mr. Goodman? Are you all right?" He saw the two intruders standing inside the exhibit display with the statue. "Hey! What the hell is this tonight, Grand Central Station? Get out of there," he ordered. "We're closed." He moved toward them, this time with his pistol drawn. His eyes darted over to Josh, but he was lost deep in thought. "I'll call the cops, Mr. Goodman."

Jack raised his hands while looking down the barrel of Max's gun. The commotion they had created was one that even he himself could not explain. "I'm sorry, Sir. We'll leave immediately." He looked around for the exit.

"Damn right you will! In a paddy wagon," Max replied, calling 911 one-handed on his cell phone.

Jack became very nervous as he watched the guard fiddle with the little gadget. He had never seen such a weapon. "No, really, Mister. We didn't mean any harm. Which way out?" Jack asked.

"How about backwards—the way you came in," Max said snidely while pointing the weapon at the door.

Kelly grabbed Jack's arm. "Let's go, Jack. We've taken enough of their time."

Josh raised his hand. "Put that gun away before someone gets hurt, Max. And put the phone down. That won't be necessary." He looked them straight in the eye. "Will it, Mister…?" He waited until Jack filled in the silence.

"Sullivan," Jack replied. "Jack Sullivan."

"And your friend is…"

"I'm Kelly Wilson."

"Well, I'm Josh Goodman," he said, extending his hand. "Pleased to make your acquaintance." Josh could see that Max was puzzled. "I'll see them to the door, Max. You go ahead and finish your rounds."

"I don't mind bustin' them, Sir," Max offered.

Josh shook his head. "No, now go on, in case there are any other stragglers in the building."

"You're the boss," Max said, shaking his head in disagreement as he left.

Josh looked pensively at Jack and Kelly, still mystified by their spontaneous appearance but certain he was on to something fantastic. A moment of silence passed while the three studied each other. Abruptly Kelly broke in. "Jack! We have to catch up with Bodecker!" As if late for a forgotten train, the two dashed for the exit.

"Hey wait!" Josh cried out.

"Thanks, Mister," Jack hollered on the move.

"It's Josh, Josh Goodman, and I still have some questions!"

"Sorry, we can't explain now. We have to catch the two men who just left," Kelly shouted, pushing through the doors.

Josh started to chase them, but they were younger and faster. By the time he reached the stairs, they were flying out the front door into the congested street. And when Josh finally reached the sidewalk, they were gone, two more figures blending into the bustling mass of humanity. Max came running out behind him. "They got away, didn't they?"

"'Fraid so, Max."

"I shoulda cuffed 'em, when I had 'em in there. You won't mention my oversights to the director, will you, Sir?"

"No, of course not, Max." Josh paused, only half listening. He looked curiously at the sky. The lightning had stopped. Then he continued, "No harm was done. Let's just say it never happened."

"Thank you, Sir," Max said gratefully, but Josh did not hear him. His mind was a million miles away, thinking about Jack and Kelly and their mysterious appearance. His eyes were focused on the crowd, hoping to get a glimpse of them in the distance. There was something more than the way they'd arrived. All four of the stragglers had been wearing very old fashioned clothes. Curious.

Max looked in the other direction, then turned to say something to Josh, but he was gone, vanished into the flow of pedestrians. Max found himself alone in the crowd. They moved past him as if he were not even there. He looked up at the clearing sky, then pulled his collar up to protect his neck from the wind. It now seemed like any other cold, blustery December night in New York City.

CHAPTER THIRTY-FOUR

Jack and Kelly wandered through the crowd on Fifth Avenue. It was windy between the buildings and cold enough to form mist when people spoke. Their lack of winter coats and ragged looking clothes made them all the more conspicuous in the dichotomy of well-dressed people. Some joyfully strolled and shopped the post Christmas sales, while others moved hurriedly, cutting through the gridlocked traffic to get to their destinations.

The swarm of activity had Jack rubbernecking in all directions. He stared first at the beggars perched miserably on the store steps, jingling their cups for change. Beyond the beggars he spotted a black man tapping out a rhythm on a conga drum. Then came a woman who waved her arms wildly while conversing with herself and collided with him. "Excuse me," he said, but the woman continued on obliviously, ranting and raving as she went.

Jack noticed many others were carrying on conversations with small boxes in their hands. They looked like the same gadget that the guard at the museum had used. Jack grew suspicious. "What's with all the people talking to their hands?" he wondered aloud.

"They're holding something—like a radio," Kelly answered.

"They can't be. They're too small."

The thundering noise of a low rider interrupted them. The vibrating boom from the stereo reverberated through the surroundings. "Asshole!" an anonymous voice called out from the crowd.

"Nice place," Jack commented. "Ever been here before?" he asked sarcastically.

"It has been a few years," Kelly said, "but yes, I lived here, in college."

"Why am I not surprised? So where do we go?"

Kelly thought for a second. "How about to church?" Before Jack could interrupt, she added, "The church my father worked for had an office in New York, that way, just past Times Square."

"Hey, maybe some of your childhood friends are now running the place," Jack jested.

"They would be in their seventies by now." A man roasted chestnuts on the corner. Kelly inhaled the aroma. "It smells so good. I'm starved."

"Well, we don't have any money."

"Party pooper."

They kept moving. There was a siren in the background. It made Jack nervous. "Let's take cover in there," Jack said, nudging Kelly into a nearby alley. It appeared to be vacant, but neither could see into its dark recesses.

"Are you always like this around the cops?"

"It seems to be a habit lately." Jack watched the street vigilantly.

Kelly heard noises coming from the depths of the alley beyond. Her eyes adjusted to the darkness, and she saw a band of teenagers skulking in the shadows. The kids were acting oddly, preoccupied and watching the one trying to roll some sort of cigarette. Kelly tugged Jack's shirt to get his attention. He looked at the group, figuring they were too poor to afford machine made cigarettes. They made Kelly nervous, and she drew back from the group distractedly. Clumsily she banged into an empty garbage can that clanked and rattled loudly. "Oops," she whispered.

The boy rolling the cigarette looked up startled and fumbled the paper, spilling the contents to the ground. The whole gang swore harshly at him for his clumsiness. He turned on Kelly and Jack. "Look what you did, you idiots. You knocked over my pot," he said accusingly. He moved into the light, approaching Kelly, his cohorts gathering behind him for support. He was shabbily dressed in a worn black leather jacket with a chain hanging from his belt, another wrapped around his neck like a collar. His head was completely shaved and tattooed proudly on his forehead was a black swastika.

Jack and Kelly were startled and wide eyed at his appearance. They retreated at the sight of the swastika. "This doesn't look promising. The Nazis must have won the war," Jack whispered to Kelly.

"What the hell are you looking at?" the boy said, pounding his fist into his hand threateningly. He had fingerless gloves on with spikes built into the knuckles. Behind him the group looked as menacing as he did, including the girls who were dressed all in black, which contrasted against their pasty white faces but matched their heavy black mascara and black lipstick. Several had bizarre hairstyles of neon green with a swirl of hot pink.

Still, the threatening teen hesitated before Jack's larger size. Jack and Kelly were speechless in the stand off. One emboldened girl stuck her tongue out at the gawking couple, revealing the barbell of metal she had pierced through its dorsum. Rings pierced her lips, cheeks, nose and eyebrows. And more than ten studded each ear. Her short top and low cut pants exposed her midsection, which was obscenely tattooed with the picture of a woman performing a lewd sex act on a man whose organ coincided with the girl's navel, which was also pierced with a ring of gold. "What kind of place has this become?" Kelly whispered.

"He's talking to you, freaks," the loitering girl said.

The others quickly chimed in with profane gestures and verbal abuse. In moments the group had gained confidence and advanced cautiously like a cowardly mob, none having the guts to strike first, but all hoping to egg on the others to start a brawl.

Jack and Kelly retreated backwards, never taking their eyes off the pack, until they had backed onto the congested sidewalk. The flowing crowd ran them down with neither concern nor malice. A man carrying packages bumped hard into Kelly. She stumbled toward the traffic speeding by in the street. Jack saw her tumbling, but was too far to help. From out of nowhere two arms stopped her fall.

"Careful there, young lady," a man's voice said.

"Thank you," she said automatically, then looked up. "You! You're the man from the museum."

Josh Goodman smiled, then said as if he'd been searching for hours, "And you two are hard to keep up with."

Jack stepped forward. "Look, Mister…Goodman, we didn't mean any harm back…"

"Forget that," Josh interrupted. "I'm not chasing you down." He thought for a moment, then added, "Well, maybe I am, but it's not to turn you in to the police." He looked curiously at Kelly, then back to Jack. Their clothes were not only old fashioned, they were dirty and wrinkled, and the couple looked cold, lost and overwhelmed. "Who are you kids?"

"Thanks again, but we're in a hurry. We really have to go," Jack said, grabbing Kelly and leading her away.

"Go where?" Josh called, speaking to their backs. They did not answer or acknowledge him. "It's a big city and not always friendly to out-of-towners." He started to follow after them. "You look lost. Maybe I can help you get somewhere?" They didn't answer. "You look hungry," Josh said in desperation. "I'll buy you dinner."

Kelly stopped dead in her tracks. Jack stopped a second after. Josh could see he had struck a chord. "Dinner?" Josh offered again, pointing at a diner across the street. "It sure looks warm in there too."

"No!" "Yes!" Jack and Kelly both said in unison. There was a second of silence as the two looked at each other. Neither could remember the last good meal they had had.

"Well, which one is it?"

"Yes!" "No!" they said, reversing answers.

Josh gave them a friendly smile. "Come on, let's get a bite." He could see they were still apprehensive. "No strings attached. Really." He waited patiently.

Finally, Kelly turned to Jack. "Mr. Goodman is right. We are lost. We have no money, and no transportation. Maybe he can help us." Josh looked at Jack with a helpful expression.

"How do you know we can trust him?" Jack said.

"Well, how do you know we can't?" she answered.

They looked back at Josh. He put on his "You can trust me" face, as best he knew how.

"Okay," Jack conceded.

"So are you hungry?" Josh asked.

"Famished," Kelly answered with a smile.

They all started toward the crosswalk. They were on a corner of Times Square. Eight massive television screens played on the building's sides, and hundreds of other advertising signs and lights also added to the electricity of the square. They cut through a line waiting to buy last minute tickets to shows and events.

Josh talked rapidly, shooting questions one after another as he walked. There was so much that he wanted to know, so much he didn't understand about what had occurred in the museum. He didn't hear any answers, and finally turned to get their response, but they were no longer there. "Damn, they did it again," he muttered. He looked back expecting to see them fleeing, but instead they were both glued to the storefront of an electronics retailer, captivated by the display window, a wall of flat screen TVs. Relieved that they were still with him, Josh walked over. He saw them gawking with amazement.

"What are they?" Jack asked.

"These?" Josh replied with incredulity. "Flat screen TVs. Haven't you seen a flat screen before?" Josh paused, amused by Jack's awe. "Sure beats the big bulky ones, though, eh?"

"TVs?" Jack repeated the unfamiliar term to himself.

His response bewildered Josh. Kelly and Jack continued down the windows gawking at stereos, digital cameras and an assortment of other gadgets.

"Are you guys for real?" Josh asked. "You're looking as if it was the first time you've seen any of this."

Neither of them answered. When at last they crossed the street for the diner Josh asked, "So, what kind of help is it that you need? And who were those men that barreled through the museum before you?"

"Who won the war?" Jack asked without answering Josh's question.

"What war?"

"The second war."

"World War II?"

"Yes, World War II."

Josh became suspicious. That was common knowledge. But nothing seemed to be as it should with these two, so he decided to play along. "That depends on who you ask. The Germans, I suppose. There was a Cold War with Nazi Europe until a few years ago when we finally signed a peace treaty with them. We beat the Japanese, though, if that's what you meant. My turn: Who were those men?"

"They're Nazis."

"Nazis?" Josh said loudly while pushing open the diner door. The host looked at him curiously. Josh smiled warmly. "Three, please, a booth with privacy if you have it."

"This way." They followed single file to the back of the restaurant. The sound of food sizzling in the open kitchen was inviting, and the smell of it was all but overpowering. It was all Kelly could think about. They slid into a booth.

It felt good to sit in warmth and rest for a change, Jack thought, without having to look over his shoulder, or being chased, or beaten. A waiter arrived immediately with a basket of freshly baked bread. Its aroma filled the air. Jack and Kelly devoured it with their eyes.

Josh saw them staring at the basket and said invitingly, "Please, help yourselves." The rolls were hot and fresh, and the butter melted into them on contact.

"Tell us how the war ended," Jack asked.

"Why? Everyone knows the way World War II ground down."

"Please just tell us, we really want to hear it."

All right, but afterwards you have to answer my questions. Agreed?" The couple nodded as they stuffed their mouths. "Well, we were at war with both Germany and Japan, fighting on two fronts. We helped Britain out, did a big build up of troops there, fought in North Africa and Italy, then in 1944 tried to invade Nazi occupied Europe."

"What happened?"

"They knew we were coming. It was a disaster. The best port across the channel in France was at the Port de Calais and we went straight for it. The Germans had built up their defenses, held a jet fighter force in reserve, and they knew, or guessed, when we'd land. It was a disaster. Roosevelt lost his reelection bid. There was a public outcry against such loss of life. We kept helping Britain so the Germans could never invade but devoted our attention to Japan. By the time that was over a stalemate had developed in Europe. The Russian generals killed Stalin and made peace with Hitler. We agreed to withdraw our troops from Italy and North Africa if Germany agreed to stay out, and they did. Like I said, there's been a Cold War with Nazi Germany for decades. It's been a nightmare of struggle and economic depression, but in 1992 we finally signed a peace treaty with them, bringing the war officially to an end. Relations are improving. Things are close to what I'd call normal in France. That's where it stands."

Jack and Kelly looked at Josh, crestfallen. "Now, tell me your story, from the beginning," he asked. "Who are you? Why don't you know about the war, and how did you get here? I mean in the museum?" he clarified. "Because I know you weren't in there just seconds before, and then, presto—there you were."

Kelly finished her mouth full of bread, swallowed and looked at Jack, who nodded, indicating he agreed to the telling of their story. "We really are not sure," she answered.

"Not sure of what? Who you are?"

"No, how we got there, inside the building where we first saw you."

"The museum," Josh stated.

"Yes. Only moments before we were outside, on a terrace at the entrance of an abbey, part of Mont-Saint-Michel, in France…"

"France!" Josh interrupted, then waited. Kelly did not answer. She had no explanation. Finally he said, "Okay, go on."

"We were prisoners of Heinz Bodecker, a Nazi SS-Standartenfuhrer, and of a German General. I never heard his name. They held us prisoner in a dungeon there, but we escaped. When we made it outside we found Bodecker and the General with several others deeply involved in a ceremonial ritual that included the statue."

"My statuette—in the museum?" Josh interrupted again, as he poured tea into a cup.

"Yes, they were preparing themselves for the opening of a time portal, a door, into the future," Jack said steadily, watching Josh closely.

Josh nearly dropped the teacup he was raising to his lips at hearing the words. He raised his hands. "Sorry. Sorry." He didn't know what to think.

"I know, it sounds crazy," Kelly agreed. "The story about the statue was thought to be only another far fetched South American Indian legend until two months ago, or I should say sixty odd years ago." Kelly took a breath. "But it is obviously much more than Indian folklore, as you saw in the museum, when we first fell into this—time."

Josh said nothing, but urged her to continue with his eyes. Just then the waiter returned and took orders. Once he was gone, Kelly continued. "We, the Allies, wanted the statue to stay out of German hands. Informants in Europe had warned that they were headed there to get it."

"There?" Josh queried.

"The jungles of Colombia, in South America. "They…" Kelly started to say, then saw confusion on Josh's face. "The *Germans* wanted the statue so that they could travel into the future, to see and manipulate the outcome of the war if it had gone against them, and in so doing determine the future. We thought the story was ridiculous, but since the Nazis took it so seriously, we had to also. I was sent to the Picayulta's village to intercept them, to prevent them from stealing the statue." She sighed, "Unfortunately, I," she looked at Jack, "or we were too late."

"We did take it away from them," Jack interjected, as if they had done at least one thing right.

Kelly looked at him then back at Josh. "Briefly, but the Germans got it back, and took us prisoner. That's how we ended up in France."

"It has been a very difficult few weeks," Jack said humorously, now feeling better with some food in his stomach. "In fact," he continued, "this has not been my best year."

"Last night," Kelly said, "something came out of the sky, and…"

"That was tonight," Jack corrected her.

Kelly thought about it a moment. So much had happened; it didn't seem possible it could have all happened in one night. "I guess it was tonight. Tonight," she resumed correctly, "in France, something came from the sky—like a comet. It interacted somehow with the statue. There was lightning, smoke and sparks, and in an incredible exchange of energy, a passage was opened." Jack was nodding in agreement to all she was saying.

We had the same sort of spectacle in our sky this evening, Josh recalled, but did not say anything to avoid interrupting Kelly's story.

"The two Germans, Bodecker and another man we don't know, went through first. Those were the men you saw in the museum," Jack said.

"We followed them only moments later," Kelly added.

"So, why did you follow them?" Josh asked.

"We were just trying to stay alive, and get away from the General's gunfire," Jack replied.

"Yes, but mostly we were following Bodecker and his partner," Kelly corrected him, "to stop them from getting what they had come for."

"And what exactly did they come for?" Josh asked.

"A box," Jack said, "with knowledge…information about the future, we assume. Information that will reveal to them how the war ended, and whether or not the outcome had gone against them, ultimately they want to determine how to alter events in their favor. If they do return to our time with such knowledge, they will be able to change history."

"So then you also can return to—to your time?" Josh asked skeptically.

"We don't know," Kelly said, not having thought that far into the future. She looked at Jack. "We assume so. The Germans think they can."

Josh sat back on the bench of the booth and digested everything. He looked at them several times as if he was going to ask something, but then didn't. Finally, looking at Kelly, he said, "So not only are you guys from World War II, but so are those men I saw tonight? And they are German Nazis?"

Kelly nodded. "Hard to believe, isn't it?"

Josh struggled with the idea, but he had seen so much with his own eyes. He could not discount that. He looked at Kelly. "Well, all they'll learn is, they won the war in Europe."

She stared at him hard. "Did they? If they hadn't come here, how can you be sure?"

"I don't understand."

"Let's say they learned *we* won the war, that this invasion you talked about was a success. All they had to do was go back with the landing place and time. Maybe that's what they did. And we failed, or fail, to stop them."

"Then...what's the point?" Jack asked.

Kelly looked at him, exasperated. "If they did it, we can do it. If we can't stop them, all is not lost. What counts is being the last one back. Or if it didn't work that way, then going back with knowledge to help our side win."

"I could get a headache trying to think this through," Jack said.

"And what year exactly was it when you two left?" Josh inquired.

"It was 1943."

A ringing at the table next to them diverted their attention. The man at the adjacent booth pulled out his cell phone and spoke loudly into it. They stared at him as he pressed the contraption to his ear.

"I know," Josh said, not realizing what they were thinking. "It makes me mad too, when people use their cells in restaurants."

"Cells? What are they? Everyone has them, and they all hold them to their ears," Jack observed. "They're not some kind of weapon are they?"

Josh realized they were bewildered. "No they're nothing like that. They're just phones."

"Telephones?" Jack inquired distrustfully. "There are no wires."

"Cell phones," Josh said, pulling his out from his pocket. He handed it to Jack, who inspected it carefully. "You guys are really for real?" Josh concluded pensively, remembering them looking at the gadgets in the window, then thinking about their questions concerning the War, and now this awe with cell phones. "You're still in the middle of World War II, before the Calais landing, even."

"Yes, and that man giving us trouble on the street," Jack recalled, "he had the Nazi swastika tattooed on his forehead. We thought..."

"That guy, he was just a skinhead."

"Yes, he was," Jack agreed. "He had no hair on his head."

"No. I mean a radical. A weirdo, looking to stir up trouble, too stupid to understand much, but searching for a cause." Josh shook his head. "Tolerating such people is one of the prices of freedom."

Their food was served, and for the next few moments Jack and Kelly stuffed themselves as Josh looked on with bemusement. As they ate, the couple shared bits of information between mouthfuls. During desert, as Josh was explaining jet airplanes to a fascinated Jack, Kelly finally remembered something. "What about Bodecker?" she interrupted, reminding them there were more important issues to deal with.

Josh waited a moment to see if they had any plan at all. Neither said anything. "Well, as I said, maybe I can help you find him and his friend," he offered. They looked at him expectantly as he took the phone from his pocket and began pushing little buttons. "I saw them get into a taxi," he told them.

Josh paused while the phone rang. "Hello. Yes, I'm trying to locate a fare you picked up at 6:40 P.M. today in front of the Metropolitan Museum." Jack and Kelly listened, still amazed that everyone seemed to have a phone in their pocket. "Cab number 3487." Pause. "I know. I understand you're not supposed to give out the information, but the man left his overcoat, with a Rolex in the pocket. I think he'll appreciate your bending the rules." Josh waited a moment. "JFK, thanks. It's a bit out of the way." He listened. "Lost and found—okay—I'll bring it by in the morning." Josh stuffed the phone in his overcoat. "They went to the airport. Any idea where they might want to go?"

"Back to the abbey," Jack blurted. He looked at Kelly. "Remember, the abbot's crypt?" he continued. "The General told them to look for the box there. It would be waiting with—I not sure what—but it would be inside the crypt of the Abbot Jean-Claude. He instructed Bodecker to return with the box and its contents if possible."

"After witnessing history the General must have made notes of key events that led to the war's final outcome. And maybe even left specific instructions on what should be done differently," Josh offered.

"And the information is in the box!" Kelly finished.

All three sat quietly for a moment considering the implications of such knowledge.

Josh opened his attaché case and booted his laptop. Jack and Kelly had already seen so many wonders they only gawked at this fresh one. With a few keystrokes Josh pulled up the flights departing JFK to Paris for the evening, excluding those that left prior to 7:00 P.M. "If they're going to Paris tonight, they'll be taking the 10:40 P.M. flight." He looked at his watch. "It's 9:55 now, too late for us to catch that one." He tapped the keys again. Jack and Kelly watched with amazement as Josh punched his buttons and came up with screen after screen of information. "But it appears that two one-way tickets were booked only twenty minutes ago to a Johan and Fritz Mueller. They paid cash at the counter." Josh gazed at the laptop for a moment. "A quick run to Paris, not a usual trip to take on the spur of the moment, would you say? And only one way." He paused. "I'll bet those are our guys." His fingers raced over the keyboard of the laptop again.

Jack and Kelly marveled at the machine. "It's a computer," Josh explained. "Of course you've never have seen one of these either. But you will, I hope." A new screen flashed up, recapturing Josh's attention. "There's one flight at, ouch, six in the morning. But it's the Concorde so we should make up some time on them." He hit a few more keys and pushed enter. "Done. We leave bright and early. I hope you've got your passports." The two looked at him, shaking their heads. Josh smiled coyly. "Well, they would have expired by now anyway. We'll have one more stop to make then—before turning in for a nap." He paid their tab, then they walked outside and Josh hailed a taxi.

"Where are we going?" Jack asked.

"Chinatown," Josh answered slyly. "You can get anything in Chinatown."

•

A few minutes later the cab was dropping them on the crowded curbside of Chinatown in Manhattan. Jack would never have guessed he was in the United States; every sign and light was written in Chinese. They slipped through a dingy doorway leading to a stairway. Three flights up they entered the dark hallway to Cindy Ling's apartment. As they walked toward her door, an automated camera followed their every move. Josh knocked on the door. The peephole opened and then closed. A moment passed, then there was a shuffling of deadbolts and other locks before the door swung open.

"Mr. Josh," a voice said from within the obscure interior.

"Cindy," Josh replied warmly. "How have you been?"

Jack looked down to see a midget waving them into a room illuminated by red light, as he imagined a cheap brothel would be. It smelled of incense and other odors he could not recognize. He could not tell the woman's age. She might have been thirty years old or sixty. She was dressed in something resembling pajamas.

"Sorry for the darkness," the diminutive woman said, looking up at them over her glasses. "I developing photographs."

"Cindy, I need a favor and I'm afraid it is urgent."

"You know I do anything for you, Mr. Josh."

"I need passports for these two, no questions."

"That easy, of course. When you want them?"

"Immediately."

Cindy laughed. "Nothing changes with you, does it?"

Kelly could see they had a long history together. Within minutes the miniature woman had taken their passport pictures, then cleared papers from the couch and offered them a seat. She turned on the television to occupy their time. As she worked on her computer, Jack and Kelly again were captivated by the TV.

"It's like a radio with a picture," Jack said, touching the screen. Josh met his eyes, glanced at Cindy and shook his head.

"Breaking news," a newscaster announced, interrupting the regular programming. "A taxicab driver was just found slain in the parking garage of the terminal at JFK airport. The murder was particularly gruesome, one officer reporting the driver was nearly decapitated." A close-up of the taxi was being shown. Within a perimeter of police tape, the vehicle was barricaded from the public. Josh noted the number on the cab. He looked at his hand. The numbers matched. "It is unknown who committed the crime or why, but airport security is already at a heightened level."

"Hope you not need to use these at the airport tonight," Cindy said. "They will look very closely at passengers for few hours."

"No, we're okay," Josh muttered.

Beside the Chinese woman a printer kicked into action, spitting out a document, catching Jack by surprise. He jumped up, then inspected the printer closely. Cindy looked at him oddly. She pulled the document from the tray and scrutinized it carefully with a magnifying glass. "It look perfect. We only wait for pictures to dry now." She paused. "Tea, Mr. Josh?"

"Yes, thank you," he replied.

"And you, Miss?"

"Yes, please," Kelly answered.

Cindy did not ask Jack, but instead filled a pot with water. She placed it in a microwave and pushed a button. The beeps caught Jack's interest. Cindy went back to her computer as Jack moved closer to the microwave. He stared into its window, puzzled at the little pot resting inside. He cocked his head as the machine hummed. "This doesn't seem to be working," Jack said. Just then the microwave bell sounded, startling him.

Cindy returned, squeezing by him. "You strange boy," she said.

Jack noted the pot had steam coming from its spout, and when he drank his tea it was hot.

Within thirty minutes Cindy had imprinted the seal of the United States on the documents and bound each of them in a jacket. Josh took the passports and inspected them, nodding in approval. "You want me stamp a page, like you already go somewhere?" she asked, standing eye to eye with Jack who was now sitting on the couch. "Vacation to Canada last year, maybe?"

"That won't be necessary, Cindy," Josh intervened. "What do I owe you?"

Cindy looked insulted. "You owe zero, Mr. Josh. But now you go. I have lot of work, and you make me behind," she said, using her hands to move them toward the door, but smiling as she spoke.

"You're a doll, Cindy," Josh replied. "I'll call you soon."

As the door closed, Kelly asked, "Is that legal?" Josh answered her with a look. "Oh, I was just wondering."

The next taxi ride dropped them at a posh address on Park Avenue where the doorman greeted Josh as they entered. "Good evening, Ron," Josh said. "Would you arrange a limo to pick us up for JFK by 4:30 in the morning, please?"

"With pleasure, Mr. Goodman."

Once in the elevator Josh inserted a plastic card into the panel and it ascended to the penthouse. As the doors opened, he said, "I don't know your sleeping arrangements, but there are rooms there and there. Suit yourselves. Jack, I may have some clothes in that one that will fit you. Kelly, that's my daughter's room. You'll have to pardon the mess. Jena's not the neatest kid on the block. But her closets are packed with clothes." Josh looked at Kelly, sizing her up. "You're about the same size. Find something comfortable for the trip tomorrow." Kelly looked nervous as only a woman would about using another woman's clothes. "Don't worry. She's at college, and she wouldn't care anyway. There's food in the kitchen; help yourselves if you get hungry. I think I'll turn in. We've got a long day ahead of us tomorrow. And the wakeup call is in four hours."

•

There was already activity on the streets of Manhattan when they stepped outside. The stretch limousine that picked them up was spacious and provided coffee and bagels on a small service table. As they drove to the airport, Josh watched the news on the television. Jack and Kelly tried to as well, but the events of the last few days had caught up with them. Both were soon slumped over in the long seats, sound asleep.

The sound of a jet taking off woke Jack from his sleep. He looked out the window. Paralleling the highway, a 747 was on final approach. After watching the monstrous plane land, Jack could no longer rest. He stared in awe at a line of jets waiting for takeoff and then looked back at Josh.

"Airplanes," Josh said.

"Yes, I can see that. We have them as well," Jack said, "just a bit smaller." He thought of Sully's crop duster back home. "But these have no propellers!"

"They're jets," Josh replied, looking out the window.

"They are huge!"

"Not as big as these rockets," Josh said, turning back to the TV. Jack looked too. A tape of yesterday's launch of the space shuttle was playing. The huge plume of fire and white smoke flowed from the rocket as it blasted toward space. The newscaster spoke of the ongoing progress on the international space station. "We've been to the moon, you know. More than thirty years ago," Josh said, and then paused. "We became kind of bored with it, though, and haven't gone back—so we're building a space station instead." He smiled and then added, "A lot has changed in sixty-one years." Kelly stirred at the sound of their conversation. "Glad you're up, Kelly. We're just arriving at the terminal."

The sheer size of the building was enough to keep Jack and Kelly's eyes occupied, but the number of people flowing through it at such an early hour was also mind-boggling. Josh became a little apprehensive at the security screening, as the agent scrutinized the new passports closely. He hoped Cindy still knew her stuff.

CHAPTER THIRTY-FIVE

When Jack first saw the sleek Concorde II jet he was mesmerized. It looked like a rocket ship from the Buck Rogers movies he so enjoyed as a boy. The only disturbing part of the plane was the large swastika on the tail. "Why is that there?" he asked Josh.

"France remained occupied until the 1950's. The French Nazi party is still the only legal political party in the nation, and they've adopted the German swastika to show unity with the German fascists. You're going to see a lot more of that sort of thing. Try not to react to it, all right?"

The Concorde II, operated by Air France, was a second generation supersonic passenger jet. It lifted off the runway at New York shortly after 6:00 A.M. Soon after takeoff a pretty French flight attendant began a first class service of champagne mimosas, followed by perfectly prepared eggs Benedict. Jack devoured his meal as he studied the aircraft with fascination. There was yet another TV monitor in it. These boxes seemed to be everywhere. It continually updated the plane's progress, giving position and statistics such as altitude, outside temperature and air speed, which exceeded 1000 mph. In the meantime, Josh used the air phone to make arrangements with a private car rental agency in Paris.

Kelly was still very sleepy and only picked at her food. It wasn't until the attendant brought dessert, which was small, chocolate and rich, that she truly came back to life. When she had finished hers, she eyed Jack's, which he gave her.

She'd found suitable clothes, especially since it was winter and Josh's daughter had several bulky sweaters. Jack was surprised at how well Josh's clothes had fit. But what they both marveled about the most was the fabrics. They'd never seen anything like them. Not long after eating they both fell asleep again.

The supersonic jet touched down under the gray skies of Paris' Marshal Petain airport early in the afternoon. Security seemed tight as they cleared customs, but Josh commented on how much easier it was these days. The French gendarme with swastika armbands was almost more than Kelly could take, though. A car was waiting at the curbside with its driver standing patiently beside it. "Pech," Josh called.

"Mr. Goodman," the driver said. "I hope your flight was pleasant." Josh nodded as Pech handed him the keys. "She is brand new," he said proudly, looking at the special edition BMW. "I think you will like her. At least the Nazis haven't ruined cars—yet."

Pech was a good looking guy with an athletic build. His eyes could not help, but fix on Kelly, and quickly he stepped forward to open the car door for her.

"Who's this?" Kelly asked with an interest meant to get a reaction out of Jack.

Josh perceived her motive and smiled. "Pech? He's a great young man. A rugby player, very resourceful. His business is to take care of anything extraordinary that an out-of-towner might need, and do it in a moments notice." Josh pointed at the high performance BMW. "He's never failed me yet." Then he winked at Pech who was standing taller than ever at hearing the compliment.

Jack knew Kelly and Josh were just prodding him, but he nudged Pech anyway and took over closing the door for Kelly.

Soon they were speeding westward on the A13 toward Normandy. Traffic was sparse, and Josh stayed in the passing lane of the toll highway.

Kelly looked at the speedometer nervously. It read 240. The other cars appeared to be standing still on the highway. "Isn't 240 miles per hour a little dangerous?" she suggested apprehensively.

"These are kilometers per hour, not miles per hour," Josh said to reassure her. "In miles per hour we are only going 145." Kelly's eyes widened but she said nothing. It didn't make her feel much better, but they were in a hurry.

"How is it you could get us phony passports so easily?" Jack asked, having considered how to pose the question several times.

"I'm an antiquities dealer on occasion. You'd be surprised how often certain documents are necessary. Cindy is the best. I first met her in Hong Kong." He smiled at the couple. "But that's another story."

Jack grinned. "Okay, but tell us why you're doing this. It's costing you money and time—for what?"

Josh glanced at Jack and Kelly. "I've got money and right now I've got the time. The fact is, I believe you, and since I do, what other choice do I have? Millions have died in Russia and Europe under the Nazis. They refuse to say what happened to the Jews, acting as if they never existed, but we know, we know. If there's a chance…" His voice tapered off.

Within an hour they reached the Atlantic coast where the toll road gave way to the slower national highways. They sped through small villages lost among the hedgerows that neatly divided the farmers' fields. "If we weren't so pressed for time I'd show you the beaches here."

"Why is that?" Jack asked.

"When I told you how the war ended, I mentioned we Americans tried to land at the Port de Calais on June 6, 1944, north of here, since it was the most logical and useful place. But we found it too heavily defended. From what I understand, the beaches here at Normandy are where we should have landed. They were seriously considered but eventually rejected since there was no port. As it turned out, they were relatively lightly defended as Hitler was convinced we'd land at the Port de Calais.

Josh figured Kelly was giving him a 'wonder how he knew' glance. He couldn't see that she was napping. "Had we landed here," Josh continued pointedly, "we would very likely have won the war in Europe. Are you following what I'm saying?"

"Yes I am. Absolutely. Normandy, not the Port de Calais," Jack answered clearly.

"What are you two talking about?" Kelly asked waking slowly.

"Wishful thinking," Josh said. A few moments later he pulled the BMW to a stop at a crossing on the flatlands before the causeway leading to Mont-Saint-Michel. The skies were gray and quickly darkening with the approaching gloom of winter twilight. The three looked across the span of water toward the lone standing island. It was eerily familiar for Jack and Kelly to be back so soon.

Jack looked out past the point where the Moroccan fishing boat had dropped them off only the night before. It was nearly impossible to grasp that it had been sixty-one years ago.

The BMW rolled slowly down the causeway toward the island village. It was not the tourist season and the place looked deserted. A few cars dotted the parking area. Josh took the closest spot to the gate. Beside theirs, only two other cars looked as if they'd been recently driven.

Inside the walls they hurried through the village on the same cobbled stone streets where Jack and Kelly had been escorted by the Nazi guards. The streets now looked very different, cleared of the debris that Jack and Kelly had only recently stepped over. The boarded windows were repaired; merchandise filled their displays. At a corner there was a café open for business. It was dark inside with only a few patrons huddled over small tables, locals appreciating the winter weather, which deterred the tourists and allowed them to take back their village for a few months. Above was the window where the little girl had smiled at Jack by the Christmas candle. He wondered what had happened to her.

They continued on the uphill path to the abbey's entrance. Even in the winter the gardens were meticulously maintained, though without blossoms or leaves. The middle-aged guard just outside the gate sat in what looked like a ticket booth and in no way resembled his counterpart from the past. His highly decorative uniform was neatly pressed, but best of all, it was not German. He was well fed and looked more like a man fulfilling his eight hours of work before going home to his kids, than a man who was battle scarred, tired and numb to the sight of death. He did not even carry a weapon. "Are you still open?" Josh inquired.

"It closed at 5:00," the guard answered in a heavy French accent.

Josh was dismayed. "Any chance we could make just a quick tour through the place? We return to America in the morning and really want to see it."

The guard delivered a shrug. "I am sorry, but I cannot. The abbey will reopen in the morning."

The man's answer was emphatic, and Josh could see the decision was not his to make. They wandered disappointedly back down the path, loitering in a secluded side garden outside the fortified wall. The sky was already dark. "Well, if this Herr Bodecker is in there, there's not much we can do about it right now," Josh said.

"We could wait for him out here," Jack suggested.

"What if he doesn't come this way?" Kelly asked.

"Is there another way out?" Josh inquired.

"Not that I know of, but I'm no expert."

Jack raised his head and rubbed his neck. He stared into the dark sky. The moon was up and its light was filtering through the clouds, silhouetting the church steeple. His eyes followed the steeple down to the main building, and then continued along the length of the two hundred foot fortified wall, where the trees and shrubs of the garden met with it. Then he did a double take. He remembered this garden. The place looked so different and yet was basically unchanged, though the thicket of shrubs by the wall had not been there before. It was the garden where the General had called to Günter the guard. Günter had retreated through a door in the wall, and moments later appeared in the dungeon, inside the abbey complex where they were held.

"Well guys, I don't know what to say," Josh said dejectedly while fixing his sight on the imposing wall. "Maybe in the morning we'll find something."

"Morning might be too late," Kelly said sharply.

"If they're already in there," Jack mused pensively, "they couldn't start any digging until everyone was out and the place was closed for the night, or they'd risk drawing too much attention."

"That means at best they've just started trying to get into the abbot's crypt," Josh allowed. "So?" he added inquiringly.

Jack tuned to Kelly. She didn't know what he was getting at either.

"So…" Jack's eyes panned across the thicket by the wall, then he started toward it. "Follow me," he said, not waiting for either of them. At the shrubs he looked both ways, then plunged through the branches, disappearing into the foliage.

Kelly and Josh looked at each other, baffled. They heard rustling and branches breaking inside. Then the noise stopped. "What are you guys waiting for? Come on." Jack's voice came through the bushes. They shrugged their shoulders in puzzled agreement and followed through the hole he had entered. Jack had resumed thrashing away at the heaping pile of vines and plant debris that had accumulated by the wall over the years.

"What are you looking for?" Josh asked.

"There's a door here somewhere," Jack said, stopping to catch his breath. "I saw the German guard—Günter—last night, or whatever night it was, that we arrived here with Bodecker." He rummaged through the decaying leaves again.

Josh pulled him back gently by the shoulder. "Where does the door go?"

"When they brought us in…up there," he said and pointed to the road leading to the gate, "Günter was down here with another guard smoking. The General scolded them, ordering them in to open up the dungeon. When he was finished Günter disappeared through a small door—here—somewhere at the base of the wall."

Kelly remembered. "He was our guard in the dungeon! The door must lead into the abbey!" Kelly concluded excitedly.

"But that was more than sixty years ago!" Josh said. "It may be closed over by this time."

"Maybe, but maybe not."

"Isn't this breaking and entering?" Josh asked.

They both stopped and looked at him, bewildered. "Aren't you the guy who just falsified passports?" Kelly reminded him. He considered her words, then dove forward to help. The three worked quickly and systematically to clear the debris from the wall. "I've got something here!" Kelly whispered loudly.

"It looks like a hinge," Josh added.

"It is! It's the door."

In minutes they had cleared an old wooden door, its rotting surface sprouting mushroom-like growths from the years of being buried. There was a large old-style padlock fused with rust hanging from the steel latch, locked closed. The door had not been opened in decades. "Can you pick a lock?" Jack asked Josh.

He shook his head. "This thing is frozen solid. There is no way you'll ever open that lock again. What we need is a hacksaw or sledge hammer."

"I don't seem to have either on me," Jack said.

"How about this?" Kelly said, lifting a stout stick from the ground. "Maybe we can pry it open?"

"It's metal, Kelly," Jack said with a use-your-head tone.

She gave him a look, then wedged the stick between the two latches which were locked together, gently pulling outward to be sure it was secure. Then she prepared herself for a hard tug.

"Jack is right, Kelly," Josh said. "There's no way you'll ever…"

Suddenly there was a loud crash. Kelly fell to the ground, unprepared for the lack of resistance. The latch had pulled away from the rotten wood effortlessly. Jack looked at the hole in the door where the latch had been attached, then turned to Kelly on the ground. "You okay?"

"'It's metal, Kelly,'" she mockingly parroted. "Help me up, Mr. Know-It-All."

It took the three of them to pry the frozen hinges open revealing the pitch black entranceway. The air inside was stale and musty, as if it had not circulated in decades. Josh lit a cigarette lighter, which dimly illuminated a stone stairway. At the top was the same guard's room Kelly and Jack had stormed. It too was virtually unchanged.

Jack peered in, first to his left where a watchman sat with his back turned, smoking with his feet up on the desk. Through the door beyond were the entrance and the great inner staircase leading to the church above. If Bodecker were here it would be up those stairs. Jack pulled back and put his finger to his lips. "We can't go this way," he whispered.

They backtracked to a dark corridor leading off the stairway. Josh gave his lighter another strike, then the three started along the passage in a tight huddle. The steps here were carved from the rock foundation and led them ever higher.

"Do you know where you're going?" Kelly asked.

"No, but this has to lead somewhere," Jack answered confidently, then he turned the corner and almost ran into a brick wall. "Or maybe it doesn't." A hole had been picked through the wall, but boards blocked the passageway. A mouse squeaked, then scurried from their feet into a gap in the barricade.

"It keeps going through there," Josh said.

Jack kicked at the boards. One shattered easily, and he quickly pried away the others, revealing a hole in a brick wall. He squeezed through it, finding it just as dark on the other side. He felt the walls with his hands, then said, "The tunnel gets narrower." Outside Josh was perspiring as he felt the tightening twinge of claustrophobia. "But there's a light up ahead."

"How far?" Josh asked nervously.

"Fifteen, twenty feet. I'm almost there." Jack poked his head through the opening. It was an abandoned ventilation duct in the chamber wall just below the ceiling. He scanned the empty room. A low watt incandescent light dimly illuminated it. Jack worked his way out of the hole and dropped to the floor. "Come on," he said, "it's clear."

Josh went first at Kelly's insistence. She had heard him hyperventilating and he did not argue. Once he was through the opening she followed. In the larger room Josh drew a deep breath. The air was stale, but he was content to have the space. The dim light disclosed a mosaic of headstones, which occupied most of the space on the walls, and there were several in the floor. "It's a crypt," Josh said. "The resting place of centuries of past abbots and monks." Jack knelt down and blew the dust from the one beneath him. "What does it say?"

"Pierre du Blois, 1216-1277."

"He died over seven hundred years ago," Kelly whispered. It seemed natural to lower her voice in a room full of dead people. They stood in silence, surveying the room. The faint sound of a pick and shovel working above broke the quiet. "Do you hear that?" Kelly whispered.

Completely still, they tuned their ears. The soft clinking of tools resonated in the stone ceiling. "Sounds like digging," Josh offered.

"It's Bodecker," Jack said. "They're in the church above us, digging under the altar of Jean-Claude-what's-his-name. We must be in the older part of the crypt. The newer church was built over it."

"Hey, come in here." Kelly's voice came from the next room. "There are stairs leading up, and the picking sound is louder this way." Josh and Jack joined her, and then the three went up the stairs. At the top they discovered a wrought iron door barricading the entrance from the cathedral into the crypt but found it unlocked. Beyond it a wide draping cord, meant to stop tourists from advancing, was all that kept them from entering. With no sign of guards, they casually stepped over it and entered the huge sanctuary. Once they were inside, the echoing sound of the tools was even louder.

Jack saw Kelly looking upward to the towering columns stretched high above which supported the vaulted ceilings and decorated gothic capitals. She swayed momentarily and stumbled backwards into the metal barrier support. Its clanging noise resonated loudly through the church. Kelly stood the sign back up in its place as if the act of cleaning up would make it all go away. The echoing clamor scared Jack and Josh out of their wits. "Sorry," she said, shrinking back. "The Knights Room," she added skittishly, patting the sign and pointing to its words.

Their look required no words.

•

From here they knew their way passing through the dining hall and up to the cloister, the same garden where they had observed Bodecker and the others on the terrace, beckoning the powers of the statue. "I think they're in there." Jack pointed to the church at their left.

They opened the side door and quietly entered the church. Inside, they saw Bodecker standing over an open hole where the

413

altar once stood. The voice of his companion could be heard. He was handing up a box to Bodecker, who took it and brushed the dirt off. For a moment they heard the big German's voice saying, "*Guten*, Schmidt. *Guten*."

Kelly and Josh crawled between two pews toward the middle aisle to get a clearer view, while Jack stayed on the side aisle, considering how to get the box away from Bodecker. At the end of the pew Kelly cautiously looked around the old wooden seat to steal a look at Bodecker. Her eyes bulged and her gut convulsed at what she saw. Less than at arm's length from her was the body of a dead monk, lying in a pool of his own recently spilled blood. His eyes, still open, stared back into hers. His torso had been split open from the groin up the rib cage, allowing the contents of his body cavities to spill out in a pile on the floor by his side. The stench hanging over him and his expression of horror etched in Kelly's mind.

Repulsed by the smell and gruesome carnage, Kelly heaved, jerking back uncontrollably, and bumping into the pew behind her. The heavy wooden bench scraped noisily on the stone floor. "Shhh," whispered Josh. The screeching bench had caught Bodecker's attention.

"*Ruhig!*" he snapped to his colleague. With the box in one hand and a pistol in the other, he slowly started a search along the pews for the source. Jack hid himself behind one of the colossal Romanesque columns, bumping into a large candle stand. He caught it just before it fell over. Bodecker made his way down the center aisle searching for intruders. Kelly and Josh quietly scurried backwards to the side aisle, but before they reached it, the sound of Bodecker's boots casually stepping over the monk's brutally maimed corpse caused them to stop. Kelly looked over her shoulder.

There was Bodecker staring straight down on them and smiling. Kelly and Josh crouched under the bench but it was useless. "Miss Wilson, I underestimated your tenacity," the Nazi said with admiration. "I will not be so careless this time." He replaced his pistol in its holster and pulled out a knife still bloody from its earlier use. "Get up! Now!" he shouted in a quick change of mood. He moved forward, directing them with a wave of his hand to step out into the side aisle and move toward the altar. As they did, Bodecker said, "You found a new friend, I see. Did Mr. Sullivan come to an untimely demise?"

Kelly caught Jack's eye, where he hid behind the pillar she was passing. He held his finger over his lips and the heavy candle stand in the other hand. As she stepped away from the column to divert Bodecker's attention and said, "Günter fatally wounded Jack in the dungeon as we escaped."

"And poor Günter? I assume he did not fare well either?" Bodecker asked as if concerned.

"He died, too."

"Miss Wilson, you are not a good person to associate with; everybody who does seems to die." He turned to Josh. "You should pick your friends more wisely. A poor choice such as this can be the cause of your death."

Josh backed up nervously not knowing where to go. Bodecker read his indecision and lurched forward, thrusting the knife toward Josh's groin and unknowingly exposing the back of his head to where Jack was hiding. The sound of the brass candle stand crashing over Bodecker's head was loud. And it sent his stunned body to the stone floor. The box too dropped to the floor. Almost at once shots rang out from across the church as Schmidt, Bodecker's partner, rushed toward them, shouting something in German.

"Quick, let's get out of here!" Jack said. Bullets ricocheted off the stone walls.

The three of them started for the front door, then Kelly turned back. "The box! I'm not leaving without it." She scooped it up the bullets barely missing her. Bodecker, in a stupor, lifted himself from the floor as she passed. She stepped on his shoulders, slamming him back to the ground, then bolted for the exit.

"Kill them!" Bodecker shouted to Schmidt while reaching for his own gun.

Josh was first to fly through the front door leading to the terrace as bullets splintered the wood in the massive door. "Hurry!" Jack yelled, holding the door open. Kelly rushed through the threshold with the box in her hands. Jack slammed the door closed and slid the base of a wooden sign through its handles.

Following the exit arrows to the left of the church, they moved toward the inner staircase, which led back down to the village. Around the corner they rushed, bolting down the spiraling stairs. Halfway down they came upon a wrought iron barrier with a gate, locked for the night to keep people from entering. "Bad idea!" Jack said, looking at the other two staring through the bars.

In unison they ran back up to the top of the steps. There was a short stone wall. The sign read *"Gautier's Leap,"* named after a prisoner who in desperation threw himself to his death instead of allowing himself to be executed by his captors.

"Not a good idea either," Josh said breathlessly as they looked over the vast open drop-off. Behind them they heard the crack of boards being broken by Bodecker and his companion. "Back there," Kelly said, pointing to the place from which they had just come. "We passed a small door by the gate."

Suddenly, sparks darted and fragments splintered off the stone wall next to Jack. They were immediately followed by the rapid cracking sound of gunfire. Again, like a school of fish, they ran down the stairs. They found the small door, leaped through it and followed narrow stairs back down to the subterranean chambers of the abbey. Frantic stomping followed them from the passage above. Jack, Kelly and Josh rushed into a chamber with a window to the outer wall. Jack slammed a door behind them but it was old and flimsy. He shoved a watchman's chair under the knob. "I don't know how long that will hold them."

It was the chamber that housed the wooden wheel used to haul the rail cart up the steep wall, providing provisions to the monks. Jack recalled it from the day before. "The cart! We'll use it to get down! Quick, get in!"

Josh looked out the opening to the ground below. "You've got to be kidding," he said.

They all contemplated the drop. Bodecker's shouts grew louder. He fired his pistol in the stairway. At the sound of the bullet ricocheting its way down the passage and splintering through the flimsy door, they all jumped onto the cart, but found it wouldn't budge.

"It's stuck!" Kelly cried. "That board in the spokes is keeping us from moving." Jack scrambled back out of the cart and worked on the stop board to get it out from the wheel, the weight in the cart was making it difficult. As he worked it out of the far side spoke, the wheel jerked forward and the cart jolted downward. Kelly let out a scream.

"Grab the break lever, Josh!" Jack yelled. "And keep the pressure on it until I get in."

"Right," Josh replied.

At the same moment, pounding started on the other side of the door. "Hurry!" Kelly said.

Jack yanked the board out the rest of the way and jumped for the cart. Gunfire blasted the door, demolishing the knob. The chair behind it clattered to the floor. "Go!" Jack yelled as he landed inside the cart. Josh released the brake, and the cart fell away from the landing in short jerking movements. The rail was steep where they were, but farther below, the incline flattened as it reached the bottom.

Bodecker and Schmidt stormed through and saw the wheel turning. They moved quickly to the opening where the rope was feeding downward. Jack, Kelly and Josh were only twenty feet down the wall, perched in the little cart like sitting ducks. Bodecker smiled and took aim at them with his pistol. He took his time, allowing himself a moment to enjoy the prospect of carnage, then slowly applied pressure on the trigger. In the cart they all saw the pistol aimed at them and were frozen with fear. The hammer from the gun came down and there was a click. Bodecker was out of bullets.

"Faster, Josh!" Kelly yelled. The cart made larger jolting drops as Josh worked the brake lever cautiously. Bodecker cursed and threw his weapon at them. Then he grabbed the assault rifle from his accomplice. "Give me that," he demanded.

Jack was watching the ledge they'd left and saw him take aim. "Let the lever go completely, Josh! Now!"

Josh looked up at the barrel of Bodecker's gun and let go. The cart plunged wildly out of Bodecker's sight, jerking roughly to the sides, and clattered loudly down the old track as Kelly screamed and hung on for dear life. Bodecker shot wildly, emptying the magazine in a single fusillade. They all ducked inside as the spray of bullets clanged against the cart's metal sides.

They sped out of control until they hit a bump in the unused track. The unwieldy cart tipped onto two wheels. Josh lunged back for the brake lever to reapply pressure. It started to slow, but then there was a loud snap and the cart went back into a free fall. The rickety old cart banged and clamored as it hurled over loose boards. "Slow us down!" Jack yelled at Josh.

"I can't!" he shouted, brandishing the broken lever that had pierced deep into his hand.

Bodecker saw his prey and his box escaping. He saw the wooden wheel quickly turning to let out rope. He grabbed a stop board and slung it back into the rapidly turning spokes. The board locked in and the rope snapped taut, dust popping out of its stretched fibers.

Below, the speeding cart slammed to a halt. Jack, Kelly and Josh smashed into one another, with Kelly squished against the front side of the cart. She groaned painfully, then asked, "What happened? Did we hit bottom?"

Jack pulled himself up and looked out of the cart, only to discover they were still a hundred feet from the bottom. "Why aren't we moving?" he muttered. Just then the cart began to rock as the rope holding it was tugged back and forth.

"That's why," Kelly answered, pointing back up into the dark. Bodecker was descending the wall with the speed of an experienced climber.

In moments he was upon them and from fifteen feet above he pulled the rifle slung over his shoulder into his free hand. They all ducked deep into the cart. "You know this can't go on forever," Bodecker sneered.

"Hang on!" Jack whispered to Kelly and Josh, then with knife in hand, he reached blindly over the side and started sawing the rope that held them suspended on the steep incline. A shot was fired, but it was too late; the rope had been severed, and the cart plummeted downward. Bodecker, supported by the taut rope, was flung upward as the rope recoiled. His assault rifle fell out of his hand as he held the rope for all he was worth.

Below, a chicken coop had been built where the cart once used to stop. The track had been dismantled and the passage blocked by the back wall of a structure. The speeding cart smashed through the weathered boards of the coop and careened through the stacked shelves where the hens laid their eggs. Chickens flapped away squawking, and feathers flew as they hurtled through the building. Finally, they came to a crashing halt against a street light, which illuminated a cloud of dust and the settling feathers.

"Everybody okay?" Josh asked.

"I think so, but let's get outta here," Jack answered.

"I couldn't agree more." Kelly groaned. "Which way?"

"The parking lot, it's right there," Josh said. "We took the short cut."

They hurried from the wreckage, crossing three blocks to the main entrance. At the car no one looked back to see if they were being followed. "You drive, Jack," Josh said, throwing him the keys. "My hand hurts like hell."

It was well past midnight when they got to the end of the causeway, and none of them saw the other car with its lights off pulling away from the island to go after them.

CHAPTER THIRTY-SIX

Upon arriving, Bodecker and Schmidt had been shocked to find themselves in New York City. They had expected to be in Berlin, to be greeted by a subsequent generation of the successful Third Reich. Something had certainly not gone according to plan. He was not used to seeing his plans go awry.

With just two days to accomplish his mission, the task seemed nearly impossible. But he learned that with the gold they had brought and the modern day airplanes they could make it back to France in just a few hours. But there were other problems. He didn't have the box. And within less than one day the portal would close. He knew, to return to his own time, he had to be within close proximity of the statue, a few feet away at most. It was obvious there was not enough time to get back to New York, at least not the way they came.

Bodecker labored over his predicament. He was not going to get beaten this far into the mission. He would find a way to get back to the statue. He knew it. He just had not figured out yet how he would do it.

With a moment to reflect, he realized that Jack and Kelly must be receiving outside help. There was no other explanation. And it was likely coming from the man he had seen with them. If that were true, then possibly they might have a plan. He decided to follow them, to see how they, with their helper, planned to return. He kept their taillights carefully in sight, yet made certain they would not suspect they were being followed.

Exhausted, Jack, Kelly, and Josh drove without speaking for almost two hours. Josh wrapped his hand in his handkerchief and grimly bore the pain. Kelly looked at her wrist for her missing watch. "What time is it?"

Josh said, "It's close to two."

"My Gosh! We have to get back to New York by sometime today," she said urgently.

Josh straightened up. "Why?"

"Because the statue is there. Anyone displaced through time has to be within its range when the portal reopens. It's the only way to return."

"Are you sure?"

"It was in my father's notes." She paused. "When I learned of this mission, I went through some of his stuff. Stuff he had accumulated while living in South America. I thought it might help prepare me. In it there were notes, parts of what he had learned about the legend."

Josh considered Kelly's words. "Within its range? How close to you have to be?"

"I'm not sure, within a few feet I assume. There was a cloud that spewed out of the statue last time. Inside it is where we saw the portal." She considered the logistics. "I don't see how we can get back to New York City in time."

"What time will all this happen?"

"I don't know exactly, but according to the legend it is sometime after the second night."

Jack looked at the two of them through the rear view mirror. "Second night! That's great! This is the second night—and soon it will be daybreak. We're here in Nazi France, the statue is in New York, and this car is almost out of gas." Neither Kelly nor Josh responded. "So what happens to us if we are not there?" he added sounding as if he would rather not hear the answer.

Kelly shook her head. "I think we might just disappear."

"Disappear!" Jack exclaimed. "You mean—like—evaporate?"

Kelly shrugged. "We don't belong here. Only the power of the statue or comet or both allows us to exist in this moment in time. I think that's what will happen. I don't know exactly."

"What do you mean, you don't know exactly? We *need* to know exactly. This is important."

Kelly sighed. "I barely had time to read his stuff. I just skimmed it. Okay? So I don't recall that much about the details."

"Details!"

Josh interrupted, "Hold on. The problem may not be as insurmountable as you think."

"What do you mean?" Jack asked, watching the blinking light that told him they were nearly out of gas.

"The statue is not in New York anymore. It should have been returned to the Louvre yesterday."

"The Louvre? The museum in Paris?" Kelly asked. "What are the French doing with a South American Indian statue?"

"France is where it was found. Archeologists, baffled by the riddle, assume some explorer stole it from the Indians centuries ago, and then hid it away. But nobody really kno…That's it!" Josh interrupted himself. "You two brought it here!" he said proudly, solving the riddle that had plagued historians for more than forty years. "It was brought by you and Bodecker during the war. Apparently it stayed here and was lost."

"That's nice and everything," Jack interrupted, "but what about our gas problem?"

"Nothing's going to be open this time of night," Josh said. "Pull into that station there. It should open first thing in the morning."

Jack slowed down, then eased the car off the road and stopped between the pumps where he sat thinking for a moment. "If we do get to the statue and it does take us back to our time, we still have another problem to face."

"What's that?" Josh asked.

"The General and his men were shooting at us when we disappeared. Remember?"

"Yes?" Kelly said.

"I imagine they will still be there, waiting for Bodecker, and for us as we return. If we feel anything like we did when we got here, we won't be in any condition to fight back or escape." Jack was looking for ideas. "And if Bodecker gets there first, it will be even worse." Jack turned off the engine and they all sat thinking.

Behind them, unnoticed, Bodecker and Schmidt pulled over. Bodecker killed his engine to wait.

"We'll just have to find a way to get you prepared for your return," Josh said finally.

"How?" Jack asked.

"I'm not sure yet, but we'll find a way," he said confidently. "Right now, we should try to get a couple hours rest. You guys look as bad as I feel."

Four hours later it was dawn, and the gas station attendant was tapping on the window. Jack shook himself to consciousness, and lowered the window. The man sounded irritated, his words bordering on belligerent. Josh spoke up in French as he opened his door. While he ordered gas, Jack and Kelly went into the station, which was already open, and picked out snacks for breakfast. At the counter, Kelly pulled a paper from the stand. "Golden Treasure returns home," she said, slowly translating the headline. There was a picture of the little stone statue below it.

"You see? It's back," Josh said walking up behind them. "This will make it easier to get you back together with it."

"Well, I hope Bodecker doesn't subscribe to the paper," Jack said warily.

Kelly went into the restroom with Josh, saying, "Let's take a look at your hand." Ten minutes later they were en route to Paris, although their progress slowed as they entered the height of rush hour traffic. Bodecker closed the distance between them, willing to risk being spotted rather than lose the car.

"The statue will not go back on display until the curator verifies its authenticity and checks it for damage," Josh said. "It's protocol after each tour of any exhibit."

"Where will we find it, then?" Kelly asked.

"It will be at the museum, but in the basement vault."

"How will we get to it?" she said.

"They know me well there. Access won't be difficult, especially since we only need to get you close to it...it's not like we are taking it away," Josh sounded confident. "But Jack was right. First we need to get you two ready for your return home. Turn right here. We're going to a friend's place. It's a studio."

"A studio? What kind of studio?" Kelly questioned.

"A movie studio. It's part of what I do. I create special effects for the movie industry. I got started in Hollywood just when it was getting big," Josh said. "Jean Claude is a friend and, most important of all, a makeup artist. He should be able to make you two up to resemble Bodecker and his friend. That way, when you return, this General who is waiting for you with a loaded gun will think you're Bodecker and his friend, and he won't shoot you." Jack and Kelly said nothing. "It should buy you enough time to escape, or fight, or do whatever you have to, in order to survive."

Jack shook his head, unconvinced. "I might be able to pass for Bodecker from a distance, but how's Kelly going to be made up to look like a man? And how do you know what they look like?"

Josh smiled. "We've come a long way in the movie business in six decades, Jack. I can make you both look like monkeys if I want. And it isn't necessary that either of you pass close inspection, only that you freeze the General from acting, long enough for your escape. Remember, when you emerge there will be all that smoke to mask you. And as for getting pictures of Bodecker and his friend, the guard at the New York Metropolitan Museum can send me the videotapes of them from when they escaped from the building."

Jack looked suspicious. "But how can you get the video tape to Paris so quickly?" he asked, perplexed.

"I'll have it sent electronically." Jack looked bewildered. "E-mail...Internet?" Then he remembered they had no knowledge of these things. He paused, then smiled and said simply, "Trust me on this, it's what I do." He looked at Kelly's hair, "I'm afraid we'll have to crop that pretty hair of yours, Kelly." Josh pointed to the curb. "Pull up here. This is Jean Claude's place."

•

A block away Bodecker and his companion also parked and watched patiently, waiting for their return. Two slow hours passed as people entered and left the location, and Bodecker grew concerned. Had they gone out the back? Finally, he and Schmidt got out of the car and went into the building that Jack, Kelly and their unknown helper had entered. What Bodecker saw was a large room with costumes and stage props on display. A group of tourists were touring the building with a guide. Bodecker and his associate joined them.

Two floors above, Jack walked out of Jean Claude's door, the spitting image of Bodecker, and Kelly could not tell much difference between her image in the mirror and the guy she saw on the videotape with Bodecker. The makeup was uncomfortable but not as bad as either had feared. The elevator descended to the main floor, and opened into the large open lobby. The tour group was crowding at the elevator door waiting to go up when Jack, Kelly and Josh stepped out. The crowd parted to let them out. Jack's eyes met directly with Bodecker's and Bodecker's with Jack's. Bodecker was shocked by his own image. He glanced over at Kelly, who looked like Schmidt.

Jack panicked and pushed the tour guide into Bodecker, then shouted, "This way!" as he led Josh and Kelly across the entryway. The crowd gasped with astonishment as they looked at Jack, then back down at the man on the ground. They were identical twins. Schmidt took off in pursuit, pulling out his pistol as he ran. He fired the gun several times and the crowd in the building panicked.

Jack ducked behind the display of a knight's armor as bullets zinged through the metal suit. Josh and Kelly kept running until they rounded a corner. Jack grabbed the spear from the display, stepped into the open and flung it toward his assailant. The spear pierced the astonished German through the chest. Schmidt staggered backwards, his hands clasping the spear protruding from his chest, mortally wounded. *"Mein Fuhrer,"* he exclaimed, but before he fell to the ground his body simply vanished. Those on the tour group stood amazed by what they were witnessing, then one started to clap as if the show had been put on to amuse them. The others in the group joined in the applause.

Bodecker, having fallen backwards into a display, struggled to get back on his feet. Immediately he took off after Jack, Kelly and Josh, who were by now escaping to their car out front. Bodecker sprinted out of the building and ran to his car, cursing Schmidt for not being there to help. Josh slammed the BMW into gear and tore away from the curb. Bodecker followed in hot pursuit. The narrow streets were crowded with parked cars, and Josh honked constantly to clear his way.

"Hurry!" Kelly shouted, looking out the rear window. "He's gaining on us!"

"Sure he is," Josh answered in frustration. "I'm making a path for him." Just then he slammed on his brakes to avoid hitting a couple who'd walked in front of him laughing at some private joke.

"There's a main street just ahead," Jack said.

"Got it. Thanks." Josh turned the wheels hard and floored the car. It lurched and bounced over the curb and onto the sidewalk. He kept his hand on the horn the whole way knocking down several stalls and an apple stand as he went. Startled pedestrians jumped for cover cursing, but Josh hit none of them. Finally the car careened on to the main boulevard, where there was more room. He accelerated and drove away quickly.

Bodecker was boiling as he followed in the wreckage that Josh had left. The broken fruit stand blocked the sidewalk, but Bodecker was not going to slow down. Instead, he steered his speeding car only inches from the building, tearing the mirror off and creating sparks as he bounced along the brick wall. It was all up to him now. And he was not about to let these Americans prevent him from achieving his destiny. With the information they had gathered, Germany was certain to win the war. He knew it. History told him Hitler's Third Reich had succeeded, of that there could be no doubt. How glorious his future was to be! He only wished he'd had time to research it for himself to see how far he'd risen, how rich and powerful he'd become with the knowledge he was taking back with him.

Without warning an elderly woman stepped from her doorway directly in his path. Bodecker crashed into her, slamming her body against the hood as he took her life. He cursed that he was slowed even that much. The tires squealed as the car flew off the curb, entering the boulevard, and her mangled body fell away. He turned sharply right after the fleeing BMW.

The street was much wider with less traffic. Two blocks behind, Josh saw Bodecker making up lost ground. He pushed his car recklessly. Josh had to do the same while searching all the time for a way to shake the pursuing German fanatic.

"He's gaining on us!" Jack hollered. In moments Bodecker was on their tail. Just then the rear windshield of the car exploded. Kelly screamed and dropped down onto the rear seat. "Are you all right?" Jack shouted.

"Yes. That was a bullet!"

Josh glanced into his rearview mirror. Bodecker had his hand out the window brandishing a gun, and repeated muzzle flashes were sparking from it. He rocked the car back and forth across the traffic lanes, making them as hard to hit as possible. "I'm getting sick back here!" Kelly called out.

"Better that than dead!" Josh turned a corner hard, and the car skidded in a wide arc. This street was narrower and more crowded. He gunned the car anyway dodging the slower traffic. Bodecker followed. His empty pistol now on the seat beside him. He'd have to find another way to stop them.

Just ahead was the Louvre. "We're there but we don't dare stop, not with that madman behind us," Josh said.

"There!" Jack shouted. "Down the alley. Maybe we can shake him!"

Josh turned sharply and the car shot down the narrow thoroughfare. Garbage cans banged and cats scattered as the vehicle careened left and right to miss them. One garbage can was in the dead center. Josh could not miss it and slammed it squarely. The can hurled over the car. Behind him Bodecker was relentless. He entered the alley too, and accelerated with extreme and dangerous speed towards them, hoping to ram the BMW before it was clear of the narrow space. *I have him now!* Bodecker thought.

As the German's car closed in on them, Josh slammed on his brakes, then turned right onto the sidewalk of a major street. Behind him Bodecker cursed as he missed the car and the sharp turn. He flew out into the middle of the fast traffic. Struggling with the wheel, he slammed violently into the side of a tanker truck carrying gasoline. His car came to a sudden stop, wedged under the tanker as it dragged with locked brakes to a halt.

"*Mein Gott!*" Bodecker said as he realized what had happened. How could this be? He knew his destiny. He struggled to clear his head and get out of the car. He had to continue the chase. There was no doubt that he would succeed, so why couldn't he move?

Horrified, the tanker driver hurried down to check the damage. Gasoline flowed onto the car pinned beneath the truck. He saw the man at the wheel was screaming angrily as he tried to get free of the steering wheel. It held him fixed in his seat. The truck driver moved to help, but then fire erupted spontaneously when the gasoline reached the hot engine of the car. The truck driver turned to run as it exploded. The fireball engulfed everything within fifty yards. The last thing the driver heard were the German's screams over the roar of the explosion.

"Look!" Kelly shouted, staring out the opening where the rear window had been. "There's been an explosion."

"Do you see Bodecker?" Jack asked as Josh began to slow the car.

"No. His car's not behind us anymore."

"What do you think?" Jack asked Josh.

"I'd say the explosion and no car is not a coincidence. Kelly, keep a sharp lookout. I'm looping back to the Louvre. We don't know how much time you two have."

"What about Bodecker...?" Kelly stopped when she saw the two men stare at her. "Never mind. Stupid question."

Clouds had gathered and there was the low rumble of thunder. A few minutes later as Josh drove the BMW into the underground parking lot for the Louvre, there was the sharp crack of lightning. "It's starting," Jack said.

On their way Josh had called ahead to the museum and asked for Serge Rabelais, the curator. He told Rabelais he wanted to inspect the returned artifact. Rabelais' trust in Josh was absolute, and he granted him the permission without hesitation. Apologetically Josh turned down his friend's invitation to first have a drink in his office.

At the entrance Josh flashed his identity card to a guard, who inspected it, then pointed to a set of double doors that led to the service area of the museum. It was the off-season and the crowds were light.

Through those doors was an elevator where another guard scanned Josh's card with a barcode gun. This guard seemed impressed that Josh's clearance was of the highest level, and immediately he let them onto the elevator.

In the elevator, the lens of a camera twisted to focus on them. Kelly looked into the mirror inside and touched her face. "It's amazing, I look just like Bodecker's gunman."

"Jean Claude is the best make up artist in Europe," Josh assured, although he sounded preoccupied, almost distressed. His mind was more focused on the box held tightly in his hands than on the words coming out of his mouth.

"Is something wrong?" Kelly asked as the elevator started down.

"While Jean Claude was working on you...and after I had told him all that had happened...I looked inside the box."

"What did you find?" Kelly asked.

Josh wrestled with her question. His mouth opened to speak, then paused. He pondered his thoughts for a moment, teetering on the brink of speaking. Kelly beckoned him to continue, but he couldn't.

Finally he said, "Maybe I should keep it to myself."

"We should know," Jack insisted. "We need to know."

"Maybe." Josh nodded. "Some of the information confirms the Port of Calais as the Allies point of invasion. No real secret there. At least not with our hindsight."

"So you mean its all just stuff that happened anyway!" Kelley blurted. "We stopped Bodecker and it did no good."

"It seems Hitler was ready for them there regardless. He didn't need Bodecker's knowledge from the future," Jack added.

"Maybe...or maybe it was the return of this knowledge that tipped him off," Josh speculated "but there is more in this box than just that."

"More? Like what?" Jack asked.

"Weapons...like your generation has never seen before. Weapons of total destruction."

"Then of course, we should see it," Jack said.

"No, I don't think that's such a good idea," Josh continued. "Such information might snowball into bigger changes that could ultimately be worse. At this point, the outcome of the war, although terrible for us and catastrophic for many, was better than some alternatives that I can now imagine."

"So what are you suggesting?" Kelly asked.

Josh tapped the little box. "There is no doubt what the General left Bodecker to discover could change history completely—and not for the better."

"Are you saying we should leave it here?"

"Exactly. We can't risk the Germans getting this information when you return if they somehow overcome you, no matter how useful some of it might be to the Allies."

Jack suddenly grasped his point. "Everything our side needs to know is already in our heads." He looked at Josh remembering what they had talked about earlier on the drive to Mont-St-Michel. Josh winked as the elevator stopped.

"If you guys say so," Kelly conceded, figuring she missed something somewhere.

They stepped into the basement, and went through yet another security check. More cameras followed them as they were ushered into the vault. It was nothing more than a secure small room, containing the statue, resting in its display and a few other items. "I don't think we have much time," Josh said. "I wish I'd had a chance to get to know the two of you better."

"I think you're right," Kelly agreed, feeling the hair on her skin start to crawl. She looked towards the statue. "I think it's starting."

"I have a request, Josh," Jack said. "Would you do what you can to return the statue to its rightful owners?"

Josh nodded. "I'll see what is possible. You two better get closer to the statue, and I better stand back." He moved to the farthest corner as the eyes of the statue began to glow. "One last thing," he called out. "Remember International Business Machines."

"The time clock company?" Jack asked.

"Yeah, that one. They won't be making just time clocks in the future...you know what I mean. Act accordingly...and you'll do well."

"What do you mean?" Kelly queried.

"I've probably said more than I should already. Just don't forget. Good luck to you both. And change the way this war came out. For the sake of the millions who were murdered and oppressed."

Kelly walked briskly over and kissed Josh. "Thank you, for everything." She hurried back to Jack's side. Billowing smoke was now pouring from the statue's mouth, flowing to the floor and forming a thick carpet. It was like before. Josh could not take his eyes from the spectacle. The smoke grew thicker, then started to swirl, enveloping Jack and Kelly. They faced each other, and Jack reached out for Kelly's hand. Sparks darted from the statue into the dense mass and the deep drone began. It grew in volume, causing a vibration Josh could feel under his feet. There was a loud bang and a blinding flash of light. When the smoke dissipated, and Josh could see clearly again, the statue had returned to its lifeless self.

Jack and Kelly had vanished.

•

As Josh prepared to leave, he was bothered by what the future would hold. Soon others would know of the statue's powers.

That was inevitable, and the track record of the human race was not good. Greed always seemed to overcome virtue. He loosened his overcoat as his mind churned. So far only he knew. He and Jean Claude.

Five minutes later Josh was upstairs moving swiftly for the exit. "Josh! Mr. Goodman, are you satisfied that all is well?" It was Serge Rabelais, the Curator.

"Yes, thank you so much for indulging me."

"Good, then maybe now you have time for that drink?"

"Serge, I'd really love to, but I'm off to the airport. My plane leaves for New York in two hours."

"And your friends?"

"They have gone ahead."

Serge looked confused. He had not seen them, and he had been there the whole time. "Well then, some other time," he said graciously while walking him around the security station.

"You can count on it," Josh said. "I won't forget this favor. It means more to me than you can imagine." Then he passed through the doors and moved quickly to the front of a line of taxis waiting at the street.

Meanwhile, downstairs in the vault, the guard making his rounds was confused. The Picayulta statue was nowhere to be found.

CHAPTER THIRTY-SEVEN

At the terrace on Mont-Saint-Michel General Joachim Schwartz also saw a bright light. Bodecker and his assistant had been gone perhaps a minute; the American couple had leaped into the phenomenon only seconds earlier and just vanished. He lifted his weapon and contemplated leaping after them, when the light suddenly increased and even more smoke poured from the statue. The thick cloud still sparked and hissed. When the spectacle waned and the smoke settled, the General stared onto the terrace at two forms. It was Bodecker and Schmidt.

"*Guten,*" he muttered to himself. "*Wie ging die Mission?*" he asked, but neither Bodecker nor the man who went with him, Schmidt, responded. The experience had left them dazed, somehow unable to function. He became concerned for their condition and even more for the mission. A moment passed without movement. "*Sind Sie ganz recht?*" he called out.

Schwartz moved toward them, followed by his two men. Jack was stunned, but started to move, sitting up first, then checking on Kelly. The sight of her startled him at first. Then he touched his face and realized there might be a problem. He heard the General's voice behind him and avoided turning around. Kelly too started regaining her senses. Jack prodded her to come around.

Schwartz and his soldiers leaned closer to help them to their feet. But as the smoke cleared, the Germans did a horrified double take at the time travelers. They jerked back. Something had gone wrong. The voyage had caused the skin on their face to peel away from the skull. The sight of them was horrendous. For another moment Schwartz could do nothing. Kelly said something to Jack, and at that instant the General realized the two were not Bodecker and Schmidt. They were imposters. Just before the General was able to issue the order to seize them, Jack slammed one of the soldiers into the pedestal supporting the stone idol.

"Go, Kelly!" he cried, pointing toward the stairs of the terrace. "Run!"

She oriented herself and bolted as the statue fell to the ground and rolled. Schwartz leaped protectively to save it and shouted, "Seize them!"

Jack quickly followed Kelly while the second soldier fumbled in confusion.

The General jumped to his feet holding the little statue, then pointed his weapon at them and shouted, "*Halt! Anschlag oder ich töten Sie!*" He fired the weapon repeatedly, tossing it aside when it was empty. But it was too late. They were already lost in the shadows. Schwartz fumed. He looked at the fumbling soldiers. "After them, *dumkopfs!*"

Again, Jack and Kelly found themselves being pursued down the very same stairs as the day before…only it had been the future. Jack thought to himself, This *is crazy!* He heard shots behind them. "Hurry, Kelly!!" he shouted.

"I'm hurrying! I'm hurrying!" she answered running, still disoriented, but peeling the fake skin and make up from her face.

The sound of gunfire alerted more soldiers, and the General saw them falling into the chase. The group followed Jack and Kelly, in hot pursuit through the narrow streets of the Mont-Saint-Michel. "After them!" he yelled. He picked up another weapon and with the statue in hand, followed as fast as he could behind them.

The commotion drew French citizens to their shuttered windows, which they cracked open and peered through quietly. They saw Jack and Kelly fleeing frantically, followed by the soldiers and then the General, who was brandishing his weapon in one hand and the statue in the other.

Jack spotted a narrow alley. "In here!" he said, pulling Kelly into it. They leaned against the cold wall of the covey hole, breathing heavily, and in seconds heard the trampling commotion of jackboots as the pursuing soldiers went past.

Feeling they had lost them, they moved out of the alley and into another walkway, but then stopped. A wooden door blocked the access thirty feet down. "Not this way!" Jack said. It was a dead end, with houses on one side and a fifty-foot drop-off on the other.

They turned to get out, but could not. The General had cornered them. He was alone and advanced toward them with his pistol. "Get out of there!" he ordered in English. Jack looked down the alley for options. On the one side the walls hemmed them in, on the other the cliff was steep and high. There was nowhere to go.

Then the General shot his weapon several times into the air, signaling the misdirected soldiers. Jack looked out over the drop off keeping Kelly close by. He inched backward moving as far as possible from the Nazi, and considered jumping. It was a long way down.

Schwartz read his intentions. "You want to die? Have it your way," he sneered. He raised his pistol to kill them, but at that moment the same little girl, who had smiled at Jack from the window, the night they arrived, saw them trapped and pushed a flowerpot from the windowsill. It dropped on the General's head with a sickening crash. As he fell, the statue rolled from his arm, bounced across the walkway and flew over the drop-off. Jack and Kelly watched helplessly. It pitched, tumbled and bounced all the way to the bottom of the steep incline, finally landing in a half-filled pot of dirt in the quiet garden of an unsuspecting gardener. Another pot it had knocked loose fell on top of it, and its dirt covered the statue completely.

Having seen it disappear over the edge, Jack and Kelly considered going to retrieve it. But in seconds there was noise. It was the soldiers returning, and they were swarming through the streets.

"Let's get out of here before it's too late!" Jack exclaimed. He grabbed Kelly by the hand. They crossed the street back into the first alley and crouched as low as they could. The soldiers were everywhere. There was no place to hide.

"Where to now?" Kelly cried.

Jack didn't answer. There was nowhere else to go. And it seemed like only a matter of moments before they were caught. Then a door opened only a few steps from their hideaway. A middle-aged man in a black beret stepped out. He put a finger to his lips and then waved for them to hurry inside. Without hesitation they did and were quickly led to a hidden cellar. He closed a heavy door immediately behind them and all signs of their presence instantly vanished. Outside, the soldiers continued in confusion, baffled as they searched.

Kelly looked closely at the man. "Who are you?" she asked in French.

He held his finger to his lips for silence. After the soldiers passed he said, *"Resistance."*

Jack and Kelly remained in the cellar for several days. They were fed twice daily, given a bottle of wine and provided with new clothes. In the dead of night the man led them to a small vessel. It was waiting in the darkness to smuggle them across the English Channel. "He is my brother." Their friend said about the man at the helm. "You can trust him to get you to Plymouth. And, may God be with you," he added. Then he pushed them out into the black water.

Within hours Jack and Kelly found themselves on a night train for London. General Smitson gave orders for them to be placed on the next flight to Washington D.C. where they arrived late at night, exhausted, but grateful to be home and back in their own time.

General Alex Smitson, Uncle Smitty as Kelly knew him, met them at National Airport. He took them straight to his office, cautioning both to say nothing until they were securely within the building. When he heard their remarkable story, his eyes grew rounder until finally he picked up the telephone and called Army Chief of Staff George C. Marshall. "We need to meet immediately, Sir. My South American agents are back and have some remarkable information concerning the war effort." He listened. "Yes, that will do. In fact, I'd say it's ideal. I didn't know he'd arrived already." He turned to the couple. "You have a few minutes to freshen up. I'd suggest you do so."

"What's going on?" Jack said.

"You'll want to look your best for the President."

•

Jack found the security at the White House surprisingly lacking. The stone-faced Marine guards scarcely glanced at the couple, but Jack decided it was because General Smitson accompanied them. Still, the nation was at war. He recalled that saboteurs had been arrested. If Hitler knew how lax things were, he'd certainly send a team to kill the President. "Why do you think the President wants to see us?" he asked Kelly when the General had stepped away, momentarily leaving them with a male secretary that was busy at his desk.

"I don't know. I just wish I'd had time to put on some proper clothes." She fidgeted with her short hair.

"You look great," he said, and he meant it. She was alive and whole. She couldn't possibly look any better. Her hair would grow.

"You're not so bad yourself. Uh, oh, here we go."

An Army full Colonel approached and said, "This way, please." They were led down a short hallway, one both Jack and Kelly had seen many times in photographs and had never expected to see in person. Then they were ushered into the Oval Office where President Franklin Roosevelt was laughing heartily at something. Seated before the desk was a General. Standing near him was a familiar and comforting figure. "Sully!" Jack said with a broad grin.

"Good to see you live and fit, lad." Sully smiled and looked Kelly over appreciatively. "General Smitson was kind enough to send for me."

Roosevelt said, "Your uncle was just telling a story on my own Uncle Teddy. It seems he left a few details out of his exploits when he regaled us at family gatherings. How are you, young lady?" The President extended his hand, still seated behind the desk, his cigarette holder clinched between his teeth the way Jack had always seen it in the newsreels. "And this is the brave young man I've heard such wonderful things about. Glad to have you both back." They shook hands, then the President introduced them to General Marshall, who was leading the war effort and intimately involved in the preparations for the invasion of Europe. "I hear you have a story. Can't wait to hear it. Please, go on," Roosevelt directed.

Kelly looked at Jack and he nodded. In short sentences she related everything that had happened since her briefing in Washington, telling of Jack's exploits to such a degree that his ears burned. Sully looked on with pride while President Roosevelt smiled. When at last she had finished, he said, "That's quite a tale indeed. What do you think, General?" He looked at Marshall.

"What proof have you?" Marshall asked quietly.

"Just our word, sir. There were some documents, but we didn't bring them back out of fear they might fall into the wrong hands."

General Smitson spoke. "We registered another unexplained phenomenon again last week similar to the one on October 31st. This one, however, was on mainland Europe, consistent with what they are relating."

"They say the Germans are going to win this thing," Roosevelt said to General Marshall.

"Well, I agree that it's quite a story, but I'd say…" the general began.

"We've seen a Nazi France Jack interjected. It was a horrible place, and the atrocities that happened….or, that will happen, I should say, over the next forty years, are horrendous." General Marshall looked like he wanted to interrupt, but Jack kept on, raising his voice. "They are expecting you on June 6, 1944, at the Port de Calais!"

General Marshall turned white as a sheet. "How did you know that?" His voice was scarcely more than a whisper.

"It's common knowledge in the future, where we just were," Kelly said. "The Germans control Europe, millions have been murdered. We, the Allies, were stopped at the Port de Calais and all hope of defeating the Nazis ended then."

"I think we should talk about this, gentlemen," the President said, no longer grinning. "What do you say, Sully?"

"If Jackie boy says he's been to the future, I believe him. And the lass sure doesn't look like someone to bend the truth, but you'd know that bett'r than me Smitt."

"Smitty?" Roosevelt asked.

"I believe her. It's why I sent her. I don't think we can afford to ignore their information. Let me ask: Are they right about Calais? Is that the plan?"

Marshall looked for direction from the President, who nodded once to go ahead. "Essentially, yes. That is the landing spot, and June 6 is one of three projected landing dates, the second in fact. But they could have just guessed."

"Then," Roosevelt said, "so could the Germans. I suggest a new plan. At once. You see, it doesn't matter if they've been to the future or not, though I'm inclined to think they have. They know the landing place and the date. Maybe they came by it through time travel or perhaps they are liars and figured it out. Either way we have to make an alternative plan, at once."

"Yes, Sir," General Marshall said, rising to his feet. "I'll get right on it. We have an alternative landing area."

As he left the room Smitty said, "Wait outside, George. I've got more for you." The General nodded.

Then the President turned to Jack. "I hear you want to fly for our Air Corps, young man."

"Yes, Sir!"

"You should see him fly, too! He's wonderful," Kelly gushed. "Out-flying two German fighter pilots, in an old floatplane!"

"I'll see to it, son. Your country is honored to have you in service."

For a moment Jack was elated, then he remembered Lucy and her dead husband. "Thank you, Sir, but I have a small problem in Texas…"

Sully shook his head. "Not to worry, lad. All taken care of. The young lady in question came ta her senses, after her father had a talk….of sorts with her. I believe it involved a heavy switch. What ye did was self-defense. Y'er free to fight for y'er country."

Jack looked in disbelief at his uncle, then realized he was a free man. He turned to Kelly, who leaned over and kissed him.

The President beamed. "All's well that ends well," he said. "Now if you love birds will excuse me, I've got some late night work to do, and an order to sign, commissioning a certain young man to become an officer in the Air Corps." They said their good-byes then Jack and Kelly left the Oval Office hand in hand, followed by Sully.

A moment later Smitson came out. "Jack you have a week before reporting for duty. You can fly back to Texas with your Uncle." Then he turned to Kelly. "The OSS has granted you a week of R&R as well young lady."

Jack looked at Kelly. He knew she had no place to go home to. "How would you like to see a simple Texas farmer's hometown?" he asked invitingly.

Kelly's broad smile was her answer.

Then Smitson summoned General Marshall over. "Jack, one last thing," he paused. "Tell the General what your friend

Goodman told you about the landing." Kelly had left a couple parts out. The Generals looked on earnestly.

"The landing?" Jack repeated while thinking about it.

"About where the books say the landing should have been."

"Oh, that." Jack paused for a second. "Normandy. He said if we would have landed in Normandy we would have won the war."